Stained Souls

By Ferran O'Neill

Available from Discovered Authors Online –
All major online retailers and available to order through all UK bookshops

Or contact:

Books
Discovered Authors
Roslin Road, London
W3 8DH

0844 800 5214
books@discoveredauthors.co.uk
www.discoveredauthors.co.uk

Printed in the UK by BookForce International
BookForce International policy is to use papers that are natural,
renewable and recyclable products and made from wood grown
in sustainable forests where ever possible

BookForce International
Roslin Road, London
W3 8DH
www.bookforce.co.uk

DEDICATION

*For William and Ellen, James and Margaret, Sean and Mary,
never forgotten.*

*And for my Father Brian Ferran, who inspired me to write;
always in my heart. There is a little part of all of you within me.*

Author

Ferran O'Neill lives in Co. Tyrone with her husband and children, She is currently working on her next thriller 'Soul Cleansing'.

Contact the author at:
ferranoneill@hotmail.co.uk

ACKNOWLEDGEMENTS

I would like to extend my thanks to all the people who have helped in their own special ways from the time I first had ideas for writing Stained Souls, right through to its publication.

First and foremost a big thank you to my copy editor, Jo Field: without you this book would not be what it is. I will be forever indebted to you, not only for your guidance and support but for all that you have taught me. I take full responsibility for any errors and anomalies, which are all mine own!

I would also like to thank the highly regarded author: Helen Hollick, for her valued insight and friendship, and for permission to use her kind quote. Several other authors have been bountiful with advice and many kind words; I thank them too for their encouragement.

My thanks go too to my sister Maggie who has read chapters over and over without sighing and never complaining and to Geno for always being there if I need you.

I extend my gratitude to all the team at Discovered Authors, who have made this journey more enjoyable than I could have imagined.

I wish to thank my husband Dessie and our children for their love, their inspiration and their support. Guess what? Looks like Westport this year again guys!

Last but not least thanks to my Mother Dymphna whose knowledge of things spiritual and uncanny inspired the character of Sandra and a few others as well who are still waiting to be penned.

Well Kate; the long awaiting is over! Enjoy!

AUTHOR'S NOTE

The Queen Alexandra Butterfly; one of the ten accepted species of 'Birdwing' Butterflies is poisonous and is the largest butterfly in the world. With its wings open it spans up to 30cms, larger than some small birds. It is a protected species and is found in valleys rich in volcanic soil in the 'Orno Province' of Papua New Guinea.

Noted for its large eggs of which it lays around 240 during its lifetime the Queen Alexandra species takes about four months to evolve through the four developmental stages finally emerging from the chrysalis as a fully grown adult. Its collection is prohibited.

The only purpose of a butterfly's life is to mate and lay eggs; to breed.

The Parable of the Sower

A farmer went out to sow his seed. As he was scattering the seed, some fell along the path; it was trampled on, and the birds of the air ate it up. Some fell on rock, and when it came up, the plants withered because they had no moisture. Other seeds fell among thorns, which grew up with it and choked the plants. Still other seed fell on good soil. It came up and yielded a crop, a hundred times more than was sown. (Luke, 8: 5–8)

PART ONE

DISTORTING THE TRUTH

PROLOGUE

Bonfire Night, 1971: Gravesend, Kent

"Let him sleep Jack."

Repulsed by the stale sourness of alcohol and vomit carried on his breath, Beth Shaw spoke in a whisper holding the door ajar, making it a barrier between her and Jack Hynds.

For what had seemed like an eternity she had been waiting; had almost worn through the bit of threadbare carpet at the window, pacing back and forth, chewing away at her thumbnail, wishing with every beat of the mantle clock to hear the fast clicking of stilettos approach her home.

Still and silent, the last of the revellers long since gone, the street outside brought forth no such sound and as the time trailed into the small hours, the dread of hearing the unwelcome crunch of heavy steps against the pavement outside ate piecemeal into any of the hope she still held.

Just past 2.15am it was, when she'd almost convinced herself into believing he'd be passed out somewhere for the night, when the sound she dreaded had come. Plunging into her senses like a shard of ice it had sent a cold surge of frayed nerves all over her; her whole being shivered in response.

Tensing her grip, she was aware that her strength – coupled with her determination – ended abruptly at her elbows. Abandoned, her hands strained, committed to a defence that was futile against his might; strength you would not guess at from the slightness of his frame. Confronted with his face, her head wobbled as she steadied herself; tried in desperation to muster up some courage, knowing she had none. Commonsense born of experience told her not to cross a drunken man; so when he pushed the door fully open and staggered

13

past, she merely stood back, gave him ample room making sure he didn't rub against her; her skin crawling in anticipation of his touch.

"I'll keep him till morning...," she said hesitantly. "He's no trouble at all... Poor little mite! It's not right... To disturb him at this hour ..." Her voice was tentative, the words spilling out in short strings; small, insecure sentences testing the atmosphere, each one waiting for a rebuff, initiating the next only so long as the silence let them speak. Fearing for the child she would at least try; she had to.

He turned, glared, and with an intoxicated ignorance growled out, "Just give me the boy; he's mine."

There would be no more attempts from her to hold on to the child; the roughness of Jack Hynds's voice panicked her. She was afraid it had carried upstairs and woken her husband: the last thing she needed was a confrontation. Speed was the best way to deal with him; get him out as quickly as she could.

She scurried into the back room and lifted the sleeping bundle off the sofa. Feeling the child in her arms a swell of pity stirred within her. She paused, affording a few moments to fix the blanket round him. Only by looking at the beauty of the child could you have guessed the father had ever been a handsome man, his features once so fine. Bloated and reddened with the drink; his eyes all bloodshot and shifty like a rat's, he swayed at her shoulder, waiting. Against all that was maternal within her, Beth attempted to hand the boy over, her heart filled with a mixture of sadness and guilt so heavy its weight pulled it deep down into her stomach.

"Quit the mollycoddling, woman," Hynds snapped, ignorantly thrusting his elbow into her breast, ripping the child away. The blanket fell to the floor. She smothered a gasp as turning with clumsy, misplaced footing for the door he almost bounced the child's head of the wall. He merely scoffed, "It's hardening up he needs. Between you and that bitch, he's being made a fuckin' wimp."

Picking up the blanket, still warm from the child, Beth held it against her chest trying to smother the feeling of uncleanliness that stemmed from where Jack Hynds had touched her. Following him into the hallway, she watched from the door as tottering unsteadily, veering to the right of the street under the weight of the child now slung like a sack over his shoulder, he disappeared into the night.

Still listening to the uneven timing of his footsteps, she felt the hand upon her neck.

"I take it he came for him then?"

Turning to bury her head into her husband's chest she searched for consolation, unable to find any, already sure she was wrong for not putting up a fight. But there wasn't anything she could have done; at the end of the day she knew her loyalties must lie with those who were asleep upstairs; she knew enough about Jack Hynds to know that to cross him would put her family in peril.

"Come on love," her husband murmured, "you have our three little ones tucked up in bed, it's up to her to tend to that one; you look to your own."

Gently patting her arms he coaxed her back from the doorstep letting go of her to shut the door and turn the key in the lock. He'd known earlier, arriving home for his tea and seeing the extra child sat at the table, to expect an uneasy night ahead. At least an episode like the last one had been avoided. Beth had let the child go this time. Now he had to deal with the anguish seeping out over her face.

It was not right her having to deal with Jack's sort. Too good-hearted, that's what Beth's problem was, and in this case it just made her a soft touch. If he had his way the boy would come nowhere near their own son. He might be a little one now, but time no doubt would turn him into a nasty piece of work. If there was anything Arthur was sure of, it was the fact that a lowlife like Jack Hynds would be more than capable of breeding another river rat like himself.

"Sure," Arthur consoled her, "have you not always thought there was something not right about that child?"

For a moment Beth shot him a brief look of disdain, but relented: he was only fumbling with the right words, the kind he was never able to get out. She knew Arthur meant well. But the child, little innocent that he was, she thought of as one of her own. Well, most of the time; it was true what Arthur said. She had on occasion found some of the boy's behaviour strange: all the age of him and to find him suffocating her oldest girl's pet rabbit as he had. It had sickened her to see it. He had that look in his eyes sometimes, just that; a look just like Jack's. It wasn't right thinking such things about a child so small. All children started off good, didn't they? But then, with blood like Jack's running in him you'd have a hard time finding any goodness. Maybe there was enough of his mother in him to make a difference. The thought brought a qualm of anxiety. What was she going to tell her?

"She said she'd be back long before now. You've seen the welts on that child's back same as me; Jack's a crooked enough bastard when he's sober. What if he turns on him? She'll not be there to stop it."

"Well then, she shouldn't be where she is now, should she, stripping to her knickers or worse?"

No, she shouldn't be were she is, Beth thought, but even though the girl's profession went against everything she deemed proper or worthy of making ends meet, Beth, searching the depths of her soul, had found an acceptance. Not that she would say so to Arthur, but in a like case there was nothing she wouldn't stop short of herself to fend for her children.

She leaned against her husband, said, "What choice has the poor girl in what she does? It was him got her into it. How was she to know what she was letting herself get mixed up in when she came across him? A right bastard he is. Sets her up there doing that and then thinks he has the right to give her a hiding when she comes home every night. Somebody should give him a taste of his own belt."

Arthur Shaw rubbed his chin gently against his wife's neck and felt the softness of her hair against his cheek. "You're right love, I know. But there's nothing you can do, I just wish you'd never met her, that's all. He's a bad sort, not for the likes of us. Maybe she'll get some sense and leave him one of these days. Get away; back to where she came from."

"That's most likely the reason she's late. That tin I've been keeping safe for her; she's got nearly enough stashed. She'll need to do it soon, though, that child can't survive many more beatings, poor little mite. Sickening that's what it is."

Arthur Shaw shook his head, despairing of the fact that his wife was involving herself with any of it. He'd heard enough talk at the King's Head to know exactly what kind of people Jack Hynds was in with; in up to his neck; the sort that good, law abiding fellows like himself gave a wide berth, but he said nothing further. He turned off the lamp in the hall and went back to bed, pausing only to allow his wife up the stairs in front of him.

Jack Hynds dropped his son onto the bunk. He had to think; think fast. He knew they would come for him; it was only a question of time. He had toyed with leaving his boy at the Shaws' place, but in the end had fetched him back to the boat to wait for her. The child was too useful a tool to leave behind.

Time was wasting; trust that bitch to be late again! She wasn't supposed to like it, damn the woman to hell. Later and later it had got the last couple of months, yet the money she brought back didn't match up. She's screwing around; he knew that all right. Sly as a fox she was, spilling out her pathetic tears when he tried to whip it out of her. He'd find out yet who the fucker was. The hairs on his back stood on end as he thought of the bastard having one over on him – whichever one he was – then the rest of them; all having a laugh at him.

Getting out a beer he sat down on the edge of a bench and bit off the lid, he needed a drink bad: wanted a shot more than the beer. He'd sort the bitch out proper this time, after he'd got out of this mess! "Bastards!" He swore. "Double crossing bastards!" He shouldn't have told them who the boy was; that had been his mistake. He'd seen the excitement rise in their eyes. Fucking foreigners; always wanting extras.

It was McMasters's fault; did he think he was fucking stupid or something? Stupid bastard, sending his son with him to the drop. A little lad like that! How the hell was a six-year-old brat gonna be able to tell McMasters what went down?

He'd felt the boss had got wind of his little earner; sensed an atmosphere at the club; caught McMasters shooting glances at him, glances that said he knew something was going on. And it was. He'd set up a right little network of his own, it was all moving to plan. It was only a matter of time till the law closed in on McMasters and there was no way he was gonna hang around to go down with him.

And now the whole thing was fucked up!

A little over two hours ago, with the light still glowing from a bonfire a mile or so up the bank from where the drop had been arranged, he'd taken to his car, had a few beers; given them the half-hour they'd paid nicely for.

He hadn't been sure, the more he tried to see it; decided in the end his eyes were playing tricks on him. But every so often, when the glow from the distant fire gave a little more light to the blackness, he'd thought he saw the silhouette of a car in between the trees several hundred yards up the bank. It had been nothing for him to bother about; probably a courting couple. There'd been no point in leaving the warmth of the car to trudge across the muck and end up getting seen if something went bad with the drop.

So far so good; wetting his thumb he'd counted out the notes separating his cut. Not bad he'd thought. Adding the extra he'd got for the boy it had made a good enough sum. Checking his watch he'd decided to give the men another ten minutes then, raising the bottle in the direction of the trees, clinked it against the window: "Give her one for me mate, lucky bastard," he'd said.

He'd had no fear of the boy spurting out what had happened to him at the hands of the men. The little ones were always too shocked the first time, too young to understand. They'd have had plenty of time to butter him up. Hell, if he'd got away with it he could have made some use of the boy. McMasters was despised by many and quite a lot of them had a taste for the tenderness of young flesh; he was sure the two foreigners weren't the only ones who would pay over and above for a taste the McMasters boy.

The chill in the air had tightened his skin as he'd left the car and with faltering steps made his way back to the old butt of a quay where their boat was moored. Whatever the effect the drink had had on him, suddenly he felt sobered up.

It was gone!

Had the drink hit too hard on him; sent him off in the wrong direction from the car? He'd turned back, climbed up onto the muddy bank, taken a few steps to his left. Stumbling in the darkness he'd fallen over a lump of rotting wood. Cursing he'd gathered himself onto all fours, moving his weight from one hand to the next – and then he had felt it: still warm to the touch; his fingers had come up against a face. He let out a yelp.

"Fuck!" It was the boy. He'd fallen over the boy.

It hit Jack hard; like a good left hook to his stomach: the boy was too quiet, too still. Frantic, he'd groped in his pockets for his lighter, running the light over the body searching for some sign of life; there had been none.

Jason McMasters's small face had been pale; his eyes staring up at the night sky in a contorted look of shock and terror; his last pleas for his pain to stop silenced.

A desperate wail from Jack had echoed the sound of the child crying into the night. Dread sweeping over him, he'd checked again for a pulse. There had been none.

"Bastards!" Falling back into the mud, Jack had sat rocking himself steadily back and forth; a habit he had formed as a child when he was scared; really scared. Then had come the violent retches as heaving, he'd emptied his guts out over the ground. He was shaking, but not at the sight of the boy. He didn't care about the boy. In those moments that followed, he was sickened only by the taste of his own fear when he knew he'd dealt himself a death sentence!

How was he gonna get out of this one? Looking down at Jason McMasters, his only thought had been that he was as much a gonner as the boy. In the end his only answer had been to make a run for it.

Pulling the boy's body closer to the bank, he'd slipped it into the dark water of the Thames and then, having got himself up off the bank, he had headed back through the blackness to his car.

He'd expected the bitch to be at the boat waiting for him with their boy; expected to get away with both of them. Cursing, he had fetched back his boy from the Shaws'. Where the hell was she?

And now it was too late.

The thud of boots; two sets overhead. Powerless, he braced himself.

He should've took more notice of the car in the shadows. He'd have got the McMasters boy back still alive if he'd took the time to find out that Ron was watching his every move; no amount of money the foreigners had paid him was enough for him to be sat here now.

The first blow cracked his jaw. Curling his lip into his mouth, his tongue met the blood oozing from the tear.

McMasters stared down at him, piercing him with his gaze, but the man said nothing; did nothing. He never got his hands dirty; not him. Not even to avenge his own flesh and blood. It was Ron who was cutting into him. It took him a few minutes to catch on that a friend had turned foe. Another mistake; there were no friends in this kind of lark. McMasters didn't know it yet, but now that he'd finally got to see Ron in the flesh it was all too clear: McMasters had been taken for a ride.

He had realised it the instant McMasters spoke the name of the face that owned the fists – the fists that were plummeting his own face into mush – the name that spelt out terror in all their souls: 'Ron'.

This was where it ended. He'd seen the remains of those who'd been unfortunate enough to meet Ron before. Meeting Ron meant you were dead. Now all he wished was that he'd downed as much of the hard stuff as he had the beer. The last punch had sent his head cracking against the window. He could feel the blood running down the side of his face as everything began to spin around him; then the darkness took him.

The coldness of the water brought him round. He tried to move but he was bound, feet and torso to a chair. His struggling only toppled him to the floor. For a moment he caught sight of his son's head protruding from under the pillow in the bunk. His boy! A life for a life! Maybe the boy could save him yet. It was his only hope. He turned what was left of his face towards McMasters, tried to get the words out, make the offer: I've took your son you take mine. But his face was gone and he could barely see and the only sounds coming from his throat before he blacked out were gibberish.

They brought him back again. But not with water this time. At first there were just sounds, then he felt the pain and slowly he was able to focus on movement around him. The onslaught had stopped and the stench of the river water drowned it at first; but he was aware of the smell; fumes; petrol. It didn't matter any more; he wanted to black out again; he knew what his fate was now.

"Take care of it."

They were the only words McMasters uttered before leaving to watch from his car.

Wrapping himself tighter into his blanket, Jack's boy watched the flames grow brighter, burning higher and higher. He could feel the heat from the fire as it spread through the boat.

At first his eyes widened at the glow of the flames, he followed them up as they danced, listened as they crackled and hissed.

Then he heard his father. The screaming was harder, louder than ever before.

The boy cringed. Shaking, he snuggled into the blanket and stuck his fingers in his ears. Curled up in a ball he took himself off to the safe place, the field with tall grass where he ran with her, catching the butterflies in his net. He concentrated harder until he could hear her laughter, her soft voice soon blocking out the screams.

He was safe again in his mother's arms.

For a long time into what remained of the night Beth Shaw turned restlessly in the bed wondering how the child had fared. It seemed she had only just drifted into sleep when she was woken by the sound of fire engines passing the house. Burning wood; she recognised the smell; so strong that for a moment she thought it was their house that was ablaze. The orange haze behind the net curtain gave her a little relief – until she drew them back.

Just behind the opposite row of houses, the ones which backed onto the riverbank, black clouds rising above the roof tops were returning the breaking dawn to night.

Beth knew their source: they came from the derelict boatyard, just about where Jack Hynds housed his family in a rundown canal boat.

THE PRESENT

2007

1

The Old Bailey, London: Friday 13th July

The point of the needle pierced through his skin somewhere high on his shoulder. He welcomed the calming effect it would soon bring to his frenzied nerves and willed it further into his soul, praying it would release him from the grip of this crazed creature who shared his being.

Roughly manoeuvred back onto his bunk, he searched for the clock on the wall through the still open door of his cell, it was just past 6.30; morning at last. The drugs were beginning to take effect; he was already drifting thoughtlessly away. This was the way he preferred to be when his mind thought of nothing. Only sometimes, as now, he began to relive the nightmare. Perhaps this time it would be different. Please God; let it be different...

He was laughing so much that when he tried to catch his breath his rib cage ached, but what was so funny? He couldn't tell. Looking down on himself he became aware of his own nakedness; maybe that was it, but why was she laughing at him? What was it about him that she found so funny? Girls always swooned at the sight of him, but this was something new. Gasping, he looked at her mistily, his eyes wet with the tears of his mirth. She had folded into such a fit of giggles that she had keeled over on the floor in front of him. Her legs were sticking up in the air showing off her knee-high boots. They appeared to be all she was wearing.

What about Fiona, he thought, panicking. What if she were to walk in on them now? This situation he had got himself into wasn't good; not good at all. For some reason, though, the thought only sent him off into another fit of giddiness; he just couldn't help it.

A figure emerged on his left, a man, walking towards him from his kitchen and blocking his view of Katie. All he could see now were

25

her boots, but he could still hear her laughter. She hadn't managed to compose herself any more than he had. Who was this bloke anyway? And why were he and Katie naked when they had this stranger for company? Even that was funny. He didn't know why, just that it was. His throat exploded again, the laughter ripping up from deep in his belly. He blinked; widened his eyes and tried to focus. God! This laughing business sure played havoc with your ability to breath. He had to try to figure out what was going on. He squinted again at Katie, she was helpless, on the floor, her shoulders shaking. He felt another spasm of laughter, tried to stop.

Suddenly, the stranger stood over Katie and raised his arm. A knife blade gleamed in his fingers.

What the hell was all this! Startled, he tried to move. The dream had been great until now. "Hey mate; go and find your own nightmare, mine was going just fine without you," he yelled at the stranger. Or did he?

Why couldn't he hear his own voice? Wait a minute what the fuck! The knife was rising and falling, again and again. Okay; time to wake up Mark; time to get out of this. But he couldn't escape it and over and over in front of his eyes the knife kept plunging. And still he was laughing; the whole thing was bizarre; hilarious.

Blood was spraying all around him, coating everything, including himself. Why was he laughing at this? Why couldn't he stop? He bent his head to look at his nakedness, watched the warm, red rivulets running down his chest. His throat ached, he wanted to cry, he was repulsed by the tickling trickles that flowed down to his groin, slid to his thighs, a pattern of veins flowing outside of his skin.

Katie wasn't laughing any more. She was screaming. He screamed too, but no sound came out. And then Katie stopped screaming. Why are you laughing, you crazy bastard, he said to himself. But still he couldn't stop. As every spray of blood made contact with his skin his body convulsed and he was off again. What strange dream was this? There's no fear! Why am I not afraid? Why am I just sitting here watching all this? Fuck am I stupid or what. No, you're not stupid, you're having a dream. Then why am I not getting out of here? But he had no answer; he just sat on, entertained by the redness that continued to spurt like fireworks around the room each time the stranger plunged the knife into Katie's body.

He couldn't see the fireworks any more; the tears of laughter mixed with the blood were blurring his vision to a red haze. He tried to lift his arms to wipe his eyes, but they were too heavy to move. He blinked and blinked again: that was his suit; that one in front of him; he was sure it was his suit. Why was someone wearing his suit? How dare they? Who does he think he is? What the hell! He wanted to be angry, but again all he could do was laugh. God! Why couldn't he stop this? Please make it stop.

The dream began to change; his thoughts, half-formed, began to clear. He was still laughing, his sides aching – and yet it wasn't so funny any more. As he struggled with the mix of emotions vying in his head, he tried to snap out of it. What are you doing? Katie is being ripped apart in front of your eyes. Why aren't you doing something to stop it? He's not going to stop with her, is he? You'll be next!

For the first time, fear took him by the throat. He screamed; it came out like a whimper. He tried to stand up. But his body did not react he was unable to move. He was numb now all over. He tried twitching at the muscles around his mouth but couldn't tell if they moved. He was paralysed he couldn't feel anything except fear; real cold fear. His bladder released a stream of warm wetness down his legs. The red rain had stopped there was no sound. The shadowy form of the stranger, still as anything, knelt over Katie.

She's dead, he thought, she has to be dead now. Suddenly there was laughing again; a man's coarse laugh growing louder and louder, filling the room. Was it him? No. It was the stranger. Slowly the man moved back as if to stand. Then he was turning; turning around.

He gasped, frozen in terror as the face looked into his own. Nothing was funny any more. This time he found his voice, heard himself scream.

He was looking into his own face.

He had to get out of this nightmare. Wake up! Wake the fuck up. He pulled himself up; he was swaying. Using his hands, he searched for a door handle but couldn't find it. The walls were red; wet, sticky red. He couldn't stand the touch of it on his hands.

"Mark! Mark!"

He could hear Fiona calling him, her voice was strained; pleading. Again she called out his name. God! He had to get out of here. He was no longer naked, his suit was back on. It was covered in blood.

His shirt clung to his chest. He felt sick. Again Fiona called to him. She was getting closer; he couldn't let her walk in here; couldn't let her see this; see what he had done.

In front of him the door opened. There was a flash of light; her face; he took hold of her but she was trying to push past him.

"No!" he screamed at her as she struggled, desperate. He grabbed for her hands, but he couldn't get hold of them, they were tearing at him, attacking his face. He was so weak and she was so strong. He could no longer fight her off. How could she have such strength? Where were all these hands coming from? He was on the ground again. Somehow she had wrestled him onto the ground. The room seemed to swirl around him. A mass of weight dropped on his chest. Rough hands seemed to be pulling at him everywhere. Male voices were raised; their shouting gradually drowning out Fiona's cries.

He woke. The officers were subduing him, bringing him back under control. He had emerged from another nightmare.

And nothing was different.

Sleep was something he dreaded. During the first few weeks after the murder he was glad of the escape. The relentless rounds of questioning tired him out and then his short escapes to the dream world were filled with senseless glimpses of things he was never able to fix in his mind. On waking, they stayed behind; he was unable to retrieve them.

But as time passed, he was aware of more sinister memories, which eventually coaxed this terrible vision from some deep corridor in his mind.

The first time this nightmare had visited him, he had fought off going to sleep again for six nights in a row, determined not to let the darkness take him back there. Eventually, exhaustion had overtaken him and he had had to endure it again. It had visited relentlessly since, always stalking his unconscious, waiting until his wretched state could offer no resistance. No sooner had he slipped from the anxiety of one haunted world, than he was offered, bound as a sacrifice, to the tormenting claws of another. So he had made it a practice to avoid sleep for as many consecutive nights as he could, but sleep deprivation had only resulted in making him deranged. He no longer knew what was real and what was not. In those moments – seldom now – in his daytime hours when for a brief time he had felt human, he had convinced himself of a reality that he still could not fathom.

He remembered those first efforts he had made to make a case for his innocence. Driven only by a belief in himself – now absent – he had made a desperate attempt to find an explanation. To understand how he had become involved in this terrible crime. The evidence, though, was incriminating; so overwhelming that he had soon become dejected with trying.

The defence team was duty bound to side with his version of events. They had presented a united defence, but he had discerned from the beginning that it was merely lip service. Fiona had tried desperately to convince him to hire another firm, but he saw that as only prolonging the inevitable.

Right from the beginning, Fiona had remained his stalwart. She had seemed indifferent to the evidence laid before her, steadfast in her belief that he was innocent. At first it had helped him maintain his belief in himself, but gradually it had leaked away. He could not tell her about the nightmares; he was too afraid they would shatter her belief in him; unmask the monster dormant beneath his skin. To have witnessed a change in her would have been to destroy the only remaining spark within him that he was not evil. And so he broke off contact with her.

As for changing his legal team, he saw no point: fresh eyes would see nothing different. The whole thing was just a formality that had to take place because he had a right to it under the law. The world, it seemed, was already convinced of his guilt. And so was he; almost. Yet deep within him, its pulse growing weaker by the day, a tiny fragment of hope managed to survive. He tried to cling onto it, but now, even he was forgetting it was there.

Frequently, the officers would allow the doctor in to check him. He knew that the respite the drugs offered would eventually diminish. He was labelled as deranged; and that was what he had become. His destiny: a padded cell.

Outside, the city slowly dragged itself awake. Increasingly the sounds of traffic broke through the thickness of the walls. Inside, the creaking and slamming of metal doors shattered the silence. The black boots of the officers sent the echoes of heavy footsteps along the corridor outside his cell, but he hardly noticed them.

By the time he had been readied to leave the cell and walk the long walk up to the courtroom, he was no longer inside himself. Relying heavily on the support of the officers to whom he was handcuffed, he watched them pulling him up the narrow steps and pushing him down abruptly onto a seat in the box. Positioned high over the courtroom, he looked down at all those present, the audience who had come to view the psychotic creature he had become. As the last dregs of the time-release drug invaded his brain, he knew he had entered the coliseum and the lions, hungry for feeding, would soon rip him apart. The verdict was a foregone conclusion.

Head bent, he looked up from under his brows at the heads arrayed below him. His whole being shuddered as he met the hatred, almost tangible, that came at him. He saw the heads in the Press box, the hands scribbling their satisfaction; the artist sketching the scene as they waited for the jury to return their verdict.

During the two weeks of the trial, despite the interminable rain, the crowds had relentlessly waited, lining the street outside the Old Bailey each day yelling for his blood. On two separate occasions they had managed to break through the police barriers and invade the court building itself. On another they had focused their efforts on the van carrying him from the prison causing such a fracas that since then he had been confined in the holding cells below. Just yesterday, members of some feminist group had broken their way into the courtroom. Shouting obscenities, they had reached the barristers' bench before being apprehended and dragged out.

Last night he had been told that after the verdict was announced today he would remain another night in a holding cell; a decoy van would return to the prison instead. He wondered why they bothered; but at least now he had only to endure the venomous hissing that seeped into his brain from the packed courtroom. So low had his spirits sunk, he would have preferred to be thrown to the mob outside.

He considered the sentence they would hand out; despite the brutality of the crime, it had a promise of brevity. A crime committed while the balance of his mind was disturbed. He would, his brief had told him, be given treatment for his illness. Illness?

Nervous; fidgeting with the cuffs of his shirt, he wondered how obvious it was that he was drowning in his own sweat. As the whole courtroom rose and the officer beside him pulled him to his feet, he asked himself one last time how it was possible that he had committed this crime. That he had done so was inescapable; there was no point in denying it to himself any more. Again he watched the spectators; the Press spilling out of their designated area and into the public gallery, such was the national interest in this case. Like hyenas they scoured even the slightest twitch in his demeanour, eager to translate every telltale sign of his guilt into tasty morsels for their viewers and readers. The brutal and senseless murder of Katie Smyth had outraged every respectable person in the land and they were now poised to claim justice in her name. Even the scantiest details of the nature of the injuries inflicted upon her were enough to make him the most hated killer in recent history.

He remembered the day he had been led into the interview room at the station. How he had shuddered at the images slammed down on the desk one after the other. Countless times he had tried to re-live what had happened, to no avail. It was obliterated by the blackout in his mind. Only in his nightmares had it come back to him. And then it wasn't real.

At first he hadn't been able to make out whose body it was he was looking at. It took all of his effort not to puke over the table. Then in one image he saw the boots and beyond them the muddle of bloodied flesh and out to the edges, the long, slender arms; the hands outstretched, the nails still perfectly manicured. She hadn't even tried to fight back. And in a fleeting glimpse before the veil came down, he was with her again, and all he could hear was her laughter; that damned laughter that had driven him crazy.

One after another, his former colleagues had turned what for him had been fleeting flirtations, meaningless affairs, into a catalogue of sordid promiscuity. Yes, Katie had been one of many brief encounters that were common in the days when he was single; the days before Fiona. To Fiona he had been true. Since her he had had no interest in any other girl. It was the only thing now that he couldn't accept. He knew irrevocably that he would not have sneaked off for an afternoon of sex with Katie Smyth. It was the one shred of hope that he had clung to. The one indication that he was not guilty as charged. But then, according to all the evidence, he was. He had lured her back to kill her. His motive, they said, was because she was pregnant. She was not, so it turned out; but she had confided as much to a colleague or two and it had provided a reason for his frenzied attack.

He was being forced to his feet. He stiffened as cheers erupted around him; the word 'Guilty' floated over his head. He saw the bewigged head was speaking; passing sentence; the words were meaningless. The officers sat him back down. For the first time since the trial had begun no one seemed interested in him. The stampede for the door by the Press had already begun.

The only figure still sitting up in the gallery had her head bowed low. Turning as the officers helped him out of the box, he looked up to her again, but she was gone.

2

The Garden of Dr Gerry Reid, Maidstone, Kent:
Friday 10th August

"Look Daddy, it's a peacock! Look at the patterns!"

Elle is calling from somewhere high above him. The sound of her voice brimming over with excitement rushes at him and passes him in waves. He can easily believe that he is standing in the hallway of some vacant, Victorian house and the ghost of a child long dead has brushed past leaving behind its echo: innocent laughter, slightly tinny, fashioned by a spirit.

But no, he is here, shrouded, lost in a blanket of fog, until just now, melting out of its whiteness she appears as a presence; a there without there-ness. Light from the sun is beaming behind her creating a halo of white gold that edges her form. She is angelic once again. This pleases him. The blue cotton fabric of her dress flaps freely in the breeze as she bounds across the grass, arms stretched out in front of her. A transparent tumbler secured against her tennis racquet imprisons her latest catch.

Too soon, before he can answer, her voice fades and this vision melts into the mist that engulfs him once again. A black shadow creeps from somewhere beyond, eats into the fog swallowing the memory of innocence.

He is lying flat on his back, drifting; rising through the darkness. All is white once again. Today is the hottest day of the summer so far. He can feel the heat of the sun high in the sky, a searing white ball, hot against his face, burning brightly into his eyes. He cannot blink to shield himself from its intensity. It is something he has tried often, but never been able to do; to look the sun right in the eye.

Would it be harder, he wonders, to take leave of this world today than it would on any other? Would a day that was cold, perhaps duller, make the leaving any easier? He supposes it is futile to waste what are to be his last moments wondering about that.

The warm moistness oozing from beneath his head spreads further, slowly draining with it any life that is left. Is he still floating? He imagines that he is.

He knows that Elle wasn't really here. The girls have long ago grown out of catching butterflies. It is true after all then, that your life flashes before you as you die. Yes, he is dying. That is something he realises, yet strangely he feels no panic. Starved of oxygen, his brain is shutting down. There is nothing he can do. Nothing anyone can do. He is merely a spectator, as is the dark shadow hovering above him, once again threatening the light.

The fall he surmises has severed his spinal column disconnecting his brain from the rest of his body. Paralysed from the neck down, his consciousness, his final existence is slipping away, and as the reel of his life rolls past him it is as if some kind of computer is siphoning off his memories, preserving them for future reference.

The gouges on his hands are witness to an act of desperation; clutching at straws was all it had been, kind of like locking the stable door after the horse has bolted. She had told him to fix it; drawn by guilt to the tool box, he had meant to finish it before she got home.

A breeze wafts over him and he imagines lifting his head to catch the cool air against his face. In reality he can feel nothing.

Out of the mist another vision appears: the boy. He is back in his office again. Boy, man, whatever. His colleagues would have given anything for the chance to study this case. He regretted the timing himself. He watches from above, over the child's shoulders, man-sized shoulders, as kilter-fisted, the man child clutches the crayons, colouring his pages intensely. The drawings are the same as always: grass, long and green, stick people with over-sized heads holding nets with mitten-shaped hands, catching beautifully coloured, intricately designed butterflies.

"Can I see them now?"

That voice comes to him clear and distinct, which seems strange as everything else that has flashed before his eyes in the last few moments was removed; untouchable.

"Alright, but hang onto my hand. I've been repairing the steps."

He can feel the largeness of the hand grasp his as they walk into the mist. Unabated, the dark shadow suddenly grows, blocking the warmth of the sun.

"Sandra."

He does not call out her name, but thinks it instead. His last thought is of her name. For he can no longer speak; no longer see. The darkness has taken all of the sun.

The small wooden gate to the garden swings closed and the tall figure returns to stand over him, casting a shadow over his remains.

3

The Search Agency, London: Monday 8th October

Sheila McBride hesitated.

Her shoes it seemed were glued to the pavement. The people here would probably think she was crazy as well. Chin up, chin up, she told herself, a cold October sun reflecting her face back out at her. The face: there it was; the constant reminder. A story of two halves; the way it is and the way it could have been. One half could be no one in particular, one of a thousand other, middle-aged women. Someone of whom it could be said time had been kind to. Nothing there that spoke of hard times, enough traces of beauty left to believe she was just in her prime.

The other half was an affliction; a punishment. Some had even called it the mark of the Devil. There were a multitude of responses from which to pick on coming face to face with Sheila McBride. What else was there to say other than at some time in the past she had been badly burned? No one who met her really wanted to ask how.

Beside her, the road was bumper to bumper. Horns beeped furious and impatient, their revving engines spluttering monoxide fumes into the air. But to Sheila, the noise of the city was but a faint drone. She was focused, rehearsing her sentences, getting them straight in her head just as she had been doing for days, driven by a determination she had not felt in years.

Reaching for the door she was caught off guard as it swished open automatically, no effort on her part. Steadying herself she regained her composure, met with coloured walls, cream and lime. She felt the tightness in her chest ease just a little, but enough for her to notice. Nice and fresh she thought; colours that said what exactly? Sheila determined everything by its shade. Green had always been her thing, so lime counted as good.

A black, granite floor, almost glass-like, reflected the black leather of the two couches sitting on either side of the doors, and the brass plant stand in the corner full of sharp, spiny cacti. The reception area seemed, well, huge; to Sheila huge translated as success. Large prints of some of Monet's later works next caught her eye. Well, that just topped it all, didn't it? Sheila liked art, any kind of art.

She was still nervous though. It was all a bit, well, up-market – if that was the right way of saying it – what else should she have expected? Everything about England had changed. But then, so too had home in many respects. Even some of the boutiques back there were designed to emulate posh hotel lobbies.

A whole generation had been born, grown and started over since she had last lived here. Thirty-five years was a long time, and yet on another level just being here made all that was in the past – a past she had vowed never to dwell on – seem just like yesterday all over again.

Dressed in her best – a new green and blue tweed skirt suit she'd bought especially for the trip – she stiffened her back, placed her small black handbag to rest half way up her left sleeve and tugging her case along on its wheels, with one deep breath she moved forward.

There was only one young lady present behind the long curve of the desk. Sheila was relieved; only one person to cope with. The background music was rather too loud though, so with her first attempt she struggled unsuccessfully to be heard over the radio jingles and announcements; her intrusion timid even though she was trying her best to be assertive. She tried once more, this time almost shouting. "Good afternoon, I phoned earlier and was told to come in after two."

The shock on the receptionist's face confronted with hers did not stir any emotions within her. She had lived with the scars and their affect on the people she met for longer than she cared to remember. She grimaced, forcing the tight skin around her mouth to form a smile, knowing the warmth that she intended it to carry would not reach the young woman behind the desk and would be wasted. It was always like this. The young; they were always the ones who were most affected. Lack of experience, she supposed. For them the world was still a wonderful place to be conquered and explored. If only they knew the half of it; knew what lurked in dark corners waiting to take them.

Sheila waited. A few seconds passed before the young woman – 'Linda' according to the little name plaque pinned to her blouse – had recovered from the initial shock and was sufficiently composed to reply. Her voice squeaked out its welcome, the pitch artificially high as she battled to appear detached from the hideous features that faced her across the smooth, shiny teak of her desk. She probably didn't realise how hard she was gripping it to keep herself from shrinking back.

"Miss McBride, isn't it?"

Sheila nodded, smiled again even though it caused her great pain, but that was something else she had learned to live with over the years. Physical pain could be managed, lessened, with drugs, but not the pain of the soul. That festered continually, day in and day out. It was a pain that only addictions could numb. She had seen it so many times before; addictions created enough pain of their own.

The girl before her she would have placed in her mid-twenties, though it was only a guess. The jet black hair had to be out of a bottle, it was too black to be natural. Half up, half down, it was arranged in symmetrical curls around Linda's shoulders and held in place by so much hair spray – or product as they called it nowadays – that it looked as though it hadn't been washed in weeks. The eyes, their colour echoing too much coral reef to be true blue, peered out from behind a pair of thick, black plastic, rectangular glasses, which Sheila was sure were more a fashion statement than a necessity. Her attention was drawn to the girl's hands: slender, with bony knuckles sloping into long fingers that had dark tides of fake tan flowing between them as her nails manipulated the keys on the computer keyboard.

"I'm so sorry Miss McBride, but since you called, Mr Alexander, well, unfortunately, something he was unable to defer has called him away." Linda indicated for her to take a seat. Throughout the rest of the interview, never once did she look directly at Sheila again; it was to an imaginary companion sitting beside her that she directed her gaze.

"But it's not a problem," Linda added quickly. "All he would have started with today would have been a brief run through of the services we can provide you with; depending, that is, on who it is you wish to find, and I can take care of all of that for you. Now, let me see, you said something on the phone about wanting to find your child, a boy

I believe? The recent changes in the adoption laws here have made quite a difference you'll be glad to know. Now, in what year did the adoption take place?"

Sheila cleared her throat before explaining. "I'm afraid Linda, my dear, in my case there was no adoption – not one that I'm aware of, at least. It's rather more complicated than that..."

An hour or so later Sheila drifted back onto the street. Thirty minutes more and she was sitting on a train headed for Dover. She had no contact number to leave at the agency, there was as yet no reservation made at the coast. She hadn't thought that far ahead. Opening her handbag she took out a small medicine bottle filled with water. She lifted out her pill box, placing it on the pulled-down table. Taking a pill, she swallowed it down with a little sip. She had been warned to take complete rest, except for the walks, which she was supposed to increase at a steady pace to build up her strength.

Discharging herself earlier that week from the hospital in Galway, she'd phoned home to the parochial house and explained to Father Devine that she needed a few weeks more before she could come back, and although she and the good Father were as close as brother and sister, she had said nothing of her intended trip or the reasons that lay behind it. Taking the ferry she'd travelled to Liverpool and then on to London by train. This was her third day in England and already the travelling had made her weak. Flying would have been less tiring, she thought, but her consultant had ruled that out for the present. It had been one of the things he'd noted on the list of dos and don'ts that he had hastily scribbled down on the back of her medication instructions when she had insisted on leaving the hospital.

It had been seeing him there, in front of her eyes, on one of those cable stations; a tea time news report. Just a brief image, but she was sure it was him. He had been standing on the steps of the court house, his eyes piercing, so full of hatred and with such intensity that it reached into her soul, even though his glare was not into the camera, but at someone standing among the swarm of reporters and cameramen: a young woman.

Totally engulfed by the angry crowd, they had become hidden from her view. But that one brief glimpse that captured his face had been enough. Then the camera had zoomed in for a close-up. All that was visible to her in that moment, as recognition exploded within her heart and everything became blurred, was the golden crown of the woman at whom he was staring.

That was all that she could revive from the footage. The words of the news reporter had contorted into echoes as her own body had convulsed with the shock of what she was seeing. The tray she was carrying had dropped to the floor, her own limp form following it seconds later. The shock had actually stopped her heart.

Now, those long golden locks – the only other piece of the image apart from him – were all that remained still vivid in her mind: His face and that head of golden hair; hair that reminded Sheila, as she replayed the memory over and over in her mind, of how her own had once looked so many years ago.

That news report had been at the end of July. She had come to six weeks later. The drugs that had kept her under a veil of trance-like sleep as her heart regained its strength were gradually reduced and she awoke to a nurse gently calling her name, welcoming her back. Back to the reality of what she had seen.

It was him! How was it possible? But she was sure. The same glaring eyes: the same face, as if copied, frozen in time. Yes, it was him.

She had never believed them, the police officers, back then. She had imagined she could feel him alive, his thick, curly black hair; his breath damp against her breast as she soothed him before sleep. She would know if he was dead.

But they had won her over eventually. The small body, mutilated and bloated, was the right height, had the right hair. Black tufts of it, matted into clumps where it still clung to his scalp. Though the face, what had remained of it, was too horrid to bear – much like her own was now. This image had haunted her all these years and yet, all this time he was here, somewhere here; alive; grown. Yes! Yes, it was him.

The train slowing to a stop intruded on her thoughts. More people filed into the carriage. Sheila bowed her head, hunching herself over to avoid them. A woman pushed a small girl into the seat beside her. The wailing started. She apologised, feeling more for the embarrassment of the mother than for herself. Back home the locals had grown used to her affliction. She avoided the tourists in summer, keeping within the gardens of the house, ordering in as much as she could. Only in winter, as the weather roughened, was she able to roam free amongst people well accustomed to the sight of her. They no longer offended her with reactions to her plight.

All these strangers and their stares were beginning to affect her. Turning round to hide her face from peering eyes, she gazed out at the Kent countryside framed in the carriage window. It flicked past at speed; luscious and green it appeared almost untouched by the colours that autumn was painting on the other landscapes she had passed through during the last few days.

This was the place she had once loved, before cruel and dangerous people had sullied its views. Back then, running for her life, she had abandoned all those whom she once knew. She had fled from them, from that life and its memories. Even though it had been the only way to ensure their safety, her guilt surfaced daily. She had sought absolution every day since.

Thinking of her son there on those steps, the only feature that differentiated him from the ghost of his father was the birthmark, the distinct shape of the pattern it made on his shaved head. Weeks had passed in the hospital as growing in strength she had fought her way back to health, though nowhere near the physical strength that had carried her before. Her doctors were baffled by what they discovered to be a strong, unblemished heart. There was no coating or blockage of the arteries, none of the usual precursors of smoking, alcohol or stress. Shock, like a charged volt, had surged through her that day. She had kept the reasons to herself.

Images of her son unearthed deep wounds that had never really healed; awoken, they transported her back. How was it possible? She didn't know. Vividly she re-lived her initial refusal to accept his loss, the ensuing years of coaxing herself, finally, to reach the borderline of resignation: a muted belief that he was gone. The daughter she had born a short time after losing him, even though now separated from her, she could feel co-existing with her own breathing, could feel her daughter's blood running vibrantly within her own veins. She could at times imagine her laughter carried on the wind. Why, then, had she denied her son an existence there too?

Haunting images invaded her sleep, enticing guilt to infiltrate her waking hours. There was no relief in her thoughts; no glorious rejoicing for a son supposed dead, now alive, seen with her own eyes. A cold sense of dread smothered the motherly instincts within her. As fresh shoots of love tingled in her brain, a frosty apprehension stunted their growth. Like father like son, the warning echoed in her mind.

Eventually, losing the war raging in her soul, she could feel him again within her being. Not as she felt her daughter's presence, but darker, a draining dullness mingled inside her, warning, preparing her. Yes, the evil was there. She had read it in those eyes, recognised the evil behind them; recognised his father evident within him. Little, if any, of herself existed in her son. It was what she had feared most in those early years during their brief time together. Learning more and more of the dark side of her husband, she had guessed her beautiful little boy would grow up in the shadow of the brute that had spawned him. Remembering her friends' hurtful remarks, snatched asides whispered behind her back, she could see it clearly now.

So close had she been to getting him away. Then she had lost him. More worrying – and what had urged her to risk this expedition – was the thought that she had abandoned him. They would have tried to reach her, of course, the police, whenever it was that they had found him – if they had found him – but she had made herself unfindable by then. Somehow she had to track him down to explain, to save him as she had saved herself. Maybe it wasn't too late to repair whatever damage had been done.

The train stopped at another village. Sheila disembarked a stop before her intended one feeling drawn to the quiet hamlet. 'Vacancies', the fifth or sixth sign read, about a mile out, almost hidden from the road by a deep thicket of evergreens. Struggling, she managed to open the gate that closed the lane off from the main road. Something about it made her feel secure as she re-bolted the rusted metal latch. Before her the lane ran straight for several hundred yards then veered to the right, a thicket of trees hiding what lay beyond. To her left, fields still green spread out into the distance separated by lines of scraggy hedgerows. Keeping to the left she avoided the raised hump in the middle of the lane and urged on by the darkening sky as the light faded and dusk approached, walked more quickly than was comfortable.

She slowed her pace when she reached the bend in the lane,

relieved to find the Fiddler's Rest straight in front of her. It was a sprawling, white building with dormer windows jutting out in all directions around the roof. The inn at least looked welcoming, yellow light glowing from most of the ground floor windows. The entrance was covered by a square porch which sat literally out into the lane. She rang the bell and waited.

A tall, busty woman with shoulder-length greying hair and dressed in a high-necked blue sweater and loose fitting jeans welcomed her in. The entrance led through into a tavern-styled bar, most of one wall taken up by a large inglenook fireplace around which a few men in farm overalls supped over pints of stout. In the corner, a large screen was showing a snooker match that no one seemed interested in. Sheila turned quickly, facing the row of optics behind the bar and feeling inquisitive eyes piercing her back. The landlady gave her a forgiving smile as she asked for a room, offered a week in advance and said yes, she would be glad of some supper, but not until later; eight or nine pm would suit best, as long as it was no trouble.

Finding her room homely, the setting sun creating an orange glow against the cream paper on the walls, she decided to rest before unpacking. Making herself comfortable on the bed she willed sleep to come, but even with the blinds drawn it evaded her.

That first day, arriving in London, she had travelled to Gravesend. But Detective McAdams had moved on. The officer at the station thought she was mad. She could tell. He'd promised to forward the message, but she had read the scepticism on his face. She had known that no one would believe her.

A few weeks, Linda had told her at the agency. "Give it a few weeks before you call back."

A few weeks? She felt it was far too long a wait.

4

**White Cliffs Cottage, Dover – Writing Retreat of Claire
Hamilton: the same morning**

A fear so immense it urges: run! It tells you: run! Keep running!

Everywhere a brown fog, poisonous like an agitated spirit, moulds itself engulfing the room. Stinging, watery, the only things running are eyes. You are gulping, tasting mouthfuls of carbon. Gasping in air thick with smoke, which merely suffocates, catches the back of your throat. You feel hands, fumbling, clawing, reaching for you; seeking you out in the darkness. The instinct is to escape. The battle within is to survive. It diminishes fast; there is, you remember, nowhere to run.

Glass shatters, hits off your skin, pelting, pinpricks like hailstones.

Something tightens around your waist. Splinters of wood rip through your skin as you are dragged. A cooling wind ripples over your body. Greedy for oxygen your breathing quickens; too fast, too fast. Pain, hard, like a brick, thuds in your chest; rocks, jagged, pierce your face, your arms, your thighs. The wind, now strong – too strong – forces you against them.

Dropped on the ledge, shivering and bleeding, relieved to be free, you can hear it: the thrashing of waves two hundred feet below.

There is, you remember, nowhere else to go…

Running the cursor up, highlighting the words, her fingers thick and fleshy, lined with age, hover over the keys. Focusing on her left hand, she studies the set stones of her engagement ring as they glisten, catching the light from the screen. Beside it the wedding band is barely visible in the ravine it has formed in her flesh. Forever embedded, it is held tightly in place between the fluid-filled folds of her skin. Moving her gaze to her other hand, she watches the fingers, the tremors more evident than of late. She makes no attempt to steady them. Decisively she lowers one, touches the key, presses: 'Delete'.

It takes a few minutes but with slow, deep breaths, the shaking stops, her heart rate slows. At one with her heroine, the panic they shared is gone.

The phone rings; another interruption. Ring, ring, ring!

Sliding the clustered diamante clip-on from her ear lobe, she lifts the receiver and balances it in place with her shoulder, cutting the sound. Rolling her eyes in the direction of the ceiling, she focuses on a spot were the paint is stained. Rainwater has leaked in where a tile from the roof has become dislodged; something else she must remember to get fixed. It seems to be one thing after the next. So much for the builder her housekeeper had recommended to carry out the renovation work over the summer.

Rubbing the rough skin of a callus on the side of her finger, caused by a lifetime of holding a pencil against it, she releases a sigh and listens to the voice on the other end of the line: it is Jane.

She cuts across the greeting, "I promise you Jane, two months and you'll have the first draft." Pulling the receiver away from her ear, Claire Hamilton relaxes back in her chair waiting for the barrage from her agent to subside.

"No Jane, I'm not stalling. Why do you always have to think that? There were a few changes I had to make, and before you say anything, young lady, you'll like them. Nothing major, only, well, it has meant I've had to retrace them all the way back to the beginning. You know what it's like."

Swinging aimlessly from side to side, propelled by her feet in her battered captain's swivel, she lets Jane ramble on and distracts herself by picking at the tufts of horsehair poking out of the chair's torn leather arms. Her gaze wanders as she half listens, moving up to the series of post-its positioned in groups on the wall. Above them, in various sizes, a dozen eyes stare down at her; characters cut out of magazines: faces; people of differing ages and sizes that fitted the mould of her pen. Tiring of the conversation and sick of the hounding, she swings round to face the window.

"No I haven't made any change to the characters! Look Jane, for once just relax girl. Why, after all these years, do you still panic so much? You know very well that when I hand over a first draft it is always practically perfect, so there's no need to blow a fuse. Why don't you take yourself out of that stuffy office of yours and treat yourself to some lunch? Look, it's gone past one, I'll have to go. Two months, three at the most. I promise!"

She sets the receiver back down, briefly squeezes her eyes shut and sighs, her energy suddenly drained. Well, if nothing else she had gained herself an extension by slipping in an extra month at the end. Six months, though, would probably be more realistic, she was so far behind. All she had to show for the last three months were scrawled notes on the post-its and a new outline. That was it! Her career as a novelist had, it seemed, reached the point of crisis.

Out of the window, across the cliffs and standing high above the town, she can see the castle majestic against the skyline. Through its grounds the ghost of her first heroine's lover had walked, haunting the poor girl until in despair she had thrown herself to her death from its ramparts. It had been Claire's first book. Now it sat proudly on a shelf beside the window alongside all the others, fifteen of them, all romantic tragedies with a supernatural theme. She had sold millions of copies of each of them, save the last two. She had been the first lady of the genre once; now it appeared the genre was out of fashion. Her sales, despite her best efforts, had plummeted. *Blood Lust*, her last publication, had received not a single nomination for any of the top awards. Historical thrillers were the in thing at the moment: crusading knights, medieval sagas, all grounded in historical facts. To create one of substance required dedicated research, which was something Claire found tedious. The fifteen novels she had penned had evolved purely from her own imagination: they were her own, honest, creations.

Writing was her life. Even after all this time she was still instantly overcome with emotion whenever she removed the packaging from her newly published copies. Hiding away in her study, she would sit stroking her fingers over and over the cover sleeves, then turn each page, one by one, not reading the words but taking delight in the fact that they were hers. At intervals she would lift the book to her face and smell the fresh print; to her the scent was food from the gods.

At present, though, there was no adrenalin coursing through her, only a prevailing sense of dread. If this novel nose dived like the last, there was always the lingering fear - pushed to the front of her mind by her recent tumble from the top twenty best sellers list - that her publisher would drop her. The drafting of this book was becoming harder with the passing of each week and although her sense of pride, along with her fear of publishing yet another book that her reading public would not take to their hearts, was causing her anxiety, she knew that worrying about it was only a small part of the problem. It wasn't writer's block, nothing like that. It was more an apprehension about actually telling the story she had chosen. The plot was brilliant. Even Jane had thought it riveting.

The original outline lay on her lap. Her maroon-framed lenses hanging on a linked chain from her neck rested on her chest. Raising them up to the light she could see the smudges and polished them off against the soft lavender chenille of her cardigan, before planting them low on the bridge of her nose and squinting at the small print to read the outline through.

The storyline followed the journey of several young women trying to find their birth mothers. The first part of the novel she had plotted out; it was fine. What had brought her to a grinding halt was the second part: the actual search by the children, years later, for their mothers. The problem? It wasn't fiction. None of it; every wretched part was true. She herself, a long time ago, had been one of those birth mothers about whom she was writing.

It wasn't that she was scared to write it. Not any longer. The bastard who had hunted them was dead, well buried and forgotten. There were pieces of the story, though, that were still missing; parts she needed to fill in. She had also felt obliged to change some things in her version of events, small discrepancies that were necessary to protect their identities. Jane, of course, was not privy to this inner knowledge and at times, when sifting through the original outline, the tensions between the two women had boiled over. Claire had found herself cornered, giving way to some of Jane's influences merely to prevent her from realising the truth: that there was something personal behind the themes directing the plot. Tragic though some of their experiences had been – her heroine's in particular – it was with the character she had chosen to portray herself that she struggled. How was she to tie her into the storyline? In the real world there was nothing earth-moving, nothing to create pathos in telling her ending, at least not in her experience of it. There existed just an emptiness that yearned to be filled.

At around the time the child she had given up turned eighteen, Claire had registered her details with several databases held by local authorities. In recent years she had also added them to forums on the internet. She longed to be found. For almost two decades she had waited. Countless times contact had been made, but never with any success. It had all become a burden in the end; a vicious cycle of hope and longing. A churning of emotions that became swamped with despair: her own when answering inquires from girls seeking their birth mothers, or theirs when answering hers. She was never their mother; none of them was her daughter. Her daughter, if she was alive, obviously didn't want to find her. Resigned to that fact Claire had accepted defeat, but there still dwelled within her a need to explain and she held on to the hope that one day she would indeed get that chance. This novel was the product of that need. She would use this latest publication, if she managed to get it finished, to air her story.

In the last few years she had lost several friends. The effect was to make her more aware of her own mortality. Whoever knew how much time they had left? This was a question she found herself musing over more often these days. No one did, not really, though at her stage in life – sixty-two – you could count on one depressing fact: there were fewer days ahead than had already passed. Acknowledging that her time was limited only added a sense of urgency to the task Claire had set herself.

The sudden dashing of rain against the glass made her turn her gaze towards the window. The blue sky was quickly disappearing behind a mountain of grey. The cottage was exposed to the elements standing as it did near to the cliff edge. The thick walls, together with the double-glazed windows she had recently had installed, would block out much of the sound of approaching storms, but there were moments when she felt that if the tempest was bad enough, the whole lot could be sent tumbling over the edge.

"Don't be so theatrical," her husband would answer when she occasionally voiced her concerns. "Something that's stood its ground for over four hundred years will be here forever."

His soothing words did little to dispel her fears and she often wondered if this piece of cliff edge would stand the test of time. There were now only three feet of chalk grassland beyond the wire at the foot of the rear garden; three feet where not so long ago there had been at least six. Because of the erosion, they had been refused a mortgage by the bank. She'd had to pay cash for the cottage and the renovations. What more evidence did she need? But they had rented it for years and when the landlord had put it up for sale, she couldn't risk losing it. So they had bought it, even though it had tied up all their savings and forced them to sell off the two houses they rented out.

Despite what had happened here – the fire and its aftermath – this was the place in which she had always found her inspiration; the place where she had first discovered she could write. True, the winters here could be rough and although the isolation suited her during the summer months, she found the lonely winter nights depressing. Not only that, but they brought with them a tendency to stir afresh too many ghosts from her past.

Flicking on the lamp, she paused for a moment to look at the framed photographs of her family. Motherhood, eventually, she had enjoyed with her sons and though she had longed for another girl, one had never come. It was something that had always saddened her and that she now regarded as a punishment from God for having rid herself of her first child. She studied the smiling faces of her children: cherished memories of days at the beach; decorating Christmas trees; even the tears shed – not by them, but by her – on their first days at school. They filled her heart with feelings of warmth that nothing else could ever come near. Yet ever present was that constant aching, that constant need to know what experiences she had lost, experiences that would never be hers. She did not even know her daughter's name. Nothing; she knew nothing about her. Oh yes – she had made guesses: Sarah, Julie, Annabelle, perhaps Anita? Could it be, she wondered, that by some strange quirk of fate they shared the same name? But then, which name? There were, after all, three from which to choose. How much did that fact complicate her accessibility – the name changes?

She had sat on park benches over many summers dreaming up images, scanning the faces of children, watching little girls pass by pushing dolls in miniature prams. She had dreamed up a replica world for her own little girl, panicked by the thought that even if she came across her daughter she might not know her. For the first ten years, when the new school term started, she had parked across from the school gates examining the faces of the little girls their mums brought to school. In time it had become a tortured addiction; any one of them could be her daughter. In her lowest moments she could easily have allowed herself to snatch one. She had never acted on the impulse, though at times, studying the mothers, she had felt bitter anger. Was one of them the usurper, stealing hugs, accepting the love and loyalty of a daughter who was not theirs, but hers?

Perhaps it was a godsend that she had become pregnant with her eldest son when she did, for she had known by then that she was no longer sane. She alone had known the desperation that clawed beneath her skin. Such had the strain become in her heart that who knows what she might have done had she not had her son to distract her? A man parked across from the school scrutinising little girls as she had done would have raised suspicion, but she, a kind, smiling, well-dressed woman, melted into the scenery. It would have been so easy; too easy.

Looking back now, the memory of it all sent a shudder down Claire's spine. Years later, after the boys went to boarding school, she had resumed her vigils, but then it had not been the children, but the young mothers who were the focus of her attention. Time had passed and guilt had rooted in her heart. If only she had been stronger.

Moving her hand to stretch out the wrinkles in her neck, Claire knew she had to leave some sort of explanation, tell her story; find some way of communicating her love. Somewhere in the future she envisaged her estranged daughter, though still faceless to her, sitting reading about her feelings. Claire prayed that she would come to understand, come to realise that sometimes you just don't have any say in what happens, that strength is sometimes impossible to find. It wasn't important that the lines between truth and fiction were blurred in the book's pages. Everything was there if you looked for it. The sympathy she craved would be found because, as mistress of the pen, she would create it. The pages were filled with words. Manipulated to serve her purpose, they would become a paper chain; a link that once read would bond their fates. In effect, her book was a letter to her daughter.

It had been immensely difficult. As she had struggled through yet another summer, all the scenarios she had created to carry the story into the present had got her thinking. She had to keep reminding herself that this book had to sell. The element of suspense in her original draft, she realised, fizzled out in the second part. It needed something; something more gripping. So, for the last few months she had done a period of research – something she had never needed to do before. She had interviewed trained counsellors; grownup children searching for lost families; re-united families, and despondent adults whose hopes of happy reunions had been dashed. These she had found the most harrowing, getting lost in their anger, her own denied a second time.

Various lines of thought, though, had emerged during her research. To what extent was blood thicker than water? Could the bonds between blood siblings and adopted siblings become as powerful as natural ones? What about the long-standing debate of nature over nurture? What were the effects on siblings, for example, when someone else appeared without warning on the doorstep claiming to be their mother? The question had also occurred to her: what feelings of resentment would exist? What if the adopted child had not had a happy life? Of the many angles there were to work the plot, the latter intrigued her the most. At times it worried her too, but it was a fantastic angle to mould. The idea had come to her as the autumn rains had begun to encroach into the last of those long summer days. What if an adopted child had such a terrible time it was only interested in seeking revenge? The consequences of this would make a much more haunting tale. That was when she had scrapped the half-finished first draft. It was this that had really held her back.

She swung back round to her desk, stared into the blank screen and thought of her characters all wrapped up in their own problems. They were based on her former friends. She knew nothing much about their present lives – at least, not their personal lives. She had come across them from time to time, those who had made their way up the social and professional ladders. There were a few of whom she knew a little, but soon she would know everything. The notices would be in Friday's papers, presented in the code they had all agreed on for emergencies. They would not be missed. Unnecessary now, of course, to use a code, but it gave it a touch of mystery. It was an Agatha Christie moment that she'd thought up: old acquaintances invited to dinner in an isolated mansion all with their own secrets hidden in their past. The thought made her smile.

The sky beyond the window now matched the dark grey of the sea. There would be no ferries sailing out tonight, she thought, studying the choppy waves tumbling closer towards the cliffs. Returning her attention to the outline pages, she continued to read. She needed a twist in the tail. Closing her eyes she entered her characters' world, immersing herself in their lives again, reliving their memories, feeling their hopes, their fears.

Late afternoon passed unnoticed into evening, and then, out of nowhere, born of her gift, spiralling from her own inspiration, he came into her line of vision. Lunging forward, her eyes blinked open and she smiled. Her creation: a figure so obsessed and deranged that he would move through the pages exacting his revenge, began to form in her mind. Stretching back in her chair, she blanked out the room, her imagination taking over to give him a face and extending to his environment.

Earlier that morning, walking Chiko, her Labrador, along the Samphire Hoe below her cottage, soaked from sea spray, the harsh October wind beating hard, stinging slaps on her face, she had been reminded of a place she'd once stayed in for a book signing. The place itself was so beautiful she had since returned, often, for long weekends, but during that first stay one stormy weekend, three novels back, the ragged outline of the coast together with the harsh winds and sea had created such an atmosphere that she'd known she would use the setting one day. Now, opening a drawer she rifled through its contents, her fingers shaking with suppressed excitement. Once Jane got hold of the first ten or so chapters everything would be okay, like it used to be under her pseudonym, she would be back on top. Her fingers close on her collection of blank picture-postcards – it was her habit always to pick some up everywhere she went. Gathering the cards she placed them on her desk one by one, laying each one beside the other, studying them for a time.

Satisfied at last, she switched to a new file on her computer, flexed her fingers and began to key.

5

"Now, how does that look, Gracie?"

Rachel angled a hand-held mirror from behind. Rounded mounds of buttery blonde hair formed into perfect layers, not a strand out of place.

"Just look at ye; sittin' there. Sure ye look grand enough to be the Princess of Monaco herself."

Gracie smiled as the mirror moved behind her, following as she turned her head left and then right. She congratulated herself for stopping at the chemist before coming to the hairdresser's, and picking out a golden blonde rinse to lift her two-week-old highlights. But she had to admit, without help she couldn't have made it look this good herself. It was wonderful what these girls could do with your hair. She felt good. A little twinkle appeared in her eye.

"Did I ever tell you girls about the time the Princess came here?"

Midway through a shampoo and facing in the opposite direction, Trisha, the other stylist, rolled her eyes. Rachel leant forward and smiled into the mirror meeting Gracie's reflection. She was well used to intercepting just at the right time and quickly too. Before Gracie had a chance to clear her throat Rachel began re-telling a shorter version of the story. Gracie's seemed to have become more long winded with every telling of it – or maybe it was just because she had told it so many times it seemed longer. Indeed, Rachel felt almost as if she had witnessed the event with her own eyes, even though it had all taken place well over twenty years before she was even born.

"How beautiful ye'd a looked too and only fifteen and chosen because ye were her namesake. The Princess and him her husband, the Prince Rainier, came to visit Croagh Patrick back in what was it, sixty one? And when ye handed her the posy she bent down all smellin' a roses and ran her hand along yer cheek – with the glove off too… ah… sure, ye must have felt on top of the world?"

Lost in the memory of it, Gracie smiled. How popular she'd been because of the honour. Offers of courting coming from as far a-field as Ballinrobe. She'd been a bit of a looker too, back then. Yet out of all of them suitors she'd gone and settled on the worst rotten apple in the barrel.

Rachel slipped back towards the sinks and busied herself tidying up the carousel trolley. Gracie continued reflecting, staring into the mirror, totally lost in her thoughts, her attention moved from her hair to her face. Her heart quickly sank into her stomach: there was nothing to escape the ravages of time when you looked into the mirrors in this place. Pushed up against them you couldn't step back. Magnified before her eyes every line marked its memory: tiny broken purplish threads close to the skin's surface, blotches etched into her complexion. It seemed with every visit their number had increased. Once puffy, now hollow, her cheeks had sunk to form two jowls on either side of her chin. Long gone were the pouting, raspberry-stained lips of her youth, all that remained were colourless cracks. They looked like they felt as she slid her tongue between her lips to moisten them; shrivelled, horizontal stalks, dried up in the life of the seasons, verging on the doorstep of winter. Silently she sighed; only them as were rich could magic away the wrinkles of experiences best left forgot.

If she put enough by every week, though, she could pay for a dose of that Botox stuff and just about in time for her next birthday too. She would have to phone up about it first though, just to make sure that at fifty-five her skin wasn't past it. She leaned in closer to the mirror. Her breasts, she supposed, weren't all that dropped south. Well, thanks for small mercies, and her face wasn't as bad as Patti Reilly's, hers was as tough as old boot leather, Gracie mused silently to herself. That woman: passing herself off for forty-eight, well, really, she thought, pursing her lips and giving a disapproving shake of her head: her that sat beside me the whole way through school, taking herself all the way to Newport to get her HRT from the chemist there. Annie Maguire's worked in the back there all her days, nudging me arm in the queue for confessions, month before last, to tell me all about it. Patti didn't think anybody knew her there, did she now?

Small world it is after all, Gracie told herself smugly, a quick wink at herself in the mirror. Someday I'll drop her right in it!

Gracie had cut out the advert the week before for a place in Castlebar. Maybe that's too close to home, she thought. I could always use a false name, though, when I make the enquiry, no harm in that; none at all. She'd splashed out on a new compact too. It was tucked in her handbag: a black, glossy case, it lit up all bright when you opened it, for touching up in the dark, like in cars and things. Fifty euro all but a cent! She savoured the amount in her head. Fifty euro, fifty! Hope that he's suffering from motion sickness in his grave! She spared him a thought, watching her reflection smile as her hand motioned a cross under the apron. Neither would she be trying out her new compact in the dark either. No! I'll make damn sure there are plenty of faces around me when I take it out in the ladies' toilet at the dinner tonight.

For years she'd been an object of pity. Now an emancipated woman she was better off than the rest of them. Gracie O'Hara wasn't tied up behind a pinny any longer. I'm not under the thumb of anyone now, can buy little extravagances like that, now that there's no raidin' of me purse for the beer money on weekends.

Weekends. Wasn't it strange, she thought, all this time wondering what it would be like to enjoy them and still I get to feelin' on edge come the Friday evening. Wasn't able to find me purse this morning, was I? Still prone to hiding it. Well, old habits die hard. She released a sigh, touching her fingers to her cheek bone, mocked: all these'ns and their advertising, promising the earth to flipping old idiots like meself.

Seeing Rachel had come over to stand behind her, Gracie spoke to her reflection. "Sorry love, just wanted to take a good look at it. It'll be one hell of a miracle though, if it survives that tempest out there. Wicked it is, wicked. Pity too, after ye making such a good job of it and all. But, well, we can't have it all now, can we, dear?"

Rachel intervened, loosening the plastic apron from Gracie's neck. "At least it's not raining, yet!"

Gracie opened her purse taking out a twenty-euro note then dug deeper finding a two-euro coin for a tip and handed it all over to Rachel.

Without warning there was a series of thuds as the wind pounded against the salon door and windows, a succession of gusts threatening to bring the glass in around them. Gracie waited a few moments for it to subside then stood with her face up against the salon window peering out. She could get a taxi, but then, on Friday evening they'd all be booked up doing runs in and out of Castlebar. There was nothing else for it, she would just have to walk.

From where the salon was situated just on the edge, where Quay Street joined Peter Street, Gracie had a direct view of the Octagon. It formed a central place in the town with most of the town's streets running off it, the stone monument standing in the centre. The seats placed around it were empty and beyond this, the pavements lining the road were also deserted; it was as if the place was a ghost town. She ran her gaze up the Portland Stone figure of St Patrick, erected in recent years to replace the figure of George Clendening, a long dead dignitary of Westport, the old statue of Clendening having had the misfortune to be used for target practice by Free State troops during the civil war. I don't doubt I'll be getting me own head blew off me before I get home, she thought, as again the wind buffeted against the glass, its ferocity making her jump back.

Behind her, the hum of the hooded drier started up. Trisha indicated to Rachel that she was slipping into the private room at the back for a smoke. Helping Gracie into her coat, Rachel drew closer lowering her voice.

"Now, I'm not one for talking behind a body's back, but she was in here early on this afternoon before the wind started getting up and, well, just looking at you here now, well, I've just got to say it to ye." Rachel glanced around to check that the other customer was still out of earshot under the drier.

"Well, that so-called friend of yours and mine, Mrs Reilly, her and all her airs and graces, well, don't be going and putting me in it, but I just have to say, well, ye look a good ten years younger than she does, and her still not fifty!"

Gracie left the sanctuary of the salon with her feet almost dancing as she headed up the street. She was bowled over by the compliment Rachel had given her. Poor Rachel, she thought, she is only engaged to be married to the auld bag's eldest son! What a sentence that would be for such a nice young lass. Heaven knows, I served a long enough one of me own.

In her pocket the bleeper went off, interrupting her thoughts. "Damned technological paraphernalia of a thing this is." Muttering under her breath, Gracie took it out to press the button. "Flipping hell, three times in one hour it's gone off. Come here; go there; fetch this; do that; instead of asking nicely. What's wrong with using the bloody phone! That flipping Reilly woman and all her bright ideas! I suppose she'd had one pinned to poor Jimmy Reilly since they was invented. If he'd got sent t'hell at the end of his days, sure he'd a thought it t'be heaven for sure!"

The walk up Quay Street was a trying one that quickly dampened her mood. She thought of Michael as she walked, his trip back to the States was running on more than he had planned. She wished he'd hurry himself up and get back. Sure it was one thing to cover for Sheila. Maybe it was that 'Priest's Housekeeper' was a position to set some tongues wagging, but looking out for Michael was what suited her best. It was almost as if he allowed her to mother him. What an odd pair they'd become, each leaning on the other salvaging something of a life to deal with what they'd each lost.

Even thoughts of Michael, though, couldn't lessen feeling the strain as her legs struggled to carry her, taut now, stretched against the steep rise out of the town. Taking the brunt of the climb, they felt close to snapping. Walking into Quay Road, she passed the stonemasons and knowing the worst of the hill was almost past and it would be a little easier on her legs, she allowed herself a faint sigh of relief. Keeping tight against the stone wall that would shelter her all the way down to the bay, she urged herself on, thinking that soon she would pass the hotel and be able to see the girls setting the tables in preparation for the parish dinner later on.

Across the road she saw her own terraced house come into view. Well, it was as good as hers. The letter had arrived this morning from the Council. The keys she would collect on Monday when she signed the lease. There was always a room at Michael's house if she wanted to take up his offer, but this was one dream she'd held on to for so long she intended to see it through. A place all to herself that wasn't fouled by the odour of smelly socks or strewn with bits and pieces left lying for her to pick up, and last but not least, a place not blighted by the pungent smell of morning-after alcohol; a sanctuary all to herself.

Very nearly lifted off her feet halfway across the road, she stopped for a few seconds in front of the brick wall. Running water, oil heating and a fully fitted kitchen were things she had always longed for as well. Little kiddies on both sides of her, these she had dreamed of once, too. An ache thudded in her chest. She turned and walked on.

That's the easy bit over, she thought, her pace speeding as the path swept downwards towards the modern holiday lets. She had already passed the mini-market when she remembered the daily paper and doubled back. Folding the paper into her bag she bought her lotto ticket, then remembering she'd smoked her last cigarette with her coffee out back in the salon, she bought a packet of ten Majors and headed back out into the storm.

Stopping at the corner, she pulled the loosened scarf closer round her head making a tight knot against her chin, attempting to save her fresh cut-and-blow-dry from the strengthening winds. She could puff it up again later. Following the road, a solitary figure, she met no one. The shops and cafés along the quay were closing up early, the scant scattering of out-of-season tourists having wisely disappeared into the bars or opting for their particular hotel's entertainment, leaving the storm to invade the empty streets at will.

Clew Bay harbour behind her, Gracie battled on, still muttering complaints to herself. Crossing sides at the pub past the fork in the road beyond the harbour wall, she decided to tackle the shortcut up the hill and over the fields. She estimated it would take a good ten minutes off her journey. Time was in short supply this evening.

Climbing higher, the tail of her coat flapping against her legs, she became more exposed to the wind. A sharp stone pierced into her ankle and she winced for a second before continuing her struggle over the uneven ground. Maybe she should take up driving now that things were different. There hadn't been any point in it before. She'd have spent her time driving to and from the pub to pick him up in the evenings. Now that she was getting a blow-dry regular like, it would come in handy being able to just pop into the car. No more waiting on buses. Yes, she would book lessons next week. No more battling the elements on evenings like this.

The wind was a constant force pushing her backwards, slapping hard against her arthritic frame making her want to cry out in agony, but breathing was enough to cope with; for now she was just about managing by turning her head to the side and gulping in what air she could. All around her the wind howled. It was an invisible greatness; a force pushing her back, only to scoop her up and plunge her forward, toppling her to the ground. Ripping at thick, reedy clumps of grass, she held on tight to prevent flight. Undeterred, she struggled back onto her feet and fought her way forward, trying to pick out level bits of ground on the rough grazing pasture that was strewn randomly with sheep droppings and rocks.

With October midway through, the weather had desolated the landscape. Darkness was coming down fast with giant beasts of blackened clouds looming forbiddingly against the shoreline below her. She could just about pick out several figures standing against the wall of the bay, arms stretched out trying to fly in the wind. Stupid Americans! Sensible people came in the summer. On summer evenings the skyline was captivating with beautiful gold and red sunsets. A succession of gales had all but stripped naked the trees and they now haunted the sky below her, spooking the air and intensifying the pitch of the wind. Like banshees wailing they cried into the dying evening foretelling their tales of doom.

She cursed herself for not being quick enough in coming up with an excuse when the good Father had asked her to give a hand helping out with the old bugger for yet another few weeks. Why couldn't he be retired to his own parish? Wasn't it just typical? Her that had been lumbered all her life, lifting and laying, cooking and cleaning for one nasty, good for nothing, lazy blackguard, now to be hoodwinked into taking on another. If only Michael would hurry up and get back it could be somebody else's problem. She had made it clear from the start that days weren't a problem, but all of a sudden she'd been burdened with the evenings. Yes, hoodwinked! Must have seen her coming! Message from above! "Keep that Gracie O'Hara toiling on her knees! Keep her away from the bingo hall on Thursday night! Let that friggin' old bag Patti Reilly snatch the ten thousand euro instead!"

At the cattle gate she rested to catch her breath. And to think I'd just been set free not but six months ago, she thought, and the farm drunk into the ground. Ten thousand would have patched it up nicely. It was mine for the taking. She realised she'd just thought ill of the dead yet again and set about crossing herself several times over. Ten candles she was lighting every morning after Mass; payment to keep him six foot under or deeper. "Hunt ye I will the rest of yer days!" All them that waited on the Reaper around his bed had heard him curse her. His dying promise; probably the only one in his worthless life he would keep too! She reminded herself. And to think the undertaker thought I was joking when I told him to make sure he nailed the lid down tight. I wouldn't put it past Tom O'Hara to make a deal with the Devil to get walking the Earth again. Killed the auld bugger to know he was leaving it first. She crossed herself again.

Reaching the lane up to the cottage, she grunted, noting the absence of smoke from the chimney. Oh! Her and her fancy red nails are too good for lighting fires! This time she did not cross herself, sure that the good man above knew as well as she did why Patti Reilly wanted her nights kept free, and her the talk of the town for years.

There was the man himself. Gracie paused, shaking her head. The ignoramus lay slumped in the armchair, his mouth catching flies. Face red as a beetroot. A whisky bottle drained to the last drop sat on the table. Hmm! Courtesy of Patti Reilly, no doubt. I'll give you a good piece of my mind! Just you wait, she complained to herself, then wondered how he had been fit enough to bleep her.

Standing over the snoring mass she gave a silent thought for her old friend. Sheila McBride will be made a saint for sure when she dies, looking after them at the parochial house then running back over here to tend to him. Was it any wonder she'd dropped with a massive coronary. They'd been told she was due back home this week. Poor thing has probably taken a turn for the worse, Gracie thought. She would have to ask the good Father Tom about her later.

The parish dinner was due to start at eight and himself here was supposed to be at the top table. Well, he wasn't going to recover in time to go. That was, she supposed, a blessing in itself. She wouldn't have to get him there. No point pressing a shirt for him either, she decided. She was running late as it was. It was best to plough on with what she could. She'd light the fire then, first, and leave the old priest where he sat. Years of experience of lifting one drunken fool reminded her that they were often best left where they fell. Besides, she was too old now to lift a weight like that.

It was close on seven when she turned off the pot of stew. The fire she'd lit had not taken long to lift the damp off the cottage. Mellowed a little, mostly thinking of the dancing ahead, she took pity on the old priest. She would fill a hot water bottle. After all, heaven forbid that he would catch a chill, which he was sure to do after hoity-toity Patti Reilly had left him freezing all day. She'd make sure the town gossips didn't go making a mistake and pointing their fingers at her.

The water boiled, she filled the bottle, keeping enough water back for a cup of tea. Everything was taken care of. "Right," she said to herself, "I'll have a cuppa and a few little puffs then sort his bed." Lifting the *Irish Times* she caught sight of the novena at the top of the page: "To St Brigit," she read it aloud. "We pray for your intercession: Thursday 1st November, White Cliffs Cottage, Dover, Kent."

"Mmm…!" Gracie, exclaimed under her breath, surmising that St Brigit being associated with fertility and all, it must be folks trying for a baby. It must have cost a pretty penny, the space on the front page. I wouldn't have put in me address if it were me, she thought, what with peeping toms and all that. But then, I suppose that's why they've put it in the *Irish Times*, don't suppose it's in the English one. Wonder if our blessed saint will do her bit? She certainly didn't intercede for me where babies were concerned – not with the ten thousand euro, neither. She set the paper back down on the table and rinsed her cup.

Kent. She thought about it as she checked the lid on the water bottle. England. How different her life would have been if she'd gone with Sheila McBride all those years ago. One thing for sure, if she had she wouldn't have done what Sheila had and come back here. Quiet people the McBrides though, and I suppose that after the accident, scarred for life with a face like that, Sheila felt she needed home more. Terrible affliction that must have been, Gracie mused, especially in her day, and her being such a beauty too.

An almighty howling sounded as she carried the bottle into the bedroom at the back of the cottage. She found herself ducking her head fearing the roof might cave in. The lights were flickering. All I need now is a bleedin' power cut, she thought.

Suddenly the room was plunged into darkness just as she'd bent over to fix up the bed. But the room didn't stay dark. There was light. It was dim, too dim. More light grew behind her, low from the floor, another sourced from beside her.

Panic grabbed her heart.

"Hello Sheila," the voice said.

Still bent over the bed, Gracie turned, the nervous twitching about her mouth resulting in a partial smile. "Sure, I'm not Sheila!"

From beneath the shadow of the low ceiling, the figure stepped out. He had been waiting all evening.

6

Craven House near Canterbury, Kent: Friday 19th October

"Holding the opened bottle of Merlot in the doorway, Simon Alexander paused, vexed to find Richard still sitting where he had left him half an hour ago. The evening had started off so well, or so it had seemed. Richard had even arrived early, and Mrs Webster, for once, had made an effort to be pleasant to his partner for a change, much to Simon's relief.

In a few hours, following an early dinner, they should have been heading off together for the airport: the weekend in Vienna to celebrate their first anniversary he'd announced several weeks beforehand; a surprise for Richard. But shortly after arriving, when Simon had been in the middle of a call from a client, he had detected a change in Richard's mood: his lover, brow furrowed as if deeply annoyed, had suddenly taken to pacing the floor and shortly thereafter had announced that he wasn't going to Vienna. No explanation, nothing. 'Go on your own or not! I don't care,' he had said.

Richard could be like that sometimes. Simon hadn't had time to dwell on the let down. Richard had shrugged him off as Mrs Webster had announced dinner, which he had eaten alone as Richard hadn't followed him to the dinning room. Richard's dinner had sat untouched until Mrs Webster, deeply annoyed at the snub, had abruptly snatched the plate back to the kitchen.

Simon entered the sitting room and headed towards the drinks cabinet for a wine glass. All he had done was take one short call, what was the problem with that? Just because Richard didn't let his business interests conflict with his private life didn't mean he had to follow suit. The call had been important: Fiona Reid was fragile; her brother was dead, she needed support – and if this lady she spoke of, in the village of Higham, had fresh information perhaps the mystery surrounding her birth could be solved.

Simon set down his glass and apprehensively approached Richard; how could he change his mind? They needed this time away; of that he was certain. "What is it with you and these things anyway?" he asked, trying to sound casual, leaning forward to rest his head on Richard's neck.

Richard Noble gave no reply reacting to Simon's touch by moving his head away from him. Sitting the wrong way round astride a bentwood chair, his chin resting on the back of it, he gazed into the conservatory, eyes transfixed on the vine. Behind the glass it clung haphazardly to its wires, a tumble of pale green foliage. It was taking all of his attention. Almost all; he had been aware of Simon's restless presence behind him for some time. Pitiful! He thought as he felt the madness growing within him seeking possession of his mind, squirming, demanding to be released and hungry for control.

Wait! He willed himself to placate, to hang on, to watch the miracle of metamorphosis on the vine, but it was becoming harder to contain them, these souls he carried who were zapping his strength, taking over his mind. Souls without purpose; they were draining him. It had taken him years to finally win over their trust and coerce them into letting him lead the way.

And then there was the girl, this Fiona Reid. Her very existence had thrown him; caught all of them off guard. Confusion engulfed them and in its wake, each one trapped inside the other, Richard was powerless to control them. Their voices had risen to a cacophony in his head as they fought, each one vying for supremacy. But he had won in the end, his will was the strongest. He had brought order out of the chaos; worked out a way to end their rage. Then, just when they were all settling down and learning to co-exist, he had lost control and made a mess of things. Richard was smart though. He had been able to cover the mistake. At least, that time.

The urge to kill grew greater within him.

Up until now he had managed to blank out the over-pronounced sighs from somewhere in the room behind him, but inside his skin he knew the rage would not subside. These butterflies, 'things' as Simon called them, had reminded him of what the priest had taught him; they showed him how it should be. The human race had sullied itself; forgotten its purpose; broken the natural hierarchy handed down over generations. One had to look to nature to be reminded of the rules, so had said the priest.

This present intrusion from Simon he had expected for more than a few minutes, but Simon was easy to ignore. Before him, released from the chrysalis, a new life was unfolding; there was nothing Simon could do to deter him from witnessing it. Without moving his gaze from the vine he turned his head slightly to avoid the musty aftertaste of wine from Simon's breath as it invaded his space.

"I'll go on my own Richard," Simon said into his ear. It was meant as a threat. "This will be our last evening together for two whole weeks! Don't you think we should be making the most of it?" Simon's hands had begun to massage into his neck seeking to arouse him, pleading of a need.

Richard tightened his grip on the chair. For Simon the moment of birth had passed unnoticed. He knew it was beyond the man to realise the importance of the scene unfolding before their eyes. Simon had become materialistic; rendered immune to the Queen Alexandra Birdwings and their spectacular beauty. People who have everything appreciate nothing.

Yes! It is special tonight, Richard thought, fighting off the distraction as sweaty fingers dug their way deeper into his skin willing him to respond.

In front of him, wings fluttered.

Richard shrugged his shoulders irritably, his hands gripped hard on the chair back. His feet, angled at either side of the bentwood's legs, pressed against the edge of the frame that held the glass divide between him and the tropical garden. Inside himself he battled for control: the instinct within him to defend his position against the threatening urge to kill. Poised in anticipation, the excitement bubbled like lava in a volcano, heating his blood; intent on taking a life.

Wings fluttered.

Built in microphones amplified the sound throughout the room.

"You're playing hard to get aren't you? You're jealous because I'm heading on to Frankfurter after Vienna?" Simon snapped.

Jealous!

Richard's eyes remaining focused on the vine.

Fuck this bastard!

Simon was an imbecile, but a necessity; he'd had his uses – access to these beauties being one of them. That trip of his had come at a perfect time in fact. Everything was falling into place: the woman in Ireland; with her too he had not faltered. He had heard her admit to her barrenness.

Inadequate creature!

His journey had not been wasted. Though not the prize he had sought, she too was part of his mission. He would have to return to Higham again. The phone call Simon had taken earlier had been vital to his plan, the gods favoured him; the wheels were turning once again. The key was there, he was sure of it. This trip of Simon's would give him the time he needed. This time nothing would hold him back. This time he would succeed.

Roughly, Simon drew away from him. He heard the clink of glass on glass; at last, a respite; Simon was filling another glass of wine.

"You know; sometimes I think you're more interested in them than you are in me," Simon scoffed, slurring his words as a knock on wood distracted him and he turned in the direction of the door.

It opened and Mrs Webster entered the room. Fixing a thick, woolly green hat down over the pink and blue rollers in her hair, she excused herself for interrupting. "Everything's locked up save the front door; you'll make sure not to forget to lock it after you set the alarm when you leave won't you?"

Simon nodded, taking a sip of his wine. She continued buttoning up her coat. "Your taxi into town is booked for ten minutes to seven. I'll see you Monday fortnight then, Sir. Have a good trip."

Simon gestured a wave of thanks and she smiled at him. Backing out of the room she glanced momentarily at Richard, sat with his back to her. Suddenly he turned; his eyes intense, a cold vivid blue. Her smile faded in an instant. Hairs stood on her arms, a look of disapproval deep-rooted on her face. The door swung closed sharply behind her.

Simon pulled his shirt sleeve back and looked at his watch before returning his attention to Richard. "I don't think she likes you!"

"Is that a fact?" Richard stood up from his chair, heard the slam of another door followed by the revving of a car, its motor fading fast into the distance. Finally they were alone. He smiled at Simon. "She doesn't know me, so what is there to like or dislike?"

He had waited patiently for tonight: Simon Alexander was no longer needed; their affair had run its course. Over a year ago, as Richard Noble, he had introduced himself, asked Simon, 'Can you help me find my mother?' Useless prat Simon had turned out to be. Later, Richard had accidentally bumped into someone else; someone as determined as he was: Fiona Reid. She, he knew, would find her for him.

Richard! He could summon him when he needed to. The best thing about him was that he didn't exist; none of them did. Nobody knows me, he laughed into himself. Nobody! He was nobody and yet everybody all at the same time – but always invisible. It was how he survived: his was the face that fronted them to the world and he had taken care to disguise that too.

This task he was about to perform was going to be so easy; it always was. It was time for Richard to disappear from Simon Alexander's life as if he had never been there in the first place; and he hadn't been, not really, because after all, who was Richard Noble? That's right: he was nobody. He contained his excitement. Simon was nothing to him now but an inconvenience.

He removed his jacket, draping it over the chair back. Slowly he undid the buttons of his shirt and let it fall to the floor revealing his tanned presence; teasing his prey. His inner excitement finding its way to the surface of his face, he met Simon's eyes with his own.

Simon, momentarily stunned at the sudden change of heart looked around the room.

"Here!"

Simon, uncertain, thought he'd much prefer the bedroom.

"Why not? We're alone: just you, me and our little friends the Birdwings. You're not going to act all shy in front of them are you?" Scoffing Richard taunted, moving a step closer.

Simon faltered, taking a step back instead to sit on the couch. Damned butterflies! He'd always felt pushed aside by his father, they'd always taken first place. Story of my life, he thought. I finally find someone special for me and here we go again, he just happens to be in love with the damn things too. But despite his disdain, Simon was already removing his tie as Richard stood before him, fully unclothed. Simon's gaze panned down from his lover's shaved head to the tanned, hairless body. His fingers tingled at the thought of touching it. He wanted Richard so badly now; he hurried to undress, desperate to be naked too. Readied, he ran his hand through his blonde hair, sweeping it back. The cow lick inherited from his father quivered for a moment before flopping back into place over his left eye. Lying back, Simon formed himself into a pose, one arm reaching out for the stem of his wine glass, he drained the last of his wine.

"No, not the couch; in here with them," Richard said, opening the door into the heated garden.

"You are acting weird tonight," Simon replied, getting off the couch, "but if kinky is what you want, who am I to argue?" He followed Richard into the garden, his steps eager; hope spreading over his face: was there a chance his lover would make it to Vienna after all? He passed through the door closing it behind him. This was a side of Richard he'd not seen before. He liked it too; he began to wish away the next two weeks....

"Sorry about the hold up, Mr Alexander, traffic's hell tonight."

Waiting in the shadows of the darkened hall for the cabbie to climb the steps and lift his cases, he pulled up the collar of his coat, stepped out and turned his back to lock the door.

"Just these two, then, Sir?"

"Yes, and be careful with them!"

The cabbie looked up wondering what was up with Simon Alexander tonight; the man was usually one of his more pleasant fares. He shrugged to himself: none of his business, people needed their privacy; he'd not put his nose in where it wasn't wanted.

Out of the zone of the sensors they were suddenly shrouded in blackness as the security lights blinked off. Slamming the boot, the cabbie walked around to the side door and opened it. No smile; no thanks; the form's certainly bad tonight, he thought. He held open the door and screwed up his nose, waiting.

Head down, Alexander came forward, looping a scarf around his neck and pulling down his hat as he bent to get into the car, snapped, "Straight to the airport; I'm late!"

He had his orders; he started the engine. He looked in the mirror as he made the turn out of the drive, the gravel crunching under the wheels. His passenger was blatantly not in the mood for gossip; he was hunched in the seat, his nose buried in a handheld computer.

Behind them, Craven House was a darkened mass in an even darker sky. Vacated, it was quiet except for the sounds picked up by the microphones, amplified into the sitting room: soft, fluttering of wings and the sound of droplets, falling one after the other onto the vine leaves, staining them; a deep red varnish over the green.

7

It was an art to him; the torture.

There were two sides to it: to be the dealer or to be the recipient.

As a child he had accomplished perfecting strategies to survive the brutality that had become part of his daily life. It had taken time to find an escape and until then he had writhed from every punch, cried out at every boot until his small form had succumbed.

'When you are scared close your eyes,' she had said. 'Picture my face and it will all go away.' He released a cynical laugh: her words had become treacherous, their memory inciting a fire of hate inside him. She had always said that, he remembered, but that last time she had lied. He had waited, scared of the strangers, terrified of his surroundings; tried over and over to do what she said, keeping them closed for longer each time, tightening the muscles around his eye sockets for all he was worth, as hard as he could until his head ached. But it hadn't changed anything. And she had never come back. Closing his eyes had made no impact, no matter how hard he tried, and unlike her, nothing else around him ever went away.

Concentration: that was how he had mastered it.

He remembered the first time it had worked. Drifting from unconsciousness he had become aware of the bruises; battle scars. He had examined them, counted them, but that time he had not been present to receive them. He had finally succeeded in escaping to the enchanted land – the place she had told him about that was filled with little people. Leprechauns were his first friends in this lonely new life. When his sister was old enough to understand, he had found fairies in it for her too. From then on he was strong, but still he longed for her; his mother, wanting her warmth; her smell.

Hidden in corners he had watched, listened to grown men, covered his ears to lessen their screams; their cries for mercy. Bloodied, strung up like carcases of beef, they gasped for air, whimpered faint pleas for it to end.

The first time he'd done it he'd felt nothing, but then he'd been an angel of mercy. Exhausted, they had not struggled. By hanging them upside down he managed easily to stuff their airways; the end always came quickly then, a few jerks and then stillness. Soon he had become intrigued with these corpses. Often they were left for days. When circumstances allowed it he would return, survey the changes decay had made to their forms. He soon realised it was he who had the power.

The smart ones spurted out what was needed of them, he had realised this as he watched them. They had wanted it over and for them death came quickly; the nudge of a muscle in the forehead and life was gone. The others were stupid; struggling for life. They were not like him, they couldn't concentrate: you had to concentrate! Some he had tried to teach, reviving them with cold water, instructing them; but they never listened. Their incompetence angered him. He would tease them, lifting the bucket up covering their heads. For some it ended this way; drowned.

He looked down at the latest recipients of his torture that were lying on the floor.

The man had given no indication that he felt any pain; that he had taken care of. There was not much blood: his bones so brittle had merely crumbled underfoot.

Crunch! Crunch! Crunch!

Not now! I've business to take care of.

Her, the woman, she had suffered. Pathetic creature, he thought; she could have lessened their suffering. But no; women he had learned were for the most part treacherous. It was a female gene thing; she couldn't give him the answer. She carried that gene, the one he sought to stamp out; she too had sown her seed on barren ground. He knew all about her. His visit to the Priory had yielded much – just not enough.

He lifted the man, limp almost weightless, and placed him back on the bed.

"It took you all this time to find out a woman's love is hollow."

Hollow; an air head!

I would have made it quick; but no, she wanted you to suffer. All she had to do was tell me, but she didn't!"

Stupid bitch!

He ran his gloved hand over the man's eyes, closing them. Bringing his head down closer to the man's face he whispered in his ear. "Don't worry!" As he spoke a smile appeared on his face; it did nothing to melt the coldness of his eyes. "I made her suffer too."

I can vouch for that! She suffered. Loads of suffering!

Leaving the camera still running, he tidied up the room. It was wise to examine the clean up in case he missed something. Not that it worried him; he could always fix any problem that occurred. He would, after all, be back.

Didn't find out much though, did you? It would seem somebody's a step ahead of you!

He looked at the woman. Long ago he had realised they were inferior beings; now he despised them. His memory was perfect; he should have known hers would fail her. That other bitch was at fault, though; it was her who had taken the answers. He had read it in the woman's face; witnessed in her the moment of realisation as it became apparent to her: the knowledge that she'd misplaced her trust. There was no reason to annoy himself about it; it just meant he couldn't stay here longer.

Pity!

Pity!

He liked to wait with them. The way their eyes changed amused him; at least he'd got that on tape. It was time to go. He knew her routine; she would be leaving soon. The briefcase would be left in the hall as it always was. Women were creatures of routine.

The night remained cloaked in darkness, the ground still wet from the frequent showers, but his plastic suit prevented the dampness from reaching him. She passed by unaware that he was there, her route unchanging through the park in the direction of the graveyard. He tensed, fighting off the rage that swelled inside him every time she was close.

Not now! He warned himself against springing out of his hiding place. Remember; she is a means to an end.

One day soon, you too sister will pay! When I find her – and I will find her – long before you do!

Did you say sister? Jenny is our sister! Jenny!

Enjoy playing with her, he told himself; she hides it well but she is falling apart.

Savour her anguish until the time comes; soon.

Soon! Goody! Goody! Goody!

Edging his body against the wall, he slipped over the top of it. The house was in darkness. The other one wouldn't pose a problem; she was hooked on the pills; he would be in and out in seconds.

8

Maidstone, Kent: the same morning

Sandra Reid bolted upright; tangled curls clinging to her face dampened by her sweat. She swiped them back, tucking them behind her ears. The grey marl of her vest sandwiched between her breasts was wet. Drawing her knees up, she sat in the foetal position, rested her chin and stared straight ahead.

The familiar neon lights; the picture: a Marilyn impostor spread provocatively over a flashy red, open-top car. It adorned the wall at the foot of the bed. Her bed; she was here; at home, safe in her own bed.

It was her darkness... not his.

Reality slowly filtered through. It was the shrill ringing of the alarm clock that had pulled her from a haunted sleep. But as usual, the sudden move to reach the damned thing and switch it off distracted her from her most recent train of thought, obliterating in that instant any hope of interpreting the nightmare from which she had just been rescued.

Part of her felt relieved; the braver part, agitated with succumbing to rescue, wanted to know what things lurked there. To conquer the fear, she knew she must come to terms with the contents of these dreams. Why did she think of them as dreams? They existed; part and parcel of each twenty-four hour cycle. Memories: bad ones; ones that her inner consciousness had so far banished successfully; buried too deep to touch.

She could just about make out the outline of the boxes lined up against the wall: most of her belongings, all readied and packed. The events of her waking hours were a big enough problem to understand. Why bother overloading her mind by trying to decipher the web of haunted images salvaged from the deep recesses of the night world: her night world – at least, the one she inhabited. God knows, she thought, if the days are anything to go by then someday soon I am going to find myself walking around in the dark. That was something she wanted to avoid.

The loud echoes of the alarm were drowned out by the sound of birds chirping on the honeysuckle arch in the garden below. Nature: it was such a great healer. Sandra imagined them fighting for a space on the little birdhouse that Gerry had tied to the top of the archway. Had she misjudged him after all? Had he foreseen that she would cling to these little creatures for some kind of sanity? Too little, too late; there would be no turning back the clock.

The things that had passed between them on that day – that last day – the words they had used to claw each other – were now their parting farewell. Lifting a dry pillow from the other side of the bed – his side – she hugged it to her, burying her head in it as if it would comfort her. Had she finally done it? Pushed him over the edge in the same way that she had driven away everyone else in this house? She tried to block him from her mind. What was done could never be undone.

He had changed, but how could she have known? She couldn't bear much more of this guilt. "Gerry..." Almost like a sign she accidentally let his name slip out. He would not hear her. For a moment or two she closed her eyes tightly, willing herself to lift the weighted sadness that his name now invoked; a love that was gone, but not gone; a love that for some reason had fizzled away.

She had finally accepted that fact; there had been no point in dragging it out. So why was it she felt she wanted to hold him now? She had pined like a lost puppy for his attention until the longing had waned. Hung in limbo, her feelings had changed and she had come to despise him. The way he averted his eyes so as not to meet hers and drew back when she tried to touch him had become unbearable.

There had been only one way to end it, the purgatory she had endured. She had not expected him to crumble as he did. That was not the Gerry she had grown used to; the one she had struggled to disentangle herself from; the one who had cried as she left, pleading for her to stay. Shocked, she had walked out.

Neither had it been another of her hysterical outbursts. For the first time in so long she had felt alive. Leaving the house that day, her hastily packed cases thrown angrily into the boot, her head had been clear. 'This is *me*,' she had told herself. 'Free!'

But now it was she who was the monster; the fake. She may not have been with him when he spiralled into a drug-induced fall from the fire escape – had he slipped or jumped? Did it matter? Either way he was dead – but she was certain it was her force that had pushed him. Every moment now spent in this house full of memories – memories that had once served to lift her spirits during the hard times – now foreshadowed bouts of depression, and these she was finding increasingly hard to shake off. To her, this place resembled a garden: once it had been carefully tended, now it was overgrown; to touch anything was to grasp at thorns that pierced as they wounded.

Reaching for the pill bottle beside her she had almost tipped two into her hand before she realised what she was doing. No way! Not going back there; two years of floating in and out of it had got her nowhere. There had to be another way: why did it have to be so hard, she thought searchingly.

Turning in the bed, Sandra pulled up the covers, decided she could spare another half-hour; she was starting back today; needed to get some sleep. She yawned, moaning as her jaws cracked. The sides of her mouth felt to her tongue like a miniature 3-D model of the Grand Canyon! She must have been chewing them in her sleep.

Listening to the quietness of the house sleeping soundly around her, she thought of the girls; of Fiona; hoped their dreams weren't as bleak as her own. What would they think of her if they knew the truth? Tears trickled silently off her cheeks and into her hair.

Faint, but recognisable, the creaking of the front door brought her flow of thoughts to an abrupt halt. For a few moments she waited; had she heard the sound at all?

The creak came again and Sandra knew she had not been mistaken. Someone was in the house. Who?

Suddenly the air around her felt cold.

As lightly as she could, moving her limbs like a spider, she climbed to the other side of the bed hushing in vain the squeaking of the springs. Grabbing up her dressing gown hanging from a hook on the back of the door, she flung it on. Poised behind the door, her ear pressed against the wood so tightly it hurt, she took a few deep breaths. Sweat springing to her hands transferred to the brass doorknob making it slippery. She strained to hear; heard nothing save the mechanisms humming inside her: the rasp of her breathing, the rapid thundering of her pulse. At least they were still churning, she thought; that in itself was something; the fear gripping her now felt damned close to stopping her heart.

Gathering her courage, she eased herself around the door onto the landing. For years she had lectured the girls about leaving the hockey stick abandoned outside the closet door. For once she was glad of it.

Weapon in hand, she made the first floor landing.

Startled by the sudden onset of the security alarm, she tried to straighten herself, what use was she going to be in this state, shaking from head to toe? 'Come on you terrified housewife you!' she scoffed inwardly, 'some detective you are!'

The noise of the ringing cut into her head; she couldn't think clearly; needed quiet; needed to keep track of where he was in the house – she assumed it was a 'he'. Surely the noise of this damned ringing drilling into her head had to be having the same effect on him?

She was in no-man's land, half-way up, half-way down. She had to make a move, one way or the other. Pushing the terrified housewife to the side, she made a run for the foot of the stairs. As she made the turn at the bottom, the drilling dwindled to a whining drone followed by the faint beeping noise of the buttons. Whoever it was knew the code, then. It should have been a relief. It wasn't. All her nerve ends were screaming at her that this was a burglar.

'Get it together Sandra!' she told herself sternly. 'You've done this hundreds of times before! But not here,' she argued with herself, 'not in my own home.'

Did he know she was there? Had he heard her? She didn't know. Even the short breaths she was managing to take felt as though they were being amplified. She stopped by the kitchen door, leaned for support against the narrow piece of wall beside it. Why hadn't she stayed upstairs, she chided herself. Her mobile was right beside the bed. How could she have been so stupid! Pushing herself away from the wall, she ineffectually wiped each sweaty hand on her dressing gown; tightened her grip on the stick and held it up.

'Right, this is it,' she coaxed herself. 'You can do this; just keep focused. Prepare.'

She sucked in as much air as she could to expand her lungs, hesitated for a moment more, then charged into the kitchen, stick held high behind her right shoulder ready to swing, adrenaline pumping, roaring...

9

Fiona screamed.

Narrowly missing her startled burglar, Sandra diverted her aim, hitting the edge of the counter instead.

Fiona remained standing, pinned against the units, a look of shocked bewilderment on her face. Dressed in a baby-pink velour tracksuit that exposed her tanned midriff and tiny waist, she pulled off her peaked cap, threw it on the table and with both hands massaged the flatness out of her hair. Like many women, she'd had it newly-styled in an attempt to cut out someone she couldn't get out from under her skin.

Sandra stared at her, thought, 'I'm going crazy!' It was the first thing that flashed across her mind: that she had finally flipped. Fiona! Her sister-in-law; it was she who had come through the door and set off the alarm. Of course; she went jogging three mornings a week. Sandra knew that. What had possessed her to forget it this morning? She felt worse than stupid and without speaking, sank into a chair, tried to slide the hockey stick out of sight under the table and wished the floor would open up and swallow her along with it. Aware of the embarrassing silence, she rubbed her hands over her eyes; cast around for an excuse to explain her behaviour.

Fiona was already grabbing mugs from the dishwasher, examining them as if nothing had happened. "I think tea would be a good idea right about now. Don't you agree?" She said it in such a matter of fact way, but that was Fiona; well accustomed to her sister-in-law's frequent episodes of acting strangely. Crockery rattled as the rack slid back out of sight. "Why am I the only one in this house who remembers to switch on the dishwasher when it's full?" she said. "Earl Grey; or perhaps I should recommend Camomile?"

Sandra, noting the light-hearted cynicism in Fiona's remark, thought she was probably expected to laugh, but she couldn't. Instead, she rolled out several possible excuses for what had just happened. As they tumbled out of her mouth she wondered who she was trying to convince: Fiona or herself.

Rinsing mugs in the sink, Fiona turned to reach for a tea towel. "I thought we had put all these sorts of episodes behind us?" It was more a statement than a question. Seeing that Sandra was still clearly dishevelled, Fiona paused, lightened her tone. "Oh, come on! Don't look so embarrassed. Look, don't you worry yourself about it." She poured water into the mugs, the spoon clinking against the sides as she stirred the tea bags to speed up the release of flavours.

Watching her, Sandra knew her sister-in-law was trying to appear calm; take it in her stride, but though it was something she had become used to doing, this time she was failing to hide the underlying panic beneath her customary everything-is-so-under-control exterior. It made Sandra feel even more stupid. Fiona would think she was starting to fall apart again and none of them needed that; not now. More than ever, as sisters-in-law and as long time friends, each needed the other just as much. They had spent the last few months feeding constantly off each other's strengths. Death when it touched you blurred everything around you.

"Look, it's been a tough time for us all lately," Fiona said. "It's probably the stress starting to show itself again. What has happened to us, all of it, from your attack – how it affected you…" her voice trailed away as she set the mugs on the table, taking a seat before continuing.

Sandra nodded; let her talk.

"What happened to Mark; and then Gerry hiding his illness like that; keeping it from us – both of us – and losing his faith…" Fiona paused, glancing towards the window, her eyes fixed on the distance as if searching for answers.

"And that's the hardest thing for me to take in," she went on. "It's why he gave in; has to be! Nothing else would explain it."

Sandra kept her head bowed, focusing on her mug, knowing that Fiona couldn't bear to voice the fact that Gerry had committed suicide, overdosed on opiates, freed himself of it all and left them behind to pick up the pieces.

Fiona, sitting opposite, looked down at her hands, stretched out her fingers and examined her nails.

Tears filled Sandra's eyes. She raised her head to hold them there, only to see that Fiona's eyes had clouded too.

In a swift movement Fiona turned away, briefly raised her fingers to wipe her eyes, but was unable to hide a long drawn out sigh. For a few seconds she sat with her back to the table, then swinging round, got to her feet and moved to stand behind Sandra's chair, grasping her sister-in-law's shoulders with both hands and leaning over her head.

Sandra knew that some remark Fiona thought of as witty was coming out next; that she was doing her best to lighten their mood. She always tried.

"It's not as if I'm going to call up the white coats and get them to haul you away," Fiona gave a forced laugh. "Just forget it. Like most of the things we used to go through with you, we'll probably have a good laugh about it one day. Well; sometime in the distant future at least. You're just on edge. This whole business is like a Clare Hamilton thriller; it's unreal."

Fiona was right. How was it possible for so much misfortune to land on one household? Feeling her sister-in-law's hands warm on her shoulders, Sandra stared into the mug; no milk; her tea was black; black like the depression that had settled in the pit of her stomach, a weight pulling her down. She imagined some great vampire-like beast – some kind of evilness personified, given form – its vast, blackened wings spread wide as it swooped downwards into their lives seeking them out. Its shadow had fallen on them: its blackness enveloped their home blocking out the light; its claws were rooted within their foundations. Devoid of the warmth of healing sunshine they were enclosed beneath it, suffocating. No matter what happened now, even if they managed to loosen the grip of this beast and find a way back to the light, their landscape was changed; forever blighted.

It had all started with the kidnap; that had been tough enough to survive. She'd fought hard to deal with accepting the things she'd endured during her days of captivity; fooled herself into believing she was a survivor. A ticking bomb, she had realised too late, was what she had become. The explosion when it came had almost blown her apart; the rawness of the wounds once opened, she finally admitted to herself, were so slow to heal.

There was so much that she now understood about the world of a victim. She had a real insight: up close and personal; an insight and a knowledge that she wished she didn't have. But she was getting there; back to the place where she once had been – or so she had thought – only now she was not so sure and all she had were doubts. Where was that place now? Most of it had gone: her life as she knew it.

Like Fiona said, it was unreal, all that had happened. Why had he done that terrible thing? How could she not have seen the signs? Wasn't it those who couldn't cope who flipped? He had always been so controlled. So, why? Why had he done it? She couldn't even think the 'S' word herself now; the act that went against everything he had believed in. The note he'd left hadn't explained; not really.

Upstairs, a message bleeped on her mobile, the sound just about audible. Fiona moved away and went back to sit at the table, sipped at her tea – it would be cold by now, Sandra thought. She went to push herself up, changed her mind. She would retrieve the message later. There was a possible buyer due before ten and the house was a mess. She couldn't think about that just now; her mind was elsewhere.

Midway through her recovery their lives had been thrown into turmoil once more. Fiona, for whom they had convinced themselves there had not yet been created the perfect pattern to sew together a perfect man, had stunned them. Following a whirlwind romance she was on the verge of announcing her engagement to her boyfriend, Mark Jakes, when her hopes of a happy future had been shattered, and all of their lives turned upside down yet again. Fiona's 'perfect man' had become deranged, lashed out at one of his female colleagues and in a frenzied knife attack, had killed her.

It had taken some time to find a way forward after Mark's trial. The atmosphere that surrounded them was unbearable. Fiona was defiant in her support of him. The trial had been fast-tracked to take place in July. Mark Jakes, though, long before this had cut himself off from her, refusing to take visits, then, as the trial was closing, he had started returning her letters. But Fiona remained undeterred. She insisted time after time that he was innocent. What she based this on neither Sandra nor Gerry could tell. She was in denial; it was as simple as that.

It had angered Gerry, her defiance; her unwillingness to accept reality. To him it was the final straw in a long line of events that had ruptured the foundations of their relationship. Right from when she was little he had protected Fiona, his little sister. As time passed he had gradually learnt to take a back seat in her life. She was one of those people who thrived on excitement; could handle anything. With a promising career in television she'd packed herself off to America and worked her way to an anchor seat on TV USA, on of the largest TV news channels over there. After fifteen years of it she'd come home. Gerry thought his role as protector would just pick up again were it had left off, but Fiona had other ideas.

Even before the murder, Sandra could see cracks appearing in their relationship. It became commonplace for Gerry to utter despairing remarks concerning various plans Fiona was making. It seemed strange that he had become so at odds with the direction his sister's life was taking. Sandra thought it all stemmed from the time Fiona had confided in them that she wanted to find her natural birth mother. Gerry's reaction had been one of rage, which had astonished Sandra. Even when they were in private he had refused to expand on why he was so angry; kept his reasons closeted. She thought maybe it was because he felt that Fiona was distancing herself from him. Perhaps he regarded her actions as a betrayal to the memory of Alice, the woman who had adopted them and in whom they had found so much love: as much if not more than might have existed had she given birth to them herself.

In all her attempts to reason with him, Sandra had gained no insight to shed any light on the reasons behind his disapproval. She knew there was more to it: he was her husband, she could tell, as she could always tell when he was holding something back. The adoption issue had worried her too, but for another, more personal reason. She had decided to screw the lid down tightly on that. She felt it was best, given Gerry's true feelings, not to climb that mountain unless she had to. And having discovered a facet of her husband's nature that she'd not known about before, she had hoped for her own sake that she would never have to. Some skeletons were best kept buried. Where Gerry was concerned that worry was over now; not that she felt particularly relieved, but anyway, it was her skeleton; not part of their past at all – at least, that's what she kept telling herself.

Sandra sighed; picked up her mug, put it down again. Needless to say, as it turned out Gerry was right in the end. After months of searching, Fiona had traced her birth mother, only to discover that she had died many years before. It had been such a let down; Stella Jones had developed Huntington's and had been dead for some time. Gerry's prophecy that no good would come of it had unfolded for Fiona when she was advised to get herself tested for Huntington's, their doctor hinting that there was a high risk of her developing the disease herself in mid-life. That was when Fiona had discovered that she could not possibly be Stella Jones' natural daughter. They said then that there had been a mix up in the adoption records, they could not explain why, but finding her real mother now was going to be next to impossible.

Sandra believed Fiona had lost interest after that. At any rate she never mentioned it again and Gerry refused to discuss it further. As far as they were concerned she had abandoned her quest. With the murder of Katie Smyth and Mark's trial, there was plenty to keep her occupied. The adoption crisis had certainly been put on the back burner then.

"I'm ready for a shower."

Fiona's voice broke into Sandra's thoughts. She looked up, saw that Fiona had finished her tea, tried to smile. "It must be cold out there these mornings," she said in an attempt to make conversation, aware that her thoughts had been wandering. She admired Fiona's dedication to maintaining her physical fitness; perhaps that was her secret, Sandra thought: healthy body, healthy mind and all of that. A stranger would never have believed what Fiona had been through over the last year. Her sister-in-law didn't wear it on her face; not like Sandra wore it on her own; so many new lines all those awful things had drawn – at least, they were what she blamed for all the new features to her face.

"It's not that bad; once you get the first half-kilometre out the way you don't notice the cold. Why not do a run with me on Friday? It would do you good!" Fiona urged.

Sandra considered the proposal for a second or two, pictured herself panting in an effort to keep up, crawling up the front step as they reached home. She shook her head, "No; no thanks." It would at best leave her shattered – provided that it didn't kill her first! Besides; the thing about running – or walking come to that – was that it gave you too much time to think. She had promised herself to steer ahead this week. There was so much to get sorted out; most importantly this house. None of them wanted to stay here any longer than was necessary: a constant reminder of who they had lost and what he had done here. An Estate Agent was due at 9.15. When he left there would be a 'For Sale' sign in the garden. A good omen perhaps that they already had three viewings booked. Probably by developers: so what; she couldn't bring herself to care.

While Fiona went off to shower and dress for work, Sandra sorted breakfast then sat with a list of 'must do's'. As usual it was endless; always was.

"No sign of Sam and Elle getting out of bed yet then?" Fiona asked, sauntering back into the kitchen, putting her laptop down on the table and leaning over it to butter a piece of toast.

"Probably have to wake them myself before long; it makes it such a long weekend this not having classes on Mondays," Sandra replied, setting down her pen and reaching for her mug of fresh coffee, adding, "they've had another rift; they're not speaking."

Fiona nodded. "I wondered how long the truce would last. What is it this time? It seems more serious than usual."

"You've stayed with us long enough by now to know the routine," Sandra shrugged. "It was a white belt last time. You know Sam counts her stuff as sacred. Elle knows it too, but she just can't help herself; she's a born tease." She paused, shot Fiona a quizzical glance. "Talking of that white belt, though, wasn't that the one you were wearing when you went out last Saturday evening?"

Munching on her toast, Fiona released a long smile, her eyes twinkling.

Sandra shook her head, "You're as much of a minx as Elle – and you know it too! If it wasn't impossible I'd swear Elle gets her genes from you! Well, I suppose it won't last forever, and at least the cat fights are silent for the moment."

Fiona turned her head looking up the hallway as if checking for eavesdroppers before speaking. "Whatever it is this time I don't think it has anything to do with the norm. I heard them last night snapping subdued snarls at each other. Your name kept cropping up, but I couldn't make out what it was about and Elle was sobbing for ages afterwards. I popped my head round her door later, but she was sleeping by then. Couldn't help noticing that she was clutching a piece of paper – a letter or something. I tried to sneak it off her to see what it was, but she started to stir, so I left it."

Sandra screwed up her face in disapproval. "Fiona Reid! You are incorrigible. Whatever is going on between them, like usual, they will try to drag us in to take sides. Ignore them; it'll be over something stupid, it always is – and what did you think you were doing trying to sneak a peek at something of Elle's that's probably private? Honestly! Sometimes you're as bad as they are!"

Fiona shrugged, "I was only trying to help. But seriously, Sandra, I get the feeling that something more than nicking accessories is going on between those two at the minute and I think this time you need to interfere!"

Shaking her head, Sandra smiled, "I'm not that stupid Fiona; they'll be onto the next row by tomorrow whatever last night was about. Take my advice, learn to ignore it; they're teenagers!"

They sat across the table from each other, the laptop most of the time hiding Fiona from Sandra's gaze. Periodically Fiona popped her head up from behind it with a smile, made some witticism before returning her attention to the screen. It continued to amaze Sandra how she carried it off. No one would ever have guessed the hell that must be raging inside her sister-in-law. It was only in the aftermath of Mark's trial that her misery had finally broken through the barrier she had erected to contain it – and even then it had taken only a few weeks for her to close up again and lock everybody out.

Through the dark days of the trial, Fiona's resilience had simultaneously amazed and terrified them. Perhaps it was the fact that she and Gerry were slightly removed from Mark Jakes that had enabled them so easily to accept what he was. But not at first. Sheer disbelief had accompanied their understanding of the events as they were reported. It shocked Sandra that they had welcomed this monster into their home, shared more than one bottle of wine over this very table. Every time she thought of him sitting there it made her want to scrub it clean again. She looked at the top of Fiona's head, bent over the screen; wondered yet again: how did it make her feel?

There had been many cutting rebukes sent flying at them since Mark had first been arrested and Gerry, always Fiona's protector, hadn't quite been able to suppress his own feelings of revulsion, so all attempts to intervene and help her through it had always ended in Fiona pushing him further away. Sandra had just got stuck in the middle; bombarded on two sides she had taken on the role of peacekeeper, tactfully listened to both, careful never to voice any supporting opinions and praying frequently that it wouldn't destroy them all.

For months she had tiptoed around them; now Fiona was doing the same around her. It grieved her how Fiona's and Gerry's relationship had disintegrated; so much so that by the time he took his life they were completely estranged. They had walled each other off, only speaking in front of the girls in an attempt to hide the huge gulf between them. It hadn't fooled anybody — least of all her. She could tell quite easily that Fiona had longed to repair the damage.

Sandra knew that these early morning runs took Fiona in the direction of the graveyard, as much as she knew that the redness around Fiona's eyes came from the tears she shed whilst sitting at the side of his grave; that she cried for him to forgive her, cried for him to come back.

Married to Gerry for just eleven years, Sandra couldn't measure her loss against that of Fiona who had shared her whole life with him. Sandra clasped her arms about her middle suppressing a shiver. What would Fiona think of her if she knew it was she who had taken him away; that it was her fault he had gone? That walking out on him had driven him over the edge? Her sister-in-law would never again be her friend. Fiona had kept her secret safe all this time, a secret kept from her own brother; one they knew would have destroyed his trust in both of them had he ever found out. But it hardly mattered now.

How was Fiona able to crack on with her life; put it all behind her as she apparently did? It was hard not to envy that ability. It was as if she had individual little file boxes in her head for everything she encountered. Had she accustomed herself to taking out only one file at a time, always taking care to close it up again and put it back before dealing with another? Sandra inwardly shrugged. She couldn't do it that way. For herself she had just one big box that had been lifted up as in a whirlpool, mixed up and emptied in a massive pile on the floor. She had lost the ability to focus or take interest in anything. By nightfall she would become dejected and no longer care that Fiona was holding it all together so much better than she could. Sandra viewed the kitchen around her: early morning chaos. So much to do.

By nightfall she would have got through another day; for now it was as much as she could do.

"Tell you what!" Fiona was closing her laptop and getting up from the table. "I can get a few bits and pieces cleared up before I head out. Most people, Sandra, try at least to make a good first impression. Just because we're praying for a quick sale doesn't mean we shouldn't aim for a good price!" She was looking at Sandra; seeking approval.

Sandra was jolted from her thoughts, "Oh, well... okay. Are you sure you have time? It is getting on a bit."

Fiona had set her case back in the hallway. "Don't worry; I have a little extra time. I've kept the morning free of appointments, there's somewhere I have to go." Already she was gathering up abandoned packaging from the counter tops, evidence of last night's takeaway; flinging them in the bin; wiping down the surfaces. Within minutes she had managed to make the place look relatively tidy.

"Right; that's made a difference don't you think? I still can't believe how those two up there spend half their day in bed." Fiona checked her watch. "Shouldn't you go and get dressed? You'll have the agent here in a minute."

She lifted her case, said, "I'll catch up with you later," before gliding up the hall with her usual elegance that always reminded Sandra of a swan, but watching her, the part of her that Sandra wanted most was a share of her confidence.

10

**Police Headquarters, Sutton Road, Maidstone:
the same morning**

"Damned things," Detective Superintendent Jeff McAdams muttered under his breath, waiting a moment for his stomach to settle after the lift jolted him onto the floor, the ever-present voice in his ear chiding him that if he lost a few pounds he'd be fit enough to take the stairs. His breathing was laboured as his huge frame struggled to cope with the excesses that ready-mades and takeaways were adding to it. He made his way to the left end of the corridor that housed the Serious Crimes Team.

Known to all as 'Grizzly', at fifty-five and one inch over six foot, Jeff still managed fairly easily – mostly due to his dress sense – to hide his age. The nickname was borrowed from a character out of an American TV serial. Apparently there was a startling resemblance – or so his colleagues had told him, and the name had stuck, outrunning the serial by several decades. The kinks in his shoulder-length, sandy-coloured hair, the worn out brown cord reefer jacket and the boot cut jeans were 'trendy and friendly,' or so Angie, his late wife, had always remarked as she hugged him before they'd departed their home for work each morning.

Viewing the open plan office he realised his meeting with the Chief Super had run on longer than he had thought: all the desks were abandoned except for one; Detective Sergeant Stevens sat hunched over his monitor tapping out his reports at a furious pace.

From the swishes and clanging of metal, Jeff could tell Christine was busy filing. In a few weeks she would be off on maternity leave, her temporary demotion to office duty, though, had not dampened her enthusiasm. She endeavoured as always to give as much in here as she did out in the streets.

He passed unnoticed into his office, quietly closing the door, needing a few minutes to run over all that had passed between him and Chief Superintendent Millar. Earlier, driving in to Maidstone, he had been so sure, so determined; had known where his future lay. Now Millar had offered him a proposition and he needed to think it over; share a few quiet moments with Angie to hear what she thought was best for him; let her have her say. In that department at least nothing much had changed: it was still Angie who told him what she thought he should do; her voice in his ear same as always; he just followed her orders. She may have been gone for going on three years, but he didn't feel the need for it to be any different; she was, after all, always right.

Unlocking the bottom drawer of his filing cabinet he removed a thick green bundle of files bound with elastic. Holding it in one hand while using his other to push the remaining folders forward, he retrieved a single greyish file hidden at the back. Taking a seat, he did not bother to flick the light switch; instead grabbed the blind cord opting to adjust the Venetian strips just enough to direct light onto the files, which he placed beside each other on the desk. With a hand on each he slid them apart, then reached into his breast pocket. The envelope – his resignation – remained unopened as it had done throughout his meeting with Millar.

The months he had spent negotiating with his brother in Stafford to acquire the cottage where he was born, and where he wished to return to in his retirement, had called into question how feasible it was for him to think about fitting back into a life he had left behind in his youth. If he were honest, their tedious conversations had served merely to remind him that he and his brother had never actually enjoyed each other's company much at all. Suddenly he could see with total clarity that the emptiness he had felt since losing Angie had eaten into him, affected his thinking; fooled him into imagining he wanted company. Somewhere inside this old head of his he knew he would not be able to stand it.

With one hand on his face he pulled the skin on his jaws down towards his chin, replaying in his mind his encounter with Millar. Jeff had been half expecting it for some time; even he had cause to question his reasoning in the way he had handled the 'Borrower Case', as they called it. Seven women – all victims of a kidnapper – taken over a period of three months; each had been held for no more than forty-eight hours, then left to be found in public areas. All except the last victim; for her the pattern had deviated. Nobody had had the foresight to imagine that the aggressor's tactics would change, but they had, and Jeff's once promising protégée, DI Sandra Reid, had paid the price. He should have been aware of the possibility, but he had failed and for that he would never forgive himself. Now there were rumblings from above. Leading a specialised team attached to the country's most successful force was a great position to hold – for as long as you managed to hold onto it, Jeff thought with a wry grimace. He had survived until now; had battened down the hatches in the initial months, tried to steer through the stormy waters, but had made no headway. Despite the extra officers and limitless overtime afforded when one of their own became a victim, their constant vigilance and monitoring had thrown up no leads. No new attacks could be attached to the case and two years on it had moved no further: somewhere out there a crazed maniac was still on the loose.

Eventually the size of the team had been diminished as more recent cases pushed it to the side. Officially the case's status remained open, but no man-hours could be afforded for further investigation. Jeff sighed; he had always thought his life was a well-planned book: he had intended to finish off in the post he held, spend time pottering in the garden with Angie, digging things in where she wanted them. He knew now that those chapters would never be written: life without her; demoted from his post; these were not what he had planned for. It was a different life, this one, a separate life. The closing pages were empty; lost to him. It was as if he was living a sequel, struggling to keep up with the plot.

Millar had given him a choice, though, and already he was seeing it as a second chance, a route to redemption. He was being handed a lifeline, but what worried him was that if he took it, he had little time in which to redeem Sandra Reid. From what he detected in Millar's attitude, confidence in her was all but non-existent. Had he time to change that? What was more to the point, was she able to conquer the memories that haunted her? Recovery had been a long and bumpy road for her. Physically there was no dispute; she had won that battle. Three operations to remove the pigment of the symbols tattooed into her back, though only partially successful, she had dealt with in her usual dignified manner. The ectopic pregnancy, discovered by accident during the operation, she had known nothing about until the news had been broken to her several weeks after she'd been found. That too had been dealt with. Odd that, though. He'd been with Gerry Reid when the doctors had asked him about it. One might have expected his reaction to be one of grief or shock, but the look Jeff had read in Reid's eyes had been unmistakeable: the man had been angry.

Jeff knew Sandra's apparent recovery was an illusion: the mind was always much tougher to heal and he knew she had struggled; was still struggling. It would always stay with her. At times he wondered just how much of what had happened to her in those days of captivity had really come back to her. He knew from his consultations with her doctors that over time, flashbacks would reveal more to her. It was well-documented in date-rape cases too, where drugs had been used: the slow unravelling over time; the recovery of memory previously blocked.

What effect would this have on her ability to work, Jeff wondered. He had seen it in her from the start, over a decade ago: an ability to read beyond the evidence. It was a gift and she had developed it into a rare talent. True, the FBI training in America, her degree in criminology and numerous seminars in forensics had helped her along, but he knew these were mere decorations added to her CV. The insight she possessed, which enabled her to enter a scene and translate the appearance of the dead, read the killer's mind from the way the victims had been left, still ran shivers up his spine. Instinct? Perhaps, but that only skimmed the surface. She herself had described it as a scourge, Jeff remembered, when they had talked about it over a drink one night. He had learned then that her gift had its drawbacks. 'How would you feel, Jeff,' she had asked him, 'if you walked into a room and could tell how everyone in that room felt about you? Who liked and disliked you. Who held a grudge! Please believe me it's not such a great thing after a while; sometimes it is better not to know.'

There was, he had recognised, a sadness about her eyes as she had spoken those words: a deep sadness. It was evident in her tone as well. Wasn't it typical of life, too, that great minds such as hers, at one with nature, so receptive to everything that went on around them, were inevitably the most vulnerable to life's stresses. This was what really worried him about Sandra Reid: especially now that she also had a terrible loss to deal with on top of everything else. As Jeff knew only too well, bereavement was tough enough for anyone, but suicide? That was the hardest of all for a family to come to terms with.

He tapped the envelope on his desk; thought, what do I do now? The sound of the door opening interrupted his thoughts. He watched Stevens place his reports on the large, curved desk that ate up the centre of his office. The young man had caused quite a stir on his first day a few weeks back. In his mid-thirties, suave; an inch or two off six foot, with his jagged dark hair gelled back off his face, he would have suited a film set better than the real life slogging of the force.

The Detective Sergeant became aware of Jeff's gaze: "Sorry Sir, I hadn't realised you were here or I would have knocked."

"Stevens; glad to see you're settling in. The first few weeks are always tough, but I think you'll find us all bearable once you get used to us; it just takes some time. Tell me Stevens, I believe you hold a degree in computers?"

"Yes sir, that's right. I was with the specialised computer unit for two years before I was moved to Serious Crimes with the Met; now I'm here."

"Yes, now you're here..." Jeff said meaningfully, hoping the young officer would confide the reasons for his recent departure from the Met, but Stevens was not forthcoming and he didn't like to ask the question directly. He nodded a brief dismissal; "I'm holding you back: maybe we'll get a chance to talk some more …"

Jeff knew he had touched on something, he could hear the dip in Stevens's confidence; the slight quaver in his voice as he said farewell. From the Met to here, Jeff mused. Why? He knew it was Stevens who had applied for the transfer. What was behind it, he wondered. He'd read the young man's personal file a few days ago, thought it was more than impressive. Not that he intended to look a gift horse in the mouth. In his day, getting to detective level and working your way onto a murder squad was the objective of your career. These days the computerised world and terrorism had changed all that. Criminals had moved with the times. Internet fraud, pornography, human trafficking and international terrorism; these were the areas of crime that enticed all the young talent. Reading through Stevens's file Jeff reckoned he was bright enough to find his way into Intelligence. Nevertheless, for now the lad's fresh young mind was an asset to the team.

Alone again, he lifted the worn out, grey folder and placed it in the centre of his desk. Hundreds of cases to choose from, Millar had said. It was public knowledge that every unit in the country was constantly under pressure having to lend out detectives to other units when manpower became stretched. Plans had been drawn up and now that a suitable building had been acquired, the new unit was due to open. Situated just outside Gravesend, it would become responsible for the entire South-East, reworking serious crimes that remained open in the area: 'The Historic Cases Unit' they were calling it. According to Millar, it was hoped that Jeff would take over the murder team.

Jeff's initial indecision about such a move had quickly given way to thoughts of the opportunity it represented; not least was the chance to escape the future he had so stupidly been considering; he felt again the clutch of despair at the thought of reuniting with his brother. It had taken only two floors, moving down in the lift on his way back from Millar's office, for him to see some potential in the move.

He glanced at the clock: 8.35am The Historic Cases Unit, he thought, would certainly be a challenge. He fingered the grey folder on his desk: another case he had never been able to let go; another victim he had never been able to forget. The Hynds case had been his first. He had carried the file with him over the years as he moved from one building to the next and even though it spent its time hidden in the bottom drawer, he had never forgotten the images the folder contained. Feeling a twinge of nausea in his breast, he flipped it open and drew a deep breath as he prepared to revisit the memories.

Little had he known when he began the investigation all those years ago, how it would come in a short time to intertwine with events in his own life and remain locked in place within him all that time. Removing the browned photo from its clip he took the curled image of Andy Hynds into his hand and was drawn immediately to the large round eyes, eyes that once had held the promises of life to come. He lifted the set of prints taken during the autopsy, black and grey, foreboding in nature, telling a truth devoid of hope that the reality of those promises had dealt out to the child.

"I thought you were still in the Gold meeting, Sir."

Jolted from his thoughts, Jeff looked up to see Christine; just her head, leaning round the door frame. Her hair, a silky, pure ebony gloss, framed her face; it was undeniable that she was blossoming.

"Oh, sorry Christine, I was going to call you in for a chat wasn't I."

"Sir; please tell me we're getting more time?" she said, moving into the room.

Jeff knew that their present case, that of a missing teenager, was a trying one for Christine. The girl, Tracey Cooper, was a member of her church choir. Five weeks had passed and still what had happened to her on her way home after school remained a mystery. A navy sports bag identified by her parents had been located, hidden in undergrowth close to the bus stop. Her mobile was still missing; the phone records placed it last used on the bus at 3.15pm when she called her mother to tell her she would be home soon.

"I'm sorry Christine, I tried. They've decided under the circumstances to downgrade it; the consensus is that she's probably a runaway."

"What!" Christine slammed her fist on the desk.

Jeff understood her fury. There was nothing to indicate the girl was a candidate for becoming a runaway. But there was also nothing left to lead them to suspect she was the victim of foul play. Indeed, now that she had been identified on a security tape, captured buying snacks on the evening of her disappearance, he had to agree that she had planned – or at least played a willing part – to slip away that day.

Christine would not be convinced. The Final of the All England Church Choir of the Year had taken place a few weeks ago and Christine, alongside the girl's parents, was steadfast in her belief that not for anything would Tracey have jeopardised the choir's chances.

Christine realised immediately that her behaviour was inappropriate. She mumbled an apology, "Forgive me, Sir. Hormones and stress!" she flashed him a brief smile rubbing the bump no longer hidden by her loose clothes and clearly visible. "It's just that there is something I'm just not seeing in that tape, there has to be. I know this girl and, well, there's just something I'm seeing that's not Tracey." Christine shook her head, resigned to following orders. "I'll make a summary before I pass on the file, but I can't let it go." A smirk broke over her face as she leant over to look at the images on Jeff's desk. "Looks like I'm not the only one who finds it hard to let go; those look to be from quite a while ago."

He returned her smile, "Yes, I'm just picking out a few old files; you know what it's like this time of year: long dark nights. It helps to have something to read over."

A phone rang in the outer office. They could hear Stevens's voice rising in agitation. Jeff shot a look at Christine, "What now!" He got up from his desk, pushed back his chair and made his way into the outer office, Christine on his heels.

Stevens was on his feet, bent over the desk scribbling details on his pad. He looked up as they moved towards him; put his hand over the receiver. "A village called Higham, Sir. Uniform's called it in; they got a call a short time ago from some woman who's found two bodies. They're at the address now; say they've seen enough to call it in as suspicious. They've secured the scene and are holding on to the witness." He unclamped his hand from the receiver, spoke into it, his pencil poised, "Yeah, he's here now. Okay, I'll pass it on. I've got that." Stevens, his expression grim, replaced the phone on its rest.

Jeff sighed looking around the empty room. "Where is everyone, surely the whole place isn't out on loan?"

"No sir, just four of them. Collie and Foster are in court until Friday and Allen called in sick. DI Reid was supposed to be back in today but there's no sign of her yet."

Christine turned to Jeff. "She left a message for you on Friday evening, Sir; her car's in for service and she has a viewing this morning, but she promised to get in for eleven."

Jeff raised his eyes to the ceiling; he hadn't read his messages yet. How was this team supposed to cope on a tightrope; he just didn't have the manpower. He held out his hand for Stevens's pad, scribbled Sandra's address and handed it back. "Right, Stevens, head here first and pick up DI Reid. Give her the details and drive her to the scene; she'll know the way. I'll phone her to let her know you're coming. Christine, looks like you're excused from desk duties for the day. Do you feel up to it?"

She was already at the door putting on her jacket. "You bet Sir! Meet you at the car."

Christine slowed Jeff's Bora to let a father and child cross the road in front of them as they turned into the King's Road. Tapping his fingers to the muted tune of Johnny Cash on the car's radio, Jeff watched the child gripping tightly to her father's hand as they hurried across the road. He glanced at Christine, noticed the strain on her face, her gaze on the little girl. Was she thinking of Tracey – or perhaps her own father? He knew relations between them were strained. Pregnant; not married, she had recently broken up with her fiancé and her father had been less than happy with the situation. Jeff wondered if he should give Christine this opportunity to talk about it in the enclosed privacy of the car. He cleared his throat, "Don't think I'm prying, Christine, but how are things on the home front at the moment? Has the situation mellowed any yet? Have you decided what you're going to do?"

She eased the car forward. "I keep telling myself that I'm doing the right thing keeping this baby, but sometimes I think it would be better for it if I didn't. It's just that Dad can't handle it; the way he looks at me; I can feel his disgust, his shame." She paused to change gear, picking up speed. When she spoke again, her voice was full of tears. "But the worst of it is the way he takes it all out on Mum. I've searched for weeks for somewhere else to live, even a bedsit. I don't know how much longer I can stay under the same roof with him."

Dismayed, Jeff looked away, wished he hadn't asked. "I'm sorry to hear that Christine, I really thought time would soften him, that he'd respect your decision." His heart sank to his stomach; personally he respected Christine's decision to keep her baby; admired her courage – and now her troubles were to be added to. How would she cope without the support of her family? So much for the modern society they lived in; attitudes just hadn't kept pace with it. A thought occurred to him: he'd had an annexe built onto his own house; originally intended for Angie's mother, but she'd passed away a year before they'd managed to get it finished. Now it sat empty. Perhaps it was something he could look into? Wouldn't take too much of an effort to make it comfortable for Christine and her baby. Then again, was it his place to interfere? He decided not to mention it, time being. He leaned forward to stab the radio button and they continued the journey in an uneasy silence.

Christine drew up the Bora in front of the tape. A few DCs stood about, expressions grim. One – still wet behind the ears by the look of him – was bent double vomiting up his breakfast. Jeff eased himself out of the car and headed towards the officer who was standing at the foot of the driveway. He needed a brief outline of what had been found inside.

Watching from the car, Christine saw Jeff turn quickly towards her and beckon her to follow him. It was apparent from his demeanour that something had riled him; the colour had drained from his face.

11

Maidstone, Kent: the same morning

The hammering outside had sounded the arrival of the Estate Agent, running late and in a hurry. Clutching the mallet under his arm and looking slightly red about the face, he had given a few words of advice on how to deal with the viewings and then he was gone, leaving the 'For Sale' sign duly implanted by the front gate.

Closing the door behind him, Sandra shouted upstairs in an attempt to stir the girls; remembered she had messages on her phone and paused at the small table in the hall to run through them. The first from last night was from Susan; one of her sisters. Skipping it she went on to the next: a reminder about the viewing from the Estate Agent. Did no one trust her competence at all? She glanced into the mirror over the table, sighed and headed into the snug to find her bag; came back to stand in front of the mirror again.

Odd strands of silver peeped out here and there from her tangled mess of chestnut hair. It needed colouring big time, she thought, wielding a brush and attempting to tame the tangle by twisting it up and securing it with the band she pulled from her wrist. Immediately, strands like feelers dropped back down on either side of her face. She made a mental note to phone Jenny, her stylist, to book an appointment.

Dressed conservatively in brown slacks and a matching mandarin-collared shirt that showed a glimpse of her beige-coloured camisole beneath, she examined her attire with a critical eye: too much exposed, she thought, and did up a couple more buttons. She had really let her appearance take a back seat lately and knew it was beginning to show. Opening a tube of moisturiser, she applied it liberally in an attempt to lessen the impact that age was having on her skin. Around her hazel eyes, tiny crows' feet zapped up the cream. She never wore make up; not any more; not since she had become aware that her Italian blood and olive complexion – inherited from two generations back – rendered make-up superfluous. It was a gift, Fiona said, always making out that she was envious of Sandra's naturally tanned skin, but Sandra, a few inches shorter and about fifteen pounds heavier, had always felt in her sister-in-law's shadow. Fiona constantly made the effort to appear perfect, while she did not. Not usually. Now, lifted considerably by taking a little time to pamper herself, she felt in better spirits.

She had taken a leaf out of Fiona's book and managed to turn the whole of the ground floor into a clean and respectable place in which to welcome visitors – it hadn't been that for quite some time. Her last shout had actually roused the girls. Surprised when they came clattering blearily downstairs, and wanting them to hurry up and get dressed, she shooed them back up again. It hardly mattered about their rooms. Teenagers! At least she had girls and not boys.

Just about to make a call to arrange a taxi into the station – it was the third time in as many weeks that she was without wheels – the phone went off in her hand. At first glance she didn't recognise the number, presumed it was the Estate Agent, until she heard Jeff's voice.

"Sandra?"

He sounded anxious.

"I've sent a car for you, I need you here. I know we agreed that you wouldn't be near a crime scene for a while yet, but, well... something's come up... I need your opinion, and..." his voice tailed awkwardly into silence as if he was finding it hard to choose his words.

Sandra felt an irrational clutch of fear.

"Well; there's another reason too," Jeff continued after a moment. "You need to get down here, Sandra. Look, I don't want to tell you on the phone; you'll see why later."

Sandra's hand tightened on the receiver, her skin prickling into goose bumps. Why was Jeff doing this to her; she couldn't cope with it, not now. She wasn't ready yet, certainly not today. He knew that. She drew breath to tell him so, but before she could speak, he added, "Sandra; it's Fiona!"

Something heavy lurched downwards in her stomach. "What? What do you mean?"

"The car should be with you soon; can't talk just now; I'll fill you in when you get here." The phone went dead.

Sandra stared blankly at the mobile in her hand and tried to think. She didn't understand why her sister-in-law would be near anything that involved Jeff? The research for the series Fiona was filming at the moment was finished; they'd started the studio work last week. What was going on? Jeff was obviously at the scene of a crime. That meant there was probably a death! She couldn't think about that.

She grabbed a jacket off the coat-stand and ran upstairs to the girls' room. The first appointment to view was a woman; they should be able to deal with that. As she expected, the girls were none too pleased, but she insisted. "Look, you'll manage. Please do this for me. If she wants to know why we are moving, just tell her it's work-related!"

She knew by their faces that it was what they feared. She dashed back downstairs as a car screeched to a halt in front of the house; another pulled up behind it. The viewer had arrived. Sandra made her excuses and introduced the girls, who, now dressed, had come to the front door. The woman seemed nice enough: brief case and camera in her hands; a developer – or a developer's wife. It didn't matter.

Sandra opened the squad car door. A new face: male. Suddenly she was back there again; reaching into that car helping with the map to that face; the features still blank. She blinked hard, took a deep breath.

"I'm DS Stevens, Ma'm. I was told to pick you up," he said.

Sandra didn't know whether it was the agonising over Fiona, the worry of whether or not the girls had thought to pull the covers up over their beds, or even the liberties her driver was taking with the lights, but she was feeling a bit more than queasy as Stevens manoeuvred his way through the traffic. Her instinctive reaction was to concentrate on the streets around her. Studying the overspill of commuters pushing past each other as they jostled with shoppers on the footpaths, she guessed that for the majority, mornings were always chaotic. She took some comfort in the fact that being disorganised was not a trait exclusive to her. Here and there, strapped to the lampposts, bins overflowed with discarded polystyrene from caffeine breakfasts, doubtless intended to cure the effects of clubbing the weekend through. Monday morning, and her mood wasn't all that was oppressive: skies that earlier had looked so promising loomed dark and threatening overhead.

"Where are we headed?" she asked.

"The call came in from Higham, Ma'm: two bodies; one male, one female."

Stevens volunteered no further information and Sandra couldn't bring herself to ask. Dear God! What would take Fiona to Higham? What was even in Higham? She wasn't familiar with the village at all.

Leaving Maidstone behind them, they endured the rest of the journey in silence. To keep her mind occupied, Sandra dialled up her messages and listened to the one from her sister.

"Hi Sandra, it's me Suzi. Look I just want you to know that when you're ready to talk about Elle I'm here. Okay? Whenever you're ready I'm hear to listen. That's all I wanted to say, Sis."

Whatever does she mean, talk about Elle? Sandra was mystified. She would have to call her back later. Looking up she caught a fleeting glimpse of the Larkin memorial on Telegraph Hill, which was rapidly becoming enveloped in the creeping mist. Only then did she realise that her driver seemed to know his way about, which was strange given he was new; his accent certainly wasn't local.

Suddenly, without warning, Stevens took a left, throwing her against the passenger door. Sandra gasped, annoyed. Moments later he bumped up onto the kerb, bringing the vehicle screeching to a halt. Flung forward against the seat belt, Sandra bit her tongue, cried, "You stupid fool!", turned to give him a piece of her mind, but he was already out of the car and hurrying up the driveway of a large detached house. For a moment she sat as if glued to the seat, watching his departing back. *Come on girl, no matter how bad it gets keep calm; remember to breath; stay focused.*

Getting out, she was greeted by the first drops of rain as she scanned the street. No sign of Fiona's car. A crowd had already gathered and was pressing against the tape cordoning off the road in front of the house, which was partially shrouded from view by a line of tall trees. Pushing through, she ducked under the tape and viewed the exterior of the house that was the focus of attention. The rain, heavy now, plummeted relentlessly onto window-ledges that had definitely seen better days: she had an impression of peeling, bubbled paintwork along the length of the front. She surmised from the rotting wood, clearly visible on the front door, that it hadn't seen a lick of paint in at least twenty years. As Sandra made her way up the drive winding round to the side of the house, she recognised the chrome headlights of Fiona's platinum mini-convertible. For a second the sight of it stopped her in her tracks.

"Sandra!"

Jeff's voice called to her over the noise of the rain, which in a matter of minutes had soaked through to the inner lining of her jacket. She turned in the direction of the front door. The dread of what awaited her inside prevented her from hurrying; with every step the tarmac clung like a magnet to the heels of her boots urging her to stay outside.

"Fiona?"

It was the one, solitary word that she could manage to get out, partially hindered by the lump in her throat, partially not wanting an answer to the question it asked.

Jeff nodded, "She's okay, but in a state of shock. After finding that in there," he moved his head backwards indicating that he was referring to the discovery in the house, "who wouldn't be? But there's a gem of an old lady across the street who's taken her in, insisted on giving her a cup of tea."

Sandra's legs almost gave way with relief, followed immediately with livid anger. Isn't that just typical of Jeff, Sandra thought, browbeaten by a little old lady! Why couldn't he have taken the time to let her know all that when he phoned.

She knew he must have read her expression because he was attempting to reassure her: "Don't worry, I've sent Christine to sit with her!"

Waiting for her response, Jeff was relieved that there was no trace of concern in his voice, not that he took Sandra for a fool. Possibly Fiona was in the wrong place at the wrong time, but this wasn't the first murder in which she had become entangled and Jeff's years of experience had taught him not to believe in coincidences. But for now he wanted Sandra to encounter the scene with an open mind, though he was quite sure that once she had established a train of events she would share his misgivings.

Sandra bit off what she had been about to say. Did Jeff not realize that he had misled her into believing Fiona was the victim, or was it that she had over-reacted to his call? And now here she was doing it again! She endeavoured to swallow her anger. But then again, if Fiona was okay, what else was here that he wanted her to see? There was no sign of the pathologist, and there was a surprising lack of forensic activity. What was Jeff up to? There was something else he was hiding. He knew she wasn't cleared yet to attend violent crime scenes. She didn't like the feel of this at all.

Wiping some of the wetness from her face she kept her voice calm, asked him, "What are we dealing with, then? I believe there are two of them?" leaning in towards him so that nobody else would hear, added, "and I hope you got the okay from Millar to get me here!"

Jeff waved his arm in a dismissive gesture intended to make that bit of protocol seem insignificant. "I've not had much time to go over the scene as yet. Uniform said that at first sight it looks like some sort of suicide pact. Apparently, a Macmillan nurse has been going in at regular intervals, but she got held up last night and wasn't able to get here. She did phone several times, though, and according to her, the wife said there was no change in the husband's condition. I did manage to get a bit of background on that. He was making a slow departure, evidently; the cancer had got into his bones. The nurse will be in later to give a statement, after she's had some sleep, but—"

Sandra, thinking about Fiona, had backed away from the doorstep and turned to view the houses across the street. She was aware of Jeff reaching out to touch her arm. Feeling the pressure of his fingers, she turned back, noted his kindly gaze scanning her face, the concern he was trying to hide.

"Look, Sandra," he said, "it's not how I'd hoped to ease you back in, but someone has dealt out an awful lot of suffering in there and aside from the fact that it's your area of expertise, I thought you'd better take a look at it; you'll see why. Don't worry about Millar, I'll take the flack when we get back to the station – not that there's much he can say when he's left me with a skeleton team. Do you feel up to it? It's bad in there, and I do mean bad."

Sandra nodded; what was bad any more? After everything she had confronted in the last two years she needed to re-define the word 'bad'. Whether or not she was up to it was debatable. She had become accustomed to always being ready; perpetually on edge for anything. That she might not be able to cope concerned her and it was, she knew, what was really concerning Jeff. There was only one way to find out; she gently removed his hand from her arm, "Okay; let's do it."

Suited up in the tent hastily erected by the first set of technicians to arrive, they made for the front door. Jeff patted her shoulder, handing her a pair of gloves as he let her into the house. She felt sure he was exaggerating, that this was just a dummy run to stop her from slipping back into the abyss.

Deeper inside the hall a waft of warm air hit their faces. Under different circumstances it would have been a welcome replacement for the cold wetness they had just been standing in, but it carried the stench of death and the central heating, which was on at full blast, had concentrated it. Even though she had been expecting it and was prepared, Sandra was almost overwhelmed. Her instinctive reaction was to hold her breath, but she controlled it and looked around her.

The general state of neglect she had observed outside continued on the inside. At one time this would have been a grand enough entrance hall; the sheer size of the place would have been too much for an elderly couple to maintain. The high ceilings and once beautiful, ornate cornices were yellowed, speckled here and there with brown. The heavy embossed paper adorning the walls had been painted over and bore telltale signs of cat scratches: little mounds of paint fragments and shreds of paper littered the floor along the skirting board. The mosaic pattern beneath Sandra's feet unearthed memories of visits to her grandmother's house; she too had had a fine Wilton runner up the stairs, but it had survived the ravages of time a hell of a lot better than this one. She wondered about the amount of traffic it had taken to leave it so threadbare: grandchildren?

To her left a double door opened onto what she surmised was the drawing room. At first glance it was quite uplifting, considering the general neglect elsewhere. Full of antiquities, the room portrayed a quiet and ordered refuge, a room the owner took pride in. Sandra felt an aura of peacefulness in here. The only sound came from a huge grandfather clock, the sound of its dull chord emphasised by the silence elsewhere in the house. It seemed poignantly out of place; still keeping time where time had stood still; life had stopped.

Looking around at all the photographs displayed in abundance throughout the room, Sandra thought it strange – given the state of the stair-carpet – that there was a total absence of children. It was a pictorial record of the victims' lives, from wedding photos, seaside poses and what seemed quite a recent visit abroad – France, maybe Spain – yet not one child in any of them.

"Peggy and Matt Lyons," Jeff informed her, adding to the scant details he had gleaned from the nurse.

She nodded, studying the images in front of her. Funny what you could tell from a collection of photos, she thought, as she viewed each one in turn. In one the woman sat in a chair, the man stood with his hand resting on it. They both looked uncomfortable. Taken by a professional no doubt; she was familiar with the stiff poses, she had some like these on her wall at home. Images of people now lost to her, whom she remembered only from childhood, denied access into their world.

Looking at the rest, all casual, taken on impulse, it was always the woman who appeared to be the stronger of the two; at least that was Sandra's impression as she examined them. She felt like a stranger intruding on happier times, for their life together appeared to have been happy: she could see it in the brightness of their eyes. Now she would have to see what sort of picture they made in death.

As Sandra moved to the second reception room, Jeff stepped back from the door. She could sense a nervous energy emanating from him as she brushed past. The room itself was brightly lit, larger than the first and not as tidy. A sofa and armchair partially divided the room in two. The space to one side was given over to a hospital bed, which was surrounded by various drips and machines; these were a familiar sight. She could feel a numbness rising through her: nearly three months on and still she couldn't cope with their image, didn't yet want to associate these things with death. She knew the quilt was hiding the remains of the man and quickly diverted her gaze to the opposite end of the room.

If it had been in another place in a happier time, she would have smiled at the familiarity of it. This end of the room formed a kind of office: a space crying out to be organised. Masses of papers untidily stacked filled every surface. Drawers overstuffed unable to close properly were left half open. At this point it was impossible to decide whether they had been rifled through or had always been like this. An ancient typewriter peeked out from beneath a paperweight formed by several bundles of leaflets. It was even more untidy than her study at home – if only just. There was no chair at the desk.

Sandra moved on inside the room, aware of the blaze of light from behind the door. She turned back towards the bed and saw the chair and its occupant lit up like a film set. Five lamps of various design formed an oval boundary around the corpse, the empty space in front crisscrossed with leads. It was the woman in the photos, but it was clear that age and having to endure her husband's illness had made her less of a presence than she once had been. In death she bore little resemblance to the strong woman presented in the images that had afforded Sandra a fleeting glimpse into her past. Beneath the lights, her head was stretched backwards, her eyes staring blankly at the greyness of the ceiling.

The chair was positioned in full view of the bed, but not close to it. Sandra moved a step nearer. She could feel the hairs standing up on her skin. She shook off the cold rush of terror sweeping through her, before it shattered her nerve. Her hands, sweating, felt closed in by the gloves; her fingers, reluctant to touch death, squirmed, digging into her palms. She could feel her heart thudding as she forced herself to move closer to the body, her feet automatically avoiding the leads, her nostrils closing in repugnance against the sweet, sickly odour of fresh blood.

As she stared at the corpse, flashes of Gerry, grey and lifeless pierced her brain, appearing and disappearing, taunting and terrorising. Closing her eyes, Sandra attempted to banish them; it was futile; eyes open or shut, he was still there. With all of her will she challenged them, interposed them with images of him living, pink not grey, eyes wet with sparkles of laughter, not empty and glazed over. *Come on Gerry, laugh for me; keep on laughing.* Silently she called to him, made the images of him stronger until he was there in her head; the Gerry she had loved and never wanted to disappear. And then, as suddenly, he melted away and she found she was looking not into Gerry's laughing eyes, but into the cold stare of the dead woman. Involuntarily she flinched.

Shivering, Sandra leaned closer, looked into the face, acknowledging the terror it expressed. She studied the eyes; dry and vacant; noted the brown discolouring in what had once been white.

She could feel Jeff's presence in the doorway behind her; knew he was both impatient and apprehensive at the same time as he waited for her response.

"I've bleeped Fenton," he interrupted her thoughts. "She was attending an inquest this morning, so she's a bit held up. I thought she'd want to deal with this one herself."

"I see; so that explains why you're on edge," Sandra replied, still studying the form of the woman in the chair. The front of the nightgown was saturated in blood, tucked up behind her, it exposed her legs, thin, absent of muscle.

Jeff cleared his throat. "Lift the gown, Sandra, but brace yourself for what you'll find."

She looked round at Jeff, puzzled. It was obvious the woman had been stabbed; she had seen enough stab wounds in her time. She lifted up the flowery cotton – already drying under the warmth of the lamps and sticking to the skin beneath – and saw what he meant.

In fact there was no skin: just dark, viscous organs and coagulated blood.

"Jesus!" she whispered, steadying herself.

This woman had not suffered stab wounds; she'd been cut into, but not as if ravished by a wild animal. The cuts into the skin seemed to have been made with precision, if that were possible. Motionless, fighting to compose herself, Sandra was almost unable to take in what she was seeing.

Suddenly, she dropped the nightgown; began to tremble, reflex making her turn away. What was she doing here? This was the last place she needed to be right now. Still trembling, she took another look around the room. This was what she was supposed to be good at, what she had been trained to do. She was more than your normal run-of-the-mill detective; she was a profiler, or at least she had been. But as she stood there in the middle of the room there was no rush of adrenalin, none of the buzz that was usually vibrant when she worked on a case. She felt as though she had been flung into a strange world, a horrid world. She wondered what she had ever found exciting in her work, in her present state of mind it was defeating. She wasn't good enough to do this; it was beyond her now. All she wanted to do at this moment was escape, run out of this house into the fresh air outside, feel the rain on her face, let it wash off the stench of death that was clinging to her skin.

With a tremendous effort of will, Sandra fought off the urge to run away; she had done enough of that lately. She'd always known that coming back into this line of work would be tough. She'd spent nearly two years leaning on everyone else until it had become a way of life. Losing Gerry had brought it all to a head. Maybe she needed this. Perhaps, in some twisted way, surrounding herself with death would keep her focused; keep her depression at bay. Deep inside her head she knew that at some subconscious level she was slowly beginning to accept death – principally Gerry's. This was as good a time as any to see if any of the old Sandra was still inside her somewhere, but such had been her mental torment of late, it felt as if a metamorphosis had taken place. She was like a caterpillar suspended in a cocoon unaware of its changing form until it emerged as something beautiful – except in her case, it had worked in reverse: she had changed into something ugly. This kind of work had once been her life and breath, but now she was a stranger to herself and at this moment she was not convinced she was capable of carrying off this stranger's task; at least not anywhere near to a degree of professionalism. But she knew she must or go under.

Sandra braced herself, resigned at least to try; to distance herself, be coldly analytical in gathering information, seeing things that most of her colleagues would pass over. She found her gaze drawn back to the corpse: *What are you doing sitting over here on your own?* Turning, she looked in the direction of the bed and then back at the rest of the room. The scene was ordered. There had been time to plan it. The killer was skilled; had killed like this before. She noted that the man's corpse had been left in shadow. Was that significant?

"Were all these lamps on when Uniform got here?" she asked Jeff, her gaze drawn back to the dead woman. *Why did you end up over here, alone, the star of the show yet so distanced from him? Would you not have been over there, holding on to the last, unable to let go? Who denied you that?*

"I've asked both the officers and Fiona,' Jeff said. "Uniform say they went no further than the doorway, and Fiona was clear she'd only taken a few steps into the room when she realized something was wrong."

Lifting her gaze, Sandra continued scanning the room, all the time her mind challenging what she saw. On another level she was bemused by her investigative abilities, aware of a tingling inside herself as she was carried along by the stranger co-habiting her body; a person so unlike her – or at least unlike the timorous self she had become – that it felt almost alien. This person had confidence – a feeling of self-assurance that Sandra yearned for; one that had been missing from her life for what seemed a very long time.

She looked again at the woman: judged by the state of her that she had been dead for about seven hours, though Leslie Fenton would confirm that – if she ever got here. *I think you would have been just like me, clinging on, not wanting the end to come, but you weren't given the chance, were you? Tell me Peggy; tell me; what did you see?*

Sandra leaned closer, peered into the woman's eyes, tried to visualise those last traumatic moments; the last glimpses she'd had of this world before she had succumbed to the terror and the pain somewhere between midnight and dawn. She closed her eyes and tried to retrace a picture in her head of the last moments of Peggy Lyon's life:

Tears are streaming from Peggy Lyons's eyes.
Why is this man doing this to them. It isn't right!
She watches helplessly as the figure in front of her fills a syringe and inserts it into the drip hanging on the stand next to Matt's bed.
She does not understand why he is laying out plastic sheeting on the floor. She imagines the screams and muffled cries as he lifts her husband from the bed and drops him hard on the sheet.
God help us! He is doing it; he really is going to kill Matt.
The crunching sound; she can't bear it. She closes her eyes but can't shut out the sounds; hears this evil man laugh at her. He knows she cannot close her ears.
"Concentrate!!" he yells at her.
She prays: 'God, take us away from this. Please God, take us away'.
"You can't!! Can you?" he shouts.
What does he want of her?
This can't be happening; not like this.
Matt needed a priest.
The man stops shouting and rips the tape away from her mouth; she

can feel blood trickling from her lips. She knows she is going to die too, but she cares nothing for herself – it is Matt she thinks of; only Matt.

He needs the last rights. He can't die without them. He just can't.

"Please... Please don't; you can't... Please! I told you I don't know. There must be a misunderstanding. I don't know what you want!" Her voice is cracked, barely audible.

She can hear his low, sustained, devious laughter. He means it to taunt her and it does. She can do nothing but watch.

He is gripping so hard on Matt's wrists that even though deprived of her glasses, she can clearly see the white knuckles protruding through his skin. Then he grabs at Matt's legs and slings him back on the bed, jeering.

She shakes in terror as the man turns towards her, laughing, his eyes filled with delight; evil delight. She feels ill; more ill than she has ever felt in her life. The sick feeling of despair that is taking her over is even worse, much worse, than when she learned Matt's cancer was untreatable.

Matt has stopped breathing. She knows he is leaving her. Her sore lips move as she prays. She pleads with God to forgive Matt his sins; beseeches that his soul be fit to enter into heaven; she prays that her prayers will suffice to make amends for the absence of the priest.

What does this devil want of her? All these questions; she has no answers.

The girl who came back earlier had asked the same questions. She had been polite, such a pretty girl. How can this evil be anything to do with her?

It is all wrong the information they gave her; it is they who are mixed up, not her.

Why has her beloved Matt been robbed of dying with dignity?

She is glad that his suffering is over, but his soul has to be pure: she offers more prayers for him...

She has lost all track of time.

How long had it been since Matt had passed.

She has intermittingly been allowed a sight of him, according to the movement of this evil man in front of her. She had seen several changes in Matt's colour. He had moved; sunk into the bed.

She could no longer see his face.

She is glad, though: it had changed several times since she had first been able to tell he was dead. Her last glimpse of him had scared her.

She feels ashamed; she never once in her life had cause to be scared of that gentle man, and that's what he was, a true gentleman.

She wishes this man would stop shaking her, her arms hurt so much.

She doesn't understand why he has switched on all the lights. They are bright. She is blinded by them.

She is aware of the man's figure, his shadow falls over her. Something glistens in his hand raised high above her head. It begins to descend. She sees it is a blade. Then she feels pain: burning, searing, indescribable pain. She has never felt pain like this; she screams but no sound comes out. She prays for death.

She manages to find the photo of Matt on the wall and fixes on the image of her husband; the way he used to be when they were happy, when their lives were in front of them. Matt... is he moving closer to her? Her vision is blurring, everything is fogging, white fog. Matt...

Now she is suffocating, her lungs drowning in fluid. Even though she wants to die, she feels the panicked nerves in her throat struggling for breath. Such pain!

She is loosing focus.

The white fog turns to blackness.

Then, nothing...

12

Turning away from Peggy Lyons's body, Sandra made her way blindly towards the front door; she needed fresh air.

Jeff was close on her heels. "Well, what do you think?"

She stopped by the open door, knew he was waiting for an answer, impatiently searching her face for a hint of her perception of the scene inside. "Somebody cut a hole in her, Jeff, that's what I think!"

"I know that Sandra, but why? We've got a right nutter on our hands here haven't we? This is the last thing I need right now. Give me a few moments until I can get hold of Millar and salvage some of the team."

Catching the attention of an officer below the doorsteps he shouted an order. "That cordon needs extending to either end of the street. See to it!" To Sandra he said, "Best keep the Press as far away as possible for the time being. I'll get Stevens to organise a check on the nearest institutions – you know the ones I mean – see if any of the inmates have gone walk about. You know as well as I do the usual suspects in this type of case."

Sandra nodded in agreement, but she had seen enough to know that her initial observations had only skimmed the surface. Not until Leslie had performed a full examination of both bodies, was there any point in attempting to see a purpose in the slaughter that had taken place in this house. For now, all they had was what she had managed, with her few basic instincts, to establish.

"Well, as you will have noted," she said, "there was no attempt to deform their faces, which would indicate their killer was not known to them. Also, there's no sign of a forced entry, so whoever it was seemed trustworthy enough to let in. Then there are the lamps: five of them and all centred around her, not him; as if it was staged and she was his focus. I'm saying 'he', but before you ask, yes it's possible that it could be a she; they couldn't have put up much of a struggle. I wonder if..." lost in thought, her voice tailed away.

Jeff, watching her face, said after a moment, "Well? What are you getting at, Sandra?"

She shrugged, "Oh, it's nothing. I need more time, but there are a few things I want to run past Leslie when she gets here. Hopefully it will be clearer to me then. What about Fiona? You haven't told me. Did she say what brought her here?"

"No, I, well she—," Jeff looked away distractedly as a large van and a white MR2 drew up to the tape. "I must go. Can I catch up with you later? I need to get over there," he indicated the houses opposite.

Without turning to see, Sandra knew by his eagerness to distance himself from the house that Leslie and her team of SOCOs were arriving. She nodded at Jeff to let him go, "Don't leave without me; remember I've no car."

Already on his way, Jeff waved acknowledgement, choosing to plod across the saturated grass to avoid the new arrivals coming up the drive.

Sandra waited by the steps to greet them, relieved that for the moment the rain had stopped. Faintly amused, she saw that Jeff had already crossed the road. A year or so ago, he had allowed himself to be paired up with Leslie Fenton to make up a party of four at the Kent Police Ball. Sandra had enquired on numerous occasions what had happened after they had left together that night, but both of them had remained tight-lipped. That was until one night several months later when Jeff came to dinner and having had more than one glass of wine too many, had let his guard slip. Suffice it to say that he had never slept with any woman but Angie. Leslie, he had discovered to his regret and as he had explained to Sandra, was one of those modern women who owed her assets to her profession – in Leslie' case, a surgeon's knife – not what he thought of as a *real* woman at all.

To Sandra's relief, how he had discovered this much he had kept to himself: the bedroom antics of her friends were not something that she relished to hear – certainly not Jeff's! Not much about his ramblings that night had made sense, but it seemed that he was all up for moving with the times, except that he liked his women natural:

God-made not man-made as he put it. Leslie was not the kind of woman, alas, that he was ready for, he had said with a rueful smile.

Whatever had happened between them that night was anyone's guess, but Sandra was not alone in noticing that since then, Jeff looked uncomfortable whenever in proximity with Leslie; never making eye contact and quickly finding an excuse to leave – as he had just done.

From across the road, Jeff breathed a sigh of relief. Making his way up to the house where Fiona was waiting, he was annoyed at himself for the way he seemed unable to deal with confronting Leslie, but he had trouble keeping his mind from wandering in her presence. He found he could not stop imagining what might have happened that night at her flat if he had not clumsily mistaken her bedroom door – to where she had retired to slip into something more comfortable – for her bathroom. Shocked by the vision of predatory sexuality confronting him, he had then blundered into a closet before quickly retracing his steps to the hallway. Shouting out some excuse about his bleeper and an emergency, he had run – or as he'd seen it – escaped. She was not his type of woman at all; he was on safer ground keeping to memories of Angela for company. Glancing back, he saw Leslie making her way up the drive. Face to face contact sent shivers up his spine; even at this distance the sight of her made him cringe with embarrassment.

Sandra forced her mouth to smile as she watched the senior forensic pathologist, Leslie Fenton, sashay up the drive towards her. Though well into her forties, Leslie could still turn more than a few heads in any room. Above average height, her bleached, blonde hair partially clipped up, bouncing in unison with her stride, her swaying left hip hitting against her case with every second step as, like a catwalk model, she approached the front door. In the few years that Sandra had known her, Leslie had never mentioned that there was a man in her life. Her encounter with Jeff she seemed to have put out of her mind; she was a career woman first and foremost and Sandra had supposed that forensic science was the lover that took centre stage in her life.

"Sandra! Nobody told me you were here. I thought you weren't due to come back for a while yet?" Leslie had one of those voices that was deep and sensual; the kind that men found seductive and women, soothing and friendly, but it was obvious to Sandra that she was the last person Leslie had expected to bump into here.

Registering the shock that Leslie was at pains to hide, Sandra suddenly wondered if most of the people she had worked with were resigned to the fact that she was in a downward spiral and had decided she was finished; her career over. Perhaps they were right. Were it not for Jeff urging her onwards, she would by now have accepted defeat. It was a depressing thought; she shrugged it off, saying, "Well, I didn't expect to find myself working the scene here either. Apparently it was Fiona who reported this one. Jeff called me not long after he arrived."

"Oh!" Leslie thought about this for a moment. "Is it someone she knew? Someone you both knew?"

"No. At least, not anybody I know. To be quite honest I haven't had the chance to ask Fiona yet, but I would presume that she didn't know them either, at any rate, not personally."

A bad feeling swept over Sandra as she spoke. Was that true? Why had Fiona come here this morning? Suddenly, Fiona's words came back to her: *I've kept the morning free of appointments, there's somewhere I have to go.* Sandra had thought nothing of it at the time, but on reflection, she had got the impression that Fiona's 'somewhere' was not connected to the studio. There was no point in trying to guess her sister-in-law's reasons for being in Higham; she would find out soon enough.

Aware that Leslie was looking at her quizzically, Sandra tried to focus her mind on the scene inside the house. "There are several things I want to ask you Leslie, when you've had a chance to examine the bodies. We've certainly got a tricky one on our hands here."

"I guessed as much when it was me Jeff asked for. Better get on with it then." Leslie said, seemingly as eager as ever to get started and moving towards the tent, but adding over her shoulder, "It's high time we got together for a chat, to catch up."

"I'd like that – shall I book us a table at Gianni's?"

Leslie smiled, "That'd be good; thanks."

"No problem. Next week? Why don't you text me a date when you've got a minute and I'll email you when I've sorted it."

"Okay."

Together they reached the tent and Sandra, holding up the

flap, stood back to let Leslie and her team file through. Trying to remember when she and Leslie had last met at Gianni's, she barely noticed their smiling nods and muttered thanks. Before Gerry died, she and Leslie had customarily had dinner together every couple of weeks or so. For Sandra, it had been a lifeline. Leslie had been well aware of the strained relationships in the Reid household and knew how close she and Fiona were, always taking the time to engage Fiona in conversation whenever they met, showing an interest in her career and asking about her latest project. Nor had she ever forgotten to ask how things were going with Gerry. Sandra had found it more than a relief to be able to open up to someone removed from the life that went on in their home. Hell, she thought, Leslie was a better therapist than the one she had sat with for two hours every month since the kidnap! But after Gerry's death, the dinners had stopped. Leslie, like the good friend she was, had been there for Sandra in the aftermath; a constant figure attending to her every need. But lately, they had drifted apart. Yes; it would be good to get together again and renew their friendship.

While Leslie and her team were suiting up, Sandra stood waiting against the wall. The rain was coming down again. The continual flow of water from the guttering soaked into her hair as she picked at the bubbled paintwork, dabbling her feet in the rainwater to wash off the leaves sticking to her boots. She watched as they swirled away, spinning towards the drain. When the rain eased, they would be left to rot. There was nobody left here to tend the garden; nobody to clear them away. Decay was all around her.

13

"Penny for them!"

Sandra heard the voice behind her, registered it was her driver from this morning, and swung round to him with a scowl. He was standing in the doorway holding out a plastic evidence-bag.

"Found this, it's a cat; dumped in the bin."

He had an engaging smile and was undoubtedly attractive. Feeling guilty, she acknowledged to herself that she had taken an instant and irrational dislike to the man – mostly sparked off by his driving – she should have her wrists slapped. In the car she had pulled up her defences, aware of the awkward silence, but unwilling to engage in small talk. Had she been less prickly, she might have picked up some useful information about the case. By the same token, he must have heard some choice bits of gossip from colleagues and wondered about this crazy woman he had been sent to pick up.

Adjusting her expression to one of friendly interest, Sandra reached out and took the bag from him. "Something else for us to add to the list of charges I suppose. I'm sorry, I didn't catch your name this morning; you're new aren't you?"

"Gareth Stevens, I'm here on transfer. Two weeks now, so not as new as you!"

Cheeky with it, she thought, giving back as good as she got, "Believe me, there's nothing new about me. I'm old news. If nobody's taken the time to fill you in, *that* would be something new with most of this lot!"

From the blank expression on his face Sandra knew he hadn't a clue what she was talking about. She smiled, "Never mind. Let me take this into Leslie. Perhaps you could find out what Uniform has got from the neighbours?"

He shot her a cheerful grin and saluting backed away, before turning to make his way out of the grounds. Definitely cheeky, she thought, watching him disappear behind the trees, but charming with it. There was something of Mark Jakes about him: the proverbial Mr Darcy! Tall, dark and handsome, tanned into the bargain. Sandra dwelled on the similarities and found herself wondering if he had a six-pack hidden under his shirt. Whatever was she thinking! She really did need her wrist slapped. And Jakes was a psychopath! *Mothers, beware! Lock up your daughters, throw away the keys. Find them all nice tubby, cuddly Gerrys – but pick ones that don't go and end up dead on you.*

Sandra braced herself to go back inside, she needed to find out all that she could about the elderly couple, most of all she wanted an explanation from Fiona. What was her connection to these people?

Leslie was finishing up her preliminary examination and SOCOs were all over the house gathering evidence. Todd, the leading officer with whom Sandra had worked before, was leaning over the corpse in the chair. He waved her over.

"Look at this," he pointed, "just here."

Sandra walked over, avoiding the lamps to bend over the lifeless form, directing her attention to the woman's wrists as indicated. Todd had slightly lifted the cuffs of her gown to reveal that both of them were smeared with a sticky residue.

"She was bound by some kind of tape then. Have you searched for it?" Sandra asked. She had already presumed that Peggy Lyons would have been restrained with something, whether it had been something the killer found here and used or whether it was something he – for she felt instinctively that the killer was a man – had brought with him, would help them to decide whether the killings had been planned or opportunist.

Todd nodded in the direction of the desk, "There's a cheap roll of tape in the top drawer over there. I haven't ascertained if it was the one that was used, but it's unlikely." He gave her a sideways glance, "I never thought I'd ever see an office worse kept than yours, Sandra," he smirked, "looks like I was wrong!"

God! She muttered under her breath; even her housekeeping skills were being discussed behind her back. "Well if the tape's not here then it's been taken!" she snapped. With an effort, she swallowed her irritation, softening her tone to query something she had somehow missed earlier: "The blood spray – shouldn't there be more, here, in front of her?"

Todd nodded as he waited for the woman's wrists to be photographed before bagging her hands. "Should have been a hell of a bleed out; obviously whoever cut that hole in her was standing right in line, took the brunt of it. We've taken samples off the carpet."

Thinking it over, Sandra studied the floor again.

"She took one hell of a beating that's for sure," Todd continued, "before the job the killer did with the knife, look, see here." Pulling up the sleeves he exposed the blackened arms hidden beneath.

Leslie, having finished her preliminary examination, had come over to stand beside them. "Sorry to rush things, but I have another inquest this afternoon and I've quite a few cases come in over the weekend that I have to allocate. I'll rearrange my timetable to slot these two in."

Sandra put out a hand to stay her; there were things she needed to ask before Leslie left the scene. "Can you give me any idea as to time of death?"

Leslie directed her back towards the bed. "For him, firstly, yes, and I find myself asking why the killer bothered; it seems such a waste of effort seeing the victim was almost nothing but skin and bones to begin with. He died more quickly than she did."

As Leslie took hold of the blanket lifting it back to reveal what lay beneath, the gorge rose in Sandra's throat; fleetingly she was grateful she had not eaten breakfast. The corpse was practically flattened: where there should have been a rib cage there was none; instead an ensemble of organs was interspersed with what she could only describe as pieces of broken crockery.

"Good God, Leslie, how did that happen? It's almost as if he was crushed."

"My guess would be trampled. Look here, the pressure marks around the wrist indicate possible manhandling of some sort. I'd say we were talking some time before midnight; as for his wife, closer to 2am, maybe 3. Of course, that's not to be taken as precise, but it is as close as I can call it for now." Leslie extended one gloved finger, "Again, just preliminary, but look at this. I'd be almost sure that this liver mortis had already progressed before death. Why kill a man already so heavily sedated that he would have been unlikely ever to wake? This man was in his last hours, he would not have lived till morning is my guess – definitely not tomorrow morning, anyway. With that little titbit I will leave you to it." Leslie flashed a grim smile. "I'll see you later then. Gotta run! Don't forget that dinner date!"

With that she was gone. It was all in a day's work for Leslie, Sandra thought, knowing it should have been like that for her too. Unless you distanced yourself, this job was untenable. She stood over the bed until she had to move out of the way to allow the SOCO team to get on with it; thought about leaving, but choosing instead to see what she could find from the abundance of papers strewn about the desk.

Most of it was literature for one of those pro-life groups. She soon found the couple's bank statements, all pegged together, there was organisation here of a kind after all. Moving to the filing cabinet in the corner, she found it was unlocked. Inside, the index folders were curled and wrinkly, showing their age. As she searched she mulled the word 'motive' over and over in her head.

And then it hit her; shuddering, she realized in that instant why Fiona had been here. These were records of women: women for whom the Lyonses had arranged private adoptions. Fiona! Sandra's heart sank. After flicking through them she could tell that a whole section was missing. Nearly all folders dated for the first part of 1972 were empty.

Taking the bank statements with her, she slipped out of the room. She was angry with Fiona now having realised what had brought her here. Her sister-in-law hadn't said that she'd started searching for her birth mother again. But of course she wouldn't disclose it, not with all that had happened. Could Fiona be capable of this hideous crime? God no! Surely not! *What was she thinking?* Yet she had been here; records that could possibly be attached to her appeared to be missing. *What was going on?*

Sandra took refuge in the front sitting room; she needed some space to collect her thoughts. *Don't jump to conclusions: try to think logically.* Lifting a photo of Matt and Peggy Lyons from the mantelpiece, she freed it from its frame. Searching through cupboards in a dresser she found nothing of interest. Everything in this room was so neat, so different to the room she'd just left, even the rows of leather-bound classics in the bookcase were organised by colour and size. But wait a minute! The dark blue ones weren't classics, they were photo albums.

There were quite literally hundreds of images spanning several decades. Working her way back through them, trying to decide by hair-styles and dress fashions, Sandra sought those that were most likely to have been taken in the early seventies. Turning back another page she couldn't believe what she was seeing. A face caught her attention, producing a brief spark of recognition that she couldn't explain. A young woman stared up at her from the photo; she was sitting with two women of about the same age, all of them, Sandra guessed, at a similar stage of pregnancy. Peggy Lyons stood behind them. She prised the photo out of its holder and flipped it over, there was no date. Sandra knew she had seen this woman in a photo somewhere before, but where. Perhaps it would come to her later. Sliding the photo into her pocket, she decided to catch up with Jeff. It was really Fiona who she wanted to see. They needed to talk. Talk? No, more than that: Sandra felt as if what she needed was to shout.

Outside the rain had eased again, but grey skies still hung stubbornly overhead. No mini convertible to be seen. 'Where was Fiona – surely she hadn't been allowed to leave?'

Jeff was coming up the drive. "She said she had studio time lined up. She knows she has to make a formal statement." Catching her expression, he paused, added "I've told her to bring her solicitor."

Sandra let out a gasp of dismay. "She's avoiding me Jeff, I don't believe that she's capable of that in there, but I know she's involved in some way. They arranged adoptions, the Lyonses; years ago, private ones – and I just know that's what brought her here. And that's not all. It gets worse: there appear to be records missing. Considering the mess in there, if Fiona has taken them things will not look good for her – not to mention us. You have just let her go and as of now – though we may not want to believe it – she is our prime suspect."

"Surely you're over-reacting, Sandra, look, for goodness sake calm down. Do you honestly perceive a woman being capable of what happened in there? Come on!" He pointed her in the direction of the car. "I've told Stevens to take care of everything else here, let's pick up some lunch. You look as if you could do with a drink, if nothing else."

If she were honest, Sandra welcomed the suggestion; she'd had enough of this crime scene. If she was even more forthcoming, her need to get away had more to do with the knowledge that Fiona was somehow involved with it. Sandra, in her recent way of dealing with things, needed time to sort this all out in her head before she could even begin to contemplate what she was going to do about it.

14

The West Coast of Ireland: earlier the same day

"Ladies and gentlemen, please make sure your seat belts are fastened securely, we shall be landing at Knock Airport shortly."

Although he had made the trip often, Michael Delaney was relieved. Another twenty minutes or so and he would be able to relax. He no longer enjoyed flying; indeed, since 9/11 he had positively hated it. It was a feeling he thought would have passed by now, but to his dismay it lingered on as strong as the first time he had boarded an airliner following that dread-filled day. He supposed there was therapy available to help, but he had no heart to arrange it. In a way he felt it was part of his punishment; a tiny part of all the suffering and pain he must endure, for he deserved to be punished. Time and time again he had denied his wife the new life she wanted; delayed making the arrangements, repeatedly putting it off. Had he done as she wanted and re-located when she asked him to, she would still be here. Some days he felt he was learning to live with it: all the grief and the guilt. On others he found it was almost impossible. On those days he welcomed the pain.

Leaning towards the window, he waited, watching for the vast expanse of the Atlantic to give way to the rugged shoreline of his ancestors, the land he had now adopted as his own. When it appeared on the horizon, a mass of dark-grey cliffs topped with a sheet of grass, such a vivid green, Michael felt the tension in his muscles begin to loosen.

Craning his neck to catch a glimpse of his cases, he felt three hearty slaps on his back accompanied by Father Tom's voice: "Good to have you back Michael. I hope you had a smooth flight."

Turning with a ready smile, Michael embraced his friend. "It's good to be back Father Tom; really good."

"Will you look at the colour of you," Tom teased. "Sure and the good Lord himself thought it was us needed the rain. It seemed at times it was never going to stop, and now here you are and it's still raining!"

Father Tom Devine was a small, grey-eyed man with a softly spoken accent. His thick head of hair, which parted at the side and fell over his forehead into a fringe, had turned white well before his fortieth birthday. It gave him the appearance of being much older than his forty-six years. He had a gentle nature; never one to lose his patience or show his frustration. Yet this morning, Michael could detect dark shadows under his eyes; a heaviness to his step as they walked towards his jeep.

Father Tom put the key in the ignition, but did not start the engine; instead he rested his hands on the steering wheel and sighed. "I'm afraid I've got bad news, Michael. I didn't think it the proper thing to break it to you over the phone; thought it better to tell you to your face."

Michael's first thought was that they had been turned down for the youth centre. They had been fighting long and hard for funding over the last two years and had finally raised their portion of the costs. As he prepared himself for the disappointment, he suddenly remembered that the decision wasn't due until the end of November. His stomach lurched. What then? Had something happened at the house?

"It's Gracie O'Hara," Father Tom said quietly, "I'm afraid she's dead."

Stunned, Michael turned to look at him; maybe he had mistaken what his friend had said, but Tom was looking the other way, gazing out of the window. "Dead, Father? When? I mean, how? You never even mentioned that she was ill."

Tom sighed, looked down at his hands and then at Michael. "She wasn't ill; God help the poor woman. Michael, my son, I'm afraid she was murdered last Friday night at old Father Mullan's cottage."

Michael, bemused, tried to make sense of the words. "What? How? What was she doing there?"

Again, Father Tom sighed heavily, his hands tightened on the steering wheel. "You know Sheila McBride was taken ill at the end of July? Well, since early August, Gracie O'Hara has been staying with me covering for her and Mrs Reilly has been looking in on Father Mullan. But then, a few weeks back, well, you know how the old boy relapses now and again: he took to the drinking again and Mrs Reilly asked Gracie to share the load, said she couldn't cope with him on her own."

Michael snorted, "The fair-weather queen cajoled her more like!"

Ignoring the comment, Father Tom continued, "I got a call late Friday afternoon asking for the housekeeper; didn't think much about it at the time. Thought maybe she'd ordered something or that it was private, about the house – she was after one of those off Quay Road. You knew she'd had to sell the farmhouse? Anyway, I told the caller she was at the cottage. God help me," Father's Tom's voice broke. Slowly he shook his head, the guilt written plainly on his face. "I even gave him the directions to find her."

"It was a man?"

"Yes."

"Has he been arrested; was he a local?"

Father Tom shrugged, "No, they haven't caught him yet, but whoever he was, I dread to think that one of our folk could have taken a life like that. Evil; it was evil."

"Like that?" Michael reached out to grasp Father Tom's arm, shook it urgently. "Like what? What do you mean? Don't tell me she was assaulted first? Not old Gracie."

"No; no; at least, not as far as the pathologist could detect. But it was bad, Michael, she was—" Father Tom paused, as though struggling to find words. He grimaced, "What I can only describe as 'mutilated', God rest her soul; horribly mutilated."

Michael could hardly take it all in. He had come back to Ireland to get away from a life that had him dealing with murder day in and day out. Westport was to have been his sanctuary: a safe haven; where he and Cathy could start a family. They had been only weeks away from realising their dream when she'd been taken from him. But he had honoured his promise to her and come on his own and now, it seemed, death had followed him here.

Gracie O'Hara had answered his advertisement for a housekeeper three years ago, when he had first arrived in Westport. Not that he had much of a house for her to keep; the old family home he had inherited lay derelict. It had lain abandoned to the elements since his grandfather had left for America. Michael had purchased a second-hand mobile home and placed it in the grounds, intending to restore the old house over time.

Within two months of starting the renovation he'd lost all interest. In truth, it was probably Gracie who saved him from becoming lost forever, such was the depth of the depression he'd fallen into by then. Drinking heavily, crying out night after night for Cathy, it wasn't long before his health had begun to fail. But Gracie O'Hara – good old Gracie – had taken him in hand. With a relentless tongue she had badgered him into pulling himself together. Now, as her words came back to him he wanted to laugh and weep at the same time: 'Sure and why would any half-decent woman want to be comin' back to a wrecked heap of a man like yourself? Been shackled to one most of me life and if I could I'd be gone in the morning so I would!'

She had thought he'd lost Cathy to another man and he had never explained the truth to her – at least, not until after she had introduced him to Father Tom. He smiled, thinking of her sharp tongue; but beneath it all no one knew more than he that Gracie's heart was pure gold. And as for Father Tom; he had mentored to Michael's grief; walked his soul back from the edge; the point of no return. Michael was still walking; the wounds flared up every so often, but Tom – his spiritual healer – was always there for him; so too was Gracie, who dealt with all the practicalities of life. What would he do without her? Through her he had learned everything he wanted – and everything he didn't want – to know about most of the locals, especially Mrs Reilly – her supposed long-time pal – whose husband, until his death, had owned a bar in the centre of town. It was where Gracie had mopped floors and cleaned lavatories, juggling the work with her four other cleaning jobs, his own included. Her husband, a brute of a man, had kept her company: supported at the bar by his elbows, his thirst quenched by one whisky after the next, served with all her barmaid charms by Mrs Reilly herself, who took great pleasure in deducting the tally at the end of the week out of Gracie's wages. All she had to do was point to the 'No Credit' sign framed above the till. Hence Gracie's bitterness: every week it was the same; no wages were ever due and it was Gracie who ended up digging into her purse to pay Mrs Reilly for the privilege of working there. Michael could imagine the delight of that mean-spirited woman who knew fine well she had tapped into an endless resource. But nothing lasts forever and gradually, as the years passed on, Gracie had sold increasing parcels of her land, only to watch the proceeds pissed down Mrs Reilly's urinals; the ones Gracie scrubbed clean every day. Yet, despite all this, the two women had formed something of a friendship; quite why Michael could never figure out. Perhaps because Gracie laid the blame for her hard life on herself; thought it was her own fault for being so foolish as to take marriage vows with a 'blow-in', as she referred to O'Hara – and one from the North at that! Poor, dear, Gracie; and now she had gone.

Father Tom had finally started the jeep and they were heading along the road to Castlebar. "Sergeant O'Leary has been keeping me up with developments, such as they are. When I told him I was picking you up this morning he asked if you would drop by. I think they want you to help out with enquiries."

Michael nodded. "Sure; I'll do all that I can. Poor Gracie; she had it hard. She was the last person in the world to deserve this."

They didn't speak again for the remainder of the journey. Father Tom's normally loquacious tongue was stilled, distracted, Michael supposed, at having aided the killer – albeit unknowingly.

Reaching the town, Michael was surprised when the jeep pulled into the hospital car park. "Are we not to meet Sergeant O'Leary at the station?"

"No," Father Tom said, driving round to the rear of the building and killing the engine. "He asked me to drop you here at the morgue. The Assistant State Pathologist is waiting for you here, as well."

"Aren't you coming in?"

Father Tom gestured at the clock on the dash. "No Michael; I have to get back, I'm saying Mass this morning. I'll be cutting it short as it is. I'll hold these bags of yours at the church; you can pick them up later. O'Leary will give you a lift into Westport when he's finished briefing you."

Michael watched the departing jeep for a moment, then turned towards the building and made his way along the corridor to the pathologist's office. Sergeant O'Leary was standing outside the door. "Mike; glad you agreed to come. I know it must have hit you hard when you heard about it, you being so close to Mrs O'Hara and all. Brian Quinn is waiting downstairs."

Michael sighed, "Yes we were close, though I haven't seen her in six months. The Bureau called me in on an investigation that lasted longer than I expected and, well, with the anniversary in September, I decided to stay on for it. After that I made the decision at long last to put the apartment on the market."

"You've finally let go of it then?"

Michael turned his mouth down, "Not exactly; afraid I got cold feet at the last minute. I've arranged to lease it out for another six months."

O'Leary nodded, gave a non-committal smile and led the way into the lab. As they went deeper into the building and the temperature cooled, Michael found he was dreading the sight of Gracie's body. It would have been lying in a chilling cabinet since the autopsy a week ago and it saddened him to think of her there, all alone in the darkness. Even more, it angered him that her life had ended like this; so cruelly.

Michael knew the Assistant Pathologist, Brian Quinn, having helped out unofficially with several cases over the last few years; nothing like this though. Mayo was reputedly the safest place in the world – though not any more it seemed. Brian, always jovial, extended his hand and almost yanked Michael's out of his shoulder socket in the enthusiasm of his greeting. "Glad you could come, Mike; we were wondering if you were ever coming back at all."

He led the way into the morgue, rustling in his green plastics and white rubber boots, pulling on his gloves as the doors swished open automatically at their approach. "Come on, I'm eager to see what you make of this. I don't believe this case is what we thought it was in the beginning."

Michael looked blank. O'Leary, a step behind him, took a deep breath and explained a lot more about Gracie's murder than the brief sketch Father Tom had drawn, by which time they were stood over the trolley and Brian was unzipping the bag. "We've put a lid on this so far as anyone else is concerned for the time being."

Michael braced himself, his attention moving from O'Leary to the trolley as Gracie's pale face emerged from the black body-bag. He reached out his hand to prevent Brian from unzipping any further than was necessary; he had no stomach for seeing Gracie naked to the world; he was never meant to see her that way. His chest seemed to constrict as he examined her waxen features; the gaunt, lifeless stare. For a moment he held his breath, imagining her fear in the moments before she died; heard again in his head his wife's last words to him: the same fear. She had made the call over her cell phone as she prepared to perish in the inferno of the World Trade Centre. Cathy, no less than Gracie, had been executed by an evil hatred.

"This was no depraved attack," Brian said.

Mystified by the statement, Michael's head shot up, "Eh?"

Brian corrected his choice of words. "What I mean to say is that the wounds were not inflicted by some maniac wielding a knife willy-nilly. You'll see for yourself when we run the shots. Whoever killed poor Gracie here took a knife and used it much like a surgeon, deliberately cutting out a circle of the skin of the abdomen and leaving it hanging like a flap, before carefully setting the intestines to the sides; I guess to give him room so he could reach the treasure he sought."

Michael looked from Brian to O'Leary and back again. "What the hell are you talking about?"

Before Brian could answer, O'Leary cut across him, "Brian thinks that our killer took himself a trophy: Gracie's womb has been cut out."

Michael waved his thanks as Sergeant O'Leary pulled away from the kerb in front of the church. Mass was over, but rather than go straight into the church, Michael stopped on the street to look up and down the tree-lined mall. The weather was mild for October and the trees had not yet shed all their leaves. Wandering across to the wall he sat and listened to the river. Its level was high. This was a beautiful town; he'd fallen in love with the place he now called home. Yet someone had chosen here to unleash his evil. Michael had viewed the crime scene prints; seen the horrific wounds to Gracie's body. That O'Leary had used the word 'trophy' was significant.

He stood and turned around slowly, not admiring the view, but asking himself what could be lurking behind that face; that door. Would there be another victim here or in some other town; one much like this. For there would be another victim; of that he was sure. Whether here or somewhere else; collectors always wanted more than one trophy.

15

Maidstone, Kent: later that day

The wind whistled spasmodically through the gap between the front door and its frame. Sandra shivered. After working at the office for the rest of the afternoon, she had gone back to the house at Higham and spent another couple of hours studying the room where Peggy and Matt Lyons had died. One of the constables had driven her back and as soon as he'd gone, the first thing she'd done was drag herself up to the shower. The rain hadn't ceased all day and she could feel the dampness rising around the house; this house always felt damp when it rained, she thought, descending to the hallway. Reaching up, she drew closed her tapestry door-curtain, breathing in some of the savoury aroma of fried onions that was wafting from the kitchen.

It was Jeff; she hadn't heard him come in. He was hunched over the cooker with an apron hanging from his neck. Untied at the waist, it brushed against the edge of the pan coming dangerously close to the flame that licked at its sides. Sandra stepped through into the kitchen, relieved to see Jeff reaching to turn off the gas.

"Have you been here long? Where's Fiona?"

"In the snug I believe," he said, pulling out a chair for her and indicating she should sit at the table.

"It'll be ready in a minute. You need to keep your strength up. She's gone to fetch that file she borrowed from Peggy Lyons." Sliding the omelette from the pan he brought the plate to the table. "Here; be a good girl now and eat that all up and I don't want to hear any excuses; you ate nothing worth talking about at lunch time."

Sandra didn't have the energy to rebuke him for being so patronising and she knew he was only being kind. She looked at the plate; the omelette both looked and smelt appetising, but her taste buds were not aroused. She knew she should be glad of it, but exhaustion was beginning to take over; she felt shattered. It was after

10pm and had been a long day. Not only did her feet ache, her brain seemed to have swelled, pulsating with all the horror and fear it had endured during the day.

Jeff disposed of the pan in the sink and sat opposite her. She knew he wouldn't move until she'd eaten, so she forced herself to try to stomach at least some of it. He gave her an encouraging smile. Over lunch he had broken the news that he was in line for heading the murder team, when the Cold Crimes Unit – for want of a better name – opened in mid-November. She could not deny it would be a sensible move for him, but to her it represented another familiar face leaving her at a time when, more than anything, what she needed was consistency.

"How are the girls today? Maybe I should take them up something, perhaps a hot cocoa?" Jeff offered.

Sandra shook her head, thinking it was not a good idea. "I'd rather you didn't, Jeff, Gerry takes—" she stopped, rubbing her hand over her forehead, correcting herself, "used to take them a hot chocolate every night without fail. It might hit a chord. I haven't had the chance to talk to them much yet, this evening. They have good days and bad days, much like me. Elle's putting on a brave face, it's Sam I'm concerned about. She always puts on a hard front, never lets you in there."

As Sandra spoke of her daughter, out of the corner of her eye she became aware of Sam in the hallway. She was heading for her room: her footsteps on the stairs were heavy and spaced; each one as it fell weighted Sandra's heart even more than the last.

Jeff rested his elbows on the table, his gaze sympathetic. "Don't be worrying, Sandra, maybe you need more time? Time together would be good for you all right now. If you want, I'll sort out more compassionate leave with Millar in the morning."

More time for what, Sandra thought. The longer she spent thinking about Gerry, the more lost she became. So much had separated them, driven in a wedge. She sometimes felt she didn't know who this man she was grieving for had become; everything about him had become so alien. Hell! I'm kidding myself, she thought. 'Grieving?' Who would call this grief? Guilt; that's what I'm crying over; my own guilt! She knew she was being swamped by self-pity, but she couldn't help herself. All the things she had yearned for were lost now, forever. It was the closeness she missed. Not the absence of passion: passion was something that had never entered their relationship. It must have been there in the beginning she supposed, well, romance if not passion. Gerry just wasn't the passionate type, but then, she wouldn't have described him as romantic either. Of course, even the closeness had been long gone before the end.

Aware of Jeff's frown, Sandra toyed with the egg on her plate, her mind possessed by thoughts of Gerry. He had always been an ordered person, always organised, relaxed; quite the opposite of herself. But that's the way they were. It didn't matter; they had complemented each other in the early years, everything had always seemed to be okay. She had never had cause to question or to doubt his love for her – until, of course, it all started to go wrong. Now she felt so mixed up and guilty that whenever she thought of him it was only as the vexed and bitter man he became. That was when the coldness had emerged; as if it was she who had brought the strife they'd had to endure over the last few years. Why hadn't he told her about the tumour? The change in his character had undoubtedly come from that. If only she had known. She had loved him, but that love had turned into a yearning; a need for him. This was what she was reduced to; left behind she would always come back round to caring. Yet thinking of the time before he had died and re-living being in his presence, she found he was a stranger to her yet again and the insecurities all rushed back.

Determinedly pushing Gerry to the back of her mind, Sandra swallowed a little more omelette. "Has Fiona eaten yet?" she asked, merely to fill the silence.

"She said she had."

"Oh, did she!" Sandra was still angry with her sister-in-law, had made several calls throughout the afternoon only to be put straight to voice-mail. But she'd seen the car parked at the front of the house when she'd come out of the shower and knew from Jeff that Fiona had eventually turned up at the station to make her statement, with her solicitor in tow. She had been given a time to return tomorrow morning. Until the autopsy was performed there was little point in questioning her further, Jeff had said. At 6pm, as Leslie had been scrubbing up to perform the autopsy, she was called to a stretch of riverbank on the edge of the marshlands to the east of Gravesend.

Construction workers had been dredging the water to clear debris and had recovered a body. The autopsy was rescheduled for noon tomorrow.

Sandra pushed her plate away with an apologetic glance at Jeff. "I'm sorry, I can't manage any more – and I don't want any more leave, but thanks for the offer. I think I'd rather keep on the case, at least for now. I'm slipping back there, Jeff, too much time for my mind to start playing with me again. I feel so helpless sitting here, always ending up with more questions than I started with. As soon as we find somewhere to live and get a sale on this place, it will get easier. There are too many ghosts here; for all of us. A fresh start and I'll cope better then. We all will."

Jeff reached over the table and gave her hand a squeeze. "What you said about Sam there, the front she puts on, that was always how it was with Angie. It took me all that time to finally get in there, as you put it, but I did eventually. We never left anything unsaid. In the end she was out of it most of the time, but I kept on talking and I knew she was listening, I knew she could hear me."

With every sentence his grip on her hand had tightened and Sandra knew how much it had meant to him to say. She thanked him silently. But their situation was so different. The attack on her had destroyed her marriage. So much had been left unsaid and so it would forever remain. She had tried hard to fight the negative feelings, but despite how much she tried, when they touched, she could never quite regain the warmth, the feeling of intimacy that once had always been there. He had given up on her; in her heart she had known it. During their last months together, when she would wake alone from her torment, she would tiptoe up the small flight of stairs to the landing on the third floor from where she could see the light under his study door. She could only stand and wipe her tears as the shadow of his form passed by regularly dulling the crack of light. She had felt such a burden to him; to everyone in the house.

Sandra eased her hand from Jeff's grasp, lifting her head as her sister-in-law came through into the kitchen from the snug, carrying a disk. Fiona folded her arms and leaned anxiously against the dresser, her eyes remaining focused on the floor, the disk still clutched in her fingers. Sandra couldn't miss the tremor around her mouth and the nervous twitch of her shoulders: what was coming next?

"I just don't get it," Fiona said. "I've gone through everything and it has simply disappeared!" Her head bobbed from side to side as she spoke and she studiously avoided eye contact.

Placing her hands flat on the table, Sandra drew breath to speak, but before she could get the words out, Jeff cut across her, "Don't get in a state about it now, Fiona, love. Both of you have had enough to cope with today, it'll turn up. Maybe you set it down at the crime scene this morning and left it without realising – you were in shock, remember."

"As if I could forget! No, Jeff, I did not open my case there this morning. I would remember if I had."

Sandra threw Jeff a coldly piercing look and turned to Fiona. What was she playing at? And why was Jeff being so complacent? She must have the folder, she was organised to a fault, never misplaced anything. Why would she not hand it over? Didn't she realise the position she was in; that she was implicating herself even further? Why the secrecy now, when before she had always been so open; when even her confrontations with Gerry had not deterred her? Above everything else Sandra felt hurt: they had always been so close; what had changed? She tried to think in terms of the investigation, but it was as a friend – a dismayed and angry friend – that she questioned Fiona's actions.

"I thought we were close," she echoed her thoughts. "Why didn't you tell me about Peggy Lyons? I know how important finding your mother is to you, but of all times to start this again, why now?"

Fiona, still refusing to make eye contact, fidgeted with the disk. "I'm sorry, Sandra, I know the timing is not exactly appropriate, but Stella's son contacted me Friday before last and told me he had remembered that his mother had stayed in a home near here while she was pregnant. In the months before her death when she was trying to find her daughter, she got him to take her there. He gave me the address: Peggy Lyons was the woman who used to run it." She lifted her eyes at last to meet Sandra's. "I didn't say anything to you; I knew you had enough to cope with. I realised weeks ago that you were having trouble accepting Gerry was gone, but I have accepted it." Fiona's tone changed, her anger clearly evident, "Can't you at least try to see this from my point of view? You know were you come from. You are lucky enough to have a family – whom you choose not to see. Gerry was all I had left and he's gone: I have no one!"

Sandra was perplexed at this sudden outburst. "I think it's unfair of you to bring up things like that! You know the reasons why I keep my distance from my family, Fiona, and what about the girls and me? Do we no longer fit into your definition of what 'family' means?" She glanced at Jeff, who was rubbing his hand over his eyes as if waiting for the right moment to interrupt.

"Look, you two," he jumped in, "I don't want to be getting involved in stuff that's private between you, but the file will turn up; if it's not there then it has to be here somewhere – unless you forgot to put it into your case to begin with, Fiona!" Looking faintly confused, he continued to massage his brow.

"No, Jeff," Fiona was adamant. "I know I placed it in the case after I made a copy of it last night, here's the copy. The only item I removed from the case this morning was the laptop. It was there, I tell you – and now it has gone. Someone has taken it." She looked defensively at Sandra.

Sandra ignored the look, recalling the scene in the kitchen that morning: it was true, she had watched Fiona working away at the table and yes, only the laptop came out of the case. Trying to keep her tone gentle, she said, "Fiona; just retrace your steps this morning. Maybe as Jeff says, you forgot to put it in. You've had a lot on your mind – we both have; it is easily done."

Fiona, raising her eyes to the ceiling as if she found the exercise stupid, began to recite: "It was a running day; I dressed in my tracksuit – that's right, Sam had borrowed the laptop last night and had set it on top of the unit in my room. I put it in the case before coming down. The folder was in the case then. I remember seeing it. I set the case in the hall and left for my run. I came back and oh! Yes," she threw a cautionary glance in Sandra's direction, "I was just inside the back door and had just untied my trainers when that stupid security alarm went off; I had to punch in the code before—"

Tensely, Sandra interrupted her; suddenly what Fiona had just said was wrong. "Fiona, what did you say? Go over that last bit again." As she spoke, she realised that she hadn't after all been imagining things this morning; it wasn't a panic attack – even if she did almost throttle her sister-in-law!

"As I said, I came in through the back door, switched off the alarm and was attacked by Detective Reid here."

Jeff interrupted, "I've lost you altogether now; what do you mean she attacked you?" He looked at Sandra, his brows shooting up in a query.

"It's okay Jeff; I thought I'd thrown another wobbler this morning, now I know I didn't. But I did almost manage to kill poor Fiona here, with Sam's hockey stick."

Jeff rapped his knuckles on the table, "Could someone please tell me where all this is taking us?"

Sandra took pity on him, almost she laughed at his expression of bewilderment: "When I woke this morning I heard the front door creaking, in the quiet of the house it was unmistakable, Gerry wouldn't hear tell of it being oiled; character he called it! I thought someone had broken in. The first thing I lifted was the hockey stick and then, well I came close to bringing it down on Fiona's head right here in the kitchen. But it wasn't someone breaking in, it was someone leaving! It must have been. You heard what Fiona said: she used the back entrance. That wouldn't set off the alarm – not until she crossed the beam. And it would explain the missing file."

"I didn't see any sign of damage to the door," Jeff sounded unconvinced.

"Whoever it was probably used the back door to get in same as me," Fiona said. "I'm afraid I never lock it when I leave; it's not as if the house is left empty and Sandra's an early riser. I guess whoever it was used the front door to get out when they heard me open the door at the back. Nothing else was touched." Fiona suddenly paled, murmured almost to herself, "I must have come within feet of—," she broke off, swallowed.

"What?" Sandra and Jeff said in unison.

Fiona shook her head as if clearing it. "Why would someone want to take the file? It wasn't even an official thing it was just Mrs Lyons's private notes on the girls she had given refuge to. She'd already told me it would be of no use to me in my search. But I had to discern that for myself. It was full of silly stuff really. In some of the records she didn't even use the girls' real names. She'd given them each the title 'Sister' followed by what appeared to me to be old names, like saints or whatever. Some were like something out of a medieval romance, you know; ancient, Old English sort of thing."

Sandra viewed Fiona with suspicion. Perhaps it was nothing, but Fiona was one of those people you just didn't say 'no' to. It could be she had persisted, browbeaten Peggy Lyons until she had given in to her, but something about the way Fiona was playing down the importance of the file seemed illogical. Sandra found herself thinking that Fiona hadn't had permission to take the file; had acquired it by subterfuge, slipping it out without anyone knowing. The more she thought about it, the more, Sandra was convinced this was what had happened: *Oh, Fiona, what have you done?*

She looked to Jeff, trying to discern what he was making of all this. Were his thoughts driving him to the same conclusion: that the elderly couple had died because the killer wanted the file and Fiona had taken it? But that was ludicrous, surely? And the implications didn't bear thinking about. Like Fiona, Sandra blenched as she joined up the dots. If that was true, then it could only have been the perpetrator of that horrendous murder who had been inside her house this morning. She shuddered. And the girls had been upstairs in their beds. No! No, she refused to believe it was true. Then another thought struck her. If Fiona had in fact taken the file unbeknown to Matt and Peggy Lyons, might she have fabricated this whole story about an intruder here this morning? Set off the alarm deliberately? If the information was useless why would anyone else kill to get it – and in such a horrific, insane way?

Sandra raised her hands to her hair; she was going round in circles; her imagination running wild. She had known Jeff for long enough to know that he would be asking these same questions, and although he was looking in her direction he was avoiding meeting her eyes. Had she been somehow tarnished by Fiona's involvement in all of this? She felt as if she had.

When Jeff spoke, his tone was somewhat downbeat. "You're sure nothing else is gone?"

"Nothing!" Fiona said.

Nodding in agreement, Sandra said, "No, nothing at all was disturbed in the house; I did a clean-up this morning; I would have noticed."

Jeff looked directly at Fiona, reached out for the disk. "Right I'll take that and drop it off at the station. Are you still okay to come in tomorrow morning? I'll set it up for ten o'clock."

Fiona nodded and moved for the door, pausing beside her sister in law. "I'm sorry, Sandra, I know that you have enough on your plate without me getting mixed up in all of this. I didn't mean to say those things to you. It's my fault that they're dead, isn't it? It was the file he was after. If I hadn't taken it, maybe they'd still be alive?"

Without speaking, Sandra raised her hand and briefly clasped Fiona's, acknowledging the apology that was offered. She didn't have the heart to confirm her suspicion that what Fiona surmised was most likely true. Fiona's guilt was plain to see: clearly she had not had permission to take that file.

Jeff's gaze followed Fiona as she disappeared up the hall, waiting until she was out of earshot before speaking. "Well, what do you think Sandra?"

Sandra shrugged, wondering if Jeff had surmised as much as she had, and if he had, whether he had decided to let it go for now. "I don't know; the killer was careful not to leave anything behind at the scene. And if he really was here, then anything that might have been of use for forensics will have been virtually destroyed by now. She's not in a great spot; is she?"

"There are certainly too many coincidences for my liking, Sandra. What also worries me is the timescale. Let's just suppose, for the sake of argument, that the killer really was after the file, discovered Fiona had got it, and forced her address out of Peggy Lyons," he grimaced, "presumably, if what we are surmising is correct, that is why those poor people were tortured. Then, it would appear, our killer moved swiftly from Higham to here: knew as well how to get in and out. In some ways it seems a bit far-fetched. On the other hand, it is not impossible, and that being so, I'm not so sure you are safe here."

All of these things had already flashed through Sandra's mind. She found that she was shaking.

Jeff continued, "Well it'll probably not result in anything, the amount of rain we've had today will have washed any footprints away, and as you say, you did a clean-up, but even so, in the morning I'll arrange to get the place printed; try to get a few casts taken outside and what have you, if you could leave the keys? But you've had various visitors today, so it'll be a mess to sort out," he added.

Sandra nodded; for a moment she had forgotten the Estate Agent and viewer from this morning.

"Look," he shot her a reassuring smile, "it goes against all reason that Fiona could be capable of the barbarism we saw in that house. She is not insane. We have to put things in perspective; she's not coping with losing Gerry any better than you are. Finding her mother is her way of battling through it, Sandra. Don't feel as though she's abandoned you; everybody has their own way of dealing with it." He held up the disk. "We may be barking up the wrong tree, but if it *is* all about something in that file, then somebody obviously wanted it badly enough to kill for it and as we witnessed today, enjoyed the kill. I presume you'll start as you always do, with the victims, before you begin looking at the killer?"

"Yes, I'll start on the victim profiles first thing in the morning. I'll work on the crime scene stats until we have the autopsy results and then put together what I can of the killer's profile. For tonight, though, I'm afraid all I want to do is sleep, so much has happened."

"Maybe this is too much for you right now, Sandra? Would it not be better for you to take a few days' rest as I suggested before? I could always put in for another profiler to be brought onto the team. I don't want you putting yourself under pressure. You're going to need to reserve your strength to get your family through the weeks ahead. You still have the inquest to deal with yet. I'm worried that this decision to sell the house – all the packing up and moving – is all a bit too soon for you all. Sometimes it's better to confront your demons before you move on. There's always the risk that in trying to settle somewhere new you'll find you've carried them with you."

Sandra made no move to agree. Only time would heal the wounds evident in this family. She didn't think Jeff expected her to take his advice, but he had felt pressed as her senior officer to air his concerns as he was required to; as her friend, he knew perfectly well that possibly the best medicine was to keep her mind busy.

"Will you all be okay here tonight? Be sure to lock all the doors and windows securely and don't let the girls go out unaccompanied. I'll get Uniform to pass regular patrols. If you think it is necessary, I'll somehow find the resources to have someone on permanent duty outside."

Wearily, Sandra shook her head. "No need, we'll be okay – and I'm a light sleeper. Besides, he's got what he came for, hasn't he?"

"Well, if you're sure," Jeff had already retrieved his jacket and was making his way towards the door, pocketing the disk. "I need to get this to Stevens."

"Please, Jeff, will you fight my corner with Millar? I need something to focus on if I'm to come out the other end of this in one piece."

"You realise he'll want another evaluation from the psychologist?"

"That's okay with me, though I don't see the point: before Gerry died I'd been seeing Dr Graham regularly since... well, you know; more than two years of psychobabble and where did it get me? It's in here Jeff, the cure," Sandra tapped her head, "and I'm the only one who is going to find it."

Jeff smiled at her as he raised his arm in a farewell gesture. "That's my girl; good to hear you've actually taken on board what Lewis Graham was trying to tell you all that time – even if you did fail to realise it! Get some sleep, you'll need it. I'll see you in the morning."

She showed him out, securing all the bolts and chains on the door before doing the same to the back one and checking all the ground-floor windows. A saying that Gerry had often used popped into her mind – she was 'locking the stable door after the horse had bolted'; for some absurd reason it made her smile.

Sandra spent the next two hours just sitting alone in the snug thinking of Gerry, lost in memories aided by the gallery of family snaps that filled one wall. Gerry's face smiled out at her from most of them, by the time she got to the last few she was managing to smile back at him. She kept asking her self why; why had this happened to them? Why now? So much was unfinished, undone. Why had it all gone wrong for them? She began to catalogue all the disasters that had happened to them – as Fiona had said this morning, it was unreal, like a Claire Hamilton novel. It had all started with the kidnapping; then Gerry's cancer; Mark Jakes turning out to be a lunatic, and Fiona's .... Sandra paused in her thinking and frowned. That was when everything had really begun to turn upside down: Fiona's search; her finding the wrong mother. Had Gerry's attitude, the change in his temperament, been affected by the tumour as she'd thought, or was there something else? What was it that had driven him to take his own life, abandon his family? The operation, his consultant had since informed her, would most likely have been successful. It would have extended his life for months, perhaps years, with treatment. Had he done it to punish her? If that was so, why had he chosen to punish the girls along with her? Suicide! He knew what a selfish act it was. It always came round to this. Anger. It was what coloured all her memories of Gerry.

Now, on top of it all, another murder – one that had connections to Fiona! Their home had been invaded – though none of them harmed, thank God. They hadn't even known about it until now. Sandra wasn't sure she could have got through the day if she had found out this morning. But surely it was crazy to think Fiona capable of being involved. Wasn't it? What on earth was in those documents? Why would someone go so far to kill to get them? Suddenly it hit her: it was almost as if someone didn't want Fiona to find her mother. That was strange: she had often felt that Gerry didn't want that either. Why *was* that?

Exhausted, Sandra couldn't think any more. The clock above the fireplace ticked away the last minutes of the day. She stared at its hands wishing them forward into a new day. All she wanted was for this one to be over. When tomorrow came, would anything feel different or would she want to send it back? With these thoughts, Sandra drifted into a restless sleep.

16

The Same Evening

Kneeling in front of the white marble fireplace he lifted the heavy clay Buddha out of his way. With a few thumps the false panel gave way and he set it to the side. Opening the Gladstone bag at his feet, he retrieved the specimen jar; raised it up to the light noting the presence of fibroids and old scaring from some previous surgery. Not such a pleasant one, he thought, but only to be expected considering the age of the donor. He placed it into the hollow of the hearth next to the other one.

Nailed to the wall at the back of the hearth, its edges a little curled by time, a photograph of a small girl stared back at him. Her eyes were as dark as her hair. Falling in ringlets over her shoulders it was pulled back from her forehead and secured with a thick red bow, exposing all of her face. She was not smiling and he remembered that she never had. Sitting on a chair, her little hands grasped tightly together, she posed for the camera. Almost invisible, the track of a tear could be traced where it had run down her cheek. Her frown bore no defiance: her eyes large and round were like those of a terrified animal brimming with fear, not of the unknown so much as an expression of defeat. It told of a sadness, a knowing of exactly what was to come. No, there had been no reasons to smile in that house. But she was in his house now. This was her shrine.

A little doll lay beneath the photo. One of the few items of hers he had left. The eyes were gouged out and it was missing an arm, its dress tattered and grubby. Holding it to his face he wept, drawing deep breaths into the cloth, searching uselessly for a remnant of her scent. Slowly he lowered it and gently running his hands over the doll's face, put it back in its place. Almost hidden in the shadows, propped against the side of the grate, lay several story books: Cinderella, he decided, and lifting it out cleared his throat, his voice softening as he spoke. "I'll have to go out later, so I'll read to you early tonight. I know this is your favourite. He drew breath and began to read: "Once upon a time…"

He closed the book. She always fell asleep before the end. He liked to think she was dreaming; he could imagine her dancing with the glass slippers on her feet. The woman had arranged ballet lessons twice every week before it happened. From outside the window he would watch her dance the *Nutcracker Waltz* to the stereo in their living room. The woman had cared for them; for a time at least they had thought that. But then, when he had eventually told, she had punished him. Her fault had been to love the man who was to blame for their nightmares. She knew what went on in the dark of night, night after night, in that house. After that he had despised her; she was like all women in the end: weak.

He had made her pay though. Her body had been so terribly mutilated that the casket had had to be kept closed. But then, so had hers, his little rabbit. He shook his head trying to get rid of the image, the carnage. The woman had never taken her out at night before. He threw his gaze to the ceiling: why? Why that night? He began to cry again. Wiping his arm across his eyes he looked again at the photograph, gently touched her face with his finger. "Goodnight little rabbit, sleep softly."

He lifted the battery-light from where it rested and changed the batteries; he had to make sure the light never went out: the darkness always gave her nightmares. Replacing the panel, he set the Buddha back in front of it. He rose to his feet, his mood subdued as he paced the floor. His quest had required that he forfeit sleep two nights in a row. But it was worth it; finally he was getting somewhere. He had waited so long for revenge and now he could almost taste its sweetness within his reach; their reach. He paused in front of the mirror, noticed the darkening rings around his eyes. He would have to do something about those.

What had taken that damned bitch so long getting round to it? he thought. He didn't like this waiting; dangling on a chain like that stupid locket she always wore around her neck! What pleasure it would give him to hold her mouth open and force the locket down her throat; listen to her gurgling; feel every spasmodic retch as she struggled and fought for air. The picture of it in his mind was irresistible; enough to release a surge of feelings that danced spuriously around in him arousing the darkness in his nature. He clutched at his stomach, the strength of their unleashing so great that he was unable to quell them as they raced through him like a volcanic charge, exploding up into his rib cage, buffeting his heart.

Dropping to his knees he gripped the spasm it produced, embracing himself in an effort to make the moment last. His shoulders rose, straining against his head; he saw the room clouding; swimming around him and he was forced to let it go: the screaming release of his orgasm travelled throughout the flat. While it lasted he could feel her throat; catch it as she choked. Yes! Feel her wriggling under him, grasping, holding tight to him, gripping in her desperation, her eyes pleading for release. Yes! He would watch the sparkle die, drowning in burst vessels; witness the shocked recognition in her pupils as she finally understood. Yes! He wanted her to know it!

He had the process perfected; the timing was crucial. He knew exactly the pallor of her skin; the changes that would come. Knew the exact length of time she could last. Then he would wrench it back, tempt her with a reprieve. She could look at him; remember his face, look into his eyes and see inside. Her eyes bulging, she would beg, croaking, froglike, for it to end. Yes; it would end, but not until she knew what it was like to feel the fear; that fear that once he had known. It was not her life to live; it should have been his sister's, his sweet little Jenny. Night after endless night he had watched her suffering, her struggle to survive. The anger within him intensified, he screamed now in agony at the memory. His tears began to fall again, his knees weakened beneath him. Sinking back, he sat rocking; slowly; methodically; eventually crying out, "Jenny; Oh, Jenny. I'll make it better, Jenny. I'll make her pay, I'll make both of them pay!"

He turned to look at the enlarged photograph that he had pasted to the wall. A reincarnation: evil bred onto evil; fate had cloned her. He cleared his throat almost singing the words, mimicking in the voice he would never forget. *"Don't be afraid. Don't be afraid, I'll be back soon. Close your eyes. Close your eyes. Picture my face; can you see my face?"* He stopped abruptly, his rage unleashed from the depths of his soul as he screamed: "Yes Mummy, I can see your face, you're smiling Mummy!"

In one swift movement he rose to his feet and lunged at the image, fists bunched, arms jabbing the air as he continued ranting. "Fuck you! Lying bitch! You never came back did you? You kept her safe didn't you? What was so special about her? It was you! It was you who killed my Jenny!" His fists plummeted relentlessly against the wall. He growled, deranged, punching over and over until he could no longer see the face that was now smeared with blood from his knuckles.

Exhausted, he flung himself face down across his desk and lay there staring listlessly at the knife. Lifting it, he raised himself and ignoring the stinging in his hands brought the blade down hard into the wood, twisting the point, digging it deeper, unable to stop the hatred, the anger scorching through him. Suddenly he released his grip, pushed himself away from the desk and reached for the bloody face on the wall, tearing it down and ripping it to shreds.

"Enough!"

Composing himself, he sought calmness, bringing his breathing back under control as he strode to the other end of the room and flicked the light switch. From the fireplace a halo of dim light surrounded the hearth. "I'll be back, soon Jenny. I keep my promises," he whispered.

He walked through to the bathroom and removed the layers that hid him from the world, setting them down on a stand beside the rest of his collection of disguises. He removed the coloured contacts and paused to look in the mirror at his eyes. He did the same with the teeth, rinsing his mouth and spitting into the sink.

Showered and shaved, he took his daily supply of pills, applied a fresh fake tan and went to bed, setting his alarm for 1am, it was now 10.30pm; a few hours that was all he needed. His eyes had to be rested, they needed to be alert. He had records to search.

At 2.40am, he turned the key in the office door, crossed the black, granite floor and made his way by torchlight into the storeroom on the next floor, switching off the alarm as he went. He had possession of the key until the following Friday; he was almost there. He'd already found three of them; only two more to go; time to get busy. He raced up the stairs: time was of the essence; the hunt had finally begun, but every day brought him closer. No one could stop him. He was untraceable; after all, who would they look for? He didn't exist!

"Watch out mamas, here I come!" Tinged with ridicule, his maniacal laughter echoed through the darkness as it reverberated from one empty office to another. The only reaction came from the tiny needles of the cacti in the corner of reception: momentarily they stiffened as if sensing there was something evil in the air.

17

The Pier, Gravesend: Tuesday 23rd October

Chief Superintendant Leonard Millar stepped out of his car, drizzly rain immediately forming glassy droplets on his overcoat. He checked the time 7.41am, he was late. His face was stern, his mind focused on this impromptu meeting that had been arranged late the night before. He noted the Jaguar was on the opposite side of the road and that the chauffeur was snoozing, peaked cap pulled down over his eyes.

Nodding politely at passers by, Millar made his way to a bench near the pier railings. She was there, waiting, almost hidden by the mist: Lady Clara Smith-Stevens. The call had taken him by surprise. What could she want after all these years? He took a seat beside her.

"I wasn't sure you would come, Leonard," she said, handing him a lidded coffee.

He welcomed it; there was a nip in the air. "A problem; you said on the phone we had a problem. People like us don't like those, do we?" He hadn't meant to be facetious; it was the effect she had always had on him.

She looked at him briefly before taking a sip from her cup. Time, he saw, had been kind to her: a few lines aged her eyes and her hair was not black anymore; he assumed the caramel blonde disguised grey, nor was it as shiny as he remembered, but that was about all that had changed.

"No we don't," she agreed pleasantly. "How long is it now? 35 years?" She kept her gaze on him.

"Just over that; hard to believe isn't it?"

She smiled. "You've done well for yourself Leonard. Chief Superintendent now, I see, quite an achievement. Have you heard from Emerald yet?"

He frowned, snapped back, "I'd rather you didn't call her that!"

"Touch a nerve does it?" She smiled looking straight ahead into the fog. "We're a bit like this place, you and I, Leonard; all spruced up and re-generated. Money can do a lot to change the surface, but the history is still there lurking beneath it all. We can't rub out the past. You know that as well as I do; the day comes for all of us when we must deal with it. Skeletons start rattling their cages in the end, Leonard dear, no matter how deep we think we've buried them. They seem to have this need to be let out into the open!"

She was mocking him and he knew it. It was a part of her nature; a part he had never warmed to. He tried not to be riled by it. "That was all a long time ago. She – I mean we – are different people now, all of us who are left. Why would she contact me? She hasn't done so in years. Why now? There's no need to drag up the past – especially not when it causes so much heartache."

"I don't think she had much choice. Things are happening, Leonard. I think the past is coming back to haunt us all." She got up, threw the polystyrene cup in a nearby bin and walked over to the railings, resting her arms on the wet metal.

He followed suit, keeping his hand in the pockets of his coat. He had received the invitation from Clara the same day he'd read the notice in *The Times*. He had known instantly to connect one to the other. "It's nothing; a coincidence," he said. "Nothing to do with us; it all ended with that crash: McMasters; the girl; both dead. It was over then."

She looked at him, then beyond him across the river; the mist hid all that existed around them. "I heard from Sheila a few weeks ago. She's been ill. Intends coming back."

His face tightened. Why would Sheila have written to her and not him? "Back where: Here? What for? Why now?"

"You sound scared, Leonard. Afraid your secrets are about to catch up with you?"

He turned his back to the railings, looked around him then turned towards her, gripping her arm, his face tense. "The child's dead, Clara. I pray for her soul every day. Sheila knows all that happened in the past: she was a part of it after all. We came to terms with it all a long time ago. She wrote to me for a time, trying to ease the pain."

Angrily, Lady Clara pulled back, releasing her arm from his hand and shaking her head. "Become religious have you Leonard? Is there something on your conscience? I *know* that car was tampered with; I attended the inquiry. I lost both my parents that night. I very nearly lost my son too, remember!"

His hand found the arm of her coat again, this time gripping it tighter. "How dare you!" he spoke with controlled fury. "Do you think I would have harmed her deliberately: my own flesh and blood? Your son survived. I lost my daughter!"

Lady Clara looked slowly down at his hand on her arm, not flinching from his roughness. As slowly, she lifted her gaze to stare into his face, her eyes filled with mistrust. He knew old memories were stirring her. They were stirring him too. Quickly he loosened his grip and turned back, leaning his arms on the railings. The deep horn of a tug bellowed hollowly out of the fog.

She waited for it to pass. "Someone betrayed us. Someone led him straight to us. I've often thought about you, Leonard, how it was you ended up transferred, gone just like that. Out of reach when she needed you most."

"Sheila ran: you know that. You girls; you may have been pawns, but Frank and I – and the others – we were no better off than you. There was no special counselling in the force then like there is now. The three of us were working under cover. There was no training given in those days; no warning that playing a part soon becomes more real than reality itself. Sheila and I – we were just two people thrown together who became too close. That's all there was to it!"

"It hardly matters now, Leonard, even if it was you or one of your colleagues. I know how brave you three officers were. If things are meant to be, then they will be. I of all people should know that! We knew one of you had betrayed us. Think about it: that guy 'Ron' – until that night when the flames threatened to envelop us and she risked her life to pull us free – we thought at first he was an invention: a bogey man made up by McMasters to keep us all in line. It was a smart move on his part. Simple in the end, wasn't it, making sure that nobody ever got to see Ron's face until he was sent to kill them. Dead people can't talk can they? But you three were the only ones who knew where we were; we knew then that one of you had to be this 'Ron'."

Millar started, grabbed the railings.

"Oh, I know it wasn't you!" Clara said. "Sheila told me as much when she came to the funeral five years later. Said she had seen Ron's face, that it was him who set the fire. She knew who he was, but she refused to tell me, even then. She must have kept track of him, though. About twenty years ago a notice was placed in the obituaries: 'Ron is dead!' He's dead and gone; nothing for any of us to worry about now. But coincidences don't just happen by themselves, Leonard. There is always some form of manipulation behind them. That is why I needed to talk to you."

Deep in thought, Millar followed her as she left the railings and made her way back to the bench. Seated, she withdrew an envelope from her pocket and handed it him. "There are pieces of our story I need to fill you in on."

Standing in front of her, he was puzzled by the change in her. Her tone had softened, she sounded unusually gentle, almost sincere. He reached for the envelope.

"Please, Leonard," she said, patting the seat beside her. "I think you had better sit down."

18

Maidstone, Kent: the same morning

Sleep had come eventually some time in the early hours, but not for long. The scourge of her faithfully recurring nightmare had ensured that as so often before, Sandra had awakened in the full throws of panic, crouched on all fours and gasping for breath. That had been long before 5am It was still dark at 6am when all the members of her subdued household gathered at the breakfast table. Instead of the usual chatter between herself and Fiona, they merely exchanged desultory words as necessary for the practicalities of the day ahead. There was an underlying feeling of uncertainty between them, which on Sandra's part stemmed from the aura of guilt that surrounded her sister-in-law. For all of their adult lives, Sandra had trusted Fiona like a surrogate sister. As much as anything, what she felt was a sense of betrayal and it hurt.

There was no direct conversation between the two girls either. Elle's nose was stuck in a book: she was competing for a part with the local Shakespeare Company for their production of *King Lear* next spring and was concentrating on her lines. The auditions at the Mary Clarke Theatre School, which she attended, started today. The school fees were yet another reason why they needed to downsize their home: Gerry's manner of death had forfeited all his insurance policies. Sandra noted that Sam, sat opposite, was glowering at her sister over the breakfast table and wondered if Fiona had been right; maybe there was something going on between them that went deeper than their usual cat-fights; Sam's glare seethed with resentment. Sandra sighed: she supposed she would have to sort it out, whatever it was; but not just now.

Promptly at 7am, a horn blasted outside: the mechanic returning the car. Relieved that she would not need a driver at her disposal again today, Sandra arranged to pick Fiona up at 10am and leaving her brooding on her own at the table, set off to drive the girls to the train station.

Still early, the motorway was empty of all but the occasional car and a succession of large haulage lorries. Sandra's shoulders tightened in automatic response as they thundered past in the fast lane. She tried to make conversation with the girls, spluttering a trail of reassurances over her shoulder that she was always there for them and that one day they would find the answers; one day they would understand. She had been making remarks such as these for the last three months. As always, in her own ears they sounded like platitudes. How could she guide her children along the path to accepting what their father had done, when she was unable to negotiate it herself? Inwardly, as always, there ran a simultaneous trail of thoughts: *God, how low can I get, using concern for them to cover up my own distress? Get it together girl; keep your mind off the fear.* Talking herself out of irrational anxiety was a coping mechanism; she had found it to be her best weapon against the sudden onset of the panic attacks that had dogged her for the last few years.

As yet another lorry cut too close into the lane in front, Sandra fought to control her fear. Trembling, palms sweating, she forced herself to grip more tightly to the steering wheel, only too aware that she was liable at any moment to explode into full panic mode. Most of her journeys followed a similar pattern. Instances like this morning, when she had the added responsibility of the girls in the car, were what she dreaded most. Just in time, she remembered to control her breathing: it was her most important ammunition; it slowed her down, calmed her. A snatched glance in the rear-view mirror brought at least some consolation: Sam and Elle appeared oblivious to her. Their heads turned away from each other they seemed lost in reflections of their own, staring unseeing out of opposite windows. Soon afterwards, with a sigh of relief, she pulled into the station car park.

"Come on Jeff, let's get this thing started," Sandra muttered to herself, turning away from the screen perched on the wall of her office. The Press Conference had already run on too long. She lifted the bundle of pages from her desk to re-read her copy of the initial report on the crime scene. Massaging her temple, she finished her coffee and endeavouring to shrug off her tiredness, stared down at the neatly printed words. Most of what she had unearthed at the scene related to the wife. There was little to learn of Matt Lyons: it seemed as if he had taken a back seat in their affairs; he had left behind only a shadow. Tidying the mass of papers and replacing them in their folder she was struck by the pathos of it: in reality it is the paper trail we leave behind that takes precedence over everything else, she thought.

Until now she had been a shadow too. For the first time it hit her that she knew practically nothing of her own private affairs. Gerry had been the book-keeper of their lives. She closed her eyes, searching in darkness for a way to banish these thoughts. She had to keep focused on the case today, not on Gerry; but despair had her in a stranglehold. There were so many things she had to sort out; it was all too much to bear and was smothering her. She wondered if Fiona would help her to sift through the boxes of paperwork that presently awaited them in Gerry's study. They had agreed to go through it all tonight, but that was before.... Her eyes filled with tears. She tried discreetly to pat them away, drawing in a deep breath to discourage more from following in their tracks.

"Are you okay Sandra?" Christine had come into her office without her realising.

Be strong you have to be strong! Avoiding eye contact, she made a motion with her hand to indicate 'up and down' and placed the file in Christine's outstretched hands. "No I'm fine, really, Christine; bad morning that's all."

"Oh; one of them – commiserations – I've become somewhat of an expert on those myself lately!"

Sandra got up from her desk her eyes drawn to the swell of Christine's stomach. "I'll bet you're counting down the days. Just before Christmas you're due aren't you?"

"I wish it was all over, Sandra, to be honest. I feel like an invalid most of the time."

Managing a sympathetic smile, Sandra said, "You'll have forgotten all about feeling like this in a few weeks." As if she was some kind of expert on the trials of pregnancy, she thought with an accompanying pang of guilt. Still, even now, so much guilt!

Christine smiled her thanks as they made their way into the incident room where the team was beginning to gather.

"Right, people, let's have some order in here," Jeff strode in behind them and made his way to the front. She could see he was in a foul mood; there were dark shadows around his eyes where lack of sleep had left its mark. Gradually, the noisy buzz in the incident room subsided as everyone found an available seat. Many of the heads in front of her Sandra didn't recognise, knew that most of them had been pulled in from other stations to bolster the team. Clutching her zipped case in front of her, Sandra stood at where she judged was a safe distance, on the periphery by the door.

Jeff cleared his throat: "Firstly, let me thank Christine for putting everything in order so efficiently," he indicated the array of boards across the room, before swiftly turning back to his team and pulling a swivel chair towards him, changed his mind and rested his weight on a desk.

Sandra fixed her gaze on the blow-up of Peggy Lyons's corpse. Posed in her chair, the dead woman stared disinterestedly into oblivion from a board on the wall. Once again, Sandra pondered on the arc of lamps and, as when she had first seen them yesterday, wondered if they had been placed deliberately, almost theatrically, as on a stage. No disrespect to you, Mr Lyons, she thought, but you were just taken along for the ride. It was your wife he was really after; why? That's what I really need to know. Why?

Her thoughts were interrupted by the Chief Super entering the doorway and coming to stand beside her. Wishing she had taken a front seat after all, she tried to conceal her discomfort and concentrate on what Jeff was saying.

"I know most of you were here late last night, but some of us were here into the small hours, so no grumbling please! It seems we've got a head start with this one: there have been considerable developments overnight. Yesterday," he gestured to the photographs, "this appeared to be a savage but senseless murder. Now, hopefully we can get a few answers from the information that Miss Fiona Reid, the young lady who had the misfortune to come across this scene, has kindly disclosed to us."

To Sandra his choice of words seemed tinged with scepticism; she was convinced she could detect it in his tone. It made something tighten in her stomach.

Jeff held up the sheaf of notes in his hand. "You all have copies of the case summary Christine has put together, so far as it stands, so let's bring ourselves up to date." He nodded to Christine, "Right then, over to you, Christine."

As Christine stepped forward to talk through the details of the crime scene, Sandra caught a gesture from the Chief Super to Jeff that he wanted a private word. As he backed out of the room, Millar threw her a discerning glance then, seeing she had caught his gaze, said, "DI Reid; nice to see you back with us." The coldness of his tone belied his words.

Automatically, she attempted a polite response, but the words stuck in her throat. Millar's eyes held no warmth; there was something going on with him today. Caught in his unfriendly stare, she realised he fully intended her to feel his sarcasm as, after a slight pause he added the word, "Again!"

Jeff gave her arm a quick, encouraging squeeze as he brushed past her, pulling the door closed behind him. Whatever Millar wanted to say to him was apparently for his ears alone. Sandra brought her attention back to Christine, listening as she explained the train of events so far as they had been able to establish them. The team was made aware of Fiona's involvement; the borrowed file and the subsequent discovery that it had been taken from her home by an unknown intruder and was still missing. Sandra focused her gaze on another of the blow-ups, prepared for a few cautionary glances. Most of the team scattered throughout the room would be familiar with the recent goings on in her family life. It was another reason why she should have sat up at the front. She waited uncomfortably for them to turn round and seek her out, but none of them did, for which she was grateful.

She was prepared for possible scenarios concerning Fiona's suspect status. In both her professional and private opinion she deemed Fiona's position precarious. So far, any evidence placing her as a suspect was, for the time being, circumstantial; the autopsy would be the deciding factor. Sandra could only pray that it steered them in another direction and opened up further avenues of investigation.

As a profiler, it was the crime scene itself that introduced Sandra to everything she needed initially. What she gleaned from it should equip her with sufficient knowledge to present a plausible theory; a guide to the purpose of this horrific crime. This in turn should enable her to begin building a credible evaluation of the person or persons who had carried it out. She knew from experience that jumping to quick conclusions frequently led in the wrong direction and that it was unwise to involve her personal opinions at this stage. She would concentrate on the facts as they became established. Her next step would be to find out all there was to know about the victims and their possible relationship to their killer. What had been the catalyst to connect them to each other? Her personal feelings in this case would have to be held at bay; whatever the consequences she would deal with them later. As always, the job would come first; at least, that was the way she intended it to be.

Having briefly acknowledged receipt of Fiona's copy of the stolen files and explained the Lyonses involvement in adoptions many years before, Christine stood down and Stevens took the floor. He flicked on the overhead projector and fed in a list of names. As Sandra read them she remembered what Fiona had said about a medieval romance, and had to agree: it was weird!

1. Sister Mary Ethelberg
2. Sister Mary Bertha
3. Sister Mary Aya of Mons
4. Sister Mary Aelfled
5. Sister Mary Brigid

There were a few snide remarks from the middle of the room. Stevens threw the culprits a cautionary stare before continuing. "It is clear, firstly, that these names attributed to the five records in question are not to be found on any certificates that might reveal the identity of the individuals concerned. From what we have been able to deduce from other records found at the house, they refer to women who, sometime in the first part of 1972, arranged for their babies put up for private adoption. Unfortunately, the information disclosed in the files was recorded in such a haphazard manner that they are unlikely to yield all that would be necessary to perform straightforward searches to identify these women."

There was a buzz in the room. "Looks as though some of the nuns from one of the local convents have a few questions to answer about the skeletons in their closet," one said. There was a subdued chuckle.

"Maybe they got a bit too friendly with the local vicar; the

Press will love this when it gets out," said another. "Think of the headlines!"

Sandra identified Keith Jones, another recent addition to the team. His gauche remark drew a few cackles from his fellow male officers, but Stevens, Sandra noticed, had a face like a brick. He took a step forward and looked as though he was about to give Jones a good smack on the mouth – which in her view was no less than he deserved. But it seemed that Stevens had won the battle to suppress his anger, for though still somewhat flushed, he stepped back and patted the air to settle the room.

"I think it safe to assume they were never intended to be used as part of an identification process, but were more for the personal use of Mrs Lyons herself; perhaps to aid her failing memory and to keep alive the times she had shared with the young women. Why she gave them these particular aliases – or why they needed them – we can only guess. Was it something about these women themselves? Maybe something about the identity of the men who fathered the children they gave birth to? It could be either – or neither."

Sandra was impressed with Stevens's performance, a true master of the stage. She almost felt he had found something heart-wrenching in this case: there was a slight tremor in his voice. Looking up as Jeff came back into the room Stevens paused for a second before continuing.

"Using a variety of search engines it will eventually be possible to identify the women on this list and track them down. I have underlined potential identifying markers, which I'm afraid won't help us initially. Normally, to start a search like this we would have indicators such as mothers' maiden names, birth dates and such like to narrow our search parameters. Sir…?" Stevens made way for Jeff to address the team.

Heads turned in unison as Jeff spoke from the doorway. "People: Mr and Mrs Lyons were the victims of an intended robbery."

"I thought robbery was ruled out, Sir?" Keith Jones was apparently baffled by this statement, "has Fiona Reid admitted stealing the files then Guv?" he added.

Jeff raised his hand to halt Jones and glanced up at the blow-ups before turning back to his team. He looked sombrely at their faces for a moment, holding the silence.

"What we do know is that whoever carried out these barbaric murders had another purpose in mind: he wanted those records. Wanted them enough to kill to get them, but that's not all he wanted. Remembering the scene he left for us yesterday, it is clear that murdering Peggy and Matt Lyons was always part of his plan; we are talking here of a sadist. The fact that the couple had lent the files to Miss Reid I fear only added to their suffering. Evidently, by torturing them, he got the information as to the whereabouts of the files out of Mrs Lyons before he killed her."

Jeff pointed to the sequence of events lit up on the screen. "From the timescale as we see it, after leaving Higham he made his way to Maidstone and in the early hours entered the home of DI Reid here and removed the files from Fiona Reid's briefcase while she was out of the house. And before I go any further," Jeff paused, "I think we should remind ourselves to be thankful that the theft was not discovered while it was being carried out..." He looked again at the blow-ups, not needing to express in words the fate that all were now reminded could so easily have befallen their colleague and her family.

After an uncomfortable moment in which Sandra could have heard a pin drop, Jeff moved forward and looked at random into the faces of his detectives. "Why? A motive! That we don't know. What we do know is this: the killer needs something from these files. We need only to look at the results of his callous act to see that he is desperate. What motivates him and who or what is he so desperate to find? That, people, is what we must find out." Jeff had taken to pacing across the room as he spoke, his hands clasped behind him. He stopped, turning swiftly, leaning both hands flat on a detective's desk, his stare moving again from one face to another.

"The biggest lead we have is the theme of adoption. Was the killer one of those adoptees? Perhaps – like Fiona Reid – he is a lost child searching in anger for a mother who abandoned him? Until we get results from forensics we cannot know that the killer is male; could as easily be female: a mother making sure she is not found, perhaps. But why, we do not know." He had moved back to the overhead projector, stood now, tapping his pen on the list of names as he spoke, "It is imperative we find this killer before he makes his next move but we must source our priorities. These women we have every right to believe may be in grave danger. We must identify and protect them. We are lucky insofar as we have the expertise and manpower to dwarf whatever resources are available to the killer."

Jeff looked across at Stevens who was lounging against the side wall. "Stevens here will split you into groups; most of you will be spending long hours in front of screens. It appears that until we identify these women this enquiry will be for the better part electronic. Ironically, these women gave up their children prior to the changes in the adoption law; in fact just shortly before it. Stevens has also discovered that there is no national database for adoptions, so it appears we have our work cut out. Jones and Warren; you can continue with the local interviews and access the traffic footage for the route to DI Reid's house during the night before last. The rest of you know the ropes. Keep in mind we don't want to have to put any more snaps like these up on the boards!"

"Right then – that's enough time wasted for now. Get on with it." As the team began to disperse he called, "I want all senior detectives back here at 6pm for a debriefing. Sandra, can I have a few words?"

She followed Jeff back to his office and waited while Christine handed him a beaker of water. Searching his pockets, he retrieved a small bottle of pills. "High blood pressure," he muttered by way of explanation, downing one and gulping the entire beaker of water.

"Jeff," Sandra said, "I've set up a meeting with an elderly vicar at Higham, a Reverend Marshton: his name turned up in quite a number of the dead couple's papers. He is free this morning, but not this afternoon, so I'm afraid it means I can't sit in with Fiona's interview."

Jeff shrugged, "I'll be absent for that too, and you'll have to do Higham solo, but unless there's any possibility the old boy ate enough spinach to mutilate two people, you should be safe enough to handle him by yourself," he shot her a half-smile. "Millar's hijacked me to attend some select committee in the Houses of Parliament. Don't look so stunned I've been involved in several things like that in my time."

"Sorry Jeff, it's not the thought of you hobnobbing with MPs that concerns me, it's just that I told Fiona before I left that I'd pick her up and would be here for her. You know she can be highly strung when she's under pressure. Who did you have in mind for taking her statement?"

"I'll get Stevens to fetch her, and he and Christine can deal with the interview. She'll be okay, don't worry. Can you handle the vicar and still make it back for the prelim from the autopsy? It's scheduled for 2pm."

Sandra checked her watch. "Should do, but I think Marshton might be key, so I don't want to rush it. It seems he and the Lyonses go back a long way; there was a fair amount of correspondence and, more significantly – at least on paper – a possible motive too. The vicar is named as the Trustee in Mrs Lyons's Will, although numerous stipulations are attached, so in fact his only benefit as I see it is a hell of a lot of responsibilities; nothing in the way of earthly gains, so to speak. But what seems strange is that they appear to have been Roman Catholics, while he, of course, is Anglican."

Jeff's eyebrows shot up, "I wouldn't be so sure; about the motive thing, that is. He's a vicar: aren't they more into spiritual gains? Rewards in heaven, and all that! And as for the religion thing, maybe they were vexed at their own faith and it was their way of having a last say. Or maybe he was the one who was vexed! You'd best wear a vest..."

"Don't tease, Jeff, he's almost 90 – I doubt he's even got the teeth for spinach! Probably spends his days in a chair protected from chills with a blanket."

"Point taken! By the way, I've spoken to Millar. He wants you to go and see Lewis Graham, but he is tied up with this trip to London just now, so you'll have an easy ride for the time being. I don't know what time I'll get back this afternoon," he checked his watch: "Hell, look at the time, I need to get going. Mind you it's not something I'm looking forward to – a return trip with Millar certainly won't do my blood pressure any good; put it through the roof more than likely!"

19

Having survived two major motorways, Sandra turned off for the centre of Higham. She arrived as scheduled at the home of Stanley Marshton and was greeted by his sister. He had gone down to the old church, the elderly woman told her, and had left a message asking Sandra to meet him there: it wasn't far; down the hill in the old part of the village. It was easy to find; look for the orchard on the edge of the marshes.

Parked up, Sandra walked along the narrow pathway beside the graveyard, enjoying the tranquillity of the setting and the unusually warm, sunny day. All around her the sound of birdsong blocked out the muffled hum of distant traffic. The church of St Mary was a quaint old place built of local ragstone and flint; the spire like something out of a fairytale. Smiling, she thought of Rapunzel and slowed her pace to dwell on the peacefulness of the scene. It was all a far cry from her reasons for being here.

Grimly hunching her shoulders, she entered the churchyard through the lych gate and saw an army of what she assumed were volunteers. Armed with shears and secateurs, they were busily cutting back verges and taming straggling bushes and trees around the periphery of the church grounds. A man's voice shouted from somewhere above her head, "Just give me a minute to make my way down, my dear."

She searched out the voice and saw a man in a blue boiler suit and hiking boots, carefully descending a ladder that was propped against the side of the porch. Reaching the bottom, he walked to meet her, pulling the woolly hat from his head and undoing the top of his boiler suit to reveal a white dog collar.

Sandra was momentarily stunned. Surely this could not be the 90-year old she had envisaged wrapped in a blanket!

"Sorry for inconveniencing you Detective Inspector, but we must make use of this glorious day the good Lord has given us." Carefully wiping his grimy hands on his backside, he smiled and held them out to her. "I am Stanley Marshton and as you can see, I have been clearing tufts of grass from the guttering. It seems to get everywhere."

Bemused, Sandra took the proffered hands and murmured a greeting. At close quarters he bore all the telltale signs of advanced age: his turkey neck wobbled loosely within his sagging skin and his hands were wrinkled and liver-spotted, yet his grasp was warm and firm and he exuded the enthusiasm and agility of a man half his age. Definitely not what she had expected!

With Marshton guiding the way, they turned towards the entrance of the church. "I really am sorry to take up your time, Reverend," she offered, "but it appears from your correspondence with Mr and Mrs Lyons that you knew them well. I am hoping you can elaborate on some of the things they were involved in."

"Ah," he said, "a sorry business; a sorry business indeed." He walked on in silence for a moment, pausing at the church door. "Of course; I will help in any way I can, but first, would you like some tea or we have coffee?" Tapping his stomach he added, "Have to keep this old engine here stoked up."

She smiled and he took it as a yes.

"Follow me then, my dear; the good ladies here always put out a tasty spread for us workers. I'm afraid this old place is redundant nowadays, but the Church Conservation Trust provides the funds to keep it from falling down and we try to keep it tidy for visitors."

He led the way to the back of the church where a table had been laid out with plates of sandwiches covered in cling film. A biscuit tin was surrounded by an assortment of flasks and mugs. Sandra accepted a coffee and finally gave in to a chocolate finger: Reverend Marshton was not one to take no for an answer it seemed. He seated himself on a pew beside the welcoming warmth of a paraffin heater and invited her to join him, asking as she sat down, "So; you want to know about the Prioress, then?"

"I'm sorry?" Sandra, getting her notebook out of her bag, thought she must have misheard.

"The Prioress," he repeated, shaking his head and sighing. "It was a dreadful shock, what you said on the phone. I must admit I have found myself questioning the Lord's reasons for allowing my good friends to be taken in such a terrible way."

Sandra felt a surge of pity; a few minutes ago this man's buoyancy and energy had astonished her, but suddenly he looked like a very old man. It was clear he had suffered a great loss. Was his mind wandering? Before she could speak, he resumed.

"Lady Margaret Brampton: that was Peggy Lyons's official title, but she never used it. She left that behind – and everything that came with it – a long time ago."

Sandra was puzzled: that name hadn't cropped up in any of the papers she had found.

He seemed to read her mind, "No, you won't have found that out, at least not until you gain access to her private rooms at Brampton Manor."

Sandra was familiar with the Manor having often driven past its imposing facade when taking the girls to their riding lessons. "It's some sort of residential home isn't it?" As she spoke, she wondered why, if they had access to private rooms there, the Lyonses had chosen to live in that run down, damp old house in Higham. It had obviously been too much for them in their later years.

"That's one way of putting it, I suppose," the Vicar looked faintly embarrassed as he added, "but it's more like a boarding school for young teenage girls who get into trouble, if you know what I mean."

Hiding her amusement at the euphemism, Sandra nodded and scribbled a brief note on her pad: *Brampton: home for unmarried pregnant teenagers*. "Didn't I read something about the place in the local paper recently?"

"Yes. Most unfortunate: part of the facility was broken into and vandalised a few months ago, a sign of the times no doubt. Even this little hamlet suffers from hooliganism from time to time, but so rarely that it made the front pages." He reached for the flask and offered Sandra a top-up.

Setting aside her notes, she held out her mug. "Could you tell me why the Lyonses chose not to live at the Manor if Mrs Lyons had retained private rooms there?"

He nodded, taking a sip of his tea before continuing. "Quite a remarkable woman she was when I first came here. That would have been early in 1955 as I recall. Very kindly; always out and about in the village offering her time and so on. When she eventually told me of the tragedy that had befallen her, I often wondered, had it happened to me, whether I could have carried the burden as well as she did."

Intrigued, Sandra asked, "What burden was that?"

As if afraid the stone walls around them had ears, he leaned closer, said in a low voice, "She trained as a nurse at the beginning of the war. That's how she met and fell in love with Matthew Lyons. He was a doctor then, a reputable profession; you might have thought her family would be pleased, except for one thing: he was of the Jewish faith and the Bramptons were Roman Catholic."

Sandra remembered what Jeff had said earlier: had Peggy Lyons been 'vexed with her own faith' as he had flippantly suggested? It might explain why she had turned her back on her religion and named this Anglican vicar as a beneficiary.

"Though you probably don't realise the significance of that fact," Marshton was saying. "Times were different then; mixed marriages were frowned upon, especially for her sort. They were titled people after all – and her father was a stickler for propriety. He was furious: went behind her back and arranged for Matthew to be called up into the medical corps. Soon afterwards the field hospital to where he was posted took a direct hit during a raid. I have often wondered if old Lord Brampton had hoped for that eventuality."

Marshton looked down at his tea, "But I should give him the benefit of the doubt, I suppose. Perhaps he had hoped that by separating the couple their attachment would fizzle out. Whatever, when she was notified of Matthew's death, Lady Margaret told her parents that she was carrying Matthew's child."

The old man paused and stared at the floor. Not wanting to interrupt his train of thought, Sandra contained her impatience, but surely he was misremembering? The other body at the crime scene had been positively identified as Matthew Lyons, so how could he have been killed in the war. Besides, she had seen all the photographs.

At length Marshton continued, "Lord Brampton took matters in hand; thought he could turn back the clock. He arranged for the child Peggy eventually bore – his own grandson! – to be privately adopted. In his view, his daughter's reputation remained intact and they could put the whole unfortunate episode behind them."

Sandra's pulse quickened; at last she felt as if she was onto something. "Do you happen to know where this son is?" she asked, calculating how old the child would be by now.

Marshton seemed not to hear. "Punished herself for giving in to them, she did," he sighed again, shaking his head. "Let's remember it was different back then; not as free and easy as it is now. A young woman finding herself in such a predicament in those days rarely had a say in what was done. There was so much guilt and anxiety – and they were Roman Catholic too – the die was cast from the beginning. Had they not been so privileged, she'd likely have been sent across the water to Ireland and probably never heard of again. As it was, she was confined to her rooms at the Manor and few people knew she was there; it was assumed she was still working away at the hospital-" He broke off, "I'm sorry, I am not looking after you very well, my dear. Won't you have a sandwich?"

Sandra smiled, "No thanks, I really shouldn't. Please; go on with the story."

Marshton nodded, "She still blames herself, you know, even now; the Prioress. Still, after all these years; blames herself for not being strong enough to keep her baby." He looked up, his eyes sparkling with unshed tears. "I'm sorry; I find it hard to believe that she's gone. You see, the thing was, Matthew Lyons wasn't dead at all. He'd been in a coma all those months, but he returned the following year: came back to claim his sweetheart."

That little riddle explained, then, Sandra thought, but why did he keep referring to Peggy Lyons as 'the Prioress', was it some kind of nickname? Putting out a sympathetic hand to pat the old man's arm, she murmured, "I'm sorry, Reverend; this must all be distressing for you."

He gave her a watery smile and took another sip of tea – cold now. "It broke him, you know: Matthew; finding out that his son had been - for want of a better term – disposed of. He and Lady Margaret defied her father; they eloped; took off to get married despite him. They bought that house in Higham and came back there to live. Of course, they tried to find their son, but Lord Brampton refused point blank to tell them where the child had been placed. His way of making them pay, I suppose. It is all very sad. As far as I know, the Prioress never spoke to her father again. I tried to intercede for them, but he was a spiteful old man by then. He never forgave his daughter for marrying Matthew and, in his view, turning her back on the Roman Catholic Church. In the late 1950s he was taken ill and as with many people when faced with their own mortality, he felt the need to right his wrongs. He released the adoption papers just before he died in 1959 and at last they could begin to try to find their son. I did what I could to help..."

Hanging his head, Marshton's eyes misted over as if he was physically reliving it over again. "If only I could go back there now...." He pulled out a large white handkerchief from his pocket and blew his nose before continuing: "You see, it was I who encouraged her to find him. I thought if she was able to see her son and explain what had happened, she could release herself from the torment of guilt that was destroying her soul. It took two years of searching until we eventually located him, or at least, his adoptive family. Tragically we were too late. None of us had foreseen that the boy might be dead."

Sandra scribbled out the word *Suspect* on her pad. She had already realised that Peggy and Matt's son would have been too old for the profile she was building. Back to the start, she thought with a sigh. Surreptitiously she glanced at her watch. Like most elderly people, Marshton was enjoying telling his story. As she had told Jeff, she didn't want to rush it, but time was getting on. She resigned herself to listen, even though she had begun to feel that she was getting nowhere.

"He had been adopted by an American family in Ohio. His adoptive father was a military man – a General as I recall – and when the boy came of age he followed his example and joined the Marines. A short time before we traced him, he had been killed in a tragic accident during a training exercise. I travelled with Mr and Mrs Lyons to Ohio to see his grave. It was all very sad: all that hope; such a crushing disappointment. Matthew Lyons was never the same, but the Prioress seemed to gain strength. In a way the trip saved her. She spent some weeks with the couple who raised their son. They were good people and the boy's short life had been a happy one. Knowing that, and being able to walk in his footsteps was a great comfort to her and when she returned home she was a changed woman; strong again. That was when she started the Priory; it would have been in 1962."

Sandra's interest quickened: "The Priory, Reverend? What was that?"

"That was the pet name we gave to her project. She opened up her home to young girls who, as she had been, were threatened with having to give up their babies. She gave them refuge, but more importantly a say in their future: something she had been denied. When Lord Brampton died, she moved back into the Manor and operated from there. The house in Higham was used for the actual adoptions that took place. The Priory itself is run by nuns – she recruited them from somewhere up north."

"She bequeathed her estate to this little church, I gather?"

"Only the proceeds from the property in Higham; the Sisters were given the Manor and the medieval museum attached to it some years ago. It was finally recognised there was a need for it, though the Prioress had been doing it for decades."

Sandra shifted her position on the pew, which felt harder by the minute. "So, in 1972, the girls she took in would actually have stayed at the Manor, not at the house in Higham?"

"Yes, that's right," he put his cup back on the table and eased himself to his feet. "I'm sorry, I've been rambling on a bit, haven't I." Smiling down at her, he reached for her empty cup, "I can see you are ready to move, and my army will be in for their lunch at any moment. Is there anything else I can tell you, Detective Inspector?"

"I don't think so for the moment. I appreciate that it has not been easy for you. Thank you for giving up so much of your time." Standing, Sandra gestured to the laden table, "and for your hospitality."

"On the contrary, my dear, I have enjoyed talking to you. It is not often these days that I am afforded the pleasure of a captive audience," he said with a twinkle in his eye.

Sandra found herself laughing as he walked her back to her car; he really was a dear old boy. As she took a final look at the church, a thought occurred to her: "One last thing, Reverend. Did Mrs Lyons have a particular interest in St Mary's? It seems strange to me, given that she was Roman Catholic, that she should bequeath money to an Anglican church."

Marshton followed her gaze and chuckled quietly. "You don't know about the history of our little church, then, detective? I would like to be able to say that knowing of my devotion to its upkeep, it was a thank you gesture for our friendship, but I know better than that. There once was a priory here too. Let's just say that *my* Prioress felt an affiliation with the Sisters of the Cloth who lived here in another time."

Back in the car, Sandra checked her messages: an appointment had been made for her psychological assessment at 4.15pm, tomorrow. She dreaded the thought of it, but knew she had little choice if she was to continue working. Not only did she have to turn up, but she also had somehow to pass the test. She had expected a snappy rebuke from Fiona for letting her down this morning, but there was none; she was getting the silent treatment instead.

Putting the car in reverse she pulled away from the church, her thoughts turning to the questions she needed to put to Leslie. It was time to focus on the mind of the killer.

20

Whitehall, London: later that morning

"Shouldn't we go left just here?" Trailing behind his Super through the labyrinth of Whitehall corridors, Jeff was sure Millar had got them lost.

"Just bear with me, McAdams, all will be explained shortly."

Don't blame me when we end up a lot later than we already are, Jeff thought, but knew better than to say. Millar was being even more close-mouthed than usual, and beyond the hazy notion that they were here to discuss funding for the new Cold Crimes Unit, Jeff had really no idea why the Super had insisted he come along for the ride. It wasn't as if he didn't have enough to do, especially during these crucial hours of a murder investigation. A committee meeting was the last thing he wanted.

Suddenly, Millar shot through a doorway into an office. Three of the desks were occupied: two by women and the other by a bespectacled man in a grey suit. Millar strode over to him, ignoring the women as if they were invisible. From behind his back, Jeff teetered in the doorway, smiled and mouthed 'good morning'. He was rewarded with welcoming smiles from the two women before they returned their attention to the piles of paper on their desks.

It seemed they were expected: the male secretary ushered them through another door at the back of the office. Trailing casually behind, Jeff saw that Millar was surreptitiously patting himself down, straightening his tie and smoothing his hair. It was a habit of the Chief Super's that made Jeff cringe. He wondered idly if beneath the highly polished boots, Millar wore white socks with little bands to hold them up – or maybe suspenders à la Eric Morecambe; he smothered a chuckle bringing his attention smartly back to the room they had entered as a voice said:

"Come in gentlemen, thank you for coming, please take a seat."

Jeff, recognising the voice instantly: *what are we doing here in the office of a Parliamentary Under-Secretary of State?* It had to be some matter concerning the committee meeting they were on their way to, but why had the Chief Super not mentioned it? Clearly, Millar and the Minister were well acquainted; that much he detected from the looks they exchanged.

Jeff was taken aback: in the flesh, the Minister seemed much less confident, less robust than numerous television appearances would suggest. Almost timid – no, not timid, he thought, so much as apprehensive. No handshake was offered; the Minister's elbows were resting on the table; hands gripped so tightly together that the knuckles showed white. Undoubtedly a sign of stress; something was up. As he followed Millar's lead and took a seat at the table, Jeff wondered what was coming.

From the end of the table, the Minister, Lady Clara Smith-Stevens, was viewing him with suspicion. He fixed his face into an expression of polite attentiveness and waited for her to speak.

"Superintendent McAdams; I am grateful for your presence here this morning." She leaned closer, her words clearly intended for him alone: "Please understand that the reason for this impromptu meeting and what I am about to disclose to you are highly confidential. I insist that you respect my wishes in this," she gave him a tight-lipped smile. "That said, I hardly need add that nothing of which I speak in this room will be allowed to enter the public domain. There is a great deal at stake here. Do you understand?"

Jeff nodded. "Of course, Minister. I quite understand." He shot a look at Millar, but he was staring up at the ceiling. Drat the man; why hadn't he briefed him properly: something here didn't feel quite right. He studied Lady Clara intensely. He knew she was in her late fifties, but she could easily have been at least a decade younger. Her high-necked, purple twinset was adorned with a simple, yet striking string of pearls, and her hair, swept up into a neat bun, gave her an air of elegance and sophistication. She looked like an upper crust lady of leisure: more suited to sitting in a drawing room of a large country mansion than in a musty old office in Whitehall.

Easing her hands apart, Lady Clara lifted a leather wallet from beside her chair and pulled out several sheets of paper. Glancing down at them, she picked up the first and slid it across the table to

Jeff. "Before I explain why you are here, you may like to take a look at this Superintendent."

As he looked down to see what she had passed to him, a name jumped up off the page: *Aya of Mons*. Only hours ago it had been lit up on the wall of the incident room at this morning's briefing. It was the alias of one of the young women on the list that had been taken from the crime scene in Higham. Jeff drew in a sharp breath: how in the hell did Lady Clara Smith-Stevens come by this name. Quickly, he answered himself: this was about the case; the Minister was in some way involved. God! It suddenly hit him: was she a target? He shot another look at Millar, but the Super was now examining his fingernails and refusing to make eye-contact. There was no doubt in Jeff's mind that Millar already knew what was going on. It still didn't make sense to him. In what way was Millar involved with Lady Clara?

He turned his attention back to the name and read through the notes beneath it; they appeared to be a person's description: hair colour, eye colour, height, weight and so forth, presumably of this 'Aya'. Jeff frowned up at Lady Clara. Could it be that she was this person? Surely not! No wonder she was so anxious about confidentiality!

"You look doubtful, Inspector," she smiled, "but I think you have guessed correctly. Aya is the alias my mentor, Peggy Lyons, attached to me. Those little notes and references were her *aide-mémoire*. She kept one for each of her girls, as she called us. She said it was in case our children came back to look for us one day, so that she would be able to create an accurate picture for them: what we were like, our personalities, likes and dislikes, strengths and weaknesses; our very nature, if you like." As she spoke, she relaxed back in her chair. It was a large, swivel wing chair in red leather; she seemed lost in it, her hands stroking the arms as though she sought comfort from them.

"I confess to being somewhat taken aback, Minister," Jeff frowned at Millar, who had now deigned to glance in his direction, his expression faintly bored. "I was not briefed to expect this meeting," he added, pointedly.

"That was at my request, Superintendent. Your Chief and I are old friends, which is why I called him as soon as I became aware of the events that have taken place – and now this dreadful news about Matthew and Peggy Lyons. I am afraid I asked him not to disclose your real reason for being here. When Leonard told me you were leading the investigation, I wanted to talk to you personally. As you will now have gathered, the Select Committee Meeting was an excuse. Until we spoke yesterday, Chief Superintendent Millar had no knowledge of what I am about to reveal to you. Once again, I must stress that it is of the utmost confidentiality."

She stopped speaking as a small knock sounded on the door to announce the arrival of a tea tray. "Thank you. Leave it there would you? I will deal with it," Lady Clara smiled pleasantly at the clerk, who nodded, set the tray of porcelain cups and saucers, teapot, milk, sugar and a plate of digestive biscuits down on the polished table and left the room, closing the door firmly behind her.

Eyeing the tray, Jeff had to pinch himself that he was not in a drawing room as Lady Clara gracefully poured and handed him his tea, the teaspoon chinking in the saucer. It was a welcome relief that somehow dissipated the tension in the room. Jeff, declining a biscuit and sipping the hot liquid appreciatively, wondered at the fact that the Chief Super was apparently on first name terms with the Minister.

"Much of what I say may shock you, both professionally and personally – and at varying levels I imagine. Some months ago, when it came to my attention that something concerning my dealings with the Lyonses was not quite right, my son acquired a copy of the *aide-mémoire* for me – with the approval of Peggy Lyons, I hasten to add. I had a strong reason for wanting it: something I must protect."

Jeff attempted to intercept with a question, but Lady Clara raised an imperious hand to stop him, softening it with a smile: "It's a trait of all politicians, I'm afraid. We dislike being interrupted! I will take your questions when I have finished. It will make it easier for you if I start at the beginning."

Muttering a brief apology, Jeff settled back in his chair and waited for all to be revealed.

"My life today is very much removed from where it began, Superintendent. I daresay you will have read about my background?"

Jeff nodded; yes, he had: the Press had had a field day when she was appointed to the Cabinet Committee for Justice and Crime; the headlines full of rags to riches stories that he had taken with a pinch of salt. She was born in a terraced house in North Yorkshire, the daughter of a seamstress and a factory worker, had got herself to university, married well and the rest was history – so what! Jeff smothered a yawn.

"What you won't have read is that as a child one of my tasks was to fetch and carry for my great-uncle. He was bedridden by then; an interesting, much-travelled man. He it was who encouraged me to be ambitious; made me aware that there was more to life than drudgery. When he died he bequeathed a sum of money that was to be used to pay for my education. It opened up a whole new world to me, Superintendent. You must understand that back in the 1950s, it was not common for a woman of my background to aspire to a university education. I gladly seized the opportunity to better myself, but I fear my education in worldly matters was sadly lacking; I was not what you would call street-wise." Lady Clara shifted distractedly in her chair and leant closer to the table, a slight flush suffusing her cheeks.

Jeff guessed what was coming. He wondered quite why Lady Clara found it necessary to tell him her life-story, and how many euphemisms she would use to explain that she had slept around and got herself pregnant! He was aware that Millar had started to fidget with his collar and was looking rather embarrassed.

"To cut a long story short, Superintendent, mid-way through my studies at university, I discovered I was expecting a child."

Thank the Lord for small mercies, Jeff thought, draining the dregs of his tea.

"Needless to say, my family was appalled. By the time I was brave enough to bring it to their attention, I was too far gone for an abortion, so my father arranged for me to stay at the Priory."

"The Priory?" Jeff echoed, forgetting he was not supposed to interrupt. A nursing home tucked away in North Yorks, he assumed.

"Yes; the residential home for unmarried mothers that in those days was run by Peggy Lyons and her husband in Higham, although latterly it has been taken over by the Council. You didn't know?"

"Er, no, that is, we knew of the adoption angle, of course, but my team are still working on the background to the case."

"Ah, yes, of course."

Jeff noticed that Lady Clara's eyes were shining with unshed tears. He felt a sudden shaft of sympathy for her. "It must have felt like a long way from home for you," he said, feeling awkward.

"I was more fortunate than most, Inspector. Although my parents went out of their way to avoid a scandal, my dear father did not show me the door as did so many in like circumstances. He chose the Priory because he had heard it was not as harsh as some of the places where unfortunate young women were incarcerated for correction in those days. Most of them run by the Church. Thankfully, times have changed, but as little as forty years ago unmarried mothers were still regarded as pariahs. It was always we women who were to blame for our situation, you understand. You will doubtless have heard about the punishment that was meted out in the name of reparation for our sins, particularly in Ireland?"

Jeff nodded; he had seen a film on the subject on TV relatively recently. There had been a rash of heart-rending documentaries since the adoption laws were changed. He cleared his throat and shifted uncomfortably in his seat.

Lady Clara looked down her nose at him. "If you would bear with me, Superintendent; there is a point to this story, I assure you. My father kept in close touch, frequently travelling down from Yorkshire to see me. It was decided that when my baby was born, my parents would adopt him as their own and move to an area where they were not known. It was a well practised solution and I was given very little say in it. The idea was that I would return to university and catch up with my studies as if nothing untoward had occurred, beyond an unfortunate 'illness'. As you might imagine, it was very distressing for me. My son to all intents and purposes became my brother; it was quite credible: he had inherited his father's olive skin and black hair, but he had my father's blue eyes and narrow features. It was never questioned, but it broke my heart not to be able to acknowledge Gareth as my own. I was forbidden to tell him the truth and it was to my mother that he turned for maternal love, not me. I found that impossibly hard to live with. So when I graduated, I returned to Kent rather than go home and it was there I met and married my first husband." She paused, "Do you remember when Kenneth McMasters, the MP, was killed in a road traffic accident?"

Jeff started, suddenly aware that she was expecting an answer. He racked his brains and dredged up the memory. "Yes, in Kent, along with his wife and daughter as I recall; a head on collision with another car. The occupants all killed outright aside from a young boy—" He broke off, the significance of the question dawning on him, added softly, "He was your son?"

"That's right. It was the night before my wedding. My parents and Gareth had travelled down from Yorkshire. They were the occupants of the other car. My son was almost six years old by then. Quite naturally, my husband and I adopted him and I was able to be his mother at last. Fate, you might say, took a hand." She looked away, discreetly dabbing her cheeks.

Jeff found her distress unexpectedly moving; it was clear that for Lady Clara the memories were as fresh as if they had happened yesterday. He found himself dwelling on the wasted years; the grief of time lost; the hurt that was never forgotten. An image of Christine's drawn face flashed into his mind. Much had changed in this world and yet so much more had not. He must see about settling her into the extension; maybe he could make a difference. When he returned his attention to the Minister, he no longer saw her as a leading politician, but as a girl, Clara, grown into a woman; one who had never stopped loving her son. She had taken a sip of water, and had resumed speaking.

"My first husband died and I remarried rather quickly, but it was only a short time before he was taken from me too. I began to wonder if I was being punished; made to pay for the secrets of my past. A fanciful notion you might think, but I was soon to realise that this was indeed the case. Without knowing it, I had placed myself in a perilous position."

Jeff focused on her face, his attention riveted. Here, then, was the twist in the tale.

"I had never denied my son knowledge of his father. Henrique Carlosanta was a gentleman; his father was from Brazil, attached to the Embassy, but his mother was English. It was brief, our time together: a passionate liaison between teenagers. We knew there was no future in it; our worlds were so different. I never told him I was expecting his child and have neither seen nor spoken to him since." From the sheaf of papers in front of her, Lady Clara drew a photograph and passed it across the table. "This was taken in 1971, just before he returned to Brazil."

Jeff leaned forward to examine the photograph and could see immediately why a young, naive Yorkshire lass would had fallen for him: classic film-star looks; tanned skin, black hair, worn long as in the style of the day. Something stirred within him: a hint of recognition. He had surely seen this face before. He stared at it, wracking his brains, but nothing came forward.

Lady Clara looked down at her hands. "It was Gareth who first discovered the path Henrique had chosen. You cannot imagine what a shock it was – for both of us. Over the years I have relied deeply on my faith: it has been my stalwart through everything, but I find myself questioning it now. I cannot be sure that we are in danger as my son believes, but I fear so."

Still staring at the photograph, Jeff looked up briefly, "I presume your son took your first husband's name?" Something about Lady Clara's face brought to his mind the image of another face. He wished he could place it.

"Is that relevant, Superintendent? My son carries the same name as myself, but he prefers to shorten it. Please don't interrupt."

Chastened, Jeff slid the photograph back across the table and waited in silence for her to resume.

"I believe we are pawns in a most unscrupulous plan to discredit Henrique. His own position in this I have to believe is unknown to him. When I knew him he was not an uncaring man; in my heart I believe that had he known of our son's existence, he would have made contact before now."

Jeff was puzzled; he could hear Lady Clara's words, but none of them made any sense. What the hell was she talking about? What path was it that Henrique Carlosanta had taken that had jolted her faith and led her son to imagine she was in danger? And what were the events she had referred to earlier? Events? To the best of his knowledge there was only one event: the murders of Matt and Peggy Lyons. He endeavoured to contain his impatience, wishing she would cut to the chase. He sat forward, about to risk another interruption, when Millar shot him a warning glance. The Super shifted in his chair as though preparing himself for something. Jeff sat back again and waited.

Lady Clara had pulled another sheet from the folder and was sliding it around for Jeff to see. He leant forward again, his eyes widening in surprise.

"Yes, I expected that would surprise you, Superintendent.

Perhaps you can now spare a thought for me and my son and the situation we find ourselves in? I must ask you to believe that had I known beforehand of the career Henrique had chosen, I would have made every effort to acquaint him with knowledge of his son. As it transpired, when Gareth turned 30, he took an interest in locating his father. It was perhaps only natural; he had lost three 'fathers' in his life: my father and my two husbands had all assumed a paternal role for him. Eventually, he sought the help of one of those agencies that help to locate missing relatives, a place called the Search Agency here in London. Unfortunately, the particular individual assigned to his case was completely unhinged: he attacked a colleague and was later convicted of— "

Jeff, his eyes widening, cut across her: "Mark Jakes!" Two sets of eyes were directed at him simultaneously: Lady Clara looked startled and Millar shot him a warning glance, imperceptibly shaking his head.

"I didn't realise you had handled the Katie Smyth case – I assume that is how you know of this man?" Lady Clara threw a questioning glance at each of them in turn.

"Well, that among other things—" Jeff began.

Kicking him under the table, Millar cut in. "We didn't, Lady Clara. Please continue."

She looked unconvinced, but did as he said. "Well, as I was saying, this Jakes managed to track down Henrique for my son. Oddly enough, the day before Katie Smyth was killed she had asked Gareth's advice about Jakes. Apparently she knew my son was a member of the police force."

The words had barely left her lips before the pieces fell into place for Jeff. Of course! Lady Clara Smith-*Stevens*. DS Stevens was her son! He shot a glance at Millar, but the Chief Super remained silent.

"Obviously, nobody at the Agency had any inkling that the man was deranged," Lady Clara was saying. "Miss Smyth was concerned about confidentiality issues and the misuse of information at the Agency. It would seem that Mark Jakes and another client of his were involved, but the conversation was interrupted before Gareth could ascertain any details. And then, of course, it was too late."

Jeff was not aware that DS Stevens had been on the investigating team for the Katie Smyth case. It certainly wasn't mentioned on his personal file.

"He has always remained concerned about the Data Protection angle, but because of his personal involvement with Mark Jakes he had to step down in the initial stages of the investigation and as far as I am aware, no more information has come to light as to Jakes's other activities. Perhaps you might raise it with Gareth, Superintendent?"

"I most certainly will, Minister," Jeff replied.

She nodded. "However, it is not that which concerns me – at least, not directly. I noted in the newspaper reports that a Miss Fiona Reid found the bodies of poor Mr and Mrs Lyons?"

Jeff blinked at the unexpected change in direction. "Yes; she is searching for her birth mother as it happens. Now there's a coincidence, Minister. Her natural mother would have been one of your companions during your time at the Priory."

"Are you sure about that Superintendent?"

"Why yes; I happen to know that Fiona Reid was adopted in February 1972"

"That is not what concerns me." Lady Clara got up and moved towards the window. She seemed agitated, her hands fiddling with the ring on her wedding finger. "Legally I am my son's adoptive mother. There is in fact nothing whatever to connect him to me as my natural son, nor is there anything to connect me to Peggy Lyons. You do see the reasons for my anxiety, Superintendent?"

Jeff nodded, but he wasn't sure he saw at all and he wondered if she was not being a little disingenuous. She must have been screened before she was appointed, and anyway, what could it possibly matter after all these years who knew about her son's illegitimacy. A nine-day's wonder in the Press is all it would be. There was far worse went on in the corridors of power; but he let it pass. And then he remembered Henrique's photograph and realised that it was not for herself that she was concerned.

As if reading his thoughts, she said, "We have followed Cardinal Carlosanta's career closely over the last year. Do you know much about the hierarchy of the Roman Catholic Church, Superintendent?"

He shook his head: born C of E, he rarely thought about religion at all, never mind anything to do with the Pope! Angie had been the church goer for both of them and he'd only attended Easter and Christmas services because she'd put her foot down.

"When the last Pope died," Lady Clara said, "there was a great stirring among the masses for a sea-change; a more moderate, liberal Pope. We saw Henrique's face so often in the days during the choosing period. He was apparently a forerunner, though as you know, he was not elected; not this time. The present Pope, as I understand, is perhaps even more conservative than the last. A 'caretaker Pope' I have heard him called. From what I am led to believe, there is every chance that Gareth's father will be elected next time. You can imagine, I am sure, that our son is in a quandary about this."

Casting his mind back, Jeff remembered there had been some speculation in the Press that before long there would be a Pope of Latin-American or African descent. Yes; he could see that it might be a problem if Pope elect was found to have a son; an illegitimate one, needless to say!

"You see, Superintendent, it is my belief that someone or some group is trying to discredit Henrique by exposing me, while others are equally determined to prevent it from ever coming to light."

"Surely you can't seriously believe that some group within the Church has uncovered your past association? And in the unlikely event that they have, you cannot possibly believe there are those who mean either you or your son harm because of it?" Clearly, Jeff thought, the woman was paranoid. The stress of office had tipped her over the edge.

"Yes, Superintendent," the Minister said with quiet dignity, "that is exactly what I believe. Searching for a parent in a South American country requires passing through a great deal of red tape. In doing so, Mark Jakes would have left behind him a series of footprints – for want of a better word – footprints that may not have gone entirely unnoticed at higher levels. Perhaps the knowledge that my son exists is already known; known to people who see him as a threat to the stability of the Church and what they hope for it." She paused, paced by the window, came forward to the table and looked down at him. "What if I were to tell you that this Miss Reid and her late brother were members of a group called Opus Dei?"

"Hold on a minute, what are you implying!" Thrusting back his chair, Jeff got to his feet. "How would you come to have information like that?" His face flushed with the effort of controlling his anger. "Forgive me, Lady Clara, but these are serious allegations: either someone has been deliberately feeding you misinformation or you are

allowing your past unhappy circumstances to colour your judgement."
He slapped his two hands hard down on the table. Startled, Lady
Clara stepped backwards. "Where I come from, Minister, Gerry Reid
was a well-respected man. I worked with his father for a good part of
my career and I knew Gerry extremely well. And I can tell you this:
he was as honest as the day is long, always went out of his way to help
people, would never have countenanced causing deliberate harm to
anyone, and as to whether or not he and his sister were members of
some religious group, I fail to see that it is relevant." Jeff realised he
had raised his voice; knew he was overreacting. He slid his hands off
the table and looked quickly at Millar, but the Chief Super had his
gaze fixed on Lady Clara's face.

"Really, Superintendent McAdams," she said, receding to her side
of the table, "there is no need for you to lose your temper. I certainly
did not intend to demean your friends; perhaps if you let me finish
what I was trying to say?" Haughtily, she stared him down.

With a mumbled apology, Jeff nodded and subsided into his
chair.

"This group has received much publicity in recent years, not
least because of a popular, if somewhat spurious, novel," she gave
a half smile. "Even so, I am sure you are aware of the implications
and understand why I might have concluded that Opus Dei may
be involved. And for the record, I do not deal in misinformation,
deliberately fed to me or otherwise."

Listening to her, Jeff pinched his wrists just to make sure this was
real-time he was in and not some weird dream. It was real alright,
even though what he was hearing was ridiculous. He shook his head,
"I'm not quite up on religious sects and the like. I have to say that I
thought Opus Dei was a largely fictional creation, sensationalised for
the sake of a good story. But in any event, surely the fact that your son
was conceived before his father became a priest would let Cardinal
Carlosanta off the hook? Wasn't there a similar case some years back:
an Irish bishop as I recall? He is still in a red hat even though the Press
tried to annihilate him for siring a child in his youth."

"It's not quite the same thing. With all due respect, Superintendent,
the fact that I am a member of the General Council for the Church
of England rather changes things. How would that be received do
you suppose? Especially in conservative circles within the Roman

Catholic Church? Whether you give it credence or not, it can only be that I am at the centre of this. It is clear to me that Mark Jakes's enquiries brought my son to the attention of people who are close to Henrique. It is not beyond reason that Fiona Reid was recruited, possibly without her knowledge, to take care of the situation. There are two possible scenarios that could explain events that have taken place."

She'd said it again: 'events', Jeff thought. What else had happened that he didn't know about? He returned his attention to what she was saying.

"It could be that Miss Reid was manipulated by Jakes to get rid of any trace of me and my son. It could equally be that they were involved together, as partners, both intent on recovering proof of the relationship between the Cardinal and myself. It is quite possible that Jakes was also intent on blackmail."

The Minister held up her hand before Jeff could speak, "I am not making allegations about Miss Reid in this respect, Superintendent, but what if I am right? What if someone else from Opus Dei has stepped into Jakes's shoes to finish what he started? Can you afford not to take this possibility seriously? And supposing—" she broke off and glared at Millar as he cut across her.

"Yes, well, I think we've heard enough and can take it from here, Lady Clara." Clearing his throat, he got to his feet and added, "I'll speak with the Commissioner and arrange for private protection for you. I think it better that for the time being you stay at your London apartments. We'll talk with Security here. We'll need a full schedule of your commitments for the next few weeks." He looked down at Jeff and motioned to the door.

The Minister looked decidedly put out, Jeff thought, getting to his feet. Why hadn't the Chief Super let her finish. He seemed livid about something. Another thought occurred to him: why the hell had Millar stopped him from mentioning Fiona's association with Jakes. It was clear that the Super knew more about this whole business than he was letting on.

Jeff, keen to get out of this room and tackle him about it, shuffled his feet impatiently, waiting for Millar to close the meeting. Without giving the Minister another opportunity to speak, the Chief Super went through the motions of thanking her for her time, promising to keep her abreast of the investigation and reassuring her that nothing of which she had spoken would leave this office. Should the need arise to extend knowledge of her circumstances to the rest of the investigating team, he would, of course, consult with her first. That said, he walked to the door signalling Jeff to follow, leaving the Minister gazing after him with a look of chagrined disbelief.

Millar could bulldoze his way out of most situations, Jeff thought, smiling to himself. But it was clear he couldn't wait to get as far away as possible. As they retraced their way through the corridors, Jeff wondered how many more lives would be thrown into turmoil as they identified the women on their list and heard their stories. He could not imagine that any of them would come close to the extraordinary circumstances of Lady Clara Smith-Stevens.

21

Back in the car, they sat for a moment in silence, Millar tapping his hat and Jeff, for once, lost for words. He thought the Chief Super had brought the meeting to a close rather abruptly, even for him. On reflection, he thought, Millar had seemed fidgety and ill at ease throughout the meeting. It was strange for a man who was usually so self-assured and in control.

"What do you think of this Opus Dei issue?" Millar asked abruptly.

Jeff thought for a minute. "Well, as I said, I don't really believe it exists; at least, not as it has been portrayed; but that there is some religious faction – or factions – contriving either to kill or expose her ladyship? Well, she seems convinced of it; that much is clear, but if you ask me it's a bit far-fetched. DS Stevens has a lot to answer for, filling her mind with all that nonsense. I assume that's where she got it from – he's been reading too many thrillers I'd say. Mind you, on a serious note, I suppose she could be a target if some person or persons have discovered the connection. It is within the realms of possibility that someone might see it as an opportunity; a nice little earner you might say. She's worth a fortune isn't she – so is the Roman Catholic Church, come to that. Could be that's what the real target is here: the Church I mean, rather than the Minister. It would be interesting to find out what this Cardinal Carlosanta is worth, too. I don't suppose for one moment he has taken a vow of poverty! All that's a load of crap in my book."

Millar remained silent and Jeff, remembering too late that he was a Roman Catholic, hastily tried another tack. "If you don't mind me saying so, Sir, you seem to know her ladyship quite well. Can you enlighten me? Is she the type of person who has to be the centre of attention?"

"I'm not really the best person to answer that question, but from what I know of her, yes, it could be so. Why do you ask?"

"Well; it doesn't add up, does it? The way she reads it that is. If this conspiracy exists in one form or another as she had led us to believe, then why would they go after the Lyonses? Afraid I don't see it – though I suppose it depends on whether or not they identified DS Stevens—" Jeff broke off with a dry chuckle. "Who would have thought it? It must have been a shock for him and his mother when they discovered that about his father. A right pickle they're in."

Released from the tension of the meeting, Jeff felt suddenly almost light-headed. A rumble of amusement started in his throat and exploded in a shout of laughter. "I'm sorry, Chief Superintendent, but can't you just picture it? Men running around in those long brown sacks, tearing people apart: it's like something out of the Middle Ages." Becoming aware that Millar was not sharing the joke, Jeff brought himself under control, suppressed a snigger and pulled his face straight. "You're Roman Catholic, aren't you Sir? Do you know much about Opus Dei?"

Millar nodded but did not elaborate, turning instead to the subject of Fiona Reid. "It is curious that the Reid girl is connected to both cases. I think we need to look more closely at her. It could have repercussions for the image of the Force – her connection to DI Reid I mean, of course."

Jeff had guessed Millar would steer the conversation in Sandra's direction sooner or later. He jumped to her defence. "Some people attract bad luck. I doubt it is any more than that, and as for DI Reid, she is an asset to the team. She won't let this distract her."

"I hope you're right McAdams, for your sake as well as hers. We wouldn't want anything to jeopardise your chances with this new post would we now. I want you to put a tail on Fiona Reid; round the clock surveillance."

"Yes, Chief Superintendent." So that was the way of it, was it? Just as well he hadn't torn up his letter of resignation. Turning the key in the ignition, Jeff pulled out into the traffic, and thought through all that Lady Clara had disclosed. It had been a surprise about her son; that he was DS Stevens. They would have to have that chat. The young man could easily have deleted his mother's information from the disk, but he hadn't. For an instant, Jeff wondered why. It would have saved him a lot of bother. Had he known his mother was going to tell them anyway? It would be interesting to hear his views on Fiona Reid – as well as whatever it was that had bothered him about the Smyth investigation. That was yet another coincidence: only weeks after Stevens asks to get posted to Maidstone they have another murder that can be connected to him. Jeff reminded himself that he didn't believe in coincidences.

Once on the Motorway, the traffic eased; it was getting on for lunch time. Jeff glanced across at Millar, "It's all a bit… in the clouds, Sir. Maybe we're jumping the gun with this angle. I think we might be forgetting something very significant; something we already know. I really don't think Lady Clara Smith-Stevens is right; she's not the object of this investigation."

"No? She would be right about the scandal though."

"That's as may be, but don't you see? Those records that we have on the young women: they were given their aliases over thirty years ago. Our Brazilian friend, Henrique Carlosanta, hadn't received his calling then had he?"

"No; that's correct, he was a student."

"And this Opus cult thing—"

"McAdams!" Millar raised his voice. "Opus Dei is not a cult. The movement was started in 1928, not in the Middle Ages! We merely help people to reach a greater understanding of their faith through the study of the doctrines of our Church. We fund and run hospitals and schools. We do *not* run around wielding knives as in your ignorance you seem to imagine."

Jeff kept his gaze firmly on the road feeling suddenly that he had walked into a cow pat with both feet. Yet at the same time he couldn't prevent the frivolous image of the Chief Super dancing around in a brown sack and wielding a man-sized, metal crucifix. Keeping the humour out of his voice, he asked conversationally, "You're a member of this group then, Sir?" It certainly explained Millar's peculiar mannerisms. Almost immediately, he had another thought: Lady Clara had confided her fears of the very group to which Millar belonged. Jeff shook his head in disbelief; no wonder the man had looked so uncomfortable!

"Yes." Millar said shortly.

"Well anyway, like I said, it's the wrong angle for us to work this case. Look, Sir; whoever it was that Peggy Lyons was trying to protect, I think we can rule out Lady Clara. It's too long ago: back then she was just an impoverished Yorkshire lass who got herself in a spot of trouble. Whatever this is all about I have no doubt that we are going to have to delve deeper to find it! I want to access the case notes from the Katie Smyth case. Would you be able to arrange that?" He shot a glance at Millar.

Millar looked puzzled. "Why would you want them if you think it's got nothing to do with Lady Clara?"

"She was right about something, even if she wasn't aware of it. We know that Fiona Reid was connected to the Katie Smyth case, if only by her association with Mark Jakes. Now she's landed smack in the middle of this one as well. That's one too many coincidences for me, Sir. That's what I want to focus on – at least for now."

"Very well, I'll ask for the files, but remember; it is time that is important here. If there are links between the cases you can be certain the vultures from the Press won't waste any time in drawing on the similarities. All we need is for some smartarse to get hold of the names of those involved and all hell will be let loose. Talk to Stevens a.s.a.p. – I get the feeling he knows a great deal more about this case than we do. At least Mark Jakes is safely locked up, but that again poses the question: how can these cases be linked? The evidence as I remember was overwhelming. Keep your eyes on the road, McAdams."

"Yes, sorry Sir," Jeff reduced speed and swung into the slow lane to allow a large white van to overtake. "I fully intend to tackle Stevens at the first opportunity."

"Yes; well we still need to act on the possibility that the Reid girl and this Jakes could have been acting together. Even though, as you say, it seems unlikely, we have to keep in mind that Lady Clara has friends in high places. Our heads could be on the block over this if what she believes turns out to be true and we have ignored it. I agree with you in some respects. My reason for wanting a tail on Fiona Reid apart from anything else is to see if someone else is watching her. That's what I want you to focus on, Superintendent. Oh, and another thing; I want you to keep DI Reid on the periphery of this case, at least for the present."

"What do you mean exactly by the periphery, Sir?"

"I mean that until we can either implicate or rule out her sister-in-law from this investigation, I want DI Reid distanced from any knowledge that Fiona Reid is the focus of it. And that, McAdams, is a direct order."

Jeff gritted his teeth. His irritation getting the better of him, he said, "Am I to take it that you want me to lead this investigation with my hands tied behind my back? Sandra Reid is one of the best investigators this unit's ever had. You are aware of the special training she's had in profiling? She has an uncanny ability, Sir. I am loath to do without it, especially since, as you say, time is of the essence."

"I'm well aware of DI Reid's training, McAdams. I'm also aware that she is volatile at the present time. Nobody can go through what she did and come out the other end without being affected by it. She's understandably damaged. If circumstances were different I'd transfer her to a desk post: office manager or the like. But there's no getting away from the fact that we are under pressure. I've never seen resources as tightly stretched as ours are now. The sooner the new unit opens the better. I'm warning you, McAdams; don't overrule me on this one. I want you to work with Stevens as second-in-command; he's well educated, experienced and bright; you won't have any problems in that respect."

"That's a bit of a double standard wouldn't you say, Sir? He's personally involved in this too."

"Nobody will know that, though, will they? You're to keep the lid on that too. As far as the rest of the team is concerned you will tell them you have identified the third name on the list, but for reasons of security the Home Office has declared it classified."

"Nothing more guaranteed to have everyone adding up two and two and coming up with five, if you don't mind my saying so!" Biting his lip, Jeff picked up speed again and move back into the middle lane.

Millar tapped his finger on the dash to emphasise his words, "I needn't tell you that this team needs to be watertight. I trust you to see to that, Superintendent."

Jeff did not hide his dismay. He knew just how personally Sandra would take it when she realised the turn this case was taking – and there was no question that she would indeed recognise that turn. It was a second nature to her; always had been; she knew instinctively when something was amiss. He would just have to go along with it for now, though. At the minute, as far as he was concerned, Sandra was a lot saner than the man beside him. Opus Dei indeed! But orders were orders: Fiona Reid was to be his focus whether he liked it or not; his gut feeling was that she was incapable of having been knowingly involved in a crime of this nature – quite the contrary. In fact, he found he was increasingly worried for her safety.

Arriving back at the station, Jeff walked quickly ahead of Millar. All his instincts were telling him that there was something decidedly odd about the Chief Super's attitude. Was it the involvement of Lady Clara? Was he worried about his eventual promotion to Assistant Chief Constable? That had to be it; but Jeff couldn't help thinking that something else was lurking in the shadows of this investigation. He couldn't quite put his finger on what.

Leonard Millar walked at a determined pace to his office and moved straight to his desk. He was livid. He dialled the number of her private line.

"It's Leonard. It is proceeding as we had hoped, though he took some convincing. I think you took up the wrong career, my dear. You should have gone on the stage; my only fear is that you've over cooked it!"

As he spoke, he glanced up at the framed picture of the Sacred Heart. "It was unfair of you to use Opus Dei in such a way and I will state here and now that I am not amused at your lack of respect; for my faith or that of my daughter! For pity's sake; why in God's name could you not have told me before?"

On the other end of the line, Lady Clara laughed. "You amaze me, Leonard. Have you grown into a protective father overnight? There was no need – I didn't think you'd be interested: it wasn't exactly planned, was it!"

"That's hardly the point. Look here, Clara; I will not have my beliefs jibed at in this way, nor those of my daughter or any member of her family. It is her safety that concerns me. I told you we needed to tread carefully. You have not changed at all, have you; still only interested in yourself. You need to tell your son the truth. Believe me, the truth will find its way to the surface. It always does, sooner or later. If it were only me at risk of losing everything, I would blow the whole thing wide open right now. And if Sheila knows who is behind it, why didn't she contact me herself?"

"That I don't know, Leonard, but whoever it is, they seem to want more people than Fiona to suffer. Maybe I exaggerated just a bit, but it worked didn't it – and remember, I am on that list too."

"It remains to be seen whether either you or Fiona are any safer, but there's nothing else we can do for now. I still feel we would stand a better chance if we explained it all to McAdams. He is a good detective, you know, and trustworthy. I wish we could take him into our confidence; if only we knew who is behind all this; and more to the point, *why*? It's like he's reaching out from the grave."

"I think it highly likely that he is. I suppose if it comes to it and there is no other way, then we will have to tell McAdams. But I worked hard to get where I am, Leonard, and I intend to stay here for as long as I can – and you have your eyes on promotion, I don't doubt. Look, I'm sorry, but I've a call waiting. We will find out at White Cliffs soon enough. You will come?"

Leonard sighed, "Yes; yes. I'll pick you up at the station here in Maidstone on Thursday afternoon – shall we say 5pm – we can travel down together. What about the others?"

"I'll try to make some enquiries about them before then. Interestingly, Karen contacted me a few days ago. You know she is a writer now? She wanted my views on her new book. She's quite successful, evidently. Apparently I'm not the only one of us who is creative!"

Leonard heard the laughter in her voice and it irritated the hell out of him. Damn the woman! Why did he let her get to him like this?

"Leonard? Are you still there?"

"Yes. Has anyone else made contact besides Karen?

"No. I'll try to make some enquiries before Thursday, but time changes people, Leonard. They could be impossible to find. We've all hidden our past so well; they might not want to dredge it up, especially now. Only Sheila and I knew about Fiona, so it's unlikely any of them realise what is going on, but if they do, it is more than likely they will not wish to go anywhere near that damned cottage!"

"Have you considered that it might be a trap – a way of getting you all together?"

"Yes, of course I have! Why else do you think I want you to come!

This needs to be resolved, as you say; once and for all. Must go; I'll be in touch before Thursday."

The line disconnected. Leonard Millar dropped the phone, folded his arms on the table and thought about his daughter and the danger she was in. All these years she had been alive when he thought she was dead. He should have been angry at Sheila for not telling him the truth all those years ago, but he couldn't bring himself to feel that way. It was all too much to bear. Before he knew it his face was wet with tears. Racked with remembered grief, he bent his head into his arms and as so often before, replayed the scene in his head.

It was May, 1971:

The Imperial Ballrooms in Gravesend. The spotlight singled out the saxophone player. Hunched over, face straining with exertion, he held onto the note. All around him women were standing on tables, wriggling their hips and cheering. A few moments more and the drummer started it off again.

The waitress appeared in front of him, tray in hand; set his drink down in front of him and smiled waiting courteously. She seemed different from the rest – or so he liked to think. He'd already noticed the expression on her face – more so in her eyes – when an unwelcome hand tried to slip up her skirt. She was not meant for a place like this. He glanced around the dimly lit room at the cheering audience. Rock stars, footballers, actors most of them: fancy clothes, eye-catching jewels and the drink – fountains of the stuff. Then there were the suits: politicians and entrepreneurs, not forgetting some other noteworthy figures; the top brass of his own profession. None that knew him, though – of course.

Alan Cunningham he was to them. Son of an American oil magnate; educated here in England at Oxford; a rich kid with endless amounts of Daddy's money to spend. That was the story behind him. All invented months ago to get him onto the register of private members here at the Imperial. He took out his wallet, placed a crisp twenty on the tray and smiled at the girl. He did not raise his hand to touch her up as he did with the others. They were all part of the role that he played, but whatever it was about this one, he couldn't bring himself to do it to her. On numerous occasions, when she bent over to set the glasses on his table, he had caught sight of the bruised skin revealed by the plunging neckline of her top. Whoever she was, it was clear she received enough manhandling without him adding to it. He followed her movements to the other tables. A big guy, belly protruding out of his shirt had grabbed her arm. Leonard clenched his teeth as he watched the man swing back his arm and smack it hard against the back of her skirt, enough to throw her off her feet. Glasses smashed; all those at the table laughed and cheered. Two large, burly men appeared out of nowhere and lifting her to her feet escorted her away. God! He hated this place.

"Mr Cunningham; if you would, please follow me."

He looked up, was handed a card: an invitation to a private party. A nerve jumped in his stomach: this was it; he was in. He followed the waiter; side-stepping the dancers beyond the bandstand to a door at the side of the kitchen entrance. The waiter moved fast around corners, up corridors, down three flights of stairs. He entered a lift, pressed the button. Leonard swallowed hard as it jolted. As the lift descended, his stomach churned on the steak and booze he had consumed that evening. The doors opened into a casino, packed tight with men and women: the upper crust. He moved quickly, still following the waiter. Down more steps to a leather padded door. Two beefy arm-wrestler types ornamented each side. The waiter nodded at one who thumped the door twice, reached for the handle and opened the door. The waiter stood back and with a nod, Leonard passed through.

This was his aim; the other private membership he had been striving to gain. Now it looked as if the operation would be a success.

"Mr Cunningham, come in and make your self comfortable. Somebody get him a drink!"

He looked for the voice; could it be? He felt his heart skip as his eyes focused on Kenneth McMasters seated at a large, mahogany desk. Finally, after two years of trying to pin down this man: the last of the big-time gang-leaders, Leonard was poised to infiltrate his ranks. All he had to do now was act calm; not make any slips. He was Alan Cunningham: he had a one-hundred foot yacht moored at the marina. He had arranged a trip for some of his new friends in the hope that McMasters, who must be aware that the coastguard was watching his regular boats, would take the bait.

McMasters was a huge man. Probably in his late forties, but

over-indulgence with food and drink made him appear older. He had been moving drugs; dispersing them across Europe. On the outside he was clean; a third-generation MP; one of the country's most prominent businessmen. He and his brother had inherited McMasters Pharmaceuticals. Until recently, all the investigators had to go on were rumours; now they could gather the evidence they needed and put an end to this man's illegal empire; the drug ring that destroyed so many people's lives.

Leonard accepted the drink with an easy smile: it was his third brandy; he was not supposed to take more than two. Large, cream-leather couches were placed at random in this vast room, which reeked of cigar smoke. McMasters's desk was perched on a platform at one end, up a rise of several steps. The carpet was a plush, deep wine; the pile ankle deep. A shady character, tall, skinny and unshaven leant over one end of the desk. McMasters spoke to him in a low tone. Money was counted and recounted then packed into a case. The skinny fellow turned, stared Leonard down then took the case and left through a door at the back of the room.

Apparently focused on the bouquet of his brandy, Leonard surreptitiously counted heads. There were about ten, maybe twelve other men in the room. Having seen that McMasters had accepted this newcomer, Cunningham, into their company, they had turned their attention back to the young women who were variously draped on their laps. There were several, presumably supplied to keep the men entertained. Dressed scantily, lounging provocatively, their sinuous movements reminded Leonard of a nest of snakes.

With a clap of his hands, McMasters sent them slinking from the room. It was, Leonard assumed, time to get down to business.

"I'm honoured, Mr Cunningham, that you've accepted my invitation to our elite gathering."

"The honour is all mine," Leonard smiled. It was only now the women had left the room that he was able to get a good look at the men around him. His back stiffened as hard faces introduced themselves to him. This was the gang; these men all dressed in tux's. He had noted them, week after week, mingling smoothly with the clientele in the ballroom somewhere above him. Down here they seemed a lot rougher round the edges.

"I've been watching you Mr Cunningham!"

Leonard suppressed a spasm of fear; had he been found out? He tried to relax.

McMasters had moved down from the desk and taken a seat across from him. "I think I know what your tastes are. You see, if you want to be part of the action here you have to accept the little gifts that I give you from time to time."

"Gifts?" Leonard, his mouth dry, forced his lips to bend in a lazy smile.

"Patience, Mr Cunningham!" McMasters laughed and nodded at one of the men who got up and left the room. Another put on some music. More drink was served. The door opened and the man re-entered dragging someone roughly behind him. Leonard's heart sank to the pit of his stomach as he saw it was the girl. Her head was bowed; he could see she was shaking. He could feel the excitement of the men around him. McMasters stood; reached out and pulled the girl over to stand in front of him. Leonard looked up at her face; saw the tears spilling from her eyes.

"I've been watching you lust after this one, Cunningham."

He felt guilty; yes he had watched her, but he had not been driven by lust. He despised the way women were treated in this place. He was filled with an almost uncontrollable rage; an urge to punch McMasters's lights out. But he couldn't let it show; there was too much at stake here. Swirling the brandy in his glass, he smirked at McMasters. "I didn't realise it was that obvious."

"Well here she is; my gift for you. You can have her all to yourself: Enjoy! McMasters laughed and flung the girl at Leonard, "You don't mind if we watch, do you?"

She landed on top of him, her head hitting his cheekbone. His immediate concern was for her. She raised herself slowly. From above him her eyes burned into his; he would always remember that brief moment: her look of understanding that he was different from the rest of them, that he was forced into this position just as she was. Before he could react, she had undone the ties of the silk wrap in which she had been clothed for the occasion. As she pulled apart the opening, her breasts fell forward, naked and exposed.

Leonard felt himself react to what he was seeing, at the same time wishing he could reach out and cover her back up.

"Come on man! She's yours – or maybe you need some help?"

He tried to grin; "Too much booze!" he slurred. "Can I take a rain check?" As he spoke, he felt her body shudder as she knelt, straddled over him. Offered to him like a piece of meat and if he didn't perform they would ravish her like a pack of hungry wolves. Months of painstaking, dangerous police work would be wasted and he would end up dead. Leonard knew what he had to do. She was staring at him with huge, sad eyes. He read in them her message: *'Do it now. Please just do it now! Please now!'* She egged him on tussling with his zip, releasing his erection that, despite everything, was ready for her.

He raised her to her feet, lifting and turning her, he gently pushed her into a kneeling position, hugging her tightly against the chair-back so that he shrouded her from view.

Entering her from behind, his face pressed against her hair, he thrust into her, the raucous cheers all around them drowning out her cries. He turned his mouth to her ear, his sweat mingling with her tears as he whispered over and over until it was done: *"I'm sorry, I'm sorry, I'm sorry…"*

22

Maidstone: later on Tuesday 23rd October

Sandra was out of breath by the time she reached the morgue. A quick glance at her watch showed she'd probably missed most of the autopsy. Peering through the glass as she pulled on her protective suit, she realised that Harris, Leslie's assistant, was heading towards her pushing a covered trolley: the remains of Matt Lyons, she read on the tag as he stopped. She stood back as Harris hit the plastic box on the wall to open the doors. Sliding past him she nodded at Stevens as he looked up from his perch on a stool by the autopsy table. Sandra took up position beside Leslie, who was speaking into the microphone hanging from a beam above her head.

"Case number 378," the pathologist said clearly, adding in a side whisper, "he must have been trying to save me some work! The opening cut on this one is clean; almost professional."

Returning to the task in hand, Leslie inserted the scalpel, cutting beneath the dead woman's breasts and instantly created a Y shape: the killer had already cut an oval to open up Peggy Lyons's belly. Sandra shut her eyes, feeling the snap of the breast plate in every one of her bones. For a brief moment she wasn't sure if she could bear to stand her ground.

Leslie was peering into the cadaver's chest. "I've just told Stevens here that traces of ordinary salt were found in and around the mouth."

What did that mean? Sandra wondered: *preservative or cleanser*? She took out her pad and scribbled a note as Leslie was handing the vital organs to Harris for weighing.

"Aha!" The pathologist bent over the cavity. "Now then; I wonder what you will both make of this." She stood back, "Have a look!" As Sandra and Stevens leant closer, she said, "Do you see? There's no womb," she directed a questioning gaze at Sandra.

So? Sandra thought, surprised when Stevens sped to the other side of the table to gain an unobstructed view. Why should that excite him? Quite a number of women had lost their wombs by the time they got to Peggy's age.

"You mean she's had a hysterectomy. Hardly unusual," Sandra said for his benefit.

"No, I'm afraid not. There's no old scarring around the tissues, just fresh wounds; quite ragged cuts here too, I might add."

Sandra gasped, horrified by the implication: "You mean the killer has taken it?"

"I fear so," Leslie agreed.

Then we might have a collector on our hands, Sandra thought, dismayed, her stomach heaving. She was puzzling about the ragged use of the knife to obtain the womb when the outer cuts and been so neat; almost professional Leslie had said. Was it significant? Had it been deliberate, or had the killer been rushed at the end?

"Wait a minute what's this!" Leslie had moved her attention away from the cadaver's mutilated stomach and Sandra, seeing the area where the pathologist was now focusing her attention, had to remind herself that it was mandatory to examine all orifices. Even so, she was gripped by an overwhelming surge of embarrassment for the deceased woman on the table. There was no dignity here; Peggy was like a piece of meat on a butcher's slab.

Leslie brought up her hand, something cylindrical clutched bloodily in her fingers. Taking it over to one of the sinks, she used a swab to clean it off. "It looks almost like a chrysalis only it's way too big."

"A chrysalis?" Stevens asked, exuding an air of suppressed excitement. "From where exactly did you retrieve it?"

"In what is commonly called the birth canal," Leslie answered dryly, shooting a concerned glance at Sandra.

Sandra was sickened. They had shared some nasty discoveries over this table in the past and now it looked as if this case would be another twisted one. Given Peggy Lyons's age, she had not expected this killing to be sexually motivated. She glared at Stevens feeling that his reaction was somehow inappropriate.

Catching her gaze, he said "Can I leave you to it here?"

Sandra was surprised; he had seemed almost to be enjoying this autopsy. "Okay, but where are you going? Leslie is not finished yet."

Treating them both to a gorgeous smile, he moved to lift his notes from the stool, at the same time pulling off his plastic suit. "I'm going to look up a butterfly expert; I've got a hunch. Leslie, would you have that chrysalis thing readied for examination?"

"Sure, will do; I'll get Harris to see to it right away." As the door closed behind him, Leslie shot Sandra a knowing look and smiled. "Is Millar letting the girls have a say in choosing the new recruits these days? What a dish! I don't mind admitting I have had some decidedly naughty thoughts since he got here."

"Now, now; cradle snatcher! I thought you were into more mature men."

"Hell girl, I'm not that old. Besides, a little spice now and then works wonders. Quality rather quantity every so often doesn't do us any harm," she smirked, added, "even if it does always end too quickly! Is he here for long?"

"I really don't know much about him. It's funny, though; he reminds me of someone. There's a tinge of familiarity about him – as if we've met before somewhere."

"Oh, I'll be getting familiar with him alright: tonight in my dreams – you can be sure of that!" the pathologist laughed returning her attention to the table.

Sandra understood Leslie's apparent need for levity. She had been the same; once. If we don't laugh, we'll cry, she thought, perching on Stevens' vacated stool to add to her notes. The true extent of the unspeakable pain the victim had suffered was clearly evident. Sandra found she was shivering; suddenly, the room seemed unbearably cold. She spared Peggy Lyons a final look of sympathy as Leslie went to the sink to cleanse her hands and Harris proceeded to sew up the cavity.

Moving through to the office to wait, Sandra re-read her notes: 'Salt in mouth; womb taken – ragged cut – trophy? Object in birth canal – chrysalis.' *What message was the killer sending?* Stevens seemed to be on the ball. Shit! Sandra slammed her notebook down on the desk. She'd forgotten to ask him about Fiona's statement; how had it gone? She checked her mobile; there were still no messages.

Leslie pushed open the door with her elbow, a mug of coffee in each hand. "Jeff phoned earlier to see if you were here. He actually stayed on the phone long enough to tell me he thinks you would appreciate some company. I think he's worried about how you're coping. Do you want to talk about it? Have you fixed our dinner date yet?"

"Sorry, not had time, but I haven't forgotten." Sandra shrugged; a guilty reflex. She knew she ought to try to explain what she felt; that she needed to keep her torment to herself. There was a time when she used to confide in her friends, but now she felt too exposed. Leslie had settled into her swivel chair, crossing her legs. She had changed into her trouser suit and Sandra detected the scent of Estee Lauder's *Pleasures*. Leslie always used it liberally to mask the odour of formalin that clung to her from the morgue.

"Should you be here at all Sandra?"

"I need to keep busy or I'll go crazy."

"Well, if you think that's best, but I'm worried about you my friend."

"Please don't be." Sandra felt like a cornered animal. Everyone wanted to help, but there was nothing they could do. She needed to escape. She looked up at the clock on the wall. "Heavens; is that the time? I'd better get back to the station. Look, thanks for the coffee. Will you fax over a copy of the report so far as it stands?" Gathering her things, she moved to the door.

"As soon as it's ready and I'll highlight the necessaries for you. Remember, if you need to talk you only have to lift the phone."

Leslie watched the door close behind her and sat for a moment, lost in thought. Shaking her head, she muttered, "Poor girl, you've no idea what's ahead of you. God help you." She sighed heavily, swivelled round to her work station and proceeded to write her report.

23

Jeff strode into the incident room a minute before 6pm Sandra was sitting with her back to the door on one of the desks beside the window, gently swinging her legs. She looked across the room. It reminded her of school: the same mess at the end of a day; bins full of sandwich packaging and squashed paper cups; chairs cleared of occupants gone for the day, all save a few uniformed officers recruited from downstairs and staring bleary-eyed at computer screens.

The continuous hum of the photocopier sounded from the corner where Keith Jones was gathering up a sheaf of papers. He crossed the room towards her and took a seat nearby. Sandra managed to afford him a slight nod that was neither enthusiastic nor disparaging. She studied him as he bent to tidy his notes. His vibrant ginger mop fell unkempt about his face. His pointed goatee and finely shaped moustache always made her think of an Elizabethan courtier; all he needed was a pair of tights and a ruff! The association brought Elle to the front of her mind: she wondered how the audition had gone today.

"So where's the new boy?" Jones asked her.

"Following up on something at the morgue."

"What do you make of him, Sandra? I can't help noticing he seems to get on well with you ladies. Suckers for a handsome face, you lot."

"What's wrong Keith? Afraid he's stealing the limelight? You'll have to stand in line at the club on Friday night. He'll be away with the pick of the crop while you're still eyeing up the stragglers."

"You think so? We'll see about that," Jones leered.

Sandra was relieved to see Jeff heading towards them. It saved her from giving way to the irresistible urge to tell Jones exactly what she – and most of her female colleagues – thought of him. He was an unsavoury character: the type who thought he was God's gift and that every woman was merely waiting her chance to drop her knickers for him. He had moved to Jeff's team from Vice some months after Sandra's attack and she had taken an instant dislike to him. In her view, he had become too much like the pimps he'd grown used to dealing with; a mind like an open sewer. It had come to her ears that in the days following Gerry's death, Jones had passed some derogatory remarks – he thought of them as jokes – about her marriage. For that alone she would have disliked him. For the sake of team stability, she kept her thoughts to herself, but was grateful to Christine for keeping her informed. It helped to know what you were up against and who your friends were. Jones was certainly not one of them.

She turned to greet Jeff, masking her weariness with a wide smile. After what Leslie had said, she didn't want him worrying about the toll the autopsy had taken.

He acknowledged her greeting, his eyes widening in surprise. "Anything show up on the traffic footage, Jones?" he put the bundle of papers he was carrying on the desk that Sandra was sitting on and leaned his buttock against it, one leg tucked behind the other.

"Not a thing, Guv, this boy – if he is a boy – must have known his way about. Nothing! Not even a cat's whisker moved outside DI Reid's house last night."

"It's still possible he slipped around the back to get away. Sandra thinks she heard an intruder around dawn, that right?" He swung round to Sandra, who nodded. "Right, go over the tapes again, Jones. You must have missed something."

"But—" Jones bit off his objection as Jeff drilled him with a glare. "Yes, Guv."

"Let's move on, then. Sandra, anything come out of your meeting with Marshton? And what about the autopsy? Did Leslie uncover anything that we can work with?"

"A few bits and pieces, nothing substantial." With a quick look at Jones loitering beside them, Sandra shot Jeff a pleading look. For some reason, she couldn't bring herself to discuss Peggy Lyons's womb and birth canal with Jones's ears flapping beside her.

For once she was glad of Jeff's sensitivity. He directed his gaze at Jones, "Was there something?"

"No, Guv."

"Then get on with it, will you?"

"Sir," a sheepish grin spreading over his face, Jones backed away.

Sandra breathed a sigh of relief and Jeff seated himself on the vacated chair. They discussed the prelims of the autopsy and touched on the profile she was building. The actions of the killer were almost certainly those of a lone, probably male attacker. Jeff seemed relieved; less so when she added that he was possibly a collector; a serial killer. She highlighted the indicators putting them up on the board, stressing her conviction that they needed to locate the women from the list as quickly as possible.

"So, you think the killer is the grown-up child of one of the mothers who gave him up for adoption, rather than someone acting on behalf of the women themselves?"

Sandra shook her head, "I can't rule the mothers out yet, Jeff. Nor can I rule out siblings. It could be that someone is trying to prevent a scandal, but I've a feeling it's more twisted than that. There were no indications of sexual assault as such, that is to say, no semen, but the insertion of an object deep into the vagina obviously has sexual connotations. And yet I'm not getting that kind of vibe from this scene. There's more to it, something I'm not seeing." Sandra shrugged, "I've a way to go yet, Jeff. Sorry."

"I wouldn't expect otherwise, Sandra. It's early days."

"I obtained quite a bit of background from Reverend Marshton. It seems that Peggy Lyons was intent on giving these women a start in life. She was generous; motivated by kindness; wanted to help. Remembering her own situation, I think she hoped they would keep their babies rather than give them away. Indeed, there is every possibility that at least some of the women kept their babies and moved on to build successful lives for themselves. What makes it so difficult is that by the very nature of their circumstances, it is likely that whoever they were, they will not want to be found. Especially if...."

"What?"

"Well, it's just a theory, but supposing, for example, that one or more of the women have achieved some kind of celebrity status in later life. It is this possibility, however remote, that prompts me to raise the prevention of scandal as a possible motive."

As always, Jeff was impressed by Sandra's perspicacity. With so little to go on she had already come very close to hitting the nail on the head – at least as far as Lady Clara Smith-Stevens was concerned. It was too good an opportunity to miss; reluctantly, he took it and told Sandra what he could. Feeling like a Judas, he explained as much as he was permitted to tell her. The intervention from on high, he said, did not allow him to reveal the name of the one woman that had now been identified: the third alias on the list.

"Well – there you are then. Like I said!" Sandra's eyes glinted with satisfaction. "But how did this woman get to know of the list? We've got it under wraps, surely?"

Jeff looked down at his feet, momentarily embarrassed. He hated to lie; damn Millar. "She read about the murder in the papers, recognised the names. I suppose there are quite a number of women out there shaking in their shoes, afraid their secrets will come out over this. If we don't make any progress locating them in the next few days, we'll have to consider using the media to get them to come forward."

Sandra shifted her gaze from Jeff's bent head and looked out across the car park. It was plausible she thought, wondering how many women out there had secrets like that; managed to keep them hidden from the world. She'd kept one too; if she hadn't had an abortion she might have ended up on a list like that... She slammed the lid down on the thought. No; don't go there. Quickly she grasped at something else to think about. *Aya of Mons: I wonder who you are.* It seemed strange to Sandra that she was not considered sufficiently trustworthy to be allowed into the circle of knowledge. She detected in Jeff's demeanour that he was not telling her everything. There was almost a tremor in his voice; a kind of shifty expression that did not suit him at all. She had thought he was her friend. Suddenly, she was not so sure.

Sandra watched a car's headlights swerving out of the car park below. She hated this time of year, the evenings drawing in. Inwardly she shrugged, turning her gaze back to the room. Okay; if this was the way it was going to be, she would just have to play along with it. She knew in her heart the way it was. The way it really was. Knew that Millar had laid down the law. She had no doubt that it was because of Fiona. *I'm regarded as a liability because of her.* Well what else could she have expected? Poor Jeff!

She straightened her back and turned to face him. There was some good news that had been overlooked and she had kicked herself when studying the list of names a short time ago. Why had she not thought of it sooner: "That's two names down then!" she said.

Jeff looked up at her puzzled; doubtless relieved that for now she was masking the disdain he expected to see. "I'm sorry?"

"It should have occurred to me this morning," she said. "Stella Jones. Fiona had already traced her, remember? Several years ago. She had died a short time before. One of those aliases has to refer to her. It was her son who led Fiona to Peggy Lyons. We just need to figure out which is her alias. I'll phone Fiona and get a number for Stella's son to see what her real name was; Stella was her stage name she was a ballet dancer in her day."

"Good, at least we're narrowing the field. Where's Stevens I expected him to be here?"

"He phoned in half an hour ago, he's got some expert examining the object Leslie uncovered during the autopsy. It seems it really is a chrysalis. I'd no idea they could be so large. A few tests need to be run, but it seems it was recently opened and even more interesting, it's of a rare tropical butterfly that could only have come from a specialist collection. The species is known as 'Birdwing' and it wouldn't breed naturally in this country."

"Now that's more like it!" Jones intervened.

Sandra jumped, nearly falling off the desk. She hadn't heard Jones creeping up behind them.

"A real lead at last: our killer either keeps butterflies as a hobby or has access to some anorak's collection." Jones smirked.

His nearness set Sandra's teeth on edge. "Either one or the other. Though Stevens did mention its collection is prohibited."

"Did you turn up anything more on the footage, Jones?" Jeff asked.

"'Fraid not, Guv. Nothing."

"Right; go home and get a good night's rest. Tomorrow I want you to put together a list of places that might be capable of housing such collections: public and private ones. Compile a list of individuals with access to butterflies and follow up on them. You can talk to

Stevens in the morning; get him to fill you in on the particular species involved."

Jones shrugged on the jacket that was draped over one shoulder and bidding them a cheerful goodnight, left them to it.

"Sandra, you'd better get on too. Oh! By the way, I meant to ask, how'd this Marshton fellow come across? Reliable, you think?"

"Not what I had expected at all. He's certainly not one for convalescing under a blanket. Agile as a monkey in fact! But yes – despite his wrinkles, he's as reliable as they come. Actually, I've been thinking about Peggy Lyons: her choice of names for those young women."

"As it happens, I've got something here that PC Blake accessed off the net." Jeff rummaged in his papers, gave up. "They're not made up names as I'd thought. Evidently they all existed in ancient times: Roman Catholic abbesses from various orders, medieval for the most part – or even earlier. Strange aliases to choose."

"It's not all that strange, in fact." Sandra moved down from the desk and pulled a chair over beside him. "Got time for a history lesson?"

Jeff settled back in his chair. "No, but you're going to tell me anyway!" Sandra grinned at him and he found that he was enormously relieved. He had expected her to be in a state after the autopsy. "Go on then."

"Peggy Lyons had a great interest in the Sisters of the Cloth, as Marshton called them. The modern-day version of her home for girls, which she called the 'Priory', is run by nuns even now. But in ancient times, the little church of St Mary's in Higham actually was a priory. The thing is, if you go back before the Reformation – before Henry VIII made himself head of the Church so he could marry Anne Boleyn – any of the medieval priories would have been Roman Catholic in origin. This was a Catholic country then. Hence the list of Catholic abbesses, who all happen to have belonged to various orders; it is not so much the aliases that are odd, as why they were given. The question here is why did Peggy single out this particular handful of girls? What was so special about them? All the other records have proper names and contact details; I checked through them at the scene yesterday. It's obvious that she was trying to conceal something;

but why? I begin to think that there is some meaning to the aliases Peggy meted out. Take this 'Aya of Mons', for example."

Jeff sat forward, intrigued. "What about her?"

"She was generally known as the patroness of lawsuits: she symbolises the power of women to rise above the conditions of their times. What we call the glass ceiling! It seems this Aya was concerned to protect women's integrity, encouraging them to pursue whatever they wanted to achieve. I won't press you to divulge anything you can't, but I am following a hunch here, Jeff. Would I be correct in thinking that this woman you have identified has a job in the legal profession?"

Jeff was stunned. He should have picked up on it already. Or should he? As always, Sandra had impressed him. "Why yes, I suppose her position does fall within those parameters," he admitted. "But Sandra, Mrs Lyons wrote these things down over 35 years ago. The woman in question, as far as I know, was appointed to her position only 5 years ago – that is, unless—" Jeff broke off, his mind working overtime. "Look, Sandra, I think you might be onto something here. I'll find out first thing—"

With a clatter, the door banged open and Stevens came rushing through it, headed straight for them. "Sorry, Sir, got stuck in the evening rush."

Jeff nodded and pointed to a chair. "As I was saying, I'll find out first th—" Again he broke off, suddenly becoming aware that Stevens might be able to tell him sooner than that. His mother must surely have told him about her life after Peggy Lyons set her on the road to prosperity. If he could ascertain that she trained as a lawyer, it might help to deduce what profession the others were in; make it easier to trace them. He would have to get Blake to do some more research. "Look, Sandra, I think we have got as far as we can on this for tonight. Tomorrow I want you to get all you can on the Jones woman. See if she ever told her family of the other girls she met during her time at the Priory. As you say, Peggy Lyons must have had a reason for singling out this particular group of women. It can only be that she wanted to protect their real identities; the question is, why?"

Jeff noticed that Stevens was getting up off his chair and motioned him to stay put. He turned back to Sandra: "Here, while you're at it you can look into this as well. A Miss Edith Hollander was a midwife employed for a time by Peggy Lyons. She might not be lucid enough to be of much help; got her telegram from the Queen a few months ago! She's a resident at Haven's Rest in Rochester. I've spoken with the Matron there and she'll expect you in the morning. You can take Christine with you if she comes in at all tomorrow. The body pulled from the river at Gravesend yesterday afternoon was identified this morning as our missing girl: Tracey Cooper. Christine went with her parents to formally identify the body; she's taking it hard: Sad business! Now get yourself off. And try to get some rest. I will see you when you get back from Rochester."

Sandra nodded, "Okay, you're the boss."

Jeff turned to Stevens. "Right then, Detective Sergeant: my office; now. I think it's time we had that little chat, don't you?"

Jeff's tone stopped Sandra in her tracks. It was the same one he used when addressing a suspect – or reprimanding a junior officer, and then only rarely. Curious, she loitered, tidying her notes and watching over her shoulder as Stevens disappeared behind Jeff into his office. What had Stevens done to ruffle Jeff's feathers? She felt an unwelcome touch of sympathy: it appears you're not in anyone's good books today, Stevens, she muttered – apart from Leslie's, of course! She retrieved several of the photographs taken from Peggy's albums. They might come in useful to jar the elderly midwife's memory. Sandra had the feeling she was on a hiding to nothing; almost as if Jeff was deliberately finding her jobs to do that took her well away from the office. Did he think she was incapable after all? Was she? She shrugged; she was exhausted, most likely she was being paranoid. The midwife could well provide a lead. And Stella Jones too if only she wasn't dead – but there was the aliases angle to look into. She would reserve judgement on Jeff's motives for now. She pulled on her coat and swinging her bag over her shoulder, walked out of the incident room, passing PC Blake, the desk sergeant, hunched over his computer. She called out "Goodnight", but he was apparently oblivious to everything but what was on his screen. As she left, she heard Jeff's raised voice coming from behind the closed door of his office. She was not into eavesdropping; she ignored it and walked on.

"You may or may not be aware that I had the pleasure of a private meeting with your mother today." Jeff raised a hand as Stevens opened his mouth to speak. "Let me finish. I don't much care for upstarts in my team, Stevens, especially ones with their own private agendas." Jeff stood behind his desk and glared at the young man for a moment before continuing. "I've learnt over the years that a good team requires certain things, uppermost amongst them is something called loyalty! It is one thing to have a certain level of healthy competition between officers, but to have a member of my team sneaking around behind my back, making use of an investigation to further his private needs… words fail me! Let me make this absolutely clear: it just won't happen; I'll not have it; not on my watch!" Jeff banged the desk to emphasise his words, remembering that he had done this to another member of the Smith-Stevens family only that morning. It seemed like a long time ago. Abruptly he sat down. "What do you have to say for yourself?"

Stevens shifted in his seat. Jeff was pleased to see that he looked decidedly uncomfortable and was nervously swallowing; his Adam's apple was bobbing up and down like a yoyo.

"I'm sorry, Sir, I know how it must look to you but…," Stevens' voice tailed away.

As usual, having had his say, Jeff's temper rapidly subsided. Millar had more or less ordered him to keep Stevens closely involved with the case. He showed a lot of promise; Jeff didn't want to dent the young man's initiative. "Look son, you're lucky that I've had a few hours to digest all of this. But it has put me in a difficult position; one that I'm none too happy to be in. You have a colleague – and I might add that she is a first-rate officer – heading home now and questioning my confidence in her because she knows she's being sidelined on this case. That concerns me more than you could imagine and I hope for both our sakes it is not going to defeat her. Right now, Sandra Reid needs her confidence boosted. With my hands tied here, I'm knocking it down. I need to fix that and soon. So, DS Stevens, why not tell me your side of things and then we'll look at how we can work on this investigation of yours together?"

Jeff set back and listened as Stevens pretty much covered everything Lady Clara had disclosed that morning. He did; however, raise some interesting questions concerning the Katie Smyth murder, but it was clear to Jeff that Stevens possessed no new information on the Higham murders or the women on the list. One thing he did discover was that Stevens had not raised with his mother the spectre of Opus Dei. When Jeff mentioned it the young man looked both startled and incredulous. The idea must have come from Lady Clara herself, then. Odd that.

Having let a chastened Stevens off duty for the evening, Jeff decided to take a break. He needed to get home; relax for a time. He pushed himself up from the desk, noticed that the red light was flashing on his phone and sat down again. Better pick up his messages.

The first was from an old colleague from years back: Tony Hardy. He jotted down the number Tony had left. It was ages since they had spoken; was Tony still a serving officer or had he retired by now? Jeff shrugged; he would doubtless find out later. The second message was from the desk sergeant at Gravesend Police station. He noted that number down too. He would contact them from home. He stopped at Constable Blake's monitor before he left the incident room. "Can you do something for me, Blake?" He had to say it twice before the young officer heard him.

"Sorry Sir!" Blake looked up, a receptive grin spreading over his face, "Certainly, Sir. More research?"

Jeff nodded: "A Brazilian cardinal by the name of Henrique Carlosanta." Jeff watched as Blake drew a notepad towards him and scribbled down the name. "I need to know as much as possible. Date he entered the priesthood; time spent in England – stuff like that. Oh! And keep it under wraps will you. Take it home with you and slip it to me in the morning."

"Will do, Sir."

"Thank you." Jeff knew he could rely on Blake's discretion. A bit of a nerd, but a good officer. God, it had been a long day. He made his way to the lift; changed his mind and walked slowly down the stairs, his mind going back to Lady Clara Smith-Stevens a.k.a. Aya of Mons. Something about her was not right. But what?

24

Michael took his cappuccino and the extra shot of espresso to a seat at the window. After returning home last night he'd spent several hours revising the file on the case and had, quite literally, slept on what he'd read. He had woken in his study with his arms folded over an image of Gracie; her insides splayed out over the bed where she had died.

The small café was quaint: polished wood floors; bright yellow walls dotted with colourful pottery plates and framed posters of Irish writers along with castles and other tourist attractions. The smell of fresh baking mixed with brewing coffee filled the air.

He was waiting for Father Tom to change out of his vestments following Mass. The café was just around the corner from the church. Dropping his satchel off his shoulder, Michael sipped at the cappuccino until there was enough room for the espresso and poured it in.

"Has no one ever explained to you about the dangers of too much caffeine, Michael?" Father Tom pulled up a chair.

"I'm fighting jet lag and struggling to get over the time change and you're going to tell me to drink cocoa I suppose?" Michael chuckled.

"I would prescribe sleep, my son; a good long sleep."

Michael dismissed the advice with a smile. Sleep was something that would not come easily for some time to come. Knowing Tom as he did, the nights were long for him too: "A case of the pot calling the kettle black if you ask me!"

Father Tom set a bunch of keys on the table and slid them over to Michael. "Can I ask why you're wanting to borrow Sheila's keys? Aside from the fact that she hasn't lived in the house for a very long time, what are you expecting to find that has anything to do with Gracie's murder?"

Michael played with the keys in his hand. "Well, Tom, maybe I'm wrong, but—" he broke off, took another sip of cappuccino, transferred the froth on his lips to his sleeve, continued: "What can you tell me of Gracie's past? It's strange you know; for a woman who knew everything about everybody around here, she never spoke much about herself. Like I said, I could be wrong, but tell me: am I right in thinking Gracie never left this town; lived her whole life within its boundaries?"

Father Tom nodded. "Far as I know that would be about right. I know for a fact she didn't drive. Her husband wasn't a Westportite; came from up north – a blow-in, as I told you – but I suppose you heard plenty about him before now?"

Michael grimaced: " More than enough. I think she was relieved more than anything else when he died."

Glancing out of the window to wave at a young man walking past, Tom nodded. "Sad isn't it, the way some people spend their lives? But Gracie accepted the one she was given; rarely complained; went about with her pal, Mrs Reilly, to the bingo and the odd dance. That's where she was going on the night that... but anyway, all this still doesn't explain where Sheila fits in."

"Well the point is, Tom; Sheila was the housekeeper wasn't she. I read over your statement about the phone call. The caller, you said, asked for the 'housekeeper' – he didn't ask for Gracie by name."

"No; he didn't; and I'll tell you something else that's been bothering me about him, Michael: his accent."

"Could you place it?"

"That's just it. I tell you; the thing about these parts is that for a good few months of the year, I have a visiting flock to preach to and, well, they'll be from all ends of the country, you understand. I've got to recognise practically every dialect from one end of Ireland to the other. I couldn't place his at all, Michael. There was something about it; not quite right; almost like someone in a film."

"Manufactured you mean; like a put-on?"

"I guess that's what I mean. Maybe he's spent time in several areas, picked up bits of this and that dialect; could be that as well." Father Tom sighed. "I don't know, Michael; I stood in front of those poor souls this morning and what can I say to them? The apprehension; the fear; I could see it in their faces. When I think that someone capable of an evil like that is somewhere about here, walking amongst us, I find it hard to know what to say to myself, never mind them!"

Michael leaned closer, said quietly, "Look Father; there's not much I can divulge at present, but I think we can be sure he's long gone. And it's a safe enough bet that he's not from about here."

"How can you be sure, my son?"

"I'm sure for a start that he has killed before; we will find other murders on the books that are similar in nature, I am certain of it. That being so, when was the last time you heard of one like this anywhere in Ireland?"

"Ah. I see what you mean." Father Tom thought for a moment. "And what about Sheila? Where does she fit in?"

"That's what I want to find out. There's always something that connects the victim to the killer. A crime like that is unlikely to be random. How well travelled was Sheila?"

Father Tom's expression changed and Michael knew he was on the right track.

Later that day, Michael, accompanied by Sergeant O'Leary and for a short while by Father Tom, searched Sheila's room at the parochial house. It was large and airy, decorated with flower-patterned wallpaper and furnished with a selection of highly polished, matching rosewood furniture that included a bed and a double wardrobe. It also had a comfortable thick-cushioned sofa with a TV taking up one corner. As Michael quickly discovered, the room was devoid of any of Sheila's personal effects. Much like a guest room, as though someone had been there for a short stay, there was a small selection of clothes, toiletries, a few books; but that was it. Yet Sheila had lived at the parochial house on and off for almost twenty years. Where was her past?

"I'm not quite sure where you're coming from Mike," O'Leary stood back from a chest of drawers, his arms folded. "Even if, as you think, Gracie was in the wrong place at the wrong time, what would have been so different about Sheila McBride? Had she been the one who was murdered, I mean. Wouldn't it have been just as senseless?"

"Possibly; possibly not." Michael was disappointed. There was nothing here. They moved on to Sheila's family home, which was about half a mile out of town on the Newport road. The house had been turned into two separate flats. The bottom one was let out on a long-term lease to Paddy O'Farrell, a local artist, whom they met in the drive unloading suitcases. He had just returned from a trip abroad. He had taken on the lease about six years ago, he said, and never saw much of Sheila. She had never let out the top flat during his time here, but from time to time she spent a few hours in it herself; cleaning he had supposed. He hadn't seen her in a long while.

Father Tom went off to tend his flock, and Michael and O'Leary spent the next few hours searching Sheila's flat. O'Leary wandered about studying paintings; opening and closing wardrobes and cupboards whilst Michael sat for a time in each room, getting a feel for the woman whom he suspected had been the intended victim. The flat was filled with a mixture of furniture, all of it dated; it had probably belonged to her brother. The kitchen, though, was a more recent addition, put in during the renovation when the house was divided into flats.

Michael was again disappointed. Perhaps his hunch was wrong; maybe it had been a random killing after all. There was nothing here that set Sheila McBride apart. It could be the home of any other woman of similar age and intellect living alone. The photographs on the mantelpiece were all pre-sixties: black and white portraits of family members; nothing recent. What did he expect? Sheila would not have been the type to pose for snaps. Yet all his instincts told him there had to be something here; something that had drawn the killer to this place; to Sheila. There had to be a link. Where was it?

"She's got a great selection of books, I'll give her that." O'Leary had opened the top button of his shirt and loosened his tie. The heating had clicked on at 4pm and the flat was getting quite warm. "She'll be well enough read if she's made her way through all of these." He fingered through the titles in the built-in bookcase: history of art; medieval history; politics; religion; some of this stuff's real heavy."

Michael glanced up from the writing desk where he had taken a seat. In a drawer he had found a brown envelope that appeared to be quite old. Emptying the contents he watched as a pile of yellowed newspaper clippings fell onto the desk. Puzzled he studied them, leafing his way through the pile.

O'Leary moved over to stand beside him, and read out loud the headline of the first cutting on the pile: *Bonfire Night Fire Claims Two*

Lives. "She lost her husband and son in a boathouse fire in Kent," O'Leary said, added, "that's how she got her scars."

Below the caption, a photograph showed the burnt out remains of a boat that appeared to be still smouldering against a riverbank. Michael checked the date: 1971; almost 36 years ago. He read on: *Mother weeps as family is wiped out.* His gaze travelled back to the crowd of onlookers. In amongst them, though much younger and her face partially hidden, he thought he recognised Sheila McBride. Clearly she was grief-stricken: her body was limp, held upright by the people on either side of her, one on each arm. He studied the picture more closely: the smoke rising from the boat; the fire engine; the array of hoses crisscrossing the ground. Sheila's scarred face flashed into his mind. If she had received those injuries in that fire there was no evidence of them here. Wouldn't she have been rushed straight to hospital if that were the case?

"Didn't you say she was burned in that fire? Look Todd; look at her face."

"That's what she told everyone," O'Leary said, lifting the cutting to examine it more closely. "Why would she say that if it wasn't true? Why would she do that?"

"Who knows?" Michael was sifting through the other cuttings, passing each one to O'Leary as he read them. Most were of the fire. Evidently arson had been suspected at first. There had been a tradition of boat burning in Gravesend, a practice going back for centuries, apparently. It was concluded that a group of revellers, drunk after the bonfire night celebrations, had thought the boat disused and set it alight. A later cutting carried the report that the police investigation was now centred on one of the victims. It seemed that Jack Hynds, 35, had been involved in drug smuggling and other outlawed activities. His son, aged nearly six, had been with him on the boat. Both bodies when recovered were barely identifiable. Poor Sheila! Obviously she had dropped her married name to avoid publicity. She would hardly want to be associated with a man like this Jack Hynds; but to have lost her son like that. Michael shook his head in pity. Once again he wondered about her burns. There was nothing here to explain it.

The next cutting was much later: a report of a car accident in another part of Kent: *Six Die In Unexplained Head On Collision.* The date was July 1978. The cutting had been torn off carelessly; there was no further information beyond a list of those who died.

"When did Sheila McBride come home to Westport?" Michael asked, scanning the names.

O'Reilly thought for a moment. "In the mid-eighties as far as I know; but she lived in Dublin for a good time before that. Worked in a hospital run by the Church; you know, a rehab centre for winos, druggies and the like. She came back here after her brother died, she had quite a sizeable inheritance, property mostly: the family house and lands, a few holiday cottages, even a pub in the village, but she closed it down. As I recall, she told me she'd left England a short time after that fire, so that would have been in the early seventies. Then, of course, she had that heart attack; she was in hospital in Galway for quite a time after that."

"Any of her family involved in that RTA, do you know?"

Checking the cutting Michael handed him, O'Reilly shook his head. "I don't know any of the names. Maybe they were friends of hers."

Michael shrugged; there was no knowing what Sheila's interest was in the car accident, but she must have kept the clip for some reason. The next was a piece torn from a personal column dated 1st August, 1988. A ring had been penned round a simple boxed notice that in large, bold type read: '**RON IS DEAD**'. Who the devil was Ron? Following a hunch, Michael re-read the names of the people involved in the car accident; there was no 'Ron'. He wondered idly why Sheila had ringed it – presumably it was Sheila – it must have some significance for her to have kept it, but there was no way of telling what that might be. The remainder of the clips were all novenas to St Brigit. No dates; the pleas varied from one to the next. Michael had seen many of these in the local paper. Sheila McBride had most likely cut them out as part of a personal record of her own novenas. It was something of a practice in this part of Ireland.

"What do you think Michael?" O'Reilly said, peering over his shoulder.

"There certainly seems to be a story behind it," Michael tidied the pile of cuttings, returned them to the envelope and handed it to the Sergeant. "But only Sheila can tell us what it is. I would like to get in touch with her, but I gather she left no contact number and refuses to carry a mobile. She told Father Tom she was taking a few weeks away.

Perhaps she told someone at the hospital in Galway where she was going; it's worth a try. In the meantime, I'll talk to old Father Mullan and see if he has remembered anything more."

O'Leary shoved the envelope into his jacket pocket. "Right; well I'll get onto this station in Gravesend; see if they can dig up anymore about the fire that killed her husband and son. It should still be in their archive given her husband's record. Who knows; maybe they can shed some light on how she got those scars. Can you imagine it! Sheila McBride of all people, married to a gangster. I just can't see it myself. It makes you think, though; why *did* she lie about her scars?"

25

Broadmoor Top Security Hospital: Wednesday 24th October

Despite the thick fog still lingering from the night before, Jeff, accompanied by DS Stevens, was on schedule to arrive at Broadmoor before lunch. He couldn't stop thinking about the Katie Smyth case and what Stevens had told him yesterday. It seemed that vital evidence may have been overlooked – at least according to DS Stevens, and Jeff had no reason to doubt him. It seemed the young officer had gone with his team to the crime scene where the prime suspect was being held while they waited for forensics. Learning it was Jakes, Stevens had taken a quick look around the premises and had then, quite properly, declared his association with the suspect. At which point, he was ordered by his superior officer to leave the scene – a bit over the top in Jeff's view – and disengage from further involvement in the case. He had left prior to the arrival of the SOCOs whom he heard later had been delayed on route by an RTA. According to Stevens, by the time they eventually arrived at the scene, all trace of fresh condensation in the bathroom, which in his subsequent report he cited as indicating someone had recently taken a shower, must have evaporated. He did not learn until much later that it had been missed.

Certainly, the detective who replaced him at the scene could not have been blamed for overlooking it at the time, Stevens told Jeff. Such was the amount of blood soaked into Mark Jakes's clothes that nobody could have denied he was present when Katie Smyth was killed. Given that he had been found still clutching the knife and clearly in a state of shock, the scene of crime had centred on the living room where the murder had taken place.

Despite Stevens' belief that his observation in the bathroom was important to the investigation, it was deemed an unnecessary complication in a case that was otherwise cut and dried. How could Mark Jakes have taken a shower? He had made no attempt to clean up the scene and he was covered in blood – later confirmed as the victim's blood. Denied access to the investigation, Stevens had to wait until the trial to hear what the autopsy had uncovered: the viscera they retrieved at the scene from the mess that had been Katie Smyth had been missing a uterus. The medical report explained that although relatively rare – one in every ten thousand female births apparently – the victim had quite probably been born without one. This, however, was in direct contradiction with the statement made by Simon Alexander, her boss, who gave evidence at the trial. He had said that at the time of Katie's murder, it was rumoured around the office that she was pregnant and that Katie had told some of her colleagues that Mark Jakes, whom she had previously dated, was the father. In the event, the defence never raised questions about this apparent contradiction as not long after the trial had started, Jakes had changed his plea to guilty and the defence centred on insanity. Stevens had thought no more about it until the Higham autopsy, when he had been struck by two possible connections: the missing womb and Fiona Reid.

All that Stevens had told him churned over and over in Jeff's mind. Now they had another female murder victim minus a womb and they knew that Peggy Lyons's had been cut out by her killer. Had Katie Smyth's been similarly wrenched from her body? If so, it was too much of a coincidence to ignore. It was also now clear to Jeff that Lady Clara Smith-Stevens had used her position to have the trial fast-tracked; very interesting he thought; very interesting indeed. There was more to this case than met the eye!

Stevens was staring out of the windscreen. Jeff checked the clock on the dash; they were in good time. "I wonder if your mother could possibly be right about the involvement of some religious cult group?" Jeff mused out loud. "I still can't bring myself to believe that Fiona Reid is involved though; it's circumstantial."

"I'm not sure, Sir. One thing I am sure about: these murders are the actions of a depraved mind. I mean, just look at Jakes! I knew him – or at least I thought I did – albeit on a professional rather than a personal basis, but even so. And look at what he did to that girl! I would never have guessed he was capable of that."

Jeff wound down the window as they reached the security gate, handed out his identity card and waited for access. "Problem is,

Stevens, Jakes is locked up in here. So what are you implying? That someone is following his orders – or is it a copycat killing do you think? Surely not! And anyway, why Peggy Lyons? The only plausible theory for Jakes or whoever to be interested in a woman like your mother would be opportunistic – blackmail. Meaning no disrespect, but quite frankly, who cares these days if someone a long time ago had a love child? We're living in secular society, Stevens. Your mother's concerns about a religious group; it just doesn't add up; it's like something out of a Dan Brown novel that my wife always had her head stuck into. No; something else is going on here; has to be!"

"I don't know, Sir. But we've got connections, I'm sure of it: we can link Fiona Reid to both cases; missing wombs to both cases. We'll be able to study the crime scene photos later today and both autopsy reports, maybe then we'll see something more that will give us an edge."

It was clear when they saw him that Mark Jakes would be no help in furthering their case. Jeff cringed as his gaze fell on the wreck they brought into the interview room. There was nothing to remind him of the suave young man he had met from time to time at Sandra's dinner parties. The once gleaming, black hair had turned to a greasy, lacklustre grey; the muscular physique had melted to flab; the once handsome features were unrecognisable, buried beneath a puffy, unhealthy pallor. Handcuffed to a chair that shook to his tremors, Jakes sat bent over, his head shifting continually from side to side, his bloodshot eyes swivelling as he looked intently into each corner of the room in turn, as though some unseen predator was circling to pounce.

Sickened, Jeff indicated to Stevens to switch on the tape.

In Rochester, Sandra left the nursing home two hours after she had arrived, having gained very little knowledge about any of the girls who had stayed at the Priory. Edith Hollander looked every inch a centenarian, her mind no longer capable of understanding what was asked of her. As Sandra had placed the photographs of the young women in front of her, the old midwife had received them alternately with tears and joy. At regular intervals, her eyes closing deep in their shadowed sockets, she had floated off clearly lost in a different time.

Sandra had found herself having to wait patiently maybe fifteen minutes at a time for the old woman to come back. It had been a wasted effort, as she had known it would be.

As she turned her keys in the ignition, she stole a fleeting glance at Edith Hollander. Her carers had wheeled her into the bay window of the common room and left her sitting there. She looked utterly lost; so alone. A shiver prickled Sandra's arms; must be the fog, she convinced herself. The morning was decidedly chilly after yesterday's warm sunshine. Pulling out of the drive, her throat aching with compassion, she turned in the direction of Herne Bay, where Stella Jones's son owned a newsagent's shop.

When she had got home last evening, Fiona had been in a state of nervous exhaustion and had retired early to bed having said very little about the interview. It had been enough; however, for Sandra to know that Stevens had given her sister-in-law quite a grilling, particularly about her involvement with Mark Jakes. This morning, while Fiona was still in bed, Sandra had received an early call from Jeff to tell her that Christine had called in sick. She would have to go to Rochester on her own and was she okay about that. Sandra had taken the opportunity to bend his ear about Stevens' handling of the interview, but he had sounded edgy and was noncommittal, abruptly ending the call.

Thinking about it on her way to Herne Bay, Sandra found she was becoming increasingly angry with DS Stevens. What call had there been to drag up Mark? As if Fiona hadn't been through enough. Why was Stevens concerning himself with Jakes anyway? It was history: he should be concentrating on the Higham case. But surely they couldn't still consider Fiona a prime suspect? Yet if not, why did she feel they were focusing in on her? Was she blinding herself to Fiona's involvement? Something was going on, Sandra just knew it. She was angry with Jeff, too: he was sidelining her; she was sure of that now. But why?

Peter Jones was not much more helpful than Edith Hollander. All she got from him was that his mother had run a ballet school before was taken ill – Sandra already knew that. Stella Jones was her stage name; she had been a professional ballet dancer before becoming pregnant with the daughter she gave up for adoption. The only useful piece of information was Stella's real name: Ethel Platt.

Sandra was disappointed; it was among the files that sat untouched back in Higham, so she was not one of the Sister Mary's they needed to identify.

With time to kill until her late afternoon appointment with Dr Lewis, and feeling she had nothing to show for a whole morning's work, Sandra reluctantly put in a call to Keith Jones. She might as well follow up on the butterfly angle. It was turning out to be their only solid lead.

He gave her a couple of addresses. She drove to the nearest, 'The Butterfly House', on the border between Suffolk and Kent. A group of schoolchildren were clogging up the entrance when Sandra arrived. She battled her way through, presented her credentials at the information desk and was shown into an office behind the counter.

Peering over his wire-framed spectacles, Professor Giles Hanley, the resident expert, seemed a cheerful soul. He was a balding, rotund little man, his stomach out of all proportion to his height. Over-indulgence was also evident in his reddened nose and cheeks. He likes a drink, Sandra thought, as she explained very briefly why she was here. Keeping details to a bare minimum, she told him only that a Birdwing chrysalis had been found at the scene. She got the distinct impression that he was more upset about that than the plight of the murder victim!

"But that's extraordinary! Birdwings are terribly rare in this country. We have a small tropical planting here so that we can keep a few. Ours is supposed to be the only collection in the country. I say supposed, because specimens have been known to change hands for thousands of pounds, but they are a protected species; their collection in the wild is illegal. In fact, I do not know of any collectors in the UK who have live specimens as we do. Would you allow me to show you, Inspector?"

"Thank you, Professor; I'd love to see them." Sandra felt like a child in a chocolate factory; there was nothing more entertaining than listening to an enthusiastic expert talking about his pet subject – and she loved butterflies.

"They have become well established here," he told her as they headed for the butterfly gardens. In fact though, we had a bit of trouble with the vines at the start. Do you know anything about the species at all?"

Sandra smiled as she answered, "No, but we have a butterfly garden planted at home. It is a riot of colour in the summer. My husband chose the plants: Buddleia; Verbena bonariensis; Hebe; Salvia, Rudbeckia, Echinacea – I'm sorry," she broke off, flushing with embarrassment, "I'm getting carried away! Anyway, as you can imagine, we attracted quite a number of different kinds, though I'm afraid I wouldn't know many of their names. The children loved it when they were younger."

"Children do," he smiled, nodding in the direction of the chattering party of schoolchildren that she had passed at the gates. "I think it is the colours, mostly, but also perhaps the mystery. They live for so short a time – and they are often mistaken for fairies!"

Sandra laughed. She had forgotten until now what fun they had had with the girls. Planting out the bottom half of the garden to attract the butterflies had been one of Gerry's brainwaves. A wave of misery and longing lodged in her chest. We were happy once, she thought. Why do I always forget the good times?

It seemed the Birdwings were not on view to the public: her guide had turned away from the arrowed pathway to the public garden. They walked on to another building passing a large sign that said 'Private'.

"This is our research building," the Professor explained, heading for a door and rapidly entering a key code. "We have a breeding programme for our rare species and conduct various trials in here."

The first thing Sandra noticed as her guide ushered her in, was the uncomfortable humidity. He led her through a large laboratory, walking towards a wall of glass. It stretched from wall to wall and floor to ceiling – and through it she saw the butterflies, and gasped.

The Professor smiled at her expression. "You won't have attracted any of these beauties; I can assure you of that!"

What took her by surprise was the sheer size of them. No wonder they were called Birdwings: some of them had a wingspan almost a foot wide. They're monsters, she thought. "Are they normally so big, or do you feed growth hormones, or something?"

Giles Hanley laughed, "Good heavens no! Most people ask us that on first seeing them, so you are not alone, Inspector. But I assure you, they are not tampered with in any way. This is their natural size.

Let me present to you these amazing creatures: the Queen Alexandra, to be precise. A fantastic species, don't you think?"

"Most certainly," Sandra was awestruck by their beauty.

"This one here; wings light brown with the yellow spots and abdomen, is a female." He pointed to another, "and this one, a darker brown with those distinct blue and green markings, is a male – though as you can see, both share the vivid red on the base of the wings." He beamed at Sandra, "They are truly spectacular, aren't they. It's dreadful to think they were almost extinct last century. Their numbers are improving now, thank goodness, but not without help and dedication. You see," he pointed to the tangle of greenery behind the glass, "this particular vine grows only in certain regions, but it is vital to their survival. If the adult lays its eggs on any other type of vine, the feeding caterpillars are poisoned by it. It is a fact that nature seems to have overlooked, for in other respects they are well equipped to survive and deal with predators; venomous in fact."

"Really? I had no idea. They always seem such harmless, delicate creatures."

"The species indigenous to the UK are, but not these ones. We established this group in the early 1960s, before the ban came into force on their exportation. This is the only group – that is to say; the only legal group – in the country."

Sandra was totally absorbed in what he was saying; her gaze following the fluttering creatures behind the glass. She had to remind herself why she was here. How did these butterflies fit in this investigation? There had to be something symbolic in the killer's act of inserting the chrysalis into Peggy's birth canal. That would be so whatever the species; but here the choice of butterfly just had to be significant – if only because of its rarity. What was that significance? She became aware of the Professor standing beside her, proudly admiring the Birdwings, almost as if they were his own offspring. They were in a way, she supposed; he had bred them after all. Offspring... a frisson of excitement caught at her mind as she repeated the word to herself. Trying to keep her voice steady, she asked, "You said that if the eggs are placed on the wrong vine they perish?"

"That's right; most certainly. The destruction of the rainforests led to the species' near demise." He turned to her with a smile, "It seems Nature had not allowed for that eventuality!"

223

Nature; offspring; nature; offspring... the words chased each other round in her head. Sandra caught her breath as, for the first time in this case, she felt the buzz that always fizzed in her veins when she made a breakthrough. Peggy Lyons had helped women to give their babies away; adoption fragmented the natural order of things; muddled the line of heredity: *the eggs were laid on the wrong vine!* Was this the message the killer was sending? Sandra's excitement went out like a damp squib. If so, it had implications for Fiona's possible involvement. Her sister-in-law had been adopted; not only that, but for some reason her adoption had been muddled; the records lost – even more fragmented. This wasn't the direction Sandra wanted to take this case in. Every step seemed to bring Fiona closer to the centre instead of taking her further away. Yet much as she wanted to refute that, she was certain she had found a key. The Parable of the Sower came into her mind: the seeds sown on fertile earth grew strong, the ones strewn on stony ground failed. She was convinced this had to be the message. The killer had given her a clue; he was justifying his actions. Was she making of it what he intended? Was he motivated by anger or self-pity? Or both?

She tore her gaze away from the Birdwings and drew out her notebook. "I'll need a list from you of the names, addresses and contact numbers of everyone who has access to these butterflies. Have you noticed any chrysalises missing?"

"No, Inspector, not at all. Nor would I expect to. I am the only person with access to this particular species. Such is its importance that I care for them by myself. As I said, they are part of a preservation study."

"Well then, Professor, I'm afraid you will have to answer some questions for me."

26

Offices of Dr. Lewis Graham, Maidstone: later that day

Whatever you do, Sandra; don't blow this. Think before you speak; think before you speak. Chanting the instruction like a mantra under her breath, Sandra dragged her feet, taking her time to climb the steps to Graham's office. She had come here regularly during her leave of absence after the kidnapping. Here he had winkled out her innermost thoughts, the fears and emotions she had tried to suppress. She knew she was foolish to imagine she could cover up what was churning in her mind right now. He would see straight through her in no time at all – he always had.

He was waiting for her, reaching out his hand to offer his condolences. "It's been a while Sandra; I was sorry to hear about Gerry. I can only imagine how that must have affected you on top of everything else."

As he walked to his armchair by the window, Sandra made a face at his back. *So; we're getting straight into it are we!* How should I feel right now? How should I react? If I were the grieving widow, what would I say? But I am grieving – aren't I? She said nothing. The silence seemed interminable. She spewed out some words to fill it: "Yes; it was a terrible time; not something I ever contemplated having to deal with; at least not in the way that it happened."

"I expect not," he relaxed back into his chair and gestured for her to take a seat facing him. They were separated by a small coffee table, a clipboard and a lean pile of glossy magazines reflected on its polished surface.

Originally from Edinburgh, Graham's accent was still strongly Scottish. He was dressed casually in jeans with an open-necked, striped brown shirt. On his feet he wore brown loafers, but no socks. His black hair was long, drawn back into a pony tail: he looked like an ageing hippy. He and Gerry shared the same profession – had shared, she corrected herself with a pang – but were as different as chalk and cheese. Gerry had always dressed conservatively: never possessed a pair of jeans in his life, preferring chinos, which were always light in colour with little turn ups; shoes that were always highly polished, smart shirts and always a tie. His fastidious conservatism had irritated Sandra at times. As the image came into her mind, Sandra found to her surprise that she would give anything to be irritated by Gerry right now.

"I'll cut to the chase straight away, Sandra. I've been asked by Chief Superintendent Millar to assess your state of mind and present him with an evaluation – an update if you like."

Sandra raised her gaze from the floor to his face, but said nothing. She knew this already. He waited for a moment. He was a great one for silences, she thought, determined this time not to oblige him by filling it.

When she did not respond, he continued: "I'm glad to hear you took some time before going back to work, but I can't say I'm altogether impressed that you have been put on this case. Jeff has told me all about it," he grimaced. "I recommended a period of at least six months before you were put under this kind of stress. It seems what I say is of little account where your senior officer is concerned!"

Sandra forced herself to give him a bright smile. "I'm afraid such recommendations tend to be overlooked in the face of stretched resources. The team has never been so short of manpower. I can see where you're coming from, Lewis, but guess what: I'm coping really well. Surprise; surprise! Focusing on something useful instead of moping about the house must be a good thing, surely? I feel so much better." She fought off a sudden urge to tap her feet, aware that it would contradict the image she was trying to present. Catching a glimpse of her bitten nails, she promptly put her hands under her thighs, sitting on them instead. It made her feel like a naughty schoolgirl.

"Possibly, but that would depend on where you are at the moment, both in terms of your illness and your grief." He reached down to the table and lifted the clipboard. The top page contained rows of questions, each followed by a box for comments. "Don't look so worried, Sandra, there are no wrong answers."

To her surprise, she answered honestly to each question as it was asked. There didn't seem any point in lying. What surprised her even more was that nothing to which she admitted seemed to worry her.

"Good. That's the police side of things taken care of, then." He said it dismissively, in a broad Scottish accent that reminded Sandra of Sean Connery and made her laugh. Again she was surprised; she felt almost relaxed now.

Putting down the clipboard, he rested his chin in his hand for a moment and looked up, meeting her gaze across the table. "I've known you coming on two years now, and not once have you opened up to me. I'm here to help you help yourself, not to judge you, Sandra. Won't you trust me?"

She released her hands from under her legs and sat forward; the bitten nails no longer seemed relevant. "I'll try," she said.

He smiled, "Good. Can you tell me, then, how things were between you and Gerry leading up to the time he died? And before you decide whether or not to answer that, let me add a special request: I want you to be honest with me. If you can't be, I'm not interested. We might as well save each other some time."

Taken aback, Sandra sat for several minutes in silence, staring past him to the window behind his shoulder. Coming to a decision, she nodded. And then she told him everything: every damn bit of it; even the irony that the overdose of opiates found in Gerry's bloodstream had not actually caused his death; they would have done, but apparently, having taken them, he had decided to mend the fire escape. When the drugs kicked in, Gerry had keeled over and broken his neck. It was the one thing that had given the Coroner pause: why would someone who had intended to consume a lethal dose of painkillers then go out to do some DIY? Had it not been for the suicide note taken with the medical report, he might have returned a verdict of death by misadventure. Gerry had written that the tumour was inoperable, the pain unbearable and soon he would become a burden to his family. He hadn't wanted that. For the first time it occurred to Sandra to wonder why the consultant had said it was operable if it wasn't. Why would Gerry have lied about that? She became aware that Lewis was speaking.

"Why do you suppose he went out to mend the steps?" he asked gently.

Sandra thought for a moment, "Because I kept nagging him to," she said.

He said nothing; continued to gaze at her as she struggled to say the words.

"Because he thought it was the last thing that he could do for me," she said at last.

Lewis smiled encouragingly and reached beneath the table for a box of tissues.

She had not realised that she was weeping.

27

"Well; there was no chrysalis left in Katie Smyth's remains!"

Jeff, thinking aloud, moved between the blow-ups of the two crime scenes. Enlarged prints of the mutilated body of Katie Smyth had been set up alongside those of Peggy Lyons. The murders were equally gruesome and Jeff, hardened as he was, could not suppress a shudder of revulsion.

Boxes of case notes and evidence bags – all itemised – had arrived from London as requested. Jeff and Stevens had spent most of the afternoon in the incident room, searching through interview records and reading and re-reading autopsy findings. Periodically, Stevens would switch from the tape recordings of his former colleagues' interviews with Jakes, to the fresh recording they had made at Broadmoor that morning.

"No; there wasn't," Stevens agreed without raising his head.

"Could it have been missed in all the carnage?" Jeff had moved back to sit on one of the desks, but was still focusing intently on the boards.

"Possibly, Sir. Nothing would surprise me about that case!"

"Wombs..." Jeff let the word hang in the air for a moment.

"Sir?" This time Stevens looked up.

"When unoccupied they are tiny; we're so used to thinking of them in terms of babies, most of us wouldn't realise just how small they are. What I mean is, you'd have to know exactly what you were looking for and where to find it, wouldn't you."

"A good point," Stevens agreed.

"This Smyth scene, it was a hell of a lot messier than the other: total overkill." Jeff got up from his chair and moved to the board, unpinning one of the Higham photographs to study it more closely.

"Yet this one we have here was purely operational; that is to say, the killer had one purpose in mind."

"I'll give you a whole list of other differences if you want!" Both men swung round to see Sandra, who had slipped unnoticed into a chair behind them. "Like the time it took to carry out each of these murders – and that's just for starters!"

Jeff braced himself; he knew that tone of voice only too well. Sandra was in a temper, but was, it seemed, directing her anger at Stevens, not at himself. If looks could kill! Jeff thought. "Go on then," he said, "surprise me why don't you."

She shot him a haughty glance that he knew would normally have preceded a teasing remark were she not so angry. Damn Millar! She was the best investigator on his team and it aggravated the hell out of him to see her being upset like this.

"Okay, I will." Sandra began ticking off each point on her fingers. "We know that there was only a 45-minute lapse from when Katie Smyth was dropped at Jakes's flat until her boss called again to pick her up. In the Higham murders, the killer spent several hours with Matt and Peggy Lyons. Their autopsy results indicate that Matt Lyons died at least two hours before his wife. Our killer took time to set the scene: the lamps, remember? And don't forget the calls made by Matt Lyons's nurse. Peggy was sufficiently conscious to answer them without raising suspicion that anything was wrong. In the Smyth case, there was none of this staging as such. And then there's the—"

"Well; that I agree with," Jeff interrupted, still studying the boards – it was easier than facing Sandra as she was at the moment. "And another thing; there was no nudity involved with the Lyonses."

"I was just getting to that," Sandra snapped.

"I'm sure you were," Jeff shot her a smile. "The main factor, though, and it's too noticeable to ignore, is that despite the different skills evident in the way the knife was used, both women's bodies were mutilated around the area of the lower abdomen. The injuries, as you can see for yourselves, were not as frantic in the Lyonses case, but there are distinct similarities. And one of them has been bugging me all afternoon," he raised a hand, "no, hear me out, Sandra. Admittedly, Peggy Lyons was bound to a chair, but the killer had to get her there. Even at her age, I would have expected her to put up some sort of a struggle. Yet look at the wounds: not a twitch of the knife anywhere on the rest of her body. Now look at this one," using his pen he circled the area of Katie's lower abdomen. "Here, and again over here; despite the decimation, all the wounds are confined to this one area in both women."

Jeff swung round to face Sandra, wanting to see her reaction. She seemed completely absorbed in the blow-ups, her anger apparently forgotten or at least put aside. He gave an inner sigh of relief and pointed again to the boards. "Where are the puncture wounds? Katie was not bound as was Peggy, yet there isn't so much as a scratch as far as I can see; nothing in the medical report either. It seems strange to me, and believe me, I've dealt with more knife cases than I care to remember. Yet there is no medical evidence that either woman was unconscious when the wounds were inflicted. What does that say to you?"

Sandra stood and joined him at the board. "You're right; no defensive wounds at all. I had forgotten, so much has happened since – but I remember thinking it strange that Katie didn't put up a struggle; not even one of her perfectly manicured nails was broken."

Jeff nodded with satisfaction. Suddenly, he grabbed a ruler from a nearby desk and leapt over to Stevens. Grasping hold of his arm, Jeff raised the ruler above his head as if poised to make an attack.

Startled, Stevens instinctively put his arms up to shield himself and bent low as Jeff brought the ruler down hard, avoiding Stevens at the last moment.

"Yes, I see," Sandra said as Jeff, with an apologetic grin, released a sheepish Stevens. "Sorry lad; just a demonstration. It wouldn't have worked if you'd known it was coming."

Looking as though she wished the attack on Stevens had been real, Sandra said, "So there should be wounds higher up on her chest. Even her neck; her legs too for that matter; yet there was not even bruising on the arms as I recall, so how did he pin her down?"

"Exactly: that's something else that has been bugging me. What answers did your lot come up with to explain all this?" he asked Stevens.

Stevens shrugged; "It hardly seemed relevant. It was a sudden, unexpected and frenzied attack. She was supposed to be pregnant and he was about to get engaged to a well-heeled TV presenter," flushing, he avoided Sandra's gaze. "Katie Smyth was about to ruin it all for him wasn't she; so he had to get rid of her. He panicked plain and simple." Stevens gave Jeff a lop-sided grin, "I'm just playing devil's advocate here, Sir. You know my feelings about this case."

Jeff nodded.

Sandra breathed an exaggerated sigh. "Why are we wasting time on this anyway? The two cases are not connected." She walked over to the box of evidence bags and brought out the one containing the knife that had killed Katie Smyth. "Mark Jakes is in prison, it's done and dusted. We've another psycho to find in case you've forgotten; one we should all be a hell of a lot more worried about than you apparently are," she said, directing another angry glare at Stevens.

Stevens leapt out of his chair, "We can't ignore the similarities," he snapped, brushing past her as he headed for the flip chart on the other side of the room.

"Wait a minute," Sandra was staring at Stevens. "I've seen you before. Before you joined the team, I mean. I have, haven't I? You were there weren't you?"

Jeff coughed. He supposed it had only been a question of time. In fact, he was surprised Sandra had not recognised Stevens before now.

"You had something to do with the Katie Smyth case, didn't you," Sandra cried. "I saw you at the trial. No wonder you have been trying to implicate Fiona. You've drawn her as a connection, haven't you?" She flung the evidence bag back into the box and roughly pushed Stevens' vacant chair out of her way to retrieve her briefcase.

"And what if I have?" Stevens shouted back. "You shouldn't be involved anyway; you are too close to it – and you're not well!"

Jeff remained were he stood scratching the back of his head, not sure how to salvage a situation that was beginning to spiral out of control. Before Sandra could respond, he raised his voice to interrupt. "Look, you two; the best thing is to keep our minds open here. Stevens, I make the decisions around here about who does what, not you. Whatever your personal views on DI Reid's state of health, keep them to yourself. Sandra, DS Stevens has queries over the Smyth case and as we've just highlighted, something about her murder doesn't quite sit right. This is getting us nowhere and I will not have bickering on my team, get it? So let's all just calm down. Now then, how's about we move onto the Higham killer's profile?"

Jeff hoped for a bit of breathing space. He knew that before they rounded off the day they would have to discuss the role Fiona had played in both cases. The way things were, that would really set Sandra off. He breathed a sigh of relief when Stevens, looking slightly put out, subsided into a chair and Sandra nodded and opened her briefcase. He noted that neither of them apologised, but he'd let it pass – for now!

"I've not got far, I'm afraid," Sandra said, pulling out a folder. "My notes here are only part of the eventual profile. They are based on the killer's actions that I believe to be significant; that is, so far as I am able to determine at this stage in the investigation."

"That's understood," Jeff nodded.

As she proceeded to elaborate on the profile, Stevens reached out to take the folder and began reading through it, stopping to listen every now and then to what Sandra was saying.

"We can be confident that this killer is male and that he matches the common characteristics; his age anywhere between mid-thirties to late-forties. He is almost certainly a misogynist – indeed, the nature of his attack on Peggy Lyons and the removal of her uterus is symptomatic of an extreme hatred of women. It is unlikely that he has relationships with women and it is quite possible that he is homosexual," she shrugged, "but that is just a gut feeling, I have nothing to substantiate it."

"Okay, point taken; go on," Jeff said.

"Obviously, he has a trained hand with a knife, but I don't think we should be duped into believing he is medically trained. He could equally be a pathologist – at a stretch, even a butcher."

"Not particularly well trained," Stevens said dryly.

Sandra glared at him, "He wasn't trying to be careful! What is clear is that he is removed from having any common feelings of humanity: his treatment of Peggy Lyons was utterly brutal. He is confident too; took his time at Higham. Even the call from the nurse didn't rush him. I would say that he enjoyed what he was doing. Possibly even got some form of sexual satisfaction from making her suffer, although there is no evidence of that."

"Are you forgetting that he murdered Matt Lyons too," Stevens interrupted, "and equally brutally? Why refer only to the hatred of women; perhaps he hates all humankind."

Sandra shook her head, "In fact, I do not believe he tortured Matt Lyons; at least, not while the victim was still living. The mangled bones are evidence that the corpse was trampled, but I think it was more for the benefit of Matt's wife. Imagine if you will, how that must have been for Peggy..."

Sandra's voice broke and Jeff looked at her in concern, but she cleared her throat and continued.

"I think there is evidence to back this up. Remember, Matt Lyons was dying of cancer; it would have taken very little to kill him. Also, unlike his poor wife, he was on a heavy dose of morphine, which should to an extent have blunted his pain. When I was back at the scene yesterday evening, I had the SOCOs go over the living room carpet with a luminal. There was patch in the centre where quite an amount of blood had stained the carpet. I think he killed Matt Lyons there on the floor, then trampled him before lifting him back onto the bed. It was Peggy who was the focus; Peggy to whom he wanted to draw our attention. The samples will confirm if it was Matt's blood when they come through – but there's more."

Jeff shot a quick look at Stevens and was glad to see the young man looked impressed.

"To all intents and purposes, what this guy wanted in Higham was the records. This begs the question: why set up the scene in the way that he did? Why leave behind the chrysalis for us to find? I saw the things for myself earlier and you wouldn't believe the size of them. Think along the lines of prehistoric. Anyway; in my view, our killer has set himself some sort of mission, as he sees it: he has a lesson he wants us to learn. The chrysalis is itself a womb of sorts, and he left it symbolically in Peggy's birth canal. It was a message."

Jeff frowned, "Symbolic? Are you saying this mission or message has religious undertones?"

"It's funny you should ask that, Jeff, because I was reminded of the Parable of the Sower when I came up with this line of thought. But no, I don't believe there is anything religious about it as such. Why would you think so?"

Realising that he had almost shot himself in the foot – for how could he explain it to Sandra without revealing what Lady Clara Smith-Stevens had divulged, Jeff cast around for something to say, but was saved by Stevens.

"The Parable of the Sower?" Stevens grinned, "Not my strong subject I'm afraid; remind me."

Conveying his gratitude to Stevens with the slightest twitch of his eyebrows, Jeff listened as Sandra explained the attributes of the Queen Alexandra Birdwing butterfly and why she had made the connection. "I don't believe religion is what gets this guy going, Jeff, if that's what you mean. I think that his use of a chrysalis – specifically one from which a butterfly has recently hatched – is more like a sign of rebirth. It symbolises the birth of a child that has been given up for adoption; the normal line of maternal caring is fragmented, if you like. To take the analogy further: as our killer sees it, the mother laid her eggs on a poisonous vine; in other words, she abandoned her baby to its inevitable fate. Now, obviously this is conjecture, but if I am right, then he must have known that Peggy had a baby adopted, so it's certain he's done his homework. She was dead the moment she opened the door to him. Well, that is my line of thinking at present, anyway."

Jeff lifted a marker and flipped over to a clean page on the chart. Scribbling in block letters he wrote 'Smyth' to the left and 'Lyons' to the right. Below that he added 'Fiona'. In the centre of the triangle made by the names, he wrote in large letters the word 'adoption'. "Well done, Sandra," he swung round with a smile. "Setting Mark Jakes to one side for the moment, I think you have found our link. As you know, Katie Smyth worked as a receptionist at this place called 'Search'. A great part of what they do is to find parents for adopted children. Mark Jakes worked there too. We know that is where Fiona met him."

"I thought you said you were setting Mark Jakes to one side! Why do you keep returning to him?" Sandra objected. "He cannot possibly be our killer. And anyway, he wasn't Fiona's main contact; that was the Director of the agency, Simon Alexander."

Jeff nodded, drawing two strong arrows, one from Katie and one from Peggy, both leading to Fiona.

Sandra was livid, as he had known she would be, "Answer my question, Jeff," she cried, flushing with anger. "Why do you keep insisting on linking Katie Smyth's murder to this one?" She turned and glared at Stevens, but he simply shrugged and remained silent.

"Whether you like it or not, Sandra, your sister-in-law can be connected to both victims, there is no point in denying it," Jeff said.

Sandra directed another glare at Stevens. "From what I can determine from Fiona's interpretation of her interview yesterday, you seem to think there may have been someone else in Mark Jakes's flat while he was slashing Katie's abdomen to ribbons. Why do I get the feeling you think it was Fiona? You do realise, don't you, that she gave me as her alibi? Are you proposing to question me too? Do you honestly believe that I might have jeopardised my career by lying for my sister-in-law? Is my integrity at question here too?"

Jeff tensed; he wasn't aware Stevens had taken this approach with Fiona. Damn Millar to hell and back, he thought. This had gone far enough! He wasn't going to keep Sandra in the dark any longer; he would fill her in later. He moved to stand between his two detectives, "Look, Sandra, nobody is making any such allegations. Fiona must have misinterpreted what Stevens here said to her yesterday. Now, can we pool everything we have gathered so far. What threads do you see as spinning from this, Sandra?" He wondered for a moment if she was going to answer him, but at last, though clearly still fuming, she spoke.

"Well; the adoption issue is only one possible angle, but I believe it is the most likely. There's a good chance that one of the children placed for adoption by Peggy Lyons had a bad experience; fell foul of the system. So bad that perhaps he sought revenge on the woman he sees as the perpetrator. So bad that it has spilled over onto all women; but principally those who give up their babies."

Jeff nodded, "What about you, Stevens, do you go along with this line of thinking?"

"It seems quite logical to me, Sir."

Sandra gave Jeff a long look, as if she wanted to add something. "Yes, go on," he said.

"Well, quite apart from the fact that I believe our killer is male, I can vouch for the fact that Fiona's childhood was idyllic, to say the least – and while there was some mix up that has made it impossible for her to discover her birth mother's identity, she certainly landed on her feet as far as her adoptive parents were concerned." She paused, thought for a moment. "We still have to identify the women on Peggy's list, but what about our number three: Aya of Mons? Do we know if she has ever been contacted by the child she gave up?"

Jeff began to formulate an answer, but Stevens got in first. "Her child was reunited with her when he was still quite young and yes, actually, like your sister-in-law, he reports that his childhood was always happy."

Sandra shot out of her chair, knocking it over in her haste. Her face said it all. "Sorry, I've just remembered I've got faxes to retrieve." Leaving the chair where it had fallen, she turned away and strode towards the door of her office.

It was an excuse; Jeff could see that she was trying to disguise her hurt. He knew how it looked and what she must be thinking. Stevens had joined the team only a couple of weeks ago and yet he was good enough to be in the know while she, a loyal, long-serving member of the team, was not! It was clear to Jeff that daggers were drawn between these two. It was more than clear that Sandra was totally demoralised. She was not stupid; far from it. She had realised what was happening. He could not let it continue. Leaving Stevens to resume studying the tapes, Jeff went into his own office, slamming the door behind him. He had been placed in an untenable position. It was exactly as he had feared. He walked to the window and looked out across the car park, wondering what best to do. Deciding that Sandra needed some time to cool down, as indeed did he, he went down to the canteen to grab some coffee and a bite to eat.

When he came back, the incident room was buzzing having filled up with most of the team. He had sent them off for a couple of hours' break after lunch: most of them had been in before six that morning and tired minds were no good to him. Through the glass in Sandra's door he saw that she was still at her desk. He went through to his own office and picked up the internal phone. "Sandra, I want to see you in my office; we need to talk. Now, if you please." Waiting, he braced himself; she had every right to be annoyed.

Stevens stayed on to help the others sift through the lists of private butterfly collectors. He needed to contact this Simon Alexander. The man could also be placed at the Smyth crime scene; it was he who had dropped Katie at Jakes's flat; it was he who had called in the police. If Jakes had not so obviously been the killer, Alexander would certainly have been a prime suspect. In fact, there was something altogether odd about Alexander's role in all this – and, what's more, it appeared he too could be linked to Fiona Reid.

Stevens looked up the number of the Search Agency and dialled. Waiting for a reply, he wondered if Sandra Reid would take his head off his shoulders were he to ask if her sister-in-law had access to a Birdwing collection! In a way, though, he had some sympathy for her: he knew what it felt like to be sidelined and she'd had a raw deal one way and another. He couldn't help smiling as he heard her raised voice coming from behind Jeff's closed door. Yesterday it had been him in there on the carpet; now it was her turn – only this time it was the boss who was on the receiving end of the earache! She was in a filthy temper by the sound of it. Stevens had already concluded it would not be advantageous to his position to rile his colleague any more than he had to, but listening to her voice rising in decibels, he was surprised to find it excited him! Could it be that he actually fancied her? Even if he did, there was no point in following it up; she was recently widowed and still wore the ring on her finger. He avoided women with baggage like that. Sandra Reid was off limits.

The ringing tone in his ear stopped abruptly and the chirpy, female voice of Search's receptionist almost pierced his ear drum. She sounded very young; interrupting her spiel in mid-sentence, he asked to speak to Simon Alexander.

As he was talking into the phone, he saw Sandra come out of Jeff's office. Walking purposefully out of the incident room, she afforded Stevens a curt nod, a slight smile hovering on her lips. His eyes remained focused on the empty space she had left for quite a time after she had gone. Yes; he did fancy her. Off limits, he reminded himself. The shrill voice sounded again in his ear: "I'm sorry, Sir. Mr Alexander is away at present and not expected back this week."

"Do you have a home contact number for him? This is Detective Sergeant Stevens, Maidstone Police Headquarters. I'll need his address too."

"Please hold while I check."

Stevens got the distinct impression that she was covering for the boss; he could imagine Simon Alexander standing beside her desk shaking his head and putting his fingers to his lips. She was soon back, shrilling the address into his ear. As she was speaking, a constable pushed a list of registered private collectors under his elbow.

He scanned through it, his eyes widening in surprise: the contact address the receptionist was reading out on the phone was there, right in front of his eyes. Well that *was* interesting! 'Alexander' was hardly a common name: Father? Brother? Thanking the receptionist, he ended the call. "Who is this Alan Alexander?" he called to the constable's retreating back.

"Hardly of interest to you, Sir; he's a lepidopterist alright – someone who studies butterflies, Sir," he explained as Stevens' eyebrows shot up.

"I'm aware of that, Constable."

"Yes Sir; sorry Sir. Well anyway, he's been in Papua New Guinea since March. I checked. Evidently he's been working in conjunction with some American university conservation programme over there, rebuilding habitats for rare species." The constable pulled out his notebook, leafing through the pages. "Ah, yes; here it is, Sir," he looked up with a grin, "he is concerned specifically with the Queen Alexandra Birdwing butterfly. Sounds a bit—"

"What!" Leaving the startled constable standing in mid-sentence, Stevens jumped off his chair, grabbed his jacket and rushed out of the office, calling over his shoulder, "Good work!" before hastening down to the car park. The receptionist had implied that Simon Alexander was away for a few days, she had not said why. Maybe he was taking a spot of leave. Minding the shop while his brother was overseas? Must be a brother; the father would be too old for jaunts in the jungle! There was no harm in hoping he would find Simon Alexander at home. It was an incredible coincidence; too much of a coincidence. Not only was the man linked closely with Mark Jakes and adoption, but also with the very species of butterfly Sandra had described. He must surely have access to it, if only indirectly – enough to get his hands on a chrysalis?

When Stevens reached Alan Alexander's address in Canterbury, he found the house shut up and empty. Disappointed, he walked round to the back, but there was no sign of life. Drat! He would have to get a warrant. Maybe there was something inside to say where Simon Alexander had gone. Maybe by the time he got back, the man would have returned.

28

Hell hath no fury! Jeff thought to himself as Sandra, her back as stiff as a ramrod, stalked out of his office. On reflection, it had perhaps been a little unwise to remind her that out of loyalty to her, he had also held back on the inescapable fact that what Fiona had done was tantamount to theft. She'd no right to take those files in the first place. He sighed; he should have realised that mentioning loyalty would do nothing to calm Sandra down. How was he going heal their relationship? With some justification, she would never trust him again.

In the end, sidestepping the issue of Fiona, he had eventually selected the two pieces of information that he felt he could safely disclose at this time: 'Aya of Mons' was the alias for Lady Clara Smith-Stevens and DS Stevens was her son. He'd had every intention of telling her more, but her reaction to even that much was such that there was no point in adding fuel to her temper. He was caught in the middle of a lie and the more he tried to adhere to it the bigger it got.

When Sandra had gone, he sat on at his desk thinking through the events of the day. Why had the Minister directed that the investigation should be centred on Fiona Reid? What was it about Fiona that had so got under her ladyship's skin? Was it possible that through her intimacy with Mark Jakes, Fiona knew about the relationship between Lady Clara and DS Stevens? But what if she did? What was so top secret about that? It hardly mattered as far he could see, except to his team, of course! Why had he been ordered not to tell them – and especially Sandra Reid? Was it simply because of her relationship to Fiona or was there more to it than that?

He became irritatingly aware that someone was tapping at his door. "Yes! Come in."

DC Blake covertly opened and slipped through the door. "Is it okay to give this stuff to you now, Sir?"

Jeff had forgot all about the little bit of homework he'd given Blake to take home with him yesterday. "Yes, it's fine. Here, sit down and tell me what you found."

Blake smiled eagerly and sat down. "Well sir, I'll start at the beginning shall I?"

"Please do." Jeff eyed with some trepidation the thick bundle of folded pages that Blake was straightening out. Clearly he had dedicated most of the previous night to the research.

"Right, well, let's see… Henrique Carlosanta was born in 1949 in Brazil. His father was a Baron, the family having been very successful in the past. They owned one of the largest coffee plantations in the Province of San Paulo and more recently have built a hotel empire across Central and South America. I researched right back into the 19th century, Sir." Blake looked up and grinned. "You'll love this bit. An ancestor of the cardinals was very close to Pedro II who was leader of the country in the 1870's when a certain law was passed emancipating the coffee slaves. In the light of the missing wombs in our case, Sir, I thought it might have some relevance."

Jeff tried to look interested, still distracted over what to do about Sandra. "And what law was that?" he asked absently, reaching out to take the other sheets Blake had set on his desk.

"The 'Law of the Free Womb', Sir – I suppose it's a bit of a long shot, but I thought it an unusual name for a law. It meant that all children born to slave mothers were to be held in a state of semi-freedom until they were aged 21, when they would become fully free."

As Blake continued to enthuse, Jeff, flicking through several pages of downloads, found more recent interests of the Carlosanta family aiding different conclusions in his mind. It appeared that on the death of his father, Henrique had used most of the family's wealth to set up an orphan village on the outskirts of Rio de Janeiro. Groups of abandoned children were housed there in small family units. Very interesting, Jeff thought. Was the Cardinal guilty about something, he wondered? Perhaps he had known all along of the existence of his son. Could it be a form of penance for abandoning his child?

As Blake delved further into the history of slavery in Brazil, Jeff lifted another report, pausing midway down the page as his eye caught the name 'Peter Smith'. Of course! Lady Clara's first husband was a Peter Smith: a link! Goodness, and how! Skimming the page with a satisfied smile he raised a hand to halt Blake in mid-flow. "This is where it really *does* get interesting, Blake; here in the late 1970's. Good work lad! Thank you. You've answered more questions than you'll ever realise."

. Blake grinned happily, "I've found more information about the names Mrs Lyons used for aliases too, Sir, if—"

"Even better," Jeff interrupted. "Good work indeed, Blake. Could you see that DS Stevens is made aware of those, but I'll hold on to this lot here – and remember, not a word about it to anyone; nobody at all, Blake, okay?"

"Yes, Sir, absolutely; you can rely on me." Scooping up the remaining bits of paper that Jeff had pushed aside, Blake shot him another wide grin and left, shutting the door quietly behind him.

So! Jeff thought, lying back in his chair, his feet crossed on the edge of his desk. Peter Smith's foundering contracting business was miraculously saved by none other than Baron Carlosanta in the winter of 1979. Only a matter of weeks later, the Baron's son, Henrique, was officially anointed Cardinal of Rio, the youngest man ever in modern times to attain such a pinnacle in the Roman Catholic Church. At the ceremony, Peter Smith and his dashing young wife were private guests of the Carlosanta family. Jeff smiled at the ceiling; "Well, well, well, Lady Clara," he whispered. "Oh what a web you have spun!"

Sandra had been looking forward to spending some time with Leslie, but the evening started off badly: she was late getting to Gianni's and couldn't unwind; neither did she have any appetite. Whereas in the past they had found plenty to talk and laugh about, there seemed to be an underlying awkwardness between them. Their conversation was forced and everything seemed to come back to Gerry. Before the meal was halfway through, Sandra found herself wishing she had cried off. Leslie, too, seemed disinclined to linger; she had an early start, she said, and would be unavailable for a few days. She was closing up an inquiry into a case of possible malpractice concerning a hospital trust. They left the restaurant early, parting company just after nine.

Driving home, Sandra could not dispel a feeling of dread in the pit of her stomach. It had been lying dormant since the autopsy, but Leslie's parting words had brought it to the surface: "Text me if there are any developments with the Lyonses. We've seen cases like this before; there will be more!" The pathologist had shouted something else as she drove off, but Sandra hadn't caught what it was. Nor, she realised, did she know where Leslie was headed, but she had driven away in the opposite direction to her home. An assignation, Sandra assumed, Leslie was incorrigible; the early start must have been an excuse.

She hadn't needed reminding that the killer would kill again. Everything she'd recorded at the crime scene in Higham indicated that he had killed before: it was too organised; he'd taken time to set up the scene, cleaned away any trace of evidence. He was a practised killer; that much was certain. Yes; there would be more. It was only by a curious quirk of fortune that they had any idea at all as to his motive. Had Fiona not taken those files they would still be clutching at straws. It was their only lead – aside from the chrysalis, of course, Sandra thought with a shudder, and the killer had intended for them to find that. But he could not have known that Fiona had got to the files first, not until he tortured the information out of Peggy Lyons – could he? And was it just an amazing coincidence that the very files she had taken were the ones he wanted? Sandra was so preoccupied that she found she was pulling into her driveway with no recollection of the journey home.

Flat-pack boxes littered the floor of Gerry's study. The double doors of the built-in closet lay open. Inside, sitting cross-legged and engrossed in a book was Fiona. Sandra smiled at her, proffering a bottle of wine and two glasses, her earlier annoyance with her sister-in-law forgotten. "You haven't got very far without me then?"

"I can't believe he kept all of these! Not only that, but he was still adding to them, right up until the day he…," Fiona turned her head away.

Sandra set the bottle and glasses on the table. Pouring the wine she brought the glasses over to the floor and sat on a scatter cushion in front of the closet. "Here," handed a glass to Fiona. "What are they anyway?"

Fiona stared at her with an expression of stunned disbelief. "You mean you haven't seen them? They're his diaries!"

Sandra let out a humourless laugh. "Good Lord no! Didn't even know he kept them. This was always his space. I didn't intrude. You haven't actually read them have you? They're probably full of notes on his patients. Maybe you're breaking some rule of ethics reading them; patient confidentiality and all that."

Fiona screwed up her face snapping shut the journal in her hands. "Oh! That's right! Fiona the file snatcher! His patient files I presume are in those locked cabinets over there." In one of the corners of the deep sides of the closet were two filing cabinets stood side by side in the shadows. "And no I'm not prying, I'm just flicking through the pages of these recent ones."

"That's not what I meant!" Sandra sighed taking a sip of her wine. "Actually, I've realised that you taking those files from the Lyons's house was a good thing in a way. If you hadn't, we wouldn't have a clue what this case is all about! Now we can at least speculate that it is something to do with Peggy Lyons's involvement with adoption."

Fiona set the journal back into the middle of the row of similar books on the bottom shelf. "I'm off the hook then, about taking the records I mean?"

Sandra looked away, "No, I'm afraid not; not exactly." She knew as soon as she said it how her sister-in-law would react.

Fiona jumped to her feet, strode across the room and flung herself into an armchair. "I knew it! I told you this morning something was up. This has to be about Mark. I knew as soon as DS Stevens started asking me about him. The cases are connected aren't they? So Mark couldn't be the killer could he. I told you all he was innocent. Nobody would listen to me. Why could none of you see that! Why?"

Yes and you are the connection, Sandra thought, but could not bring herself to say. "Look Fiona, don't go jumping the gun! Yes, there are some similarities, but there are more differences. Everything linking the cases is circumstantial. And anyway, even Mark is still committed to his guilt!"

"How would you know that?" Fiona sat forward, "You've seen him! Haven't you?"

Sandra set down her glass and squeezed her head between both hands. *We shouldn't be having this conversation! Here we go again!*

Wearily, she raised her head and looked at Fiona. "Jeff and Stevens travelled up to ask him some questions this morning. They've accessed the case files. We are re-examining them now."

Leaping to her feet, Fiona paced the room, "Don't you see Sandra? They think the killings are similar. That he couldn't be guilty, that somehow he's been framed. Finally, God has listened to my prayers!"

Sandra got up off the floor, grabbed her sister-in-law by the arms and forced her to stand still. "Fiona, listen to me. That's not why they travelled up there. They think he's got an accomplice; that someone has some kind of a pact with him." Releasing Fiona's arms, Sandra turned away afraid that Fiona would read the truth in her eyes, but Fiona held onto her, her hands tightening around Sandra's wrists.

"Surely you don't believe that Sandra? You know that's not true!"

Fiona's nails were marking her arms; she struggled free from their grip. *Why had she said anything? Stupid; so, so stupid!* "Let me go, you're hurting me. It's not official yet, but it's you! They think that it might be you!"

Fiona stood motionless, staring at her, mouth open; speechless.

"Not me, Fiona. I don't think that. Not Jeff either, at least I don't think so – but just let's say the idea has been floated. Something else is going on Fiona. Millar has put pressure on Jeff to keep me out on the edges of the case."

"I don't believe you," Fiona said at last. Letting go of Sandra's wrists, she moved to the window, stood a few moments then walked towards the door, turned down the lights.

"I thought you had arranged for them because of the break-in, but it wasn't you was it?"

"You're talking in riddles, Fiona – and why have you plunged us into darkness for goodness sake!" Sandra took a step towards the dimmer switch, reached towards it.

"No, Sandra!" Fiona hissed. "Down there almost hidden by the trees. That car's been there all evening; two men in it I noticed it pull in behind me when I got back."

Sandra edged her way over to the window and looked up and down the street. Then she saw it. "Maybe Jeff arranged it? Well at least we can sleep easier knowing we've our own personal security. Look, forget about them. It's getting late and we're both tired. Let's make a fresh start at this tomorrow," she gestured to the filing cabinets.

Take your glass downstairs I'll stick a pizza in the microwave. There is no point in speculating what Jeff has decided about you or me or anything else to do with this damned case. But the last thing I want is for us to fall out over it. Please, Fiona."

Relieved when Fiona nodded and picking up her glass led the way down to the kitchen, Sandra took another quick glance out of the window. *The car followed Fiona home; those guys outside are not here for our protection, they're here for surveillance! Why did I even mention Mark? What kind of a picture of him does she still hold in her head?*

Part Two

Picking Up The Pieces

**"Drive towards Dover, friend, where thou shalt
meet welcome."**
William Shakespeare: *King Lear*

29

Dover: Tuesday 30th October

"'My name is Monica. I think you are my mother…'"

Anita Hunt's eldest son, Justin, heard the excitement bubbling in his mother's voice as she read the email out to him over the phone and his heart sank.

There had been so many like it ever since he could remember. He had always known of this sister who existed somewhere, just not at home with them. When he was younger it was all a great mystery; he couldn't quite figure out why his mother had needed someone else to look after her baby. He'd thought it strange that he and Scott couldn't see their sister until they were older. Even when he was fifteen and his mother had sat them down and told them the real story about how she'd got pregnant, how she was in danger and had no option but to give her baby away, they had not held it against her. But he could tell now, as the years had dragged on and one hopeful after the next had come and gone, that the strain of it was taking its toll on his mother's health. This one would be just like all the others; the wrong one.

"When did you receive it?" he asked, trying to inject some enthusiasm into his voice.

"This morning; it's her; I can feel it; this time it's really her!"

"Have you replied to it yet?" There was silence on the other end of the line. Justin thought his mother was probably weeping. A thought suddenly occurred to him: "Are you sure it's for real? I thought the agreement with the Priory place was that any correspondence had to come through them?"

"Oh, Justin, it's all right! This time everything is right. We've been sending emails back and forth all morning. It's only the mother who has to direct correspondence through official channels; children have always been free to contact lost parents directly for years. Anyway;

she's coming on Thursday. Justin you are finally going to meet your sister; on Thursday!"

"You've invited her to the dinner?"

"Why of course I have! Her space is always there for her," Anita laughed.

Justin sighed. Space at the table was not what bothered him; he and Scott had grown up with an empty table setting; a place always laid for his sister – just in case. It grieved him that their mother was building herself up yet again for what would almost certainly be another disappointment. It was like some sort of an addiction with her: she just didn't seem capable of proceeding with caution.

"I'll give you a buzz later, Justin," she said. "Sally is coming up the drive. She's helping me to organise the meal on Thursday."

"Okay. Tell her I said 'Hello and I hope she's making the gateaux as usual!' By the way, how is your novel coming along?"

"Better than I expected. I had a flash of inspiration a few weeks ago, which is actually what gave me the idea to bring the girls all back together again. It's flying along now. Look, Justin, I have to ring off. Sally's at the door. I'll talk to you soon. Bye."

Before he had a chance to respond, she had gone. Shaking his head in despair, Justin wandered through to his study, anxiety for his mother furrowing his brow.

"Wouldn't you know that damned car of ours would start acting up this week of all weeks!" Sally Burton had let herself in through the hallway. Her face was even redder than usual; a sure sign she was flustered, but still managing to look fashionably smart. She ran the local slimming club and insisted she must keep up a suitable image for her position. In her late forties, her makeup applied as heavily as always, she was sporting a new hairdo: this month black with bright red streaks through her fringe and across the ends at the back. Anita guessed she spent as much on looking the part as she earned. The spray tan that coated her skin didn't come cheap, nor did the chunky beaded chains and bracelets that jingled against each other as she moved. Shrugging off her mac, she shook it and reached out to hang it on the coat rack beside the door before looking up to greet Anita.

"Dear God, love! Whatever happened to you?"

Anita's smile dropped. Sally made her feel like a slob at the best of times. She patted down her hair aware that it was standing up on top of her head Mohican style. Walk the dog, write for six hours, walk the dog again, write until late into the night and sleep; eating snacks mostly biscuits and microwave dinners in between. This was the way she had operated for weeks. Her hair hadn't been washed since Sunday; there had only been time for a quick shower each morning – to wake her up more than anything else. She was conscious that weight was piling on; perhaps she should sign up for Sally's class, she thought with a smile. The urge to write ruled her life. All she was aware of was the tingling need in her fingers to make contact with the keys on her computer – until this morning, when that email had arrived on her screen. Now, her book forgotten, she was in a daze.

"I've been working all week," she mumbled, not meeting Sally's concerned gaze. "I'm pressed by a deadline."

"Yes. Well. I'll make you an appointment for early on Thursday morning."

Sally had put on her 'no nonsense' face and Anita couldn't help but smile. Sally to the rescue. Thursday! A spasm of excitement shot up to her throat, so sharp it made her gasp. She would have to look better than ever on Thursday: her daughter was due around three. She had arranged it that way so they would have a few hours alone before everyone else arrived. Anita turned quickly away so that Sally would not see the tears springing to her eyes. Her daughter! Trying desperately to compose herself, she made for the kitchen. "We'll have some tea and you can fill me in on your week before we start sorting the menu."

Sally followed, launching into her usual stream of chatter. A born grumbler, she moaned about her husband, her daughter and half of the town, day in and day out. She was a great study for any writer and Anita knew just how to get her started.

"How's Tommy's back this week then?"

Sally closed her eyes shaking her head, "Don't talk to me; big lazy lump…"

Filling the kettle, Anita hid a smile.

30

"Hold it there! Camera 5, zoom in close to her eyes. She's crying. That's it!"

Fiona was fighting back the tears too. She could barely hear her producer giving commands to the camera men in the studio. This was the final day of shooting on the series. Reaching out she took hold of Eleanor Williamson's hands.

"Camera 5, pan down to the hands and hold it there!"

The hands of the two women clasped in mutual sympathy and understanding filled the screen: one pair delicate and unblemished, the other wrinkled and sagged with age. The film of Eleanor's search for her parents, which had just been replayed on screen, had stirred up a host of feelings in Fiona's heart. It was a struggle to keep her emotions out of her voice.

"You're 78 years' old, Eleanor. Surely you have accepted the likely fact that your birth mother is no longer alive? What drives you to keep looking after all this time?"

Eleanor pulled her hands away and with shaking fingers patted at her tears. Turning to peer into Fiona's eyes, the elderly woman remained silent for a moment. She looked almost stunned, as if Fiona should have known the answer to the question – which, of course, she did.

The instructions from the producer to Camera 2 to get an angle jarred Fiona to ask again. "Why, Eleanor? What is it you hope to find?"

Without moving her gaze as the camera zoomed in for a close-up of her face, Eleanor answered at last; her voice steady and determined. "I need to know who I am. Before I die; I want to know who I am."

Fiona took off early for a lunch break. The morning shoot was the last of a five-part documentary due to be aired in December and entitled *Lost Souls*. Usually, work was an escape from trying times at home. The situations of the five people highlighted in the series and the closeness of their plight to her own had drained Fiona. It was Eleanor's experience that had touched her the most. Will that be me she wondered, and was still wondering as she parked in the drive at home.

All these feelings held so near the surface – for a lifetime? She shuddered; she couldn't live like that. She needed to know who she was now! There was no one left who belonged to her. Her adoptive mother and father were dead. Gerry was gone and so abruptly too. They were part of her life; she had never intended to hurt any of them, but it had always been there: the feeling that she was different.

Changing out of her trouser suit she slipped into a pair of jeans and a stripped cotton shirt, made a smoothie for her lunch and took it up to Gerry's study. Lifting a couple of his early journals, she curled herself into the alcove of the deep-set, Georgian sash window and started flicking through the earliest of the books. The pages were unlined; the writing in a childish hand. Some of the lettering was back to front, each shaky attempt travelling further down the page than the last. She smiled, reliving her first memories of her brother in his self-appointed role as her protector. She was small; about three. Mum had plaited her hair in two, each plait tied with bows. Harry, from across the road, had pulled out the bows and made her cry and Gerry, much smaller than he was, had stood up to him and demanded them back.

Tearing her gaze from the words on the page, Fiona looked down to the road in front of the house, noted that the blue Vauxhall car that had kept her company over the last two days was still there. With a shrug, she returned her attention to the journal. Unfolding a loose page she found a drawing of a knight. She set it aside and flicked to the next page. It was comforting; made her feel as if Gerry was still there; as if time had not passed. Had he ever looked back at these journals as she was doing now? When had he last looked at this very page? She could imagine his lean, tanned fingers smoothing the pages; see the slight smile lifting the corner of his mouth. It was warm sitting by the window; the sun was shining through the glass making patches of light on the carpet. Fiona felt her eyelids grow heavy. Closing them for a moment, she thought back to the last time she and Gerry had been here, in this room...

***

14th February, 2007

Gerry Reid gripped the journal, the first in a series of 35 that he'd written every day since his mother had enrolled him in junior infants. One a year: could it really be that many years ago? He moved slowly away from his desk to look down on the view from his window: St Valentine's Day again, and already the cherry trees were coming into blossom. Spring was early this year.

It had become a ritual to stand here each morning awaiting his first appointment of the day. But today was different; today it was the turn of someone else to wait on him; today he was the patient.

Flicking through the pages, he stopped to unfold a coloured drawing he had glued in; a childhood sketch of a knight clad in full armour. Underneath the page he viewed the words he had recorded. He had no need to read them: the memory of that day remained vivid in his mind as if it were yesterday. He sighed; that was the day when it had all begun.

***

14th February, 1972

It's still okay, he reassured himself, balancing on the tips of his boots. He stood on a wobbly tower of books that he had placed on a rickety chair, all in an effort to reach a sight of himself in the over-mantle mirror. The spongy padding of the seat cushion made no secure foundation, so one quick peek was all he could manage.

He had been told not to move off his spot, and not wanting to get into more trouble he steadied himself and took a huge leap, landing on his backside on the hard linoleum floor. Wincing from the pain, tears immediately welling up into his eyes, he used the cuff of his sweater to wipe them away, determinedly hushing the cry inside him for his mother. He didn't want to be told again that he was a nuisance.

Afraid they would come back at any moment he got back onto his feet and lifted the books, placing them in order of height were they belonged. He pulled the chair back to the wall and took his place on the sofa. Sitting with his head bowed, he resumed twiddling his thumbs: he was six years of age.

He wondered if it had happened yet. He swirled his eyes and tried to look down at his nose, he could only see one side of its end. He had hoped to see in the mirror.

"Whose nose is going to get put out of joint now?" That's what they all kept saying to him: Nana Brown, Auntie Ethel even the lady behind the counter in Sainsbury's had tapped the end of his nose and said this. He didn't want a crooked nose. Everybody at school would laugh at him if he came in with a deformed face. They called Benny Hampton terrible names because his eyes were crooked. He did not want to be called names. Most of all he did not want this baby to come home with them.

Gerard raised his chubby hand and fingered his nose again; it was still the same. He wondered if it would hurt much when it twisted out of joint. He didn't much care for pain; it made him cry. He would be a sissy if he cried.

"Your ma couldn't be getting a baby; you're full of lies. My ma gets a big bump every time she brings a baby home. Your ma's as skinny as a pole."

Harry Jacobs was eight. Gerard had taken him at his word, he knew about things. He was allowed to play in the next street and the one after that. Gerard was never allowed to venture beyond the gate at the end of the drive.

But Harry had been wrong because she had got it. It was right here, in a cot next to the sofa.

"Don't touch the baby Gerard. We'll only be a minute."

That's what he had been told. A minute was always a long time. Dinner took a minute; that was long. His mother talking to Mrs Kemp on the corner was a longer minute. One little look would not take that long. Gerry stood and climbed onto the arm of the sofa. He leaned over and peered into the cot. Lifting his hand he pointed his finger and prodded the sleeping bundle.

It gave off a yelp. Gerard jumped back. Harry said babies did nothing but yap. He was right about that. Leaning in again he looked at its face. It had a stubby nose, like a little pig, he poked it again. This time when it gave a yelp he did not jump back. Why did they have to have one of these anyway? He could smell it now. Yuk! Elizabeth Brown said babies smelt lovely; of powder. This one was stinking.

Gerard nearly jumped out of his skin as the door creaked open. Quick as he could he slid back into a seated position on the sofa and looked up at the lady who had entered the room. She had a bundle in her arms, another baby. Gerard tried his hardest to look innocent and not responsible for the frequent yelping that was still coming from the cot.

The lady started to rock the cot gently and in a quick minute the yelping had stopped.

"Aren't you a lovely little boy?"

She was looking at him now. It felt good, someone showing an interest in him. All anyone ever talked about at home was the new baby coming; everybody had forgotten he was there at all. The lady sat down next to him. He thought he should explain why he was there. When they visited his Nan's or other houses he was never allowed in the front room and certainly not unsupervised. That was because he liked to climb and usually broke something.

"We're here to get this baby," he explained.

As she leaned closer to him Gerard could smell the lovely powder that his mother used to cover him in; that she said he was too big for now. She had got more of it in the chemist this week, but it was not for him. It was for the baby. He wondered if the lady had got the baby on her knee in this place too. "Did you get that one here?"

The lady gave a gentle laugh and nodded. "I suppose you could say that. She's a perfect little princess, isn't she? She just needs someone special to watch after her."

Gerard's eyes lit up. A princess: A real princess. He had never seen a real princess before. The only ones he had seen were pictures in the story books his mother read to him each night. He wondered what a princess baby smelt like. There was no way it could smell bad. He leant a little closer and took a sniff. It smelled of baby powder and flowers; just lovely. Then it came to him, he could be special; everyone had said at one time or another that he was special.

"I can look after her if you'd like, I could keep her safe."

"Could you do that, special little man?"

As she spoke to him she gave his chin a little tickle. Gerard looked up at her. When she touched him he felt like he did when his Mum cuddled him. Maybe if he stuck his head in a bit closer she would stroke it too; that always felt good.

He liked her eyes. They were twinkling, shiny green eyes. The rays of light from the window made her head glow. He wondered if she was an angel. The pictures in his bedroom were like that; they were angels. Gerard had an idea, he moved back slightly and took a quick look behind her. No wings; the angels in his pictures had wings. Mum said they needed them to fly to where you were to stop bad things happening.

But she still had the glow when he looked back at her head. He knew why she had no wings; she was a magic angel. Her wings were hidden inside and she could make them come out when she wanted to fly. And besides, if anyone saw them they would take her to the church and cover her with that cold, hard stuff like the angels there; then she'd be stuck and she would never get to fly.

"What is her name?"

The lady freed one of the baby's hands and holding the little fingers she told him, "Her name's Fiona, but someone will probably change that."

Her eyes were full of tears. Gerard didn't feel good that she was sad.

Taking his hand she said, "Would you keep her safe for me? Would you make sure that no one ever hurts her?"

"I would, I would. Can we have her? I promise to look out for her."

Gerard was so excited; this wasn't any ordinary baby. She was a princess; his own princess. Wait till he told Harry about this. Harry had four sisters. They had scruffy hair and snotty noses; they definitely weren't princesses. But what if his new sister was a real princess? Harry couldn't beat that.

The lady leaned over Gerard and cupped his face in her hand. "If I place her in that cot you must never ever tell; not anyone. They will come and take her away. They are looking for her right now."

Gerard's eyebrows arched up, he so much wanted to boast to Harry that his sister was special: that he was specially chosen to guard her. But she could be taken back then and more than anything he did not want the smelly baby that was in the cot.

"Okay tell nobody, not even mother and father, especially not mother and father and never Harry. I promise."

Then the scariest thing so far of his life happened to him. The lady stood up and placed the princess in his arms. He felt like jelly. At first he closed his eyes as tight as he could, for he was so afraid he would drop her. Then he opened them to check that he hadn't. The little princess smiled at him and he felt so proud.

The lady took the other baby from the cot and laid her on the sofa, then taking the princess from Gerard's arms, she lifted her and placed her in the cot. She knelt in front of him and removed the pendant from her neck, closing it into his chubby little hand.

"Keep this close to her, it will protect her. Remember do not tell anyone our secret."

The lady picked up the other baby and looked into the cot. Gerard would always remember the sadness of her face. At the door she turned around, but said nothing more to him. She left clutching the smelly baby in her arms. And still he couldn't see her wings.

The Reid family walked proudly up the High street, Mrs Reid pushing the pram whilst Gerard walked beside scanning the street to see if anyone had noticed there was a princess in the pram. They stopped at Crafters toy shop and Frank Reid said to Alice: "We should let Gerard pick a toy, so as his nose doesn't get put out of joint."

Gerard could have whatever he fancied. He couldn't believe it; there hanging in the window was a knight's outfit: his special uniform. Knights protected princesses didn't they. They needed body armour to fight dragons and evil wizards.

It had been a special day, the fourteenth of February 1972, a new baby sister who was a princess given to him by an angel; a knight's outfit and – he knew because he felt it – his nose had not gone out of joint.

Gerard Reid walked beside the pram clutching the pendant. He knew he had to treasure it because it was special and would keep his Princess safe.

"We'll have to pick a name for her," Frank Reid said, lifting her out of the pram in their hallway.

"Fiona", Gerard piped up.

"Where did you get that name from, Gerard?"

Gerard clung onto the pendant still in his pocket. It was in the shape of a butterfly, he could feel its wings. "The butterfly angel told me she was called Fiona."

Frank Reid looked sceptically at his son, then rubbed his hand over the top of Gerard's head and smiled, "The butterfly angel, eh? What do you say then, Mother?"

"Fiona's a lovely name."

"Alright then; Fiona it is."

Gerard's mother took off his coat, hung it on the coat stand and led him into the sitting room, taking him up on her knee.

"Come here Gerard, Mummy wants a huge hug from her special little boy."

Hanging on round her neck, Gerard thought he really was special after all and so was his little sister. He would protect her from now on.

Two minutes later he had changed into his armour and had already begun his vigil beside her cot.

***

14th February 2002

Lifting one of the framed photos off the window sill, Gerry's mouth lifted in a half-smile. His childhood memories, like those of most people, were coloured by the senses of the time: the smell of his mother, the touch of her skin. And even though his perception of what had taken place was now endowed with an adult's reasoning, he still reflected on it with the eyes of a child. His belief in angels – or at least his assumption that the ones in the churchyard had once soared through the skies – was shattered when he was eight. Auntie Ethel having passed away, his father had taken him to the stonemasons to choose a monument for her grave. The whole process of changing a lump of stone into an ornament of choice was explained to him and part of the fantasy world that he lived in was lost. Not long after that, by his own deduction he worked out that his butterfly angel wasn't really an angel at all. Even now, all this time later, Gerry felt a tinge of embarrassment for his childish naivety.

Their freedom as children had been somewhat curtailed compared to their peers. Not that they had felt closeted or denied adventures – they had made their own – but always within the confines of the garden hedge. Neither did he feel that they had lost out or that their mother had been overly protective. They had become well accomplished at school and both had succeeded in professional careers. But so much of what had been real to them in the imaginary world they had created would have concerned him had he detected it in his own girls at that stage of their childhood.

Whatever he believed as a child had nothing to do with the problems he had brought upon himself, anyway. He had barely passed eighteen when his father had told him the truth about his own background. Gerry knew then that his Dad had thought he wouldn't remember much about the day Fiona had come into their lives, had failed to realise that Gerry would automatically be able to put the whole picture together and understand what had really taken place that day. No; angels were not real at all! It had all been a big con.

What he had done after that had led to this terrible position he was in now. It had been the saddest day of his life to find out that the man he had idolised all those years: the caring adoptive father, morally upright, a respected officer of the law, devoted to his wife and children, was in fact a cheat who had tricked his wife into adopting his mistress's son. It had destroyed him in Gerry's eyes. To learn that this cheat was in fact his natural father had been a bitter blow. The knowledge that what he loved and respected in him was not real, but was false, had consequences that did not take long to impose on Gerry's life.

Once his mother knew that Frank had told him, she never looked at him in quite the same way as before. The arms that had always given him warm embraces felt cold after that. After so many years when she had set aside her husband's betrayal and hidden so well the pain, which Gerry knew it must have caused her to have him around her, she no longer had to live with the lie. She had never said anything about it to Gerry, but she didn't need to. He knew he had lost her.

As an adult – and a psychiatrist – he knew this feeling of lost love had emanated from deep inside himself and that in turning away from her in his hurt, he had brought about a self-fulfilling prophecy.

But whatever, of one thing he was sure: he did not want the person he loved most in the world to have to experience this loss of love and stability.

He had always accepted that Fiona's bond with their mother was closer than his own. Once he knew why, he had decided never to let anything break it. When Frank Reid had shown him photos of the club where he had worked under cover and picked out the dancer who was Gerry's mother, Gerry at the time had taken no interest in her. If he had needed any further evidence that Frank had pulled the same con a second time, it was in the picture staring back at him. Just behind those who posed for the camera, although younger than he remembered her, was his angel. It was enough to confirm what he suspected: Fiona was his natural half-sister.

Eventually, Frank and Alice had both died, Frank having a heart attack during the early days of Gerry's first marriage. Gerry held onto his secret. Until recently it had been worth the fifteen years or so of warmth that Fiona got out of it; still able to feel the comfort of Alice's love. And although from the time this had all been made known to him Gerry had lost that; such was the love and the respect he held for his adoptive mother, he could not let her discover that she had been betrayed by Frank a second time. Gerry would not see her destroyed.

Now, for some reason – and he denied himself an understanding of why, even though he knew it existed deep inside his own heart – Fiona was intent on discovering the identity of her birth mother. He anguished at the thought of feeling rejected all over again; could not bear to lose the one true person, apart from his wife and children, who was real in his life. What he feared most, and did everything in his power to prevent, was that she would see the falseness in him; he did not want to be to her what Frank had turned out to be for him: a cheat.

Gerry set the photograph on his desk. It was one taken outside the registry office on the day of his wedding. It showed him holding Sandra on one side and Fiona on the other, with Sam and Elle standing in front. He chuckled as he thought how angelic the girls looked then, aged nine and six, before makeup, music and boys had entered their lives. But they were never a problem to him; they did have their moments, but it was all part of growing up and he, with all his experience of children in his chosen field of psychiatry, could handle all that. It was a pity he was struggling with the other two women in his life.

Massaging his fingers into his temple, he willed himself to cope with the pain growing in his head. But it would do no good. He reached for his jacket and emptied the last of the tablets into his mouth. He'd finished the bottle already and he knew it should have been far from empty. The nagging thing about that, though, was that they did nothing to ease the relentless explosions that ripped through his head. Getting up to pour a glass of water, he prayed a silent prayer that this consultant he was to see today would be able to find the cause behind the pain – and most important of all, a cure for whatever it was that persecuted him so. He could not take it anymore; he knew he had turned into a grotesque monster because of it and was rapidly destroying Sandra's love for him.

Sitting back at his desk, he tidied his case notes into their folders and placed them into his briefcase. He was in his office. It was situated on the third floor of their home and could be accessed by its own entrance by means of what Sandra called 'the iron giant'; the metal fire escape. Yes, Sandy was right; it looked ugly imposing itself against the back of the house and despite being host to the ivy that wrapped itself around most of its framework, its biggest problem was the safety of the structure – or rather the lack of it. He occasionally took consultations at home and Sandra was always warning him.

"You'll be sued for injury one of these days. Don't keep on ignoring it; you don't want me saying I told you so. It's a death trap, sitting there all set and ready to catch someone!"

Another door led out onto the upper landing, but Gerry did not think it suitable to take clients past the private bedrooms in their home. It was this door that sprung open without warning, briefly unsettling him until he saw the ray of sunshine that walked through it.

"Fiona, I didn't know you were here, shouldn't you be at work, I thought you were in court today?"

It was a little joke between them; Fiona was in the middle of shooting an English version of *Judge Judy*, due to be run overnight on a cable station later in the year. The idea was that warring couples would have their matrimonial problems sorted out on screen. Fiona acted as one of the mediators, much like a solicitor.

"Gerry," she sighed. "Try not to be such a fuss, not today. Today's a special day – or have you forgotten?"

"Fiona! Have I ever forgotten?" A smile broke over his face and high-toned, almost singing, he wished her, "Happy Birthday!"

Already he had moved towards her and taking her by the waist he swung her around setting her on his desk. He was intent to keep it upbeat no matter how she tested him. Despite the fact that they barely saw eye to eye anymore, he would not let anything spoil her day. She was doing the same: putting their harsh words behind her. She had a knack for it; unlike him. It was always Fiona's way: she never carried bad atmospheres over to new days and although lately it had produced the need for some effort on her part, she ignored his mood swings. She hated falling out with him; every new day was just that: new – and yesterdays were always gone.

It was St. Valentine's Day, she was thirty five – or at least, this was the day when they always celebrated her birthday. Tall and slender, sitting on his desk, she drew her legs up, tucking them beneath her. She was more than a picture: she was stunningly beautiful.

"Early sitting, all done and dusted by ten thirty. Which I am happy to say leaves me the rest of the day free. This is going to be a special day. I just know it. Look what Mark gave me this morning and it's only a little appetiser. The big surprise comes later. This day isn't going to go quick enough until dinner tonight. Isn't it beautiful Gerry?"

Gerry couldn't miss it; dangling from her neck instead of the butterfly locket she had worn for all these years. It was a solid gold Tiffany Heart, studded with diamonds and it was, he had to admit, beautiful; but where was the locket? Even his strongest will to hide his reservations were not enough to cover up his sudden feeling of annoyance.

"All right, spit it out," she said. "It's no use leaving it hanging there staling the air, let it out, Gerry." She was doodling on a note block as she spoke. She held it up for him as she waited for him to start destroying her day. It was a quick sketch of his face; stern features, eyebrows like triangles and cheeky horns on his head – and just for added effect, exhaust fumes rolling from his ears.

He couldn't bring himself to smile. "Where have you put the locket, Fiona?" He was striving as hard as he could to keep a light-hearted tone. He didn't want to keep hounding her, things had felt so bad lately, but it was so important to him that he kept her safe and that's what the locket had always done; kept her safe. Gone may be his childish belief in angels, but on occasion certain things had happened that left the locket as the only reason behind her still being alive at all. The irrationality of the thought failed to strike him.

Fiona grinned at him, "Look, I've still got it, next to my heart." She touched the little inside breast pocket of her jacket. But he could see that she was hurt that he hadn't complimented Mark's gift.

"I'm getting really sick of this childishness you insist on smothering me with, Gerry. I'm a big girl now. Jesus, I'm thirty five years old! When will you realise that I'm not a little girl anymore. It's suffocating me, Gerry; suffocating me." She slammed her fist on his desk and sighed before she turned her gaze to the ceiling.

"I'm sorry Fiona, it's just that I worry sometimes; I've a bad feeling—"

She stood and cut him off before he could finish. "I don't want to hear about your bad feelings. Despite what you may feel, I think today is going to be great. In fact; more than that; I've a feeling it's going to be special, really special. I won't let you do it this time, Gerry. I won't allow you to spoil today for me."

Helplessly unable to retrieve the situation he had created, as always in recent months, he let her have the last word.

She walked over to where he stood, gave him a quick peck on the cheek and left him alone again.

He picked up his case and left by the fire escape thinking it better to avoid Sandra downstairs, knowing she would be able to tell they had been arguing again. Fiona would release her frustration at his behaviour on his wife; she always did.

It was 4.50pm that evening when Gerry pulled his car into the forecourt of a petrol station. Again his head was exploding making him unable to concentrate on the road. He pulled off his tie and grabbed a tissue from a box on the passenger seat. Sweating, he battled with the confusion of all that had unfolded that day.

He had guessed for some time that there were woeful reasons for his changes in behaviour, but had never guessed the tumult that it would release in him today. He opened the window to let in some air. It sickened him, what he had looked at today, but what frightened him most of all was that it was something he could not control.

He emptied a few of the opiates the consultant had prescribed, hoped they were worth taking and turned up the radio to catch the news.

"Police have released the name of the young woman found stabbed to death today in Parkland Tower, Hill Gate North as Miss Katie Smyth. Police intercepted a man at the scene who is presently helping them with their inquiries..."

Gerry stared at the dash for a few moments before starting the engine. The name of the girl meant nothing, but the address did. Fiona and Mark lived at Parkland Tower. The bad feeling that he'd woken with that morning ached all the harder in his gut.

He turned in the direction of home and recited the prayer, the one tucked inside the butterfly locket: "Angel of God..."

***

Wednesday 31st October, 2007

The journal slipping from Fiona's fingers woke her. She was cramped in the alcove of Gerry's study, her back pressed against the window. She shivered; the sun had gone. How long had she been asleep? Had she been dreaming? Her brother's presence had seemed so real she almost expected him to be there, gently chiding her for allowing herself to get so exhausted. Bending to pick up the journal, she slid off her seat with a groan. God, how she missed him; how had it come to this?

And then she remembered what she had been reading.

31

Police Headquarters, Maidstone, Kent

Jeff slammed down the phone. He'd tried to get through to Lady Clara's office several times this morning never getting further than her personal assistant. He shouted for Stevens, who stuck his head round the door.

"Sir?"

"Would you be kind enough to call your mother for me and ask if she can spare me a few moments of her time? Somehow I don't think my messages are getting through to her!"

Coming into Jeff's office, an embarrassed DS Stevens hurriedly pushed the door to. "She'll be in meetings, Sir. Your best bet is to catch her around lunch time. That's when she always has time to phone me."

With a curt nod, Jeff waved him away. The whole team was assembled out front. The week was almost over and they had come to a standstill. That had its good points, Jeff reflected: at least there had been no more murders. Maybe Matt and Peggy Lyons had been the end target after all; then why steal the records?

This morning, at long last, the team had finally been granted permission to retrieve all the private adoption records concerning the Priory. Now the tedious task lay ahead to sift through them in an attempt to match the aliases to the real names. Could it be that the women they sought were safer staying hidden? Was it right to try to find them? Jeff banished the doubts: too late now anyway, he had set the ball rolling. He had met with several newspaper editors the previous evening and arranged for a carefully worded advert assuring of confidentiality, to be placed in today's papers. His hope was that the women concerned would see it and contact the incident room. So far, the phones were not ringing. He had even gone so far as to insert one of the photographs of the Priory found in Peggy Lyons's albums. And that was not all: one of the papers had run an update on the murders alongside the appeal. Jeff was expecting the call from Millar at any time!

Leaving his office, he walked across the incident room and checked the boards. "What have you dug up on this Simon Alexander?" he asked Stevens, seeing the name had been added.

"Not a lot yet, Sir, but I'm heading into London to the Search Agency's office now. Thought I'd see how much I could glean from Alexander's secretary and any of his associates."

"Okay. Well keep me posted. It's interesting isn't it when you look at the time line?"

"Isn't it just," Sandra said, coming up behind him. "At the end of August last year Fiona attends Search and enlists the help of Alexander to find her natural mother. Six months later Katie Smyth makes it known to Stevens here there are issues concerning privacy of information." Searching through Fiona's statement, she grabbed a marker and added several dates under Simon Alexander's name on the board.

She turned to look at her colleagues then back to the board. "The following day, February 14th, she is murdered. Mark Jakes, another employee of Search, is caught red-handed – no pun intended!"

Jeff chuckled silently to himself; at least she was in good enough form to make jokes about it today. He had explained to her yesterday that for the present his hands were tied, with pressure coming down hard from above to keep her workload light. It seemed she had accepted his explanation; certainly she was in a better temper.

"Eight months pass," Sandra continued, "and as Fiona states here, she contacts Simon Alexander to inform him she has located the house in Higham. That was on Thursday evening last. She says she intends to visit Mrs Lyons to ask for her help in sorting out the mix-up over her adoption papers, and tells him she has arranged her visit for Sunday. That night—"

The strident tone of a phone ringing cut across what Sandra was saying. They all swung round as one, but it was not the special line set up for the advert. Exchanging glances, they returned their attention to the board. Christine took the call. It was for DS Stevens.

"So," Sandra said, "Sunday night the Lyonses are murdered. Shortly after that my house is entered and the records are taken. Clearly, we need to know what Alexander's role is in all of this: He's the only other person who knew Fiona was there."

Stevens replaced the receiver. "That was a return call from Heathrow. I phoned all the airports earlier. Alexander's secretary – name's Linda – said he was on holiday and his house is all locked up, so I phoned around the airports just on the off-chance he was headed overseas. Turns out he was booked on a flight to Vienna on Friday night, then going on to Frankfurter on Sunday for some big conference on Human Rights. What's interesting is that he didn't turn up for the flight on Friday and neither has he yet contacted them to re-book."

Nodding, Jeff faced his team. "Right; let's see if we have enough to get a warrant. Stevens, you head into London. Take Jones with you. Find out if Simon Alexander uses another address. I'll talk to the Met, see if they can unearth some background concerning him and this company of his. See if the staff there can fill you in on his private life."

"Right Sir, but do you think he fits the profile? Aside from anything else, so far as we know, he doesn't seem to have been adopted."

Sandra's mobile sounded. She stepped back to the window to answer it. The call was brief. Slowly she pulled a chair over and sat down, her gaze on the window.

Assuming it was personal, Jeff left her to it and turned back to the board, tapping Alexander's name. "Maybe not, but he's all we have for now. He was the only one to know of Fiona's plans. And he wasn't on that flight. Besides, whether he was adopted or not, his agency concerns itself with adoption. Maybe hearing about the turmoil of so many abandoned children finally got to him. When we find him we'll ask him all about it! Now let's get things moving here!" He strode back to his office. The phone on his desk was ringing and so was Sandra's mobile again.

He knew before he answered that it would likely be Millar on the other end of the line. Looking up he realised that Sandra had followed and was standing in the doorway.

"I've just accepted an offer on the house," she said. "I should be pleased, and I suppose I am, but it feels strange."

His hand on the receiver, Jeff gave a sympathetic nod and held up his hand to stay her.

Sandra shook her head. "Sorry, Jeff, but I've got to go out. I am expected at Brampton Manor within the hour. There was a break-in there a few months before the Higham murders. I thought it worth checking; it might be connected."

Picking up the phone, Jeff mouthed "Okay" and waved her on; right now he had troubles enough of his own.

To his relief, the call wasn't from Millar. It was Tony Hardy, who had been out last night when Jeff returned his call. He had something on his mind and wanted Jeff to pay him a visit; thought it would be of interest seeing that it was connected to the case. He hadn't mentioned it to the detective who had visited them the evening before because his wife had only disclosed it to him later. But then he had read the paper this morning and was a bit baffled by the fact that her code name, as she called it, was included in the ad, even though the investigating team obviously knew of her whereabouts. It was only then that he had thought there was something odd about it.

What the hell...? Jeff listened, his eyes widening in surprise. Tony's *wife*? All this was news to him. He finished the call and sat staring into space. His first conclusion was that Stevens hadn't quite understood their little chat. Then he remembered Stevens had been with him until well after eight on that particular evening, so it could have nothing to do with him.

He was still pondering on this when Constable Blake, having waited for the incident room to empty, slipped into his office with more information he had unearthed on the South American Cardinal.

Placing a bundle of paper on Jeff's desk, he said, "DS Stevens thinks it's a good idea if I sift through some of the forums linked to adoption sites on the net, Sir. He thinks some of the women might have put messages up in the hopes their children would see them."

"Good idea, Blake." Jeff pulled the downloads towards him and nodded. "You didn't let Stevens see these did you?"

"No sir. I did all that at home last night, printed it out there too. I've been carrying it about folded in my shirt pocket all morning."

"Well done, lad. I will explain this angle to the team eventually, but for now it's top secret, okay?"

"Understood, Sir."

After Blake had gone, Jeff locked the papers into his desk and checked his watch. The search warrant for the Alexanders's house would take a few hours to set up. For the time being, he needed to talk to Tony. He hurried out to the car park and started the car, heading in the direction of Gravesend, a coil of foreboding curling in the pit of his stomach.

Tony Hardy was raking up leaves in his garden when Jeff pulled up at the fence. Dressed in a red v-neck sweater and beige chinos, Jeff supposed he was filling a greater part of his retirement on the putting green. His hairline had receded more than when they had last met and what remained of his hair was more white than grey. Dropping the rake he made his way to the passenger side of the car tapping the window at Jeff to unlock the door.

"Do you mind if we talk out here for a bit before we go inside, only Lydia hasn't seen the paper yet so she won't have caught on that something's not right. I don't want to alarm her."

"Of course – shall I drive us somewhere; won't she think it's odd if she sees us?"

"No, here's okay she's taking a nap in the conservatory out back." Tony got in to the passenger seat. "Look Jeff; I didn't think a thing about it at the time. Just past six it was when he called here. Flashed the identity card; seemed on the level, even knew her maiden name. Looked like a copper too; you know how you can tell one of our lot a mile off. Said his name was Perkins.

"Never heard of him," Jeff said.

"Well; I took him in. Guess I knew right away what it was all about. Fact is I'd been half-expecting it. Lydia's been fretting about it ever since we saw it on the box – about the Lyonses. Nasty business."

"What did he look like, Tony? Could you pick him out if we set up a video line up?"

Tony nodded. He had eyes like – well, do you mind that bloke who acted in that *Nazareth* thing a good few years ago? He had eyes like that. You know the kind I mean? They stand out above everything else: a real vibrant blue that doesn't look quite real."

Jeff nodded. "Contacts probably – go on Tony, what did he want exactly?"

"Well, that's just the point: never got around to asking. It was like he just wanted to take a look at us. Said he was checking up on anyone who had known Matt and Peggy Lyons. The thing was that just before he arrived Lee had dropped off Vicky and the grandkids, so it was all a bit chaotic. I led him through to the back sitting room and he walked over to the French doors to look into the garden. Vicky was down the end with Linda and the children – we keep their pet rabbits here and they'd gone to play with them. Anyway, I asked if he could be discreet. You know what I mean. Only we've never told Vicky anything about the days before she was born. She has no idea that her mother was once a hostess in a nightclub. It's not the sort of thing we would want her to know, you understand. And she knows nothing of the hardship we suffered, struggling to get away from that place so as we could get married and bring our girl up decent. We never told her anything. There didn't seem a need."

Jeff had had no idea either. Tony had been married and settled when he was moved to the squad at Gravesend. If he had thought about it at all, he had assumed Lydia was what she had always seemed: a respectable, supportive wife and mother. That she had at one time been a high-class prostitute would never have occurred to him. No wonder Tony was looking so agitated at having to divulge this information.

Tony was pacing back and forth, speaking nervously. "Smiling he was; standing watching – the children more than Lydia – just watching them playing with the rabbits – and smiling. I filled him in with our background; he already seemed to know a bit about us, like I said. And then he just turned, looked at me and said we had nothing to worry about. Said he was only interested in women who had abandoned their children. I mean, I thought it strange at the time, that choice of words. But to be honest with you, Jeff, it was the way he looked at the kids. It raised the hairs on the back of my neck, if you know what I mean. Kind of came over all funny he did. I could swear he was almost in tears as he rushed past me and took off out the front door. Weird!"

Staring straight ahead, Jeff made no comment as he tried to make sense of it all.

Mistaking his silence, Tony said, "Look Jeff, I don't want you thinking any less of Lydia now that you know about her past. You have no idea what it was like for her. I thought we had left it all behind us a long time ago. Vicky doesn't know I'm not her real father either, so keep that under your hat too."

Jeff shook his head, feeling sorry for this man who had been a close colleague for going on thirty years. Tony must have thought he knew about Vicky, but like Lydia's past, it was news to him. He patted him on the shoulder. "Don't worry, my friend. It's nobody's business but yours. Rest assured I will make sure it stays that way. But I think you haven't told me everything; there's more isn't there?"

Tony nodded, opening the car door. "Yes. I might have known you would guess that. Come into the house, Jeff, and talk to Lydia. She can tell you better than I can."

Lydia was one of those women who seem ageless: tall; her figure and her looks no different from when Jeff had last seen her, here in this room about five years ago. He and Angie had often had dinner with the Hardys, but after Angie died the invitations had gradually dried up; hardly surprising – he had stopped responding to them.

Bleary-eyed after her nap, Lydia offered Jeff a cup of tea, which Tony went off to make. When he had left the room, Lydia seated herself close to Jeff and spoke almost in a whisper. "I think Tony's annoyed with me for keeping in touch with the girls over the years. But he finds it hard to understand the bond; especially after all we went through together."

Her statement startled Jeff: "The girls?"

"Yes; the ones in the newspaper. Well, I call them 'girls'," she smiled, "but we're all old women now! We all knew Peggy Lyons, you see. Such a shock; that poor, poor woman."

Jeff's jaw dropped. For a moment he could not believe what he was hearing. "Forgive me, Lydia, but let me get this straight. You know who these women are? Where they are?"

"Of course I know who they are! I don't know of their exact whereabouts, but we keep in touch now and then."

What a stroke of luck! This was too good to be true. Was it real? Jeff wanted to pinch himself. Instead he took out his notebook and scribbled as Lydia chattered on.

"I know you've talked to Clara," she said, "she contacted me this morning – though I don't really know how she got my number. But anyway, we are supposed to meet up. It's a place called 'White Cliffs', the last place we were all together, except for the funeral in '78, of course, that was when Sheila's little girl was killed."

"This Sheila, is she one of these women too?" Jeff asked as Lydia stopped to draw breath. "The ones listed in the paper?"

"Yes, Jeff. Sheila is one. Then there was Karen and Amilee. '78 was the last time we all actually met up. All of us except Amilee; we lost her back in '72. I don't even know what names they use now. We keep in touch through coded messages in the paper – novenas – and only if something happens to deem it necessary."

Jeff had written down the names. "Necessary? In what way necessary?"

"If one of us needs a friend: we made a pact that we would always try to be there for each other. The thing is, unless you have been through what we all went through, you cannot possibly understand."

"What about the code names we printed in the paper – what were they all about?"

Lydia smiled; it looked forced: "That was all Peggy's idea. She never once queried our past; never judged us or made us feel that we had done anything wrong. She told us stories of great people, all of them with secrets. She named us after saints, you know – it was to be part of our cover when we stayed at the Priory. And we dressed in habits for a disguise in case anyone came searching for us. I suppose in some ways it seemed like a big adventure to us – until it turned tragic – we were all very young."

"So: you say Lady Clara Smith-Stevens has called a meeting? Can I suppose the others are aware then that something is happening and that is why you have all been summoned to this place," he checked his notebook, "White Cliffs?"

Lydia stood and walked over to the fireplace. "Actually, no; I think it must have been Sheila, and the notices were placed a few weeks ago. I really don't think they have anything to do with the murders in Higham."

Jeff gave Lydia an encouraging smile hoping she could explain more to him, but she remained silent, gazing unseeing at the window. He prompted her, "Tell me about the code names; why those particular names? What happened to connect you five in particular? I don't suppose..." he paused as a thought struck him. "Lydia, Tony has told me a little about your past. Tell me; did some of these girls work in a club like you?"

Lydia flushed, looked down at her feet. "I'm sorry; I thought Tony had explained. We were all from the same club; all of us!"

Jeff nodded hiding his concern. So; Lady Clara had lied to him – and to Millar what's more – she was no innocent lass from up North. She might have been at one time, but not when she found herself pregnant with her son. It occurred to Jeff that he was in a bit of a pickle. What was he going to do with this piece of information? He wondered what DS Stevens knew. Had he received the same cover story as they had about the circumstances surrounding his birth? A nasty business this was turning out to be. There was definitely something running between the lines in this case and it wasn't just middle-aged ladies who were the victims; there were other young lives at risk of being destroyed by an unsuspected and murky past.

Lydia moved restlessly away from the fireplace. "There's another set of names that we were known by. His 'trinkets' he called us. He gave us all names of precious stones. I was 'Ebony'; Clara was 'Amber'; Sheila, 'Emerald'; Karen, 'Sapphire' and Amilee was 'Jade'."

Jeff noted down the names. He looked up at Lydia. "Him?"

"McMasters."

She had barely said the name when it all fell into place for Jeff. Although he had been involved only indirectly in the McMasters' case himself, Tony had been part of a huge undercover operation. The club at the Imperial Ballroom, from where the drug baron had run his evil empire had been notorious. Yet somehow they had never been able to pin it on McMasters – and eventually, of course, he had been killed in an RTA. And bloody good riddance, Jeff thought with feeling. If Lydia had worked there, it was no wonder she wanted it kept quiet. He could see this was difficult for her; her eyes were welling with tears as she dropped her gaze.

"Most of us started the same way," she said, "working the tables. Amber – that's Clara – was there before any of us. It's strange looking back on it: I feel so dirty, even now, but we just had to make the best of it back then. We were innocents; just kids with no money; too naive to know what was happening with the drugs and everything. And mixing with celebrities, actors and the like, well you can imagine, it was exciting to us then. We thought we were so special. As long as you were treated well enough it seemed an okay way to live. And we were frightened too. Once you were in you had to keep quiet; do what he said and he would protect you. I had no idea that Tony was a copper, not until later when they got us away; you know – when the operation he was involved in went wrong."

Jeff nodded. It was all coming back to him now; the stories Tony had told him, the snippets of information about different cases that get passed around over a beer.

"Amber was his," Lydia said. "She belonged to McMasters; the most precious of stones he called her. She was also close to Frank Reid; I think they had a bit of history, but she never talked about it much."

Lydia seemed to have got into her stride and not wanting to break her train of thought, Jeff held his tongue, but what she was now revealing was dynamite. He scribbled the name 'Frank Reid' followed by several exclamation marks. He didn't believe in coincidences – remember! He continued scribbling as Lydia worked through the list, putting the names she remembered to each alias.

"Emerald, poor Sheila that is – she was Sister Mary Brigid – she just wasn't cut out for it at all. The rest of us had no one else to answer to, but Sheila was different: she had a husband, or rather a brute. Twisted he was—"

"Are we by chance talking about Sheila Hynds here, Lydia?" Jeff interrupted.

Lydia nodded, "Yes, it was him, Jack Hynds, got her to work the tables. He used to hit her about something awful, but never where it showed. You could make a good living on the tips alone. Wouldn't have done if she'd come to work with black eyes! Anyway, after a few months she caught the attention of one of the punters that McMasters had invited into to the private club; the casino beneath the ballroom. Loaded he was, and McMasters wanted to use him, so he gave him Sheila. He wasn't a regular this man; we never found out who he was. I think Clara may have known him though, she was a sly one was Clara. But then, she had to be to survive."

"What do you mean by 'gave'?" Jeff frowned, not quite understanding.

Lydia gazed at him, a wry expression on her face. "Just that; gave her to him, that's what we all became in the end, presents for his clientele."

Jeff felt his ears grow red as he realised exactly what she meant.

"What about surnames, Lydia, do you remember them?"

"Oh yes," Lydia nodded. "Amilee's was Hunter; Karen's was Howell and Sheila's and Clara's you know – but like I said, I don't know what names they use now or even if they've kept the same forenames. We changed them for our own safety. Ken McMasters; he had friends everywhere."

Jeff didn't need reminding about the dangers these girls faced; he had seen enough in his years as a copper to know what it meant to fall foul of someone like McMasters. The memory jarred on his brain. Almost he could smell the whiff of burning boat and see the body of the dead child, Sheila Hynds's son, fished out of the river barely recognisable. Had McMasters had a hand in it? Almost certainly; but there had been nothing to connect him to it at the time; with a sudden shiver Jeff remembered he had the file still locked in the glove compartment of his car. He had been so busy he had forgotten.

He was about to ask Lydia if he could see the notice that had been placed to arrange the meeting at White Cliffs, but Tony arrived carrying a tray of tea and biscuits and the thread was broken. Downing his tea and thanking them both, Jeff advised Lydia not to meet up with her old pals – at least not for a while. Best to wait until things had been sorted out; he didn't think that in this case there would be safety in numbers.

"I'll look into this visitor of yours, Tony," Jeff said as they strolled out to his car. "There's a slim chance that it's above board; wires get crossed. Unlikely, I know. I didn't want to alarm Lydia, but I think you should be extra vigilant until we know the score. Don't leave her on her own and keep the house well secured at night; windows as well as doors—" he broke off with a rueful laugh. "I don't need to tell an ex-copper all of this do I. Sorry!"

"That's okay," Tony smiled holding open the car door. "You're only doing your job. So, Jeff – what's this case all about?"

"Haven't figured it out yet, though we do have a prime suspect," Jeff answered, his gaze going back to Lydia, her figure still visible against the voiles at her sitting room window.

Moving to block Jeff's view of her, Tony shifted from one foot to the other until he stood directly in front of Jeff, the car door in between them. Placing his hands on the bonnet of the car he glanced back to the house, but Lydia had disappeared from view. "A prime suspect," he repeated. "I've known you too long Jeff; if that's the case then tell me this my old mate; why don't I feel any enthusiastic vibes from you? The chase is on, yet I can't see it in you; none of the glinting in your eyes. I haven't been gone long enough to forget how it feels, you know – that adrenalin in the blood when you know you're on the scent. What's wrong here Jeff?"

Getting into the car, Jeff reached for his seat belt. "It's a bit complicated. We're just waiting for a search warrant to come through then we'll make our move. We've got the right man, I'm fairly sure of that, but as you've detected – well, something else is niggling me about this. People are lying to me and I don't like that. There's more to this case than meets the eye."

Aware that voicing his misgivings would not make Tony feel any better about the fact that his wife might have had a lucky escape Jeff attempted to sound more up beat. "Look; take care Tony and make sure she doesn't head to that reunion. If this guy *is* our killer, I don't like the way he found his way to Lydia so easily, but if he had wanted to harm her we wouldn't be here talking about it now. Maybe he knows where the rest of the women are too. Best to stay away from them until this gets sorted out. Thanks for calling it in; it has certainly made things more clear; answered a lot of questions that have bothered me from the beginning."

Placing a hand on Tony's shoulder he urged him, "Don't worry. I'll handle all you've told me with great care. Lydia's secret is safe with me. And by the way, I might even have a proposition of sorts for you in a few months – if you can drag yourself away from that golf club of yours for a few days a week. I'll keep in touch."

Jeff drove down the road several hundred yards before pulling into a lay-by. Sheila Hynds! Well that was a turn up for the books. Now he knew why she had vanished following the discovery of her son's body: she had been pregnant and had fled. Strange thing that he had been looking at the file the very morning the call had come in from Higham. Pulling out his notebook, he glanced through the other names: one of them had to be Fiona Reid's mother, except for Sheila – Lydia had said her daughter died. If the women had planned to meet up tomorrow night there was a good chance Sheila Hynds was already in Dover. He took out his mobile and phoned Christine, gave her the address of the White Cliffs Cottage and asked her to contact the Dover station to see if someone could check the place out.

That done, he turned the key in the ignition and slid the car back onto the road: *where would Sheila Hynds go?* The only friend of hers that he had known about was Beth Shaw. Making a quick decision, Jeff put his foot down and headed for the row of terraced houses near the old docks where Beth had lived. Was she still there – was she even alive? It was a slim chance.

"Can I help you at all?"

Locking the car, Jeff looked over the roof to see a woman he judged to be in her mid-forties standing on a chair, cloth in hand, cleaning the windows of number 36.

Smiling, he strolled over. "I was hoping to speak to a Beth Shaw. Am I at the right house?"

Putting a hand on his shoulder to steady herself, she stepped down from the chair. "It's the right house alright, but you'll not find her here I'm afraid. She's in the graveyard, about a mile back up the way you just came."

Jeff had known it was a slim chance: 35 years was a long time. He wondered about her husband. "What about Arthur, is he there too?"

"Why yes; as a matter a fact he is. This is my day off; come over from Rochester every Thursday. Spend the day sprucing the place up for him; do what I can."

Jeff frowned, puzzled. "I'm sorry? He's alive then?"

"Of course he's alive. Like I said, he's in the graveyard. Sits there most of the day he does. Probably wishing for the ground to open up and pull him down beside her and one of these days he'll get what he wants: it's pneumonia he'll go down with sitting out there in all weathers."

Jeff thanked her and headed back, stopping across the road from the cemetery gate. He opened the glove compartment and flicked through the pages of the Hynds' file until he came to the statement Beth Shaw had made way back in 1971.

He was just getting out of the car when Christine phoned him back. The cottage was deserted. No sign of life about the place at all. It was a remote building perched on one of the smaller cliffs, though it appeared to have been recently renovated. The local police surmised it was owned by an out-of-towner and was probably a holiday home only occupied in the summer months. They had said they would get back to her.

Thanking her, Jeff made his way into the cemetery. He spotted Arthur Shaw immediately. Sitting on a bench, head bent, he cut a tragic figure. He seemed lost in his own world as Jeff sat down beside him, but the name 'Sheila Hynds' forced an immediate reaction.

The old man's back stiffened as he turned to look at Jeff from watery, bloodshot eyes. "I knew the first time I laid eyes on that one she was trouble. Kid dies and she scarpers. Left my missus with a ton of grief to bear on her own did that one. Swallowed her up in the end it did. My Beth never got over it."

Jeff understood loss; thinking of Angie, he listened as Beth's husband rambled out one rebuke after the next. It seemed that Beth had carried her guilt in her heart all the way to her grave. In her eyes she may as well have started the fire herself, the old man told him. She was dead fond of that little boy. She always regretted handing him over to his drunken father on that dreadful night. Slowly, the scripts written by her doctor increased until she floated from one day to the next, but they never lightened the burden. In the small hours of the night the child's little hands clawed at her through the flames, his screams cut through her head driving her insane.

She had clung on as best she could until the last of her own had left. The girls had both gone into nursing and got married. Her pride and joy, their son, David, went to university to take a science degree and took up lodgings with some of his friends. Somehow she had done it; got them all raised and off her hands. It was over, they didn't need her anymore; it was time for her to make it all better.

Jeff, still so close to his own grief, let the old man talk. He knew it was some kind of a release for him. He doubted that Arthur had talked much about it to anyone before.

The day Beth died, Arthur had come home from his shift one evening and she'd set his dinner tray on his lap as usual. It had been easy to slip past him with the bottle of sedatives. Upstairs in their bedroom she had downed the whole lot. When Arthur found her, she was still hugging to her chest the photographs of himself and their children that had always stood on the shelf by the bed. It was like they had watched over her as she took her first sleep without nightmares in fifteen years. The old man's voice broke as he explained this to Jeff.

He had guessed what she was going to do. No one knew better than him of the struggle she had endured. He alone had shared the darkness and with it the terrors that haunted his wife night after night. He had wrestled with his conscience to leave her be, let her have the peace she longed for. He'd felt her faint pulse gradually fade, slower and slower until there was nothing. It was a release, a release that he had felt as much as her. He'd felt no guilt: she had been lost to him and the girls a long time ago. All of Arthur's anger had been for his son. They'd had a sympathy card from him; that was all. Attempts to reach David at his flat in London had failed; contact it was true had diminished in the last year, but to not turn up for his mother's funeral was an insult that Arthur could neither understand nor forgive.

Easing himself up from the bench, his seamed face wet with tears, Arthur Shaw looked down at Jeff. "She's over here," he pointed.

Jeff followed him to the graveside and stood, head bent, imagining the scene: the earth falling on the casket; the distraught girls saying their farewells and leaving their father a few moments of privacy to say his final goodbyes.

A sharp wind blew against his face as he turned to make his way across to the gates of the cemetery. Holding up the collar of his coat to shield himself from the cold air, he stopped and turned back again. Separated from Beth's grave by the path was another: a small mound marked by a tiny headstone: 'Andy Hynds 1965–1971'; nothing else. Overgrown with weeds, forgotten by most, the grave bore a fresh display of carnations. Arthur Shaw murmured beside him: "I do it for her. She always brought him carnations – every month. It reminds me why my Beth chose that day out of any day to take leave of this world."

Jeff put out his hand to grasp the old man's shoulder. "I'm sorry, Arthur," was all he could say. The story had affected him far more than he would have imagined. Twenty years of walled-up hatred for a woman, who as far as Arthur was concerned had caused his wife's death, finally unleashed to a stranger. In truth, it seemed that Arthur Shaw had been grieving Beth's loss from the night she had placed little Andy Hynds into his no good father's hands.

Jeff drove Arthur back to his terrace; it was the least he could do.

He felt guilty for opening so many raw wounds – not that the old man had ever succeeded in closing them.

It was dark long before he made it to the outskirts of Maidstone. The temperature too had dropped with the sun. He supposed that was why he was shivering.

32

Residence of Bishop Thomas O'Mally, Canterbury:
the same day

His lips kissed the ring; his head remained low as the hand moved in the sign of the cross above him. "In the name of the Father and of the Son and of the Holy Spirit: Amen. God bless you my son."

Receiving the blessing, Leonard Millar remained for several minutes on his knees; in his own mind absolved of nothing; still a sinner.

The Bishop settled himself into his armchair and pulled a cord hanging by the side of the huge marble fireplace, signalling to his valet to bring in the tea tray.

Leonard's knees creaked as he raised himself to his feet.

"You should get something for that my friend, before arthritis sets in."

Leonard returned the Bishop's smile and nodded.

The valet entered, laid his burden on a table at the Bishop's elbow and with a small bow, left.

"You've been a valued member, Leonard; always remember that God forgives those who are truly penitent, whatever their crime. Try to find forgiveness in your heart. Your acts of goodness, your self sacrifice over the years will be remembered on the day you are judged. All I can say to you is pray; listen to the Lord."

Leonard studied the flames flickering around the logs in the grate and casting shadows on the hearth. Devoid of forgiveness for Clara who had lied to him, he had been praying more than ever before. For thirty years, since she had told him the little girl killed in McMasters's car had been his daughter, he had grieved. Appalled at what she might have suffered at the hands of that depraved criminal, he had been unable to forgive Sheila for not telling him what had happened to her, but most of all, he had been unable to forgive himself for allowing it to happen. Convinced of his guilt he had sought refuge in his church, had offered his life to Christ. He had attended seminars with members of Opus Dei, eventually becoming an associate member himself. All they asked in return was that he abstained from sexual intercourse and freed up his time to further the word of the Lord and spread the doctrine of the catechism. For him celibacy was no sacrifice. Without Sheila that part of his life was gone. There had never been nor, would there ever be, anyone else.

As always, the Bishop had received his request for advice with kindness. "Open your heart to God's word Leonard. Listen and he will tell you the way forward. Now you know she is alive, you have a responsibility to this child. If she has inherited your faith she will have strength, but if as you say she is in danger, she must take precedence over everything."

Leonard thanked him and walked with him to the door. As they reached it, the Bishop paused, taking Leonard's hand in his own. "For all your sins, you are a good man, my friend. You will do the right thing. I will keep you in my prayers. I must also pray for another friend of mine who was, I believe, known to you." Withdrawing his hands, he said with a small shake of his head, "He had a triple bypass several weeks ago. I'm afraid his strength never fully recovered following the operation. I speak of our dear brother, Cardinal Carlosanta; he was called home to God early this morning."

***

Craven House near Canterbury

When Jeff placed the call to Sandra he was standing in the grounds of Craven House, the home of Simon Alexander and his father. She had returned from Brampton Manor and was at home dealing with another viewing. Her visit had been worthwhile, she said: only the old office at the Manor, the one used by Peggy Lyons, had been vandalised, not the new office building, which would have yielded much greater rewards for a common thief. The break-in could only have been their man; she was sure of it.

Jeff gave her directions to Craven House and asked her to join him as soon as possible. He did not tell her why. He replaced his mobile into his jacket and took several steps across the lawn before stopping to gaze up into the night sky. Here, away from the distant glow of lights that was Canterbury, a multitude of stars was visible. He sighed deeply, dislodged a mint from a packet he'd found in the corner of a pocket and put it into his mouth. A vehicle was turning to park in front of the house, its headlights streaming across the driveway. Jeff walked slowly towards it, his breath now as cold as the frosted grass beneath his feet.

"First impressions, Bob?" Jeff quirked an eyebrow at the forensic pathologist, Robert Canning, as they took in the scene in front of them. No one had entered the tropical garden yet; no one really wanted to. The man they sought – or what remained of him – hung behind the glass in front of them. Random fluttering sounds echoed eerily around the room in which they stood.

Simon Alexander was suspended, trussed up by vines round each arm. His knees were bent, the lower parts of his legs trailed behind him. Another vine was coiled around his neck and stretched up to the light fitting, holding his head aloof. His body was puffed, his skin darkened and marbled, his insides rotting and infested; but more stomach-turning than anything else was the movement of maggots pulsing beneath the skin that was making the corpse appear to breathe.

Jeff struggled into his plastic suit. "Is it possible he could have set all this up on his own? Perhaps a bit of rough and tumble that got out of hand?"

"It's possible Grizz, old boy: I've seen several S&M's go wrong in my time. It will all depend on how the vines were tied. Have you ever made a butcher's knot?"

"Can't say I have, why?" Jeff rubbed some Vicks into the inside of his dust mask knowing that the second they opened the glass doors they would all want to retch.

"It would have given him enough slack until he put pressure on it, so if that's the way the vines are tied we could still have a possible suicide."

As far as Simon Alexander's secretary was concerned he was in Germany. She had told them they could get a spare set of keys from the housekeeper, who had met them at the house and was now making tea in the kitchen. Quick thinking from Jeff had spared her coming face to face with the fate of her employer's son. Having entered the sitting room and switched on the lights, Jeff had blocked the doorway, pushed the protesting woman back and ushered her to a room further down the hall, which just happened to be the kitchen.

"Why don't you make us all a nice cup of tea, Mrs Webster isn't it?"

She had protested. "There's no milk; the house has been locked up for a fortnight. What's going on?"

"We'll settle for black coffee then, love, looks like we'll be here quite a while."

Obviously used to taking orders she had resigned herself to the kitchen and was sitting at the table drinking a cup of black coffee when Jeff rejoined her.

He motioned her to sit back down and helped himself to coffee. It was strong, just the way he liked it; freshly ground too, a much better aroma than the one he could still smell on his clothes. Mrs Webster didn't seem to notice; her cry of distress when he broke the news appeared to be genuine.

"I left him here a week last Friday to lock up, him and that creep he'd taken up with! He was gay, you know.

Jeff nodded, but made no comment. They had got the same information from the Search Agency's secretary. The boyfriend's name was Richard Noble, evidently.

He wouldn't have been here if Mr Alexander was about!"

"Why's that Mrs Webster? Did Mr Alexander Senior not approve of his son's sexuality?" He watched as she took out a packet of small cigars and lit one, taking a long drag before pouting her lips to blow the strong fumes into the air in front of his face. He supposed it was better than the lingering stench of putrefaction on his clothes. He noted the deep creases in her skin, realised she was probably a good few years younger than she looked.

"No, that's not what I mean!" she snapped. "He's brought home several lovely young men over the years; one even lived here for a time. Mr Alexander was always fully supportive. But this one was different. About a year ago he arrived on the scene. Mr Alexander invited Simon to bring him down at weekends, but he always made excuses. Yet as soon as Mr Alexander leaves for Australia he's about all the time. Most of it spent in the tropical garden and that's supposed to be off limits even to me!"

Jeff refilled his cup. Who was this Noble guy anyway? The people at Search knew little about him yet none of them seemed to like him either.

"Had an evil eye in his head that one, always gave you a stare like; you know what I mean; eyes that glared, got into your skin and snipped you underneath!" She shivered. "Gives me the creeps he does!"

Jeff smiled at Mrs Webster, leaning towards her. "Do you think you could describe him to one of our artists?"

"Certainly I could. I could pick him out of a crowd anywhere; that bald head of his and that great big, ugly, brown birth mark lobbed on the side of it!"

Thanking the housekeeper for her help, Jeff told her a car would pick her up in the morning and take her to Maidstone to meet with the sketch artist. He assured her they would treat the house with respect and that notifying Mr Alexander Senior was already taken care of; the authorities in Papua New Guinea were probably breaking the news to him round about now. A uniformed constable was helping her out to a car as Sandra parked up in front of the steps.

"Where does this leave our prime suspect theory?" she asked Jeff, confronted by the spectacle hanging above her head. "Looks as though he was a bit tied up at the time of the murders in Higham, don't you think?"

Jeff smirked, "I'm glad you've found your sense of humour, Sandra, but I need to bring you up to date. There's coffee in the kitchen. Join me?"

The glass door opened and Robert Canning called them over. He was clad in something resembling a space suit fitted with breathing apparatus and had to lift the mask so he could speak. "Under the vine, he's been garrotted. The head's near enough severed. It's the vine that's holding him together: Definitely not a suicide!"

Jeff and Sandra moved towards the body.

"Right guys!" Sandra called to the SOCOs. "Can you all just stop where you are and clear the room: five minutes just give me five, okay?"

Everyone cleared out of the room, including Jeff and Robert. Sandra stood alone shrouded in her plastic suit and slowly turned a full 360 degrees, then paused. The chair, her eyes were drawn to it. She walked over, touched the back of it intending to run her hand along it. She noted where it was then lifted it and turned it around so that the seat was facing her. Leaning it back so that it neared the glass she noted the line marked on the glass. *You watched him! Not just him you were watching them!*

Entering the glass-walled tropics she stood beside the hanging man, much like the sole mourner at a graveside, staring downwards; still and solemn. The stench was overwhelming. The fluttering of the Birdwings added to the grotesque horror of the scene.

Ten minutes later she was drinking coffee in the kitchen listening to Jeff. Simon Alexander's hands, feet and head were bagged and sealed to preserve evidence. In a short time his remains would be on route to the morgue. There the body would be examined meticulously for evidence: traces the killer might have left behind. Sandra already knew there would be none.

"Who is Richard Noble?" Jeff asked. "Somebody has to know who he is?"

33

Police Headquarters, Maidstone: Thursday, 1ˢᵗ November

In full uniform, Leonard Millar waited to be called in to the Commissioner's office. It was just before nine.

Thirty minutes later, he had disclosed most of everything he knew. The Commissioner stood staring out over the buildings clasping his hands behind his back.

"It's a hell of a mess Millar!"

Leonard cleared his throat. "Yes Sir. I will do the honourable thing, Commissioner, and hand in my resignation, but I need to help my daughter first – discreetly if that is possible."

Waving his hand dismissively, the Commissioner moved back to his seat. "I don't want to hear about resignations, Leonard. You've just disclosed to me that one of my predecessors could have been the right-hand man of one of this country's most notorious gangsters. We can't let that get out. It could open up a huge can of worms. Seventeen people died when that undercover operation went belly up! Now you're telling me one of our own has their blood on his hands. It's a small mercy that he's dead and buried!"

Leonard intervened. "I'll have to explain it to McAdams, Sir. I don't yet understand why this is happening, but Simon Alexander's murder has to be linked; it has all gone too far."

"I agree. I'll get on the wires; give you more manpower." The phone rang on the Commissioner's desk. With an irritated frown he answered it: "I said no calls... oh... yes, of course. Very well, put her through." While he was waiting, he held his hand over the mouthpiece, looked up at Leonard and said, "Sorry – I left a message for my wife to call me. This won't take long."

Leonard nodded, transferring his gaze to the window. It was a fine, crisp morning; the sun was catching the wings of a gull gliding effortlessly in the cloudless sky.

"Darling; look something's come up," the Commissioner said into the phone. "I'm here in Maidstone this morning and I'll have to head back to London for another meeting there this afternoon. It will probably run on late into the night, so I'm afraid I'll not make it for the dinner after all."

Listening to the apologetic tone, Leonard hid a smile and transferred his gaze to the floor; he could imagine that the Commissioner's long-suffering wife was used to this.

"Of course I'll be back for the weekend," the Commissioner was saying. Smiling, he relaxed back in his chair. "I wouldn't miss it for the world.... Yes Darling, don't worry, I'll bring some with me. I won't forget. I love you too."

Replacing the receiver, he looked up a little sheepishly and raised his eyebrows at Leonard. "She's arranged a bit of a do for this weekend. We have an honest relationship, Leonard. Do you know, I think this is the first time in thirty years that I have lied to her." He shook his head, "It's something I promised myself I would never do, but in the circumstances..." he shrugged.

"Yes, Sir; it is difficult sometimes."

"Indeed." The Commissioner got up from his chair and strolled over to the window, turned back, said, "You're quite sure this is all about your daughter?"

"Yes," Leonard answered, his voice straining almost to a whisper, "quite sure."

Jeff was waiting to be put through to the desk sergeant at Gravesend who had been on duty two nights before. He had been waiting for some time; the officer on duty this morning was trying to find the sergeant's home number. Jeff could hear paper being shuffled about. He drummed his fingers on the desk in a surge of impatience. At last the phone clicked through to a ringing tone.

Waking the sergeant from his sleep, Jeff apologised and explained who he was. "I gather you have a message for me?" he said, grabbing a pen and notepad.

"Yes, Sir; a woman by the name of, er... just a minute, I think I wrote it down somewhere," he yawned. "Ah yes, here it is: Sheila McBride. She came in to the desk a couple of weeks ago: wanted to leave you a message." He yawned again.

Jeff punched his desk. "What? Why haven't you contacted me before now? What was the message, dammit!"

There was a shocked silence on the end of the phone before the sergeant replied, "Sorry, Sir. Didn't want to waste your time; thought she was some kind of a nutter, if you know what I mean – we get a few! She looked the desperate sort. Irish I'd have said from her accent. Been in a terrible accident at some time; half her face was missing; burned something awful – melted, like. Anyway, she said her name used to be Hynds; spun this cock and bull story about her son. I made a note of it, but she refused to show me any identification and, well, to be honest, I decided it wasn't worth passing on."

"Well, perhaps you'll let me be the judge of that, eh, Sergeant? What did she say exactly?" Gritting his teeth, Jeff kept his voice calm knowing from experience that he would get more cooperation that way. What had happened to Sheila in the years since he had last seen her? Whatever it was, it was not the fire that had taken her husband and son.

"It was all a bit odd. She told me to tell you that if there was any chance after all these years you had still kept a file open on her son's murder, you could close it. She said that you would spend your time better, what with all this new technology you have now, finding out who the body was you pulled out of the Thames, because it wasn't her son; hers is alive and well; she's seen him. Said she saw him on the TV news some time in late July, Sir. That was when I realised she was a bit doolally, if you know what I mean; a doting Mum lost her boy, poor soul. They can't accept it sometimes."

Jeff dropped his pen, swore; bent to retrieve it. "What day was this exactly? Did she leave a contact number?"

There was another moment's silence on the other end of the line. Jeff found himself hoping for the sound of more pages rustling as the sergeant flicked through his note book, but no such luck.

"Afraid not, Sir – and like I said, it would have been about two weeks ago, a Thursday I'm nearly sure of it; yes, definitely Thursday two weeks past. The funny thing is that on Tuesday, this guy lands at the desk from some agency in London. Says he's called Simon Alexander: the Managing Director of Search; that's the agency. Anyway he wants to know the name and the present whereabouts of the leading officer who dealt with the murder of a certain man back in '71. The victim's name was—"

"Jack Hynds," Jeff said testily.

"That's the one, Sir. Well, of course, I recognised the name straight away. The next thing he does is announce that he's helping Hynds's son to find his mother; none other than Sheila Hynds. Well that was when I realised she'd not been spinning me a line after all. Maybe I shouldn't have told him, but he seemed on the level – showed me his card and everything. The thing is, this Hynds woman didn't give me a contact number, but what she did give me was a forwarding address. Place in Ireland – I was right about her accent – Westport; it's in County Mayo, Sir. This guy said he'd got that address and had already checked it out, but she'd left."

Jeff shook his head in frustration; the sergeant was trying to cover his arse. Where did they find these incompetent dullards – and how did this one ever make sergeant? "Did you give this Alexander guy my name?" he snapped.

"Certainly did, that's why I left a message for you; thought you'd want to know, Sir. Has he got in touch with you yet?"

Jeff was blunt and to the point. "He would need the services of a medium to do that, Sergeant. Simon Alexander has spent the last fourteen days rotting away at his mansion with his head almost severed from his neck!" Afraid of what else he might say, Jeff slammed down the phone.

The light on line two immediately flashed. He picked it up, his voice still gruff. "McAdams; what is it?"

The voice on the other end was male, the accent Irish. Jeff shut his eyes and cursed quietly under his breath.

"Sorry to bother you Detective Superintendent; your team organiser put me on hold. This is Sergeant Tom O'Leary from Castlebar police station in Mayo; Ireland that is. I think we have a murder that might interest you."

Ten minutes' later, Jeff rushed out of the office yelling for Sandra. "Sandra; go pack your toothbrush! You're going on a trip. Maybe they're all dead already and we're only just starting to find them. Pack warm clothes, it might be chilly in Ireland. You're travelling with Jones – I hate to do this to you, but there's no one else freed up. Stop for a briefing before you head off." He turned back to the incident room: "People! Briefing – now if you please."

34

Another picture board had been added to the array on the walls. Put together overnight, it depicted the haunting image of Simon Alexander's gruesome remains.

"Fucking psycho!" Jones muttered standing close to the blow ups. "The man's a fucking psycho!"

Jeff agreed wholeheartedly, but made no comment. Christine was pinning a series of artist sketches to another board. She took a seat near the open window. She looked drained. Tracey Cooper's death had hit her hard. Images like the ones that surrounded her here were not really what the doctor would have ordered a pregnant woman to be looking at – and only weeks before she was due. Her mind should be focussed on the forthcoming birth of her baby, not horrific deaths like those depicted. The room was slowly turning into a real horror gallery. Christine must be wondering what kind of a world she was bringing this new life into, Jeff thought.

He sighed, scanned the boards, grimaced; turned to his team and waited, tapping his foot until he had their full attention. "Okay people; we have another murder. Victim's name is Gracie O'Hara. It's in a place called Westport, a seaside town in the West of Ireland: lamps around the body, womb cut out; no question it is our killer. Only this time he's made a mistake. She was not one of the women on our list, but he must have thought she was. I will explain in a minute how I know that." He indicated the new board, "This is a copy of the artist's sketch of the suspect, taken from eye witnesses in Westport." Jeff pointed to the image on the left. "This one is the sketch we arranged this morning with the housekeeper at Craven House, and this is another from the staff at Search."

"They are all of the same man, that's for sure!" Jones stated the obvious.

"Richard Noble," Jeff agreed. "We know what he looks like but nobody seems to know a damned thing about him!"

He looked at the faces in front of him, each one mirroring his disgust. "Right then – here's the background: in 1971 there was a fire on a houseboat at a disused dock in Gravesend. As far as we were able to ascertain, Jack Hynds and his son Andy were on the boat at the time. In any event, Hynds perished in the blaze, but we could not find the body of his son at first. A few weeks later the body of a small boy came adrift fifteen miles up the Thames. He was badly decomposed, but there was evidence of terrible head injuries; boat propellers; fish, as you'd expect after three weeks in the water. We determined from the size of the body, together with the hair colour and the fact that the only bit of clothing left on the child was what remained of a pair of underpants, that we had found the Hynds child. Andy would have been in his bunk when the fire started; we assumed he had been thrown out of the boat in the explosion so was not as badly burned as his father."

Stevens broke in, "What has the death of a child in 1971 got to do with this case?"

Jeff moved towards the list of women and pointed: "The boy's mother, Sheila Hynds, was Irish: a native of Westport."

"She's dead too then," Jones interrupted. "It's her murder we're heading to Ireland for? But I thought you said the victim's name was Grace something or other, Guv. So there were two—"

Jeff raised his hand to cut Jones off. "Shut up Jones, let me finish. It would appear our killer, Richard Noble, was after Sheila Hynds. We don't yet know why – at least, not exactly. However; as I said, this time he made a mistake. Sheila was no longer in Westport. Another poor soul – Gracie O'Hara – was murdered in her place. She was filling in as housekeeper during Sheila's absence. Noble obviously thought he'd got the right woman. But we know that Sheila Hynds travelled to England a few weeks ago under the name of McBride – her maiden name. She came here looking for her son."

"But her son is dead; you just said so!" Stevens was not alone, all the detectives looked puzzled.

"Sheila Hynds visited my old station at Gravesend soon after arriving in England. She wanted to tell me her son was alive. She had seen him during the summer via a news report on TV."

295

Sandra got to her feet. "You believe this guy Noble is Andy Hynds and that this woman Sheila is the real target then? His mother?"

Jeff nodded.

"If she's here and he's here, then why are we headed to Ireland?" Jones asked, looking belligerently at Sandra.

"I would guess to look for a trail that will lead us to Sheila, hopefully before Noble – or Hynds – gets to her," Sandra responded, quirking an eyebrow at Jeff.

Again, Jeff nodded. "Yes. We can't assume the killer has not discovered his mistake. Sheila Hynds is still at risk." He waited for the buzz to die down before continuing. "As a lad, Andy Hynds spent quite a bit of his days and part of his nights in the care of a woman named Beth Shaw. She had a son the same age. He left for university and was never heard of again. Never even went to his Mum's funeral, the father said. The Shaws were a tight-knit family; there must be a reason why the son suddenly broke ties."

Jeff looked across to Stevens. "I want you to start tracking him down. If Andy Hynds *did* survive that fire, chances are he might have kept in touch with David Shaw."

"Right, Sir," Stevens scribbled the name in his notebook, "any last known address?"

"Afraid not. Step into my office after the briefing will you and I'll fill you in on what I got from his father." Jeff pointed to number two on their list of women.

"Tuesday evening past, our friend Noble a.k.a. Hynds impersonated a police officer to visit this lady here. Her real name is Lydia Hardy. However; the killer left her untouched. Interestingly, she did not have her child adopted. So it seems she had nothing to fear from him. Don't forget, apart from Sheila – who is probably our number five – we still have another woman to locate: number one or four. Lydia Hardy has informed me that one of the girls, Amilee, died in '72.

"You mean two, don't you, Guv? There's still number three; this Aya of Mons," Jones said. "Have you got another name for her?"

Jeff exchanged glances with Stevens, said, "For reasons that I am not able to divulge at this stage, we do not need to pursue that particular name. Aya of Mons is off limits, okay?" He glared at his team, hating that he was forced into this position.

"Someone big and famous is it, Guv?" Jones voiced what they were all thinking.

"I said off limits, Jones!" Jeff shot him a look that all of his team recognised; it was another reason they called him 'Grizzly'! There was a muttered chorus of assent; Jones flushed and looked down at his feet.

Jeff nodded; "Right then, that's it, people. For the time being, all our efforts must be centred on locating Sheila Hynds. Best keep your weekend free! Sandra – can I speak to you before you leave? I'll see you afterwards, Stevens."

Back in his office, Jeff pulled the cord shutting the blinds and settled into his chair. "I hate this damned business of tiptoeing around in my own investigation!" He tapped his fingers harshly against the desk.

"There's more isn't there; I mean aside from Lady Clara Smith-Stevens being Aya of Mons. You know more than you have just disclosed."

Jeff sighed. "I can't hide much from you, Sandra, can I?"

Sandra slid into a chair and crossed her legs. "I know Fiona is somehow involved in this case, I can feel it in my gut. I mean, more deeply involved than taking those files from Peggy Lyons. One of our women is her mother; I am sure of it. You know, don't you? Is it this Sheila Hynds, because if it is, that gives me great cause for concern? Is that what you're not telling, Jeff?"

Jeff shook his head. "No; Sheila Hynds's daughter died as an infant – only five years' old. You don't need to worry on that score. We haven't got much time, so I need to fill you in on the rest of it; what I couldn't say out there. I am putting my neck on the line here, Sandra. It goes without saying that I'm not telling you this, okay?"

"Of course – how long have you known me, Jeff?"

He grinned at her. "I have discovered that back in the late sixties, early seventies, all these women worked for Ken McMasters as hostesses in his club. You've read the case files; you know the score. You can imagine what this information would be worth to the Press! Aside from that, Lady Clara has invented a sad little story for herself and I'm certainly not going to be the one to break it to her son."

Sandra let out a gasp. "God! Poor Stevens; you think he doesn't know?"

"Well I can't be sure, but I don't think so. Anyway, Lydia Hardy is married to an ex-copper; an old colleague of mine. Naturally, they want her past kept hidden too. And that's not all; there's something else running through all of this, I can just feel it!"

"Do you think Millar knows about any of this?"

"That's what's been bugging me since yesterday. That day we met with Lady Clara something was bothering him. I just couldn't put my finger on it, but something didn't seem right. Also, he seems to have it in for Fiona. I don't understand why – but that is the reason he didn't want you anywhere near this case. Like you say, it's as if she is more deeply involved than we know. There's something going on here, Sandra. I am getting to the stage where I think I shall have to confront Millar. How can we possibly solve this case with one hand tied behind our backs; it's ridiculous."

Sandra uncrossed her legs and got to her feet. "I appreciate your telling me; thanks Jeff. What's your next step?"

Jeff thought before answering. "There's a property called 'White Cliffs' in or near Dover. According to Lydia Hardy, these women are planning to get together there tonight. I think I'll drop in on them. I have a feeling, though, that Sheila won't be there. My guess is that she's more interested in locating her son than meeting old pals. This Noble guy seems to have better information than we do, but this time we'll be a step ahead of him. I want to talk to these ladies. See what their story is. I want to know as much as I can before I confront Millar. Fiona should be safe for now."

Jeff walked round to Sandra's side of the desk and leaned against it. "It's Stevens I feel sorry for. Some time soon his mother needs to tell him the truth. This is all going to come out, you know. We can't keep it hidden from the team indefinitely."

Sandra agreed. "It's dynamite. If the papers find out she was a gangster's moll they'll crucify her."

"My thoughts exactly – and Stevens too," Jeff nodded in agreement, "which will reflect badly on the Force. Maybe that's why Millar is being so close-mouthed. He doesn't know I know, yet, of course. But there's something else niggling me: Mark Jakes. It seems that Lady Clara pulled more than a few strings to fast-track his trial. I can't work out why. As I said, I've a feeling there's a great deal more to this than we are aware of at present."

Sighing, Sandra flopped back in her chair. "It's funny, you know, when I look back on it. Usually something zaps inside me as soon as I meet people; how they come across, you know? I never got that feeling with Mark Jakes, that he was a villain. Not till afterwards. He just seemed a regular nice guy. I couldn't believe it when Fiona set her eyes on someone who seemed so perfect for her. And then it all went downhill for us – and fast too."

Seeing Sandra's eyes welling with tears, Jeff pushed himself up from the desk and looked at her with concern. "Are you okay? I've been worried all week that this case is too much for you. You're coping brilliantly, so well that I keep forgetting how it must be for you. I shouldn't have put so much on you so soon. It took me months and months to learn to get through each day without Angie – and even now I barely manage it some days. Goodness knows how you are coping without Gerry. Look, I'll send someone else to Ireland – or Jones can go on his own."

"No, please don't. I'm okay. I've been bottling things up. Dr Graham says I should be more open, talk about it more, but I don't know how to tell anyone about me and Gerry."

Jeff subsided back onto the edge of his desk as Sandra wiped the tears from her cheeks. He felt a surge of compassion for this clever young woman who was his friend as well as his colleague. For the moment, nothing seemed more important than giving her the support she so obviously needed. "Just say it," he said gently.

She gave him a watery smile. "I was very convincing while he was alive that everything was fine. Since he died, I've got it off to a tee hiding what's going on inside of here," she pointed to her head.

"Which is part of your problem; that's exactly what Graham means," Jeff returned her smile. "You can tell me anything, you know you can."

Meeting his gaze, Sandra took a deep breath. "Our marriage since my attack had been nothing more than a farce. The day Gerry fell from that damned balcony I had packed up and left him; couldn't take the emptiness anymore. Since then I have blamed myself. If I had known about his tumour maybe I would have reacted differently; weighed our situation up; given him some leniency. But I am convinced that if I hadn't left him, he would still be alive. He took his life because of me," her lip trembled and the tears long held in check flooded down her face.

Fishing a clean hanky out of his pocket, Jeff leaned over and took her hands. "God, Sandra; why didn't you say something before. For goodness sake, it was him who took that decision; not you! You'll destroy yourself piling on the blame."

Gratefully dabbing at her face with his hanky, Sandra shook her head. "He was obsessed with Fiona ever since she came back. It is strange, looking back on it; her search for her natural mother crazed him. I could never understand why. I thought it was so selfish of him. Yet the more I concentrate on this case, the more that fact comes to the front of my mind. It is almost as if Fiona trying to find her mother sparked everything else off. But why – and how could it have done? It doesn't make a lot of sense." She offered him back his hanky. "Maybe if we knew who her mother was, it might explain things."

"No, you keep it." Getting to his feet Jeff placed a hand on her shoulder. "I've had those thoughts too, Sandra. I'm hoping you'll find something in Ireland. I hope too that we find Sheila Hynds alive. She was a fine young woman. Something about her was different, somehow. She had a raw deal what with one thing and another. She came here back in the late sixties hoping for a better life. Unfortunately she had the misfortune to fall into the arms of Jack Hynds and I guess that sealed her fate. I wonder where she is now; she has to be staying somewhere. By the way, I should tell you that at some time her face has been badly burned. It's happened since the fire that killed her husband. Might be something you can find out about in Ireland – what happened. Get access to her personal stuff; if we're lucky it might shed some light on the past, maybe even where she intended staying when she reached here."

Thinking about Sheila as he had last seen her, Jeff was silent for a moment. "It's sad; very sad how fate decrees the direction our lives take. Is there ever anything we can do to change things do you think?"

"I don't know, Jeff. I really don't know."

"Look," he said with a wry grin: "I know I always say there's no such thing as a coincidence in our line of work, but perhaps it really *is* a coincidence that Fiona started her search at the same time our killer started his. Maybe it's the exception that proves the rule, eh? Don't worry about Fiona; it's his mother our killer wants. If anything, he'll feel akin to Fiona; in his eyes she will have suffered like him. You know, don't you, that if he wanted to harm her he could have done so by now. He got into your house, after all. If Noble *is* Sheila's son – and it seems likely – what the hell happened to turn him into such a monster."

Sandra thought of the victims so far; the brutality employed in their demise. She met Jeff's eyes with a long look, said succinctly: "Something terrible: a lot of it; and over a very long period of time."

35

Jeff threw the folders onto the passenger seat of his car and reversed out of his space. He would return at 2pm to pick up Stevens when they were due to leave for Dover. In the meantime he was headed for home to get a few hours' shut eye. They had worked the scene at Craven House until well after 4am; he hadn't been home yet, opting for a short nap on a couch at the station. He wrinkled his nose: he needed a soak in a hot tub more than he needed to sleep. On balance, he thought with a grin, he would rather be in his own shoes than those of DS Stevens right now – and not just because of the poor bloke's mother! Stevens had the noisome task of attending Simon Alexander's autopsy.

"We're in luck today," Robert Canning said, handing Stevens a flexible space helmet complete with air tank. The pathologist was still covering for Leslie, who wasn't due back until tomorrow. "The new down-draught tables have been installed during the week. They'll help draw the stench away from you. When you're ready; let's go moon walking!"

Stevens chuckled; Robert Canning was a character alright; getting on a bit now, about the same age as Jeff. An experienced pathologist, he was not as serious as Leslie was over the table. It was the first time Stevens had tried out one of these special suits. He spoke into the mouthpiece his voice distorted. "My mother used to have an attachment hood something like this for drying her hair when I was younger."

Canning grinned and ushered him through to the lab.

The body of Simon Alexander lay on the table. The bloating and the advanced decay once again sent a shudder through Stevens. Despite the added benefit of the new suit and the modified slab with special air vents to lessen the effects of the gases, he was unable to stay the course. Retching, he left the autopsy midway through and waited for Canning outside. It was a long wait, but finally the pathologist came through to the scrub room.

"Not that you would realise it now, but that lad in there certainly took care of himself. Perfect teeth, heart, lungs and liver; all of it; if someone hadn't put an end to him he would have lived to a ripe old age. Cause of death: garrotted with a fine wire as I've already indicated. Been dead about two weeks, but difficult to pinpoint exactly. The tropical environment will have speeded up decomposition. Incidentally, you might be interested to know that the sex was rough; no old scarring, all new: used a condom – as you'd expect. I'd be surprised if we'll get any of the killer's DNA."

Stevens headed back to the station; he had much to ponder. This muddied the waters. None of the victims so far had been sexually assaulted. Was this different? Alexander was, of course, Noble's sexual partner. But then, why had he killed him? What motive could there possibly be? According to the autopsy there were no older indicators of rough sex; the ties to the wrists were post-mortem as well.

Jeff had soaked long enough. He dried himself off and fetched a fresh shirt and a pair of cords. After rummaging through a drawer he found a clean pair of socks and headed down to his kitchen to make coffee. He sat reading through the file on Hynds, making odd notes; things he wanted to follow up. He stared at the face of the small six-year old boy. This image was a coloured one, provided by Sheila Hynds just before she disappeared. He was a beautiful boy: thick, wiry black hair, skin tanned and freckled with the sun; bright, vivid blue eyes. The colour, even in this old photograph, was startling. Not contacts then; he had been wrong about that.

The autopsy prints held no comparisons. Goose skin, bloated and waxy; there had been a run of cold weather at the beginning of November back in '71; winter had come early. The deep wounds and trauma to the skull indicated the body had been caught and dragged several times over the period it had listed in the Thames. Little of the face remained. Linking what could be determined between the before and after images was no different now to how it had been at the time. The child's fingers and toes were eaten away – most likely by pike – as were his eyes. No prints were available; the child had never been to a dentist and DNA hadn't been around back then; at least, not to the extent it was now. A mistake could easily have been made. All it needed was for the body of another child of the same size and hair colour to have ended up in the water at around the same time. What were the chances of that? No other child had been reported missing in the area at the time. Strange that; if the body they had buried as Andy Hynds wasn't his; whose was it?

Jeff lifted the coloured image again and peered into the child's eyes: "What happened to you son, to bring about such evil? What hand were you dealt by cruel fate?"

***

Stoneford Hall: the Downs, Kent: 1978

The boy pulled the door to very slowly, dreading a creak. As it neared the frame he placed his thumb against the wood, then, as the door jammed against it, he eased his thumb out nipping the skin. Blood flowed red from the tear; he licked it away. Limping, he crept away from the gatehouse; away from the sleeping men he had been forced to entertain during the night. Sore and aching, he hobbled across the grass making his way up the steep grounds to the main house.

Suddenly he stopped, splashes of dew wetting his bare feet as he stood, frozen, midway up the lawn, his eyes fixed on the window: the last one on the left side of the house; Jenny's room. The light was on; a shadow passed across the window. His fists clenched, he gritted his teeth; his body convulsed with rage. No tears came; he had stopped crying a long time ago.

He was twelve. When he had first been taken he'd had nothing, they'd even left behind his name, Andy. He still had nothing. Except Jenny.

At her door he could hear the sobs. The hate boiled inside him. He overcame it and entered the room, climbed in beside her. Patting her head he soothed her. "I promise you Jenny, this isn't going to happen to you again. I'm going to make them all go away."

Elizabeth McMasters felt her body go rigid as her husband's heavy form returned to their bed. In the darkness of her world she waited until she sensed he was asleep. Feeling her way, she left the bedroom and paused in front of her daughter's door. There was no sound except for the stuttered gasps of breath that she knew followed tears of deep hurt. She knew because it had always been that way for her too. Touching the door handle, she quickly withdrew her hand. The boy had told her the truth. She turned and again feeling her way, took refuge in an empty room on the other end of the landing.

Outside, a crow cawed; the first sound of morning. Was it still dark? She couldn't tell; her world was perpetually dark. Her husband was a man to be feared; the blindness a cruel punishment. He had inflicted it on her when he found out she had found love with someone else after years of neglect from him.

It all made sense really now; the neglect. Kenneth was never interested in her; she was merely a commodity; something he owned. Through her he had got a hold over Frank, her brother. As a DI at Maidstone, Frank was useful to Kenneth. It was handy to have an insider; strings to pull now and then. At least that was how it had started. Frank was a superintendent now.

He had been there when the acid had been poured into her eyes: a double-edged warning to them both to keep in line. They'd held him down; there was nothing he could do except watch. Family was everything to Frank; he would do whatever Kenneth wanted to keep her from more harm. She knew since then her brother had been dragged deeper and deeper into Kenneth's underworld. It tore her apart to think what he must have had to involve himself in over the years for her sake.

There was nothing she could do to help the girl. Nor could she help herself. Running away was out of the question; she needed to feed her habit. It was the one thing Kenneth was good enough to supply her with; it helped blunt the pain, helped her to get through the endlessly dark days and nights: the puppet wife on the arm of the MP, Kenneth McMasters.

She'd known about Clara, the child of his mother's much younger sister. Only nine years' old when he'd offered himself as her guardian; his own cousin. Five years ago Kenneth had adopted another little girl; a replacement for Clara whose body had outgrown his needs. He liked them young. Elizabeth knew that now. She sighed; she had always wanted a daughter. She'd slapped the boys face when he'd told her about the abuse. Not out of anger. She realised that now, admitted to herself that it was being forced to face her own guilt that had made her hit him. She already knew where her husband slipped off to during the night. He'd been doing it for years, and she had been too weak to do anything but ignore it; pretend it didn't happen.

She was starting to shake. She needed another hit. Was it six or was it seven years since she had lost her own son? She couldn't remember. The drugs were good at distorting things, but not that good. Kenneth thought he had it all covered up. Something had happened that night he'd taken their son with him. She didn't know what, only that the boy he'd brought back with him wasn't her son. Everyone was replaceable as far as Kenneth was concerned. Even his own son. She'd long since stopped wondering what had happened to their child. She felt in her soul that he no longer breathed. In this house that was something of an escape. She made her way back to her room and within minutes was floating into blessed oblivion.

Jason leaned on the bonnet of the car until it clicked shut. Dumping the tools he'd stolen, he sneaked around the back of the house. It was evening. The McMasters were heading to a pre-wedding dinner. Clara was to be married the next day.

He sat in the kitchen watching the clock. The women who worked in the house entered the kitchen shortly after six. He didn't want any dinner. Two satchels were stuffed with food behind the stable. He'd raided one of the money bags from the gatehouse hours earlier. He and Jenny would be long gone before the men arrived tonight to discover the theft.

From the hall window he watched as the car started turning to take the curve of the steep drive. Racing up the stairs he stopped to watch from the balcony. The car had gained speed. He knew it couldn't slow. Faster and faster it plunged towards the main road outside the grounds. He imagined the panic within the car: McMasters bellowing at the chauffeur.

Out of the corner of his eye he saw the black Rover turn off a side road onto the main road, travelling fast; it would pass the gates in a few seconds. Another car! He hadn't thought of that! The result would be even better than he'd planned.

He stood, his eyes shining with delight as the two vehicles collided; the sharp clanging of metal on metal, the shrill thud of the impact pierced the air. He smiled, turned and ran up the rest of the stairs bursting into Jenny's room.

It was empty.

36

Ireland: Thursday 1ˢᵗ November

Sandra pulled her jacket closed; Jeff had been right about the temperature. They were being driven in a squad car from the airport just as the last light of the afternoon dulled, the sun disappearing into a thick mass of indigo clouds on the horizon, sending a shimmering line of orange across the sky. Ahead of them the pyramid outline of a mountain top came into view. Jones pointed to it. Sandra nodded, "Yes, I see it, it's beautiful."

"That's 'Croagh Patrick' – Ireland's holy mountain," Sergeant O'Leary enlightened them, his voice tinged with pride.

Soon they were in Castlebar, which turned out to be quite a large town. Sandra laughed delightedly when they stopped to let a crowd of children cross the road in front of them: a ghoulish procession of vampires in flowing black capes; small, sheet-covered ghosts; green-haired witches with brooms in tow and one or two horned red devils. They were being hurried along by a harassed looking woman carrying a pumpkin lantern. She waved her thanks at O'Reilly as he drove on.

"On their way to a party," he explained. "It was All Souls yesterday, but the hall was double-booked, so the spirits have had to wait a day for their knees-up!" he grinned.

Of course it was; what with one thing and another, Sandra had forgotten Halloween this year. Her smile faded and she suppressed a shiver. Perhaps it was just as well!

A series of roundabouts directed them into the town centre and after stopping for several red lights they eventually pulled up at the hospital. The body was due to be released to the funeral director and Sandra wanted to see it first. O'Leary had explained that in Ireland, unlike in England, the autopsies on all murder victims were performed either by the State Pathologist, Brian Quinn, or his deputy, Maria Kane. "We don't get that many murders here," he told them. "It's generally a safer place to live these days – but not for Gracie O'Hara, sadly," he added. "The funeral's on Sunday."

Brian Quinn said more or less the same thing when, having viewed the remains, Sandra and Jones met him in his office. "We don't see many murder victims in these parts; especially not like this one; first I've ever come across as bad as this in my time here."

He was a giant of a man, reminding Sandra in some ways of Jeff, his arms bulging in the sleeves of his jacket as he offered her the copy of his report. She read it through, pausing from time to time to glance up at the watching men, relieved that Jones, for once, had nothing to say.

Catching her glance, O'Leary said, "Considering the circumstances: the arrangement of the lamps; the cutting out of the womb and so forth, we brought in a consultant quite quickly; name of Michael Delaney…" he faltered as Sandra's head shot up. "You know him? He helps us out now and again; not very often; like Brian says, things like this are rare here. He's a retired FBI field agent."

Sandra gave a brief smile. "Yes, if it's the same Michael Delaney I knew him when I was in the States – and his wife, Sarah. She works out of New York; runs the head office of some telecommunications firm – or did. Have they relocated here?"

As she spoke she wondered why Mike Delaney had retired so early. As she remembered, he was headed for a brilliant career. His specialist field was the occult. She'd read recently that murders related to such practises were on the increase in the States; other countries too. There was something telling in the way O'Leary was looking at her; he gave a brief shake of his head.

"I'm sorry to break the news if she was a friend of yours. She was lost in the World Trade Centre. Michael came back here to Westport soon after. Said he was disillusioned with the whole American thing. Before 9/11 they had been planning to relocate, so he stuck to the plan and came on his own. It's where his roots are; his family emigrated from here back in the 1930s. They'd kept the house; all but a ruin it was by then. Michael's spent the last few years doing it up; quite a job he's made of it too. A distraction of sorts I suppose."

Sandra sighed, "Oh, that is bad news, poor Michael, I'm so sorry."

Michael Delaney had been paired up with her during both of her training courses with the FBI. She had actually stayed with him and Sarah for a few days following the end of the last course. Had it really been so long ago? What had happened to her promises to keep in touch? At least she'd sent them the yearly token of a Christmas card: the thought made her feel suddenly worse.

O'Leary nodded. "Actually, he's offered to put you both up tonight; wouldn't hear of you staying at a hotel."

The Delaney ancestral home sat perched midway up a steep hill about two miles the other side of the harbour town of Westport. Two magnificent, cast-iron street lamps graced either side of the drive. Smaller, less elaborate ones in pairs were spaced at intervals along the winding pathway up to the patio area in front of the house.

It was a solid looking building; square, built of stone. Two long, sash windows on either side of the double front door glowed with light. Above them were two more and in the middle a stone balcony doubling up as a porch with pillars down to the ground. Tom O'Leary raised a hand to the ring of the lion's-head door knocker, but before he could reach it, the door opened inwards and Michael Delaney stood there, a huge smile lighting up his tanned face.

Sandra breathed an inward sigh of relief; he seemed little changed. A few salt and pepper streaks had invaded his black, closely trimmed beard and short cut hair, but he was still as attractive as she remembered. Casually dressed in an Aran, turtle-neck sweater of soft grey over faded black jeans, he welcomed them in, grasping Sandra's hands in his own as if relieved to finally meet a friend after a very long wait.

O'Leary had been right, she thought, looking around her as she was shown to her en-suite room to freshen up. Michael had obviously poured his heart into the house. Subdued hues of cream and beige covered the walls allowing the restored cornices to highlight the rooms. As she made her way back downstairs, her footsteps sent whispering echoes into the marble-floored hall. Grand it certainly was, but there was something missing here. She paused at the bottom of the stairs, her hand caressing the polished curve of the banister. Was she imagining it? Was it her own sad emptiness and not Michael's that she was feeling?

Declining O'Leary's offer of a night on the town, with dinner and a few drinks thrown in, Sandra masked her delight when Jones gladly accepted. Now they had gone, she and Michael were in the kitchen, perched on stools opposite the biggest range she had ever seen and enjoying bowls of piping hot stew. The entire kitchen was bespoke; designed and handcrafted by Michael himself. He's got more cupboards and working surfaces in this one room than I've got in my entire house, Sandra thought, gazing with envy at the high quality finish. It was as if she had stepped into the cover of some glossy magazine and it felt a million miles away from the sombre tragedy of the investigation, so when Michael spoke of it, it brought her up short.

"It was the lamps," he said, "the way they were placed. That's what sparked it off for me." Collecting the empty bowls and re-filling their glasses with wine, he picked up a folder lying on a worktop and brought it to the table. It contained a set of prints of the crime scene, which he laid out for them to study.

"We didn't know about the chrysalis at first; it must have got dislodged somehow when they moved the body. A technician happened upon it at the morgue; didn't realise it had anything to do with the case. I'd actually tapped in all the particulars two weeks ago thinking we were onto a collector, but nothing showed up. Then, last thing yesterday I thought what the hell, and tried again. Hit on your murder in Kent, read about the missing womb and the chrysalis. On the off chance, I quizzed the assistant who'd been on duty that night and hey presto: one chrysalis. Only trouble is we don't have it any more. So what do you think; Is it the same?"

Sandra smiled; then took a sip of her wine. "I think you already guessed that before you phoned Jeff McAdams."

A half-smile came to his face. "Yes, well I really never expected to get called into a case like this when I agreed to help out here. Especially not one involving someone I knew; poor Gracie; I can't bear to think what she must have suffered before it ended." He tapped the image with his fingertip.

Sandra's gaze was drawn to Gracie O'Hara's lifeless form: a frail figure with pencil-like legs and arms. Pale golden hair framed her narrow face; her eyes, colourless and milky, stared transfixed at the ceiling. Her mouth was open, frozen in a silent scream, her lips crusted with white crystals. But for the difference in size, it could have been Peggy Lyons's corpse lying there.

"No bruising to the neck; no sign of struggle in the room around her. It's as if she just lay back and let him cut her open," Michael said.

Sandra nodded. "Peggy Lyons was bound wrists and feet to a chair. She was tortured for some time before she died, but again, there was no sign of a struggle. He killed her husband too, but he wasn't the focus. This woman was the first, though, and we've since found another body we think is connected. A man; we believe he was the killer's sexual partner, Simon Alexander. He would have died about a week after yours. Totally different posing though; garrotted."

Michael gave a low whistle. "He's been busy hasn't he – four murders within two weeks! If he keeps to his schedule we have to anticipate another between now and next week."

Sandra reached for her profile. Michael studied it closely, nodding in agreement. "What you know of this guy Noble matches everything you indicate here. Yet Jeff McAdams mentioned you've not been able to find any trace of his existence."

"Nothing; we're taking it from the angle that he's Sheila McBride's son, Andy Hynds. She presented herself at the station in Gravesend a few weeks ago to tell us he was alive. We all thought he was killed more than 30 years ago."

"Is that right? Dear God! Poor Sheila: it didn't take me long to work out she was the intended target and that Gracie was a victim of circumstances; in the wrong place at the wrong time. I can't help but feel I'm solely responsible for that. If only I hadn't lingered in New York there's a damned good chance the poor old girl would still be alive."

"Oh, Mike, don't." Sandra put her hand on his shoulder. "You mustn't blame yourself." As she spoke, she heard the echo of Jeff's words. Knew she would not be able to convince him any more than Jeff had convinced her, but she had to try. "Even if you had come back sooner it probably wouldn't have made any difference. From what you say of Gracie, she would still have tended to Sheila's duties; expected you to cope without her. Besides, the position of priest's housekeeper would have given her status, if only temporarily. Your presence wouldn't have changed her fate. In fact you too might have been killed had you got in this monster's way."

Despite her words of wisdom she acknowledged that he wasn't persuaded. The only hope of purging his guilt was to apprehend the killer and bring him to justice. She wasn't yet sure how she would ever purge her own. She steered the conversation back to Sheila's son.

"Apparently she recognised him on TV footage back in July. This is where it gets interesting. Also in July, a Mark Jakes was tried and convicted of the murder of a young woman; Katie Smyth. She happened to work alongside Mark at an agency 'Search' in London. Simon Alexander, the body we found yesterday, was the Managing Director. Even more interesting is that the manner of Katie Smyth's death closely resembled this one here." She pulled one of the images of Gracie towards them.

"But this guy Jakes killed her, you say. When, exactly?"

"St Valentines day – February past. He pleaded guilty and has been behind bars since then."

Michael shrugged, "So that wouldn't explain the links with this agency."

"No. It makes no sense to me at all. And yet we cannot ignore the connections." Lifting out another folder Sandra opened it and added to the display before them several blow ups of the Katie Smyth crime scene.

Mike sighed as he surveyed the gruesome images. Katie Smyth's face was covered in her own blood; her eyes too were reddened where blood had trickled into the sockets. The wounds, though, were more ragged than Gracie's. The girl's breasts sat pert even in death; silicon filled; smeared with congealed blood.

"She's naked." Mike's voice was barely audible.

"Yes; except for her boots."

Long, high-heeled boots laced up to her knees covered her legs, which were at angles and dropped back against the floor; her arms too were stretched out on either side of her.

Handing him the copy of the autopsy findings, Sandra added, "Unlike Gracie and Peggy Lyons, there are sexual innuendos in the way she is posed. She was drugged too; must have been; there are no sign of any defence wounds. Yet nothing showed up in any of her samples. It was the same with Peggy – no defence wounds at all. Have any of the blood samples your lot took from Gracie come in yet? It may explain why there was no struggle with her."

"Not yet. But there were no needle marks found on the body; then again, they might have been destroyed in the mutilation that followed. The sexual undertones set this one apart though, Sandra; it's a different signature, you know that."

Sandra looked away and sighed.

"These cases are tough to deal with," Michael said, concernedly. "How are you holding up? It's hard to cut yourself off from ones like this. I know only too well; it's always been a battle for me."

"It's not that… it's just that… well, I kept telling myself that Katie Smyth's murder had a sexual basis and however similar the cases seemed, the motives were not akin." She brought out another set of prints to add to their morbid display; several shots of the remains of Simon Alexander. "But then, when I was confronted with this…"

She waited as he examined the prints, shaking his head as if old memories of images just as ugly were stirring in the back of his mind. "A sexual motive here as well, then?"

"Yes. That's not all, Mike. Mark Jakes: I knew him personally; he was Fiona's – my sister-in-law's – fiancé."

Michael turned his head; blinked his eyes shut for a few seconds before redirecting his attention to the prints of Katie Smyth. "I'm sorry Sandra; this was a tough one then."

Sandra chewed on her bottom lip. "It gets worse than that. Fiona; she was adopted. She's been trying to locate her natural mother, which, incidentally, is how she came across Mark Jakes. She's somehow tangled up in all this."

Michael listened quietly, nodding from time to time as Sandra told him everything they had discovered: about Fiona, the records of the women at the Priory; Sheila Hynds, the Birdwing butterflies and the significance of the chrysalides.

When at last she had finished, Michael re-filled her glass, silent for a time. After a while, he said thoughtfully, "We both know that if he sees this as some kind of mission he will twist the boundaries to draw Gracie into its confines; widen his scope. Realising she was a mistake will not have weakened his resolve. You know the pattern; he'll justify it as securing his objective. You've explained something for me, though. Have a look at these."

Mike searched in the file he'd made from the cuttings found at Sheila's house and showed them to Sandra, along with the receipts for donations to the Priory. She studied each in turn, particularly interested in the receipts. They slotted another part of the puzzle into place.

"I think these explain how he tracked Sheila to Westport," she said. "There was a break-in a while back at Brampton Manor, which used to be the Priory. At the time it was thought to be a gang of local misfits out for a night of vandalism. Nothing appeared to have been taken. I feel sure that had we known to look for them, we would have found that all that was missing were the records and contact details for a generous donor in Ireland. Even if he hadn't known the name McBride, Andy Hynds would have remembered his mother's voice, known she was Irish and put two and two together."

She looked up and smiled at Michael. "I am just beginning to feel as if we are closer to cracking this one. We've located two of the five women and they are safe for now; one died several years ago, which leaves us two to find. Sheila particularly is in grave danger. Jeff has already talked to one of the women; it appears they all are supposed to meet up at a cottage tonight in Dover."

"Ah!" Michael shot up from his stool. "There's something else you should see." Leaving the kitchen he returned a few moments later holding a folded newspaper. "You said Dover; a cottage tonight?"

She nodded as he held it out, pointing to the small boxed ad at the top of the page. Puzzled, she read it, glanced at the date: "This paper's dated the day Gracie was murdered."

"Yes. Apparently, the day after Gracie died old Father Mullan was mumbling that he hadn't received his paper." He flashed an apologetic smile, explained, "He's past it; doesn't really understand what's happened. Anyway, Gracie usually brought it back from the village for him, but we couldn't find it. We checked and found that Gracie had indeed purchased a copy on her way back to the cottage that evening. It seemed reasonable to assume the killer had taken it. This struck me as so odd – I mean, why bother to stop to read the local paper when you have just brutally murdered..." he faltered, cleared his throat. "Well, I got hold of another copy. I've read it from cover to cover, over and over, trying to think why it was of interest. Each time I was drawn to this novena to St Brigit; it just seemed strange. Now, of course, you have explained it. You said Brigit was Sheila's alias?"

"Yes, but it wouldn't have meant anything to Noble then," Sandra said. "He didn't know about the aliases when he murdered Gracie, he couldn't have; not until he took the records from Fiona's briefcase."

"I would hazard a guess he knew the novena was significant. I can't think why else he would have taken it. The point is, Sandra, he knows now: which means he—"

"Knows about White Cliffs," Sandra finished, reaching for her mobile. She tried to ring Jeff; his mobile was engaged. She left a voice mail for him. Then she rang the station, spoke to the duty sergeant; asked him to alert the station at Dover. From this distance there was nothing else she could do.

Still studying the files, Michael said suddenly, "This name Noble; he'll have chosen it himself."

"Yes; it would seem so." Sandra set the artist sketches on top of the crime scene prints. They studied the face for a time in silence. It was Sandra who spoke first, "He doesn't look like a monster."

"Do they ever?"

"Perhaps not; anyway, there's nothing we can do for now except wait to hear from Jeff." Swishing the dregs of wine about in her glass, not quite sure how to approach the subject of Sarah, but feeling she had to say something, Sandra eventually spoke. Avoiding eye contact, she blurted out, "I don't know what to say; whatever I say you must be tired of hearing it, but O'Leary told us earlier about Sarah. I didn't know. I'm so very sorry. The Christmas cards I sent to you both; if you received them they must have hurt. I'm truly sorry."

Shaking his head he reached out touching her hand. "No; not at all – I still have the apartment in New York; I fly back every couple of months. I call it an insurance policy in case it doesn't work out here; only fooling myself with that one though! Just can't let go I suppose. She was – and is still – a part of me. It was in fact the cards without her name; the solitary 'Michael' that hurt much more. Not that they were meant to; but you know what I mean. In my despair it was a time of anger. It was easy to think harshly that people could just rub her out. For those first couple of Christmases I wanted to see her name there, right beside mine. At least on yours and one or two others I got my wish," he said, his eyes wet with unshed tears.

"I'm glad, then; about that at least," she said huskily, close to tears herself. Not wishing to talk about Gerry and aware it was the next logical direction in their conversation, Sandra swiftly changed tack, distracting Michael by turning back to images of Gracie. "I would like to see where it happened, Mike," she said.

"I've already arranged to take you there first thing in the morning. I guessed you'd not be content unless you see the place for yourself!" Getting up to clear the table, Michael dissipated their emotion with a teasing grin.

Sandra grinned back. "And Sheila's house too? We're kind of hoping I might find something to help us locate her before Noble finds her. Jeff is not convinced she'll show up at Dover this evening."

"Yes, of course, Michael said, as together they returned the images of all the victims' mutilated remains to their folders. "We'll do that too. Come on; let's take another bottle out to the sun room."

Sandra laughed, "It's dark; there's no sun!"

Lifting their glasses he retrieved a fresh bottle of wine from the rack. "No matter; there might be a moon! We'll open the doors; listen to the sea. Grab a couple of throws off that couch on your way out."

37

Dover: early that same afternoon

Sally Burton entered the butcher's shop; the rib-eye roast Anita had ordered the day before was wrapped and set aside ready for her. While she was there, Sally bought some sausages and a chicken pie then she headed for the bakery. The two large, fresh cream gateaux ordered at the beginning of the week were ready for collection. It was almost lunch time.

Back home, she shuffled through the back door, eased her shopping onto the counter-top in the kitchen and turned on the oven. Setting aside the roast and one gateau, she made room in the fridge for the rest. Retrieving a large roasting pan, she prepared Anita's beef, covered it in foil and placed it in the oven. Finally, she filled the kettle and cut a thick wedge of gateau.

The sound coming from the sitting room was football; the sports channel as usual. She did her best to ignore it, digging instead into the sumptuous layers of sponge and cream, savouring the sweetness: it was better than sex! Much better. Peeping through the open door she saw her husband, feet stretched out on the couch, newspaper over his face, his pot belly rising and falling. Sat in the armchair opposite was her daughter. Similarly oversized, the girl was engrossed in a book. Almost thirty years of age and no notion of flying the nest yet!

Sally thought back to the day she had first held her daughter; tiny and pink she was then. Now look what she had grown into. She was a changeling: gone was the sweet, angelic little face, the delicate limbs. Sally sighed and took another mouthful of gateau.

"Any grub up yet Ma? What's cooking; smells like Sunday roast." Her daughter had become aware of her presence.

"It is; but it's not ours. There's a chicken pie in the fridge; you'll have to manage with that. I've to leave again before dinner to help out with things up at the cottage and I'll be out all evening."

Upstairs in her bathroom, Sally knelt by the lavatory and stuck her fingers down her throat, vomiting up the gateau. You couldn't lead a slimming club unless you were slim. This way she could have her cake and eat it. She knew better than to overdo it; it never did her any harm.

Anita put Chiko on the lead and made her way back to the cottage. Her head was filled with questions. Nerves tingled like butterflies in her stomach; over and over she tried to picture the moment only an hour away when finally, after all the searching, all the heartache, she would hold her daughter in her arms again. To while away another hour, she switched on her computer, re-read the chapter she'd finished that morning: the fire; their escape. She just didn't think she'd portrayed it right. Something didn't quite fit.

A car turned up the lane. She stood as its engine cut; took a deep breath, closed her eyes for a moment, praying quietly: "Please make it right; this time, please make it be right." With more than a little apprehension, she made her way to the door.

***

The Reid's home, Maidenhead

Fiona had filled two boxes for the shredder: spurred on mostly by anger. It was a betrayal. Never before had she felt this way about her brother. Not even when their relationship had hit rock bottom following Mark's arrest. No matter how frayed the strings became that bonded them together, nothing, not even the fact that they could no longer pass even the briefest moment in the same room without snarling hurtful rebukes at each other, had ever left her feeling as angry as this.

Both of them, it appeared, had resolved to play out what were to be his last few weeks in total ignorance of each other. An undeclared truce had existed between them; somewhere, deep in their subconscious, neither was willing to sever that last thread. When everything else was stripped away, they were family; brother and sister. It had never mattered that the blood of strangers pumped through their veins for to them that fact had never arisen. Or so she thought. Their love for each other had been pure and innocent. As children growing up together they had been oblivious to the physical difference between them. By the time they were aware of it they had been old enough and wise enough to realise that such differences didn't matter; it didn't make them any less brother and sister.

In fact, as Gerry had persuaded her on the day she discovered she was adopted – and put it so touchingly perfect too, she thought, with another burst of anger – she was special. He had always made her feel special. She remembered his words; how warm they had been as he had whispered them into her ear, his fingers softly wiping away her tears. "We're on a higher plain me and you, Fiona. You were picked specially for me as I was for you. None of the rest of them can say that. They all just got landed together, not specially chosen like us."

That last thread, though, had finally snapped. He had known! He had known all along – all the way through their childhood – known that she was adopted. Why couldn't he have told her? He had also known that Stella Jones couldn't have been her mother. Why couldn't he have said? Why let her find out, and in such a hauntingly sad way: that poor woman, dead of that terrible disease?

Fiona checked her watch; nearly 3pm She tried Sandra's mobile. It was switched off. Probably still in the air. Looking around the study she focused on the filing cabinets. Why would he hide it from her: the truth? That her mother – her birth mother – had swapped her with the baby her adoptive parents were supposed to have. Why? Why couldn't he have told her that? The questions had been going round and round in her head since she had discovered this truth in her brother's journal. So many wasted years and it was all Gerry's fault.

The cabinets stood side by side. She jumped to her feet. Patient confidentiality; of course! That must be it. He couldn't tell her could he, if her mother was a patient? Above all else, he had been a stickler for that; never broken a confidence – not ever.

Frantically she searched his top drawer; no keys; she left the study, running down the stairs to Sandra's room. Flinging open the wardrobe, she felt through pockets. Moving on to Gerry's bedside locker; nothing; she slammed it shut. Undeterred she returned to the study, searched under the middle drawer of his desk, then flung herself onto the chair, staring here and there at every piece of furniture in the room.

Eventually her eyes fixed on the pelmet. Dragging a chair to the window she felt with her fingers, running them along the top. When he was young Gerry had always hidden his pocket money up here. Touching the cold, smooth metal she brought a small bunch of keys down in front of her eyes, jumped off the chair and went to the cabinets. For a moment she paused: patient confidentiality was sacrosanct. Gerry had drummed it into her for years. She hesitated, decided her needs were greater and opened the first drawer.

Focusing on dates of birth, it didn't take her long to work through the folders. It turned out that none of Gerry's patients were any older than she was herself. Swallowing the disappointment, so great she wanted to weep, she went to close the last drawer, saw an envelope lying under the sections of folders.

'Fiona Reid' – the envelope was addressed to her. At her London flat. How did it get here? The postmark was dated the February 14th. Was it a forgotten birthday card? Had Gerry been saving it to give to her?

Suddenly a shudder swept through Fiona. Slowly, dazed, she found her way to a seat. It was not only the date they had always called her birthday; it was also the date of Katie Smyth's murder. A date she wanted to forget.

She examined the envelope again. Why hadn't Gerry given it to her? Why would he have hidden post addressed to her? She didn't really believe he had forgotten. He never forgot things like that. The envelope had been opened, the edges of the flap clearly tampered with. Tearing it open she brought out a folded sheet of paper. A floppy disk was tucked into its folds. Lifting it, she turned it over; no label. Setting it aside she unfolded the letter. It was not typed; there was no address at the top; it had been handwritten in haste, the writing sloppy.

Dear Fiona

I was going to give this to Mark to give to you, but I've sent this copy to your flat just in case he doesn't meet me like he has promised.

I know I've been a bit of a puke; jealous of you and all that. But I'm over it now. Something is not right here at the agency.

I copied this disk today. I've made two copies. Simon's boyfriend had all this stuff about you and Mark. I saw it on his computer yesterday. I think he's stalking both of you. I don't know why, but when you access it; well you'll see, some of the stuff is really weird – and private.

I think Richard Noble knows I've sussed him out too. When he let himself into the records room yesterday I slipped into Simon's office and made the copy. I think he knows because when he was leaving he stopped at reception. He stood in front of me and just glared. Didn't say anything, but if looks could kill! I don't like him; he's really scary.

Anyway, Mark has taken a half day off to arrange a few things for your engagement party this evening and I said I'd meet him at your flat at lunch time and give him a hand. I wanted to explain everything to him, but didn't want to tell you all of this and spoil the party for you, so I thought it best to write to you instead.

Best not to mention this to Richard Noble – like I said; he really scares me. Goodness knows what he will do if he finds out I know what he's up to, creepy sod!

By the way; hope you two are really happy together. No hard feelings! It's obvious Mark really loves you and I'm glad for you both. I hope we can be friends.

Good luck.

Katie

White with shock, Fiona read the letter through again. What was all this about? The image of Katie pouting at Mark from behind the reception desk the first day she had arrived for her appointment, flashed before her eyes. Yes, they had a history. Certainly Katie had never missed an opportunity to let her believe there was still something between them. But it was all play acting. They had only gone out together a handful of times; it had been nothing serious; not like it was with her and Mark. From the moment they had met it had been special. Mark. Oh, Mark. God, how she missed him.

Holding the disk in her hand it still bothered her that Gerry had hidden this letter from her. A few days after the murder he had gone to her flat to retrieve her belongings; he must have lifted it then.

Switching on the computer, she inserted the disc and opened the first file: photographs; mainly of her. Standing at the window; sat at tables in restaurants; shopping; Mark and her in the park; embracing. Something coiled in the pit of her stomach. She felt sick. Closing the file she opened another. Personal information; everything there was to know about her. She couldn't understand. Where had all this come from? Was this some kind of trick? Maybe Katie was more of a minx than they had thought. Surely not! A pang of remorse swept through her as she thought of poor Katie.

The next file she hit on left her trembling, her mouth dry, the feeling in her stomach a consuming ache. More photographs; her again only smeared over red; her face distorted. It was sick.

One more; she would look at one more. Opened the file she found it was a form of diary started the previous October. She read the first entry.

Wednesday 15th October. We must be calm. Concentrate! Find the explanation.

Thursday 16th October. Fiona Reid. We know her face. We will know her history.

Friday 17th October. We hate Fiona Reid! DIE! DIE!!!!

Fiona leaped from the screen. Shaking, she backed away from the computer. What *was* this?

There was a sound from the hallway. She turned, held her breath, crept into the hall.

A stream of junk mail was pushing through the letterbox, floating to the floor.

Rushing to the door, with trembling fingers she clicked down the snib, pulled across the chain. She was so scared. The words had stuck to the inside of her eyes: Friday 17th October. We hate Fiona Reid! DIE! DIE!!!!

Last October; her first appointment with Simon Alexander; something niggled about that day in the back of her mind.

Kicking the junk mail out of the way, she noticed an envelope addressed to Sandra. It had an airmail sticker – from America. Picking it up, she put it on the hall table.

Fiona Reid! DIE! DIE!!!!

Bracing herself she went back to the computer.

38

Dover: the same afternoon

Seagulls screeched above her head. Sheila moved slowly, sand making its way into her shoes. Before her was the stark, white face of chalk named Shakespeare's Cliff. She had not known that back then; known nothing of the history of this place until a few days ago when she'd read about it in a tourist information brochure.

The cliff path was clearly visible now, twisting its way up between the rocks. How much easier it would have been, back then, had they been aware of its existence. From here, she could just see the fence at the back of the cottage perched high up on the edge of the cliff. Breathing heavily, she stopped to take a rest. Several times since arriving she had come this far; tempted each time to take a closer look. The memory of everything that had played out here was printed indelibly on her mind as surely as it was printed on her face.

Goose pimples formed on her skin. This was the weekend; today the day. Which one of them had placed the notices – and why? Someone was here. There had been a car the day before last too. Yet today there was no sign of life; the cottage seemed quiet, abandoned.

Rested, she took to her feet again, the pathway steep but manageable. She was about two hundred yards away when she heard an approaching vehicle. She slid back, pressing herself against a boulder that protruded from the rocks. Held her breath, listening.

Voices carried on the wind; she was unable to hear what they were saying. She waited until they had gone, then continued slowly upwards. The path turned away from the cottage, running parallel with the cliff for a while, meeting the road some distance from the cottage grounds. A narrow field edged the cliff, a tall hedge hiding the front of the cottage from view.

She entered through a gap in the hedge. The grass was overgrown tickling her legs as she waded through it. Coming to a halt beside a tree, again she rested; subsiding onto a large root that stuck above the ground. She was tired. It felt strange to be this close to the cottage. It seemed changed; looked nothing like it had before all that time ago. 35 years was a long time; gone was any evidence of the fire that had swept through its rooms.

She closed her eyes. She didn't want to remember, but she couldn't stop the fear. Her face ached; she heard again the crackle of flames, felt her nostrils filling with smoke. It began to play out in her mind. In the end she gave way to it and watched.

A hand is clasping over her mouth: a huge, thick hand smelling of diesel.

Not fully awake, she is lifted from her bed; her scream is muffled. She is carried outside. It is dark; the air, cold, hits her brow. Dark hair flaps across her face puzzling her until she remembers it is her own, dyed hours beforehand; part of her disguise.

A car door opens. She is released. A voice speaks as if known to her, the tone friendly. She looks up into his face; even though it is dark she knows him.

"Stay here, Clara. It won't take long."

He runs back to the house. She realises the car engine is running. She peers through the window, still grappling to understand what is happening. Why did he call her Clara? Then she realises; her hair is black now, like Clara's. He'd made a mistake. She sees the flicker of light. The sudden 'woosh' takes her by surprise; flames are licking up the open doorway of the cottage; the man is disappearing into the darkness around the side.

"The girls!"

Lunging forward she scrambles, running barefoot towards the cottage. Roaring flames; orange turning yellow against wood already blackening; hissing almost singing; above her, swirling heavy clouds of smoke force her to stop.

"The girls!" She screams, calling after the man, following him round to the back of the cottage. The roar of the flames is almost indistinguishable from the wind that is fanning them.

She shouts: "There are people inside! You have to help them; there are more girls inside!"

In the midst of all this heat, she freezes. There is no way back in. The wooden door at the back is alight; stacked against it the kindling they use for the range. Blocks of wood piled high against that; all of it alight.

She pauses, looks around; he is nowhere to be seen but she knows what is happening now; understands that he has set the fire. An engine revs outside the front, the tyres screeching in haste as he makes his getaway. Running to the outbuilding, she grabs up a spade and dashes back to a window. Head down, she drives the shovel end through the glass, sending shards everywhere about her. Using a milk churn she hauls herself up to the sill, feels her arms and legs tearing as she forces herself through the frame.

Bunching her torn nightgown up around her face, choking through the smoke, she falls clumsily against furniture as she makes her way to the back room. Enters, shutting the door against the smoke. Amilee and Lydia are there. She rouses them.

Instantly they panic, aware of the smoke, the roar of the flames. She urges them to hurry; pulling sheets around themselves, they scramble back through the kitchen. She helps them up to the window, turns, runs back into the dense smoke of the hallway.

As she forces herself past the flames, there is a whooshing sound, a bright white heat hits her face. She crumples to the floor; screaming. A gas lamp on the stairwell has exploded sending a ball of liquid flame spilling out over her face. She is burning, burning.

Crawling to the kitchen she finds the sink, splashes water over her face, finds no relief from the pain searing through her skin; feels it peel and curl amidst the stinging. She grabs a towel, soaks it in water and still screaming, wraps it around her face.

She has to try again. Back in the hall the heat from the flames attacks her face through the towel. She cannot imagine any kind of agony that could be more intense.

Upstairs the smoke is thicker; she is forced to her knees. She can hardly breath now, her mouth is full of foul taste; the air heavy with soot. Choking, she presses her face to the warm floorboards, gasps through the towel, crawls to the bedroom, elbowing her way through the doorway. Pushing the door closed behind her she seizes an armful of bedding, stuffing it under the door to slow down the smoke that is filtering into the room. She can hardly speak. Hoarsely she summons the two remaining girls, Karen and Clara. Their breathing is slow, already succumbing to the poisonous air. A thunderous sound comes from below; the heavy creaking of timber tells her the staircase is crumbling, consumed by the flames. They will not make it back down the stairs.

Again she must shatter a window. Grabbing up a chair she hurls it at the glass. Splinters fly around her in a cascade of diamonds. Blackness begins to creep from the edges of her mind. She knows she is going to die. Holding it at bay, she grabs sheets from the beds and knots them together, her fingers are shaking. She binds the ends around each of the girls, drags them, one after the other to the rear window. They are like rag dolls, heavy and helpless. The fire has not yet invaded the roof below her. The back porch breaks the drop as she lowers Clara, who slides on down, dropping with a thud to the ground. With the last of her strength she lifts Karen to the sill, careless of the splintered glass, pushes her over.

She is finished now; has nothing left to give; is almost too weak to care. Yet from somewhere she finds the willpower to climb onto the sill, feels with her toes to the small roof below; lets go. She is falling, falling. Thudding onto the ground, her ankle twisted beneath her. It is strange for she cannot feel any pain. Except for her face. She cannot breath. She claws at the towel; Amilee unwraps it. As it comes away it takes half her face with it. She cannot even scream. Her face fills her senses: she is a burning, throbbing ball of pain.

She hears a car; senses the danger as another vehicle screeches to a halt; men's voices are shouting at the front. Between them, Amilee and Lydia drag her, Clara and Karen to the rear of the garden. They crawl into the shadowed dark by the fence. The wind is strong; below them she can hear the sea crashing against the rocks. This is the only place to hide.

39

With a good few hours still ahead of them before the women were due to meet up, Jeff and Stevens reached Dover shortly before 3pm They sought out a decent looking café and ordered fish and chips for two and a pot of tea. Later, they took a walk along the pier to stretch their legs before heading up to the cottage. It was an ideal opportunity to get to know Stevens better, Jeff thought; but somehow he didn't feel much like talking and beyond airing aspects of the investigation, they said very little.

As they turned back from the pier, the evening was drawing in, the night sky thickening around them. The sun, a dusky red ball, slowly but steadily disappeared into the sea.

There were no cars in sight at the cottage; the door was ajar and light spilled out onto the front. Parked a little way up the road, Jeff doused the headlights, loosened the collar of his shirt and wound down the window. They could hear the distant shushing of the sea and the trees stirring in the breeze. Beyond that it was quiet as the grave.

"Can't see any cars; doesn't look like anyone's arrived yet, but the front door's open so someone's about," Jeff said.

"Here's one now, Sir; headlights coming up on the left."

They watched the lights coming closer; a green Clio came to a stop outside the front door. A woman got out and opened up the boot. Carrying something bulky in both arms, she staggered a little as if her burden was heavy. Whatever it was, it was covered by a cloth. Under one arm she held a square, white box. Backing to the door, she pushed it open with her bottom, shouted a cheery greeting and disappeared inside.

Jeff let the car run towards the cottage, easing on the handbrake as they came up behind the Clio.

"Okay, let's introduce ourselves," he said, getting out of the car.

He was locking the door when they heard the scream, followed by a crash. Shrill, whimpering cries invaded the quiet of the evening.

As they turned towards the sound, the woman re-emerged, clinging to the doorframe for support. Bent over, still wailing, she suddenly dropped, her legs folding under her.

Stevens reached her first bending to lift her. "It's alright, I've got you. I'm Detective Stevens and this is Superintendent McAdams. You're safe now. Can you tell me what's wrong? What is your name?"

"Sally," she whispered. "Sally Burton." No sooner had she spoken than she began to retch. Disconcerted, Stevens held her gingerly as she vomited onto the road.

Jeff slid past them into the cottage. Moments later his voice bellowed from within: "Stevens!"

Leaving the fraught woman on the step, Stevens scrambled through the front door almost slipping on a mess of roast beef and gravy. An upturned roasting dish lay in the hallway; a gravy-stained tea towel beside it; a squashed cream gateau had spilled out of a nearby box. Avoiding it, Stevens moved to where Jeff stood on the left of the hall looking into a front room.

Anita Hunt lay on the white, linen-covered table; her legs, bent at the knee, had been forced wide apart. Her long-sleeved, black shirt-dress was fanned out on either side of her, her breasts partially exposed, all but the top two buttons undone. She was very obviously dead.

The tablecloth was stained deep red where her blood had seeped through. It had spread out in all directions like ink on blotting paper. The lower abdomen was cut open, its dark contents wet and glistening. Lamps, five of them, were arranged around the body. Half in shadow beneath the table lay a dog – or what had once been a dog. Its throat had been cut, and like the mistress it had struggled valiantly to protect, its stomach had been torn open, its innards spilling out onto the carpet.

"Jesus!" Forcing the word in a strained whisper, Stevens went to push past Jeff, who raised an arm to stop him.

"There's a phone on the hall table. Get back up!"

Stevens did as he was bid.

Jeff stood motionless in the doorway of the dining room. Outside, the woman, Sally Burton, was keening and sobbing. Jeff sighed, another image superimposed itself on the one before him: the blood; Angie's legs strung up in a similar position. 1st December 1971: their only child had been a breech delivery. In his mind's eye he saw the crudeness of the forceps, noted again the absence of sound; the long-awaited sound that comes in those first moments after birth; the cry of the first breath that never came. He banished the image from his mind as Stevens came up behind him.

"What's it with the legs?" Stevens asked.

"She's given birth," Jeff explained. "He's placed her to look as if she's just given birth."

40

Dover: later that evening

It was completely dark now. Sheila, still sitting under the tree, had heard a car and hesitated for a while, undecided whether to approach the house. That was when the dog had started barking, frenzied and distressed, it had yelped, a high-pitched yelp, then silence. Her stomach lurching, Sheila had made her way back to the hedge and peered through. She had watched for a while and seen the car leaving, the sound had died away, but fear had kept her lurking there. She couldn't see anybody. There was a dim glow of light from the cottage. A few minutes passed; still there was no sound. Chilled to the bone, she had pushed herself onto her feet, rubbing the circulation back into her legs. This was silly; either she was going in or she wasn't. She had to make a decision. Then she had seen the headlights, heard a car. Moments later there was another. A green one; it was the same one she had spotted the other day.

The scream split the night. It froze her to her spot. An overwhelming sense of dread crept over her; gasping she backed away, forcing herself back into the hedge. So distracted was she that she failed to hear the rustling in the undergrowth, the snap of broken twigs. Suddenly she was aware that she was not alone. Before she could react, something jagged her shoulder. Then the darkness took her.

Sickened by the devastation around him, Jeff took a call on his mobile.

"Blake here, Guv; got something on one of the forums. Karen Howell. She gave a baby girl up for adoption in Higham at the end of January 1972. We've traced her to an address in Sevenoaks. Number 5, Cherry Grove it is. Only I've run the address through the register and there's no such person listed. I found an Anita Hunt, though.

Perhaps the Howell woman is an alias or a live-in member of staff. This Anita Hunt also owns the cottage, the one that you're headed for in Dover. What do you want us to do?"

Stunned, Jeff waited, collecting his thoughts before he spoke. He knew the Sevenoaks address; had immediately connected the name.

Shit! This would set the cat among the pigeons.

Far more calmly than he felt, he said, "Thanks Blake, it's okay, we're already on it. I'm here now. I'll get back to you."

"Okay, Guv."

The line went dead. In the distance, sirens shattered the air, coming closer. Jeff rejoined Stevens out front. He was helping Sally Burton, whom they now knew was Anita Hunt's housekeeper, into her car to wait for the ambulance. She was in shock, but otherwise unharmed. He called Stevens to one side to break the news.

They held the responding units outside, barring them from entering the cottage; the situation was delicate. Millar was unavailable so Jeff had made the call himself. 'An incident' was how he had described it; something like this couldn't be broken over the phone. He estimated it would be another twenty minutes or so before the helicopter arrived.

As directed by Jeff, the local police had sequestered extra uniforms from as far away as Canterbury. Road blocks had been set up though Jeff knew the killer was probably long gone.

He'd had a message from Sandra via the station. Sadly, it had come too late. She had evidently asked them to alert Dover that he might need back up, which explained why uniform had reacted so quickly. He sent her a text, reassured her he had received her message; hadn't time to do more just now.

Robert Canning was on his way by road; following closely behind, two SOCO units from Maidstone, but nothing would be touched until Anita Hunt's husband had been informed of her death. That was the unenviable task that fell to Jeff. Walking through the rooms of the cottage, he paused at the door under the stairs thinking it was probably a closet. Strange then wasn't it, to have a coat stand in the small hallway? He thought about this a few moments and called Stevens to his side. Trying the handle he found the door locked. Hearing keys jangle beside him he turned to find Stevens sorting through a large bunch, each of them labelled.

"These belong to the housekeeper; she has a spare set seeing as the cottage is only occupied for part of the year."

Jeff entered the small room and switched on the light. It was a narrow L-shaped room. The widest part actually ran along the back of the cottage, which must give it a splendid view out over the cliff behind. Under the window was a desk made from a thick piece of smooth, oak-stained timber straddled on several columns of rustic brick. Placed directly below the open window sat a flat-screen computer. Jeff walked over to the window and paused looking out into the darkness beyond the cottage. Through the glass he could hear the slamming of the waves against the foot of the cliffs below. Turning, he scanned the tiny room wishing Sandra was with him. It dawned on him that he missed her.

A large corkboard filled with magazine cuttings took his attention. Beside it, pale yellow post-its full of scrawled writing, numerous in number covered the wall. Jeff walked back to the desk. Beside it on its own stand was a printer; the paper tray brimming with pages printed out in prose. Lifting them he read a few lines. It seemed she was a writer: a novelist. That he hadn't known.

"Stevens; switch that thing on will you. See if you can get into her emails; anything that might help—" He broke off hearing raised voices coming from outside; some sort of commotion. Jeff sighed. What now? He went to investigate.

Stepping through the front door he came face to face with Chief Superintendent Millar. He was in a rage. His flushed face matched the red of his silk waistcoat; feet stomping, arms waving, he was shouting at a cowering uniform. "Do you realise who I am Constable?"

Millar's mouth dropped open as Jeff stepped out through the door. Jeff too, was stunned; what was Millar doing here? He was even more surprised to see, one step behind, Lady Clara. A calf-length, blue chiffon dress was visible beneath the folds of a matching velvet cloak. They were both dressed up to the nines. Jeff averted his eyes and coughed.

"What is going on here McAdams?" Seeing Jeff, Millar's voice was strained; he sounded disconcerted.

"I'll explain directly, Sir." Jeff waved back the two constables and ushered the two arrivals into the hallway. With his huge frame blocking the door into the front room, he directed them into the large kitchen cum living area, part of a new addition to the back of the renovated cottage. As they each settled into an armchair, it dawned on Jeff that the two of them must be here by invitation: guests for the evening. A twinge of anger curled in his gut. Millar had not been straight with him. If he hadn't been sure of that fact before, he most certainly was now.

"Anita is dead," he said baldly.

Lady Clara gasped, raising her hands to her face then dropping one to her bosom. A look of puzzlement spread over Millar's face.

"Anita? I don't know any Anita; we were here to meet Karen."

Jeff turned his gaze to Lady Clara; she evidently knew the name. "Anita; known to both of you as Karen. Karen Howell."

For a moment Jeff was silent as his superior officer assimilated this information. Then, glaring, he said, "I think, Sir, it's about time you told me what is really going on here."

Millar's face had taken on a pale, almost ghost-like hue. A shiver broke over him and he dropped his gaze to the floor.

Jeff shrugged, turned to Lady Clara; stared at her intently. "You might be interested to know that your son is here; he's in the study. I would add that he is out of earshot for the present."

She was obviously unsettled by this piece of information; she glanced uncertainly at Millar, who reassured her. "It's alright, Clara; I'll explain. As Superintendent McAdams says, it is high time I did." He looked around at the door into the hall. It was open. He got to his feet, walked briskly to the door and closed it, returning to his seat. Staring at Jeff, he sat for a moment as if choosing his words and took a deep breath.

Waiting, Jeff had the curious feeling that Millar was about to say, "Are you sitting comfortably? Then I'll begin..." But of course, he didn't.

"Back in the early seventies I was drafted in from Lincoln to form part of an undercover investigation. My objective was to obtain inside information on Kenneth McMasters. I and one or two others infiltrated the club from which he ran his operation. Everything was going well, or so we thought at the time. But unknown to us we had a mole in our ranks. During the six months that I masqueraded as a member of McMasters's inner group, I became involved with Sheila Hynds. Tony Hardy was another undercover officer; he was also involved with one of the girls."

"Ebony," Jeff interrupted.

Millar looked up; agitated. "It seems you already know what I am telling you?"

Jeff nodded, "Yes, but only a part. Please go on, Sir." He was conscious that Lady Clara had transferred her gaze to him. She looked extremely perturbed. And well you might, your ladyship, he thought, remembering what Lydia had said about her.

Millar cleared his throat. "Frank Reid was the superintendent who was, up to that time, operating from a distance; he did not become involved until the later stages of the investigation. The girls working the club got embroiled in some scam; blackmailing rich men they'd had relations with: rich, powerful men. As you might expect, there were pregnancies among the girls. They were young and naive; didn't take proper precautions."

He paused; a look of pained distaste spreading across his features. "Abortions were common amongst them. Not Sheila, I hasten to say. She wasn't one of McMasters's girls – at least, not at first. Before we encountered each other she waited tables upstairs."

Millar's voice had grown shaky, the words trembling in his throat. Jeff's eyes focused on the Chief Superintendant's hands; he was wringing them continuously.

"McMasters was an unscrupulous man; took pleasure in inflicting suffering. As part of my initiation…" Millar's face tensed; he appeared to struggle with his words. He gasped, folded his hands around his head as if in pain.

Jeff was alarmed to see that Millar's face was awash with tears. He looked drawn; haunted. Jeff half rose from his chair, "Are you alright, Sir? Can I fetch you anything? Glass of water?"

"No, I'm sorry. You have to understand, McAdams; this episode in my life is not one of which I am proud and I find it hard to talk about. But it has a bearing on this case. My sins have come home to roost in the most horrific way."

It seemed a strange thing to say. Jeff was reminded that Millar was a religious type; a member of Opus Dei. He was startled when the Chief Superintendent suddenly cried out.

"Dear God! Forgive me. I raped her; in front of them all. In the club beneath the ballroom; a dozen or more of them: drug runners, pimps, thieves and scum. McMasters forced me to take her like a common whore while they watched."

Jeff gasped, but made no comment. Lady Clara was, for the moment, forgotten.

"I was in a situation where I was given very little choice in how I acted," Millar went on. "I was forced to make instant decisions, and on my actions rested months of dangerous police work. We were so very close to success. Had I refused, my cover would have been blown wide open. Not only that, but it would have been worse for her; they would all have taken her; used her. And so, in a way, I was able to protect her. She became 'my woman'. She thought I was one of them; never knew until much later that I was a member of the Force. Somehow, despite it all, we forged a kind of friendship." He looked up, gave a hollow, humourless laugh. "I have tried ever since to justify it to myself in this way, but nothing can ever take away from the agonising guilt I feel. It was the hardest thing I ever had to do. You see, McAdams, I truly loved her." He hung his head; silence followed, only interspersed by Millar's strained breathing, his shoulders shaking with the effort of suppressing his emotion.

Stunned, Jeff thought back to the Sheila he had known during their brief meetings following the supposed death of her son. He had warmed towards her; she was so lovely and had seemed so brave. He could understand it would not have been hard to fall in love with her. Despite his revulsion at what Millar had just divulged, he was suddenly filled with pity for his superior officer. Would he have acted any differently in the same situation? It was impossible to say. Millar seemed to have shrunk in his chair, the man was crumbling in front of him. Perhaps his dedication to his Church was a direct result of this period of his life; had he found some sort of refuge; solace in dealing with his past? Clearly his abhorrence of what he had done was as strong all these years later as when it had happened.

"I appreciate your telling me all of this, Sir, and I realise how hard it is for you, but I still don't quite see how it impinges on the present investigation."

Millar lifted his head. Clearing his throat he glanced at Lady Clara. When he spoke, his voice was barely more than a whisper. "Sheila was carrying my child. By this time things had started to go wrong with the operation. Two of the officers under cover with us disappeared. McMasters knew something was up. By this time Tony had become deeply involved with Ebony – or Lydia as she was really called, but you know that, don't you. More deaths were discovered. We feared for the girls. Then this blackmailing thing came to the surface; apparently a senior member of the Cabinet at that time, who was a close colleague of McMasters, was approached. Jack Hynds was singled out for the job, though he wouldn't have had the brains for such a scheme; at least not without help."

Jeff noticed that Lady Clara was becoming fidgety, her eyes darting about the room. He might have expected to see some signs of distress; tears for her dead friend in the other room; not this strangely inappropriate anxiety. Her reaction troubled Jeff, but he let it pass for the moment as Millar continued speaking.

"One by one McMasters's gang members started to turn up dead; then one of the girls was found floating in the Thames. We decided at that point to get the girls away; somewhere safe. Not all would come; some took it into their own hands, fled back to their families, but five of them, all of them pregnant, were placed in the care of Peggy Lyons – Sheila among them. By this time, sixteen people had been felled by McMasters, including Jack Hynds and the boy; Sheila's boy. We had to suspend the operation; it was clear McMasters was onto us."

Millar got up and walked over to the sink, turned on the tap and splashed water over his face. Reaching for a towel, he dried himself, seeming more composed as he returned to his seat, dark splashes of water on his waistcoat.

"It all went quiet; months passed. Then, in March 1972, Frank Reid insisted that the girls were still in danger. I suppose he was right; they knew a great deal about McMasters; could have given plenty of evidence. The trouble was that he had too many friends in high places. We had nothing concrete; had never succeeded in catching him red-handed, and who would listen to a group of club hostesses, even if they had been brave enough to go into the dock. He was depraved; bestial; a paedophile – and yes, we maybe could have got him for that, but at the time it was primarily the drugs ring we were after. We didn't dare move against McMasters too soon and send his contacts underground, nor did we want to risk his getting a not guilty verdict. And so we waited." Millar ran his fingers through his hair distractedly, gazed unseeing at the floor.

"Most of the babies had been adopted by then with the help of Peggy Lyons, but Lydia, assisted by Tony's colleagues, arranged for her child to go to her parents in Yorkshire. Like I said, we were finalising new identities for all of the women involved, but before we could finish the paperwork, Frank decided they had to be moved urgently from the Priory. You see, McMasters had sussed out where they were. We don't know how. But anyway, he liked to tease his victims first; he arranged to adopt Sheila's daughter – our daughter. I had no knowledge of this until afterwards. Quite suddenly I was transferred to Birmingham. There had been a trail of murders up there. By the time Sheila wrote to tell me about it, my little girl had been legally adopted by Kenneth McMasters and his wife. Peggy Lyons attempted to block it, but to know avail; there was nothing I could do."

"As I now understand," he glared at Lady Clara, "when Sheila realised what was happening, she took steps to prevent it; she exchanged our daughter with the baby girl Peggy Lyons had arranged for Frank Reid and his wife to adopt. You know her, McAdams, as Fiona Reid. For some reason best known to herself Sheila neglected to tell me this."

Jeff's mouth dropped open. Quickly he shut it again, speechless, his mind working overtime, aware that Millar was still speaking.

"Sheila told nobody at the time; not until much later. In fact," again he glared at Lady Clara, "I have only recently learned the truth. I had assumed that it was my daughter who was killed with McMasters and his wife when their car was in a head-on collision. As you are aware, Lady Clara's parents and her son were in the other car."

Yes, you poor bastard, Jeff thought. After the meeting at Whitehall, he had looked up newspaper reports of the RTA in which Gareth Stevens had been involved as a small boy. He was lucky to be alive: the cars had been written off, the carnage horrific. McMasters, his chauffeur, his wife, and the little girl, Jenny, had been killed outright, as had Gareth's grandparents. The brakes on McMasters's car had failed. Sabotage was suspected, but never thoroughly investigated. The whole business was decidedly murky, Jeff thought. Now he suspected he knew why. Again he observed Lady Clara shifting uneasily in her seat. There were undercurrents here that he could not fathom.

Jeff cleared his throat, "They were moved then, the girls, from the Priory?"

"Yes. Once McMasters knew they were there, it was imperative to get them away. Frank Reid's family owned this place: White Cliffs; so they were moved here for a few weeks until they could be re-settled with new identities elsewhere; Peggy Lyons helped. Tony arranged for a transfer to Gravesend. He decided it was safer being closer to McMasters where he could keep an eye on him; better than always looking over your shoulder somewhere else, he said. It didn't quite go as planned though. I had been transferred to Birmingham, as I said. I never got to see Sheila before I left. She went back to Ireland; wrote over the years, told me about the fire here at White Cliffs. A few years ago her letters stopped coming and mine were returned. I imagined she had forged a new life for herself, so I stopped trying to make contact."

Jeff looked up. "And she never told you about your daughter?"

"No. As I said; she told nobody, not until after the accident that killed McMasters, and then only Clara."

"You mentioned a fire here, Sir; I understand that Sheila Hynds's face is badly scarred. Is that how it happened?"

"Yes. It was not accidental. Were it not for her, they would all have been killed. Somehow she managed to get the girls out. The cottage was surrounded by McMasters's remaining henchmen. They thought the girls were still inside, but thanks to Sheila, they'd escaped. They had to clamber down the cliff face to get away; Amilee lost her footing; fell. Her body was carried out to sea; never found." He paused, his face creasing, more tears welling.

Embarrassed, Jeff cleared his throat, "Sir, you said something about a mole—"

He broke off; the sound of the helicopter vibrated overhead. A constable rapped on the door and opened it, stuck his head round, looked across at Jeff. "Sorry, Sir, but the chopper's here."

Jeff jumped to his feet. "Thank you Constable." He turned to Lady Clara, tried to keep his voice mildly neutral. "Perhaps, Lady Clara, you could arrange some tea? Anita's husband has arrived."

Millar stood, his eyes drawn up to the sound. He raised his eyebrows in an unspoken query at Jeff.

Jeff spoke, his voice low, urgent: "Anita Hunt, Sir. I assumed you knew. Did Lady Clara not say? She is – or rather, she was – the Commissioner's wife. You didn't know?"

Richard Noble heard the helicopter going over, smiled. He could see the red lights in the distance as he took the bend. Immediately he slowed. Popped a pill into his mouth.

Approaching the checkpoint he pulled down the mirror, the light shone on his face. Looking into his own eyes, he smiled again. He expected no problems.

As the policeman tapped a torch on the window, he wound it down.

The fresh-faced constable gazed at him for a brief moment, shining the torch in the car, the artist's impression of Richard Noble clutched in his hand.

But he was not Richard today.

Fluttering his eyelashes and looking pointedly at the policeman's crotch, he lisped, "Yes Officer? Is there something wrong?"

Blushing to the roots of his hair, the young policeman hurriedly waved him on.

Out of earshot, he put his head back and hooted with maniacal laugher.

41

Westport, Ireland: later that night

Sandra retired to bed early, though she had no intention of sleeping. Scattered over the bed the faces of the murder victims looked back at her. The images of Simon Alexander set to one side with Katie Smyth; to the other Gracie and the Lyonses. Certainty was growing within her that she was viewing the actions of not one but two depraved minds. Mark Jakes couldn't possibly have killed Alexander; that had to have been Noble, but what about Peggy Lyons and her husband – and Gracie? Two killers working in tandem? The beep of her mobile interrupted her thoughts. She answered, expecting to hear Jeff following up on the brief text he'd sent earlier, but it was Suzi.

"Where are you, Sis? There's an Irish signal on my phone."

"I'm in Westport believe it or not! There was a murder here two weeks back connected to a case we're on in Kent. I meant to call you back several times, Suzi; I'm sorry, it's just that things kind of took off."

"Not to worry; I just thought I'd give you a buzz, see how things have played out with Elle."

Sandra shuffled to the edge of the bed swinging her legs over the side. It was a repro four-poster high off the floor. There was a gothic-style fireplace across the room where Michael had set a turf fire earlier in the evening. The smell of warm peat filled the room. Sandra moved towards it, curling herself into a winged chair beside the hearth; the vibrant orange glow immediately warming her.

"I've been wondering about your message on and off all week," Sandra said, "though I couldn't quite understand what you were getting at. To be honest, I actually found myself dreading calling you back just in case you were going to tell me she was pregnant or something!" Sandra closed her eyes, screwing up her face; too late to call back the words. Suzi's eldest daughter had given birth a week before her nineteenth birthday the year before – on Christmas Eve in fact. Suzi was very defensive about her daughter despite the fact that she was already part way through her first year at university in Galway, and coping well enough on her own. Any negative reference to teenage pregnancy was likely to get a scathing response. Sandra grimaced, waiting for the change in Suzi's tone, but getting quite a different one instead.

"You mean she hasn't told you yet; about her mother – about Rebecca, I mean?"

Sandra's heart heaved; the juxtaposition of the words Rebecca and mother in one sentence creating a sudden hurtful twinge in her stomach. Rebecca Reid, Gerry's first wife, had abandoned her husband and children to follow her acting career all the way to America. After the divorce she had married some big producer, but her career had never gone beyond budget TV films. That was until about eighteen months ago when, with a little twisting of arms by her second husband, she had landed a role in a TV sitcom. Beyond everyone's expectations, it had soared in the ratings and was now in its third series. Rebecca had signed full custody of her children over to Gerry and during the years since she had abandoned them, not once had she made any attempt to contact Elle and Sam. Sandra had never met her; she doubted Elle even remembered her. She had been only two. Rebecca's name was never mentioned at home. Massaging the sudden ache in her stomach, Sandra posed the question.

"What about her?"

There was silence for a few moments before Suzi finally spoke. "Perhaps it wasn't my place to interfere, Sandra, but Elle wanted advice and she didn't want to talk to you about it – at least, not until she'd got things straight in her own head that is."

"I see; straight about what exactly?"

Sandra waited for the explanation, reliving images of Suzi and Elle engrossed in conversation on Elle's bed during the two weeks Suzi had stayed on after Gerry's funeral. Sandra had happened across them several times, their conversation always breaking off as soon as she appeared: that quick shifting of shoulders; the change of subject given away by false tones of voice. It was not something Elle had yet mastered as well as Suzi. Teenage calamities, she'd assumed, neither hurt nor surprised that Elle had chosen to confide in Suzi. With five daughters of her own she was more experienced; just enough distance too. Rebecca had never come into Sandra's head; why would she?

"Elle and Sam both got letters from her not long after Gerry's death. I thought they would have told you by now?"

"No." Sandra sighed.

"Oh. Trust me and my big mouth. Ah well! Nothing there to worry about then; is there? Maybe they decided not to take up the offer. I don't think Sam was fussed on it anyway. It was Elle who was torn."

"What offer? What do you mean torn?" Sandra's mind was replaying things that had been niggling her for a few weeks now. All of a sudden she realized Fiona had been right: something more than normal bickering was broiling between the girls. Despite the warmth from the fire, she felt suddenly cold.

"Rebecca wants them to move to Hollywood! Elle was all taken up with it. She approached me because she was troubled about how you would feel; the timing and all that."

"God that woman's got a nerve!" Sandra cried. She was not just vexed; somewhere deep inside fear started to trickle through her. "Who the hell does she think she is; not a care in the world for close on fifteen years and then; at a time when they're completely vulnerable she comes waltzing into their lives as if she has some God given right!"

"Sandra. Come on. She does; she is after all their mother; their natural mother."

"That's cheap coming from you! What am I then, a fucking caretaker? Someone hired in the interim. I reared those girls. I bathed them and fed them. Held them in the middle of the night; cleaned up their cuts; not her! Even before she left them she had little to do with them. Gerry told me enough about her; she hired a nanny; a round the clock nanny for God's sake! That's the kind of mothering she did."

Suzi sighed in her ear. She had seven children in all; four from her first marriage now grown; three from her present. Her first husband, a brute, had left her near dead several times before they finally got her away from him. Austin, her present husband, was a gentle giant; they'd been married close on twenty years now. Sandra remembered little of the first being the youngest in the family. What she did know was that he had pursued Suzi relentlessly for custody. Not that he actually cared about his children, just intent on ensuring she would never be happy. The children in turn hated him with a vengeance. The strain on Suzi had left its mark. She'd had a pacemaker installed a few years earlier; was on medication for her nerves. Sandra regretted losing her temper, but Suzi's back was up and it being Friday night, she would by now have taken several glasses of wine. Inevitably, the tirade would flow.

"You're no better to claim yourself worthy of motherhood, Sandra; you disposed so easily of your own! It's one thing to leave a marriage; abandon your kids; but to deny them life; you murdered *your* baby Sandra!"

"Ouch!" Sandra's eyes closed; yes that was one way of putting it; 'murdered'. It was something she had learned to live with; a knowledge that lurked in the background of every waking moment of every single day. She had been only eighteen; it had not been love. Suzi had been her only confidante – she'd had to tell somebody. She had fled to England for an abortion. Brought up in a strict, Roman Catholic home, Suzi had been appalled. For years they had not spoken about it – barely spoken at all in fact – not until the death of their father five years ago. Suzi had mellowed by then; distanced from her Church by their refusal to annul her first marriage, though still steadfast in her beliefs against abortion. Tortured with guilt, Sandra had long ago overcome the traumas resulting from the act itself; what was done was done. But never a day went by that she did not regret it.

"I'm sorry, Sis." Suzi's voice was almost a whisper. "I didn't mean it."

"I know. What are we like?" Sandra managed to lift her own voice. "What advice did you give to Elle?"

"I didn't. Look, Sandra, at their age they will decide for themselves. It pains me the things my children had to endure. But my situation was different. Just think of the opportunities for the girls. Like it or not, Rebecca's got the power to open doors for Elle. Think how talented Elle is; you can't deny her a chance; Sam too. You've done a fantastic job with them. Look, Sis, take it as it comes; don't make them feel backed into a corner. The most important thing to remember is that if they decide to make a go of it, just take care you leave a way open for them to come back if it doesn't pan out."

Sandra thought about what Suzi had said for a long time after she had rung off. It was good advice. It didn't make her feel any better.

Her eyes were swollen and bloodshot from weeping when Jeff eventually phoned. It was good to hear his steady voice, but his news shocked her to the core; it cast a shadow over the investigation. Commissioner Ian Hunt's wife was a quiet woman; had always shied away from the limelight. Few people had known she was the renowned novelist, Claire Hamilton; public appearances had been seldom.

Jeff filled her in on the particulars, adding the bits of history that he had learned from Millar. "So after all this time, Sandra, it is Sheila Hynds who is Fiona's birth mother. It appears that Chief Superintendent Millar is her natural father – what a turn up for the books eh? He didn't know until a few days ago. It appears Lady Clara Smith-Stevens told him last week. When McMasters threatened to adopt the child, Sheila swapped her baby with the one Frank and Alice Reid had arranged to adopt. Millar didn't know anything about it. Nobody knew until much later. Then, when Millar found out that McMasters had adopted Sheila's little girl – as he thought – he assumed she had died in that car crash. He's a ruined man, Sandra. It's like he doesn't know what to feel most guilty about!"

"Did Sheila never tell him?"

"Apparently not."

Stunned, Sheila felt a clench of fear for her sister-in-law. "I'll not break it to Fiona over the phone, Jeff. I'll wait until tomorrow when I get back."

"Don't worry about her, Sandra. The house is under surveillance. Millar has doubled up on uniforms; nobody could get through. I realise now that he has been trying to protect her. That's why he wanted you off this case too; didn't want you getting too close. He doesn't know I have told you any of this, okay?"

After Jeff had gone, Sandra brought up her home number and Fiona answered almost straight away. Sandra knew from her voice that she was not only vexed, but agitated. Fiona took no time in recounting the discoveries she had made. She had already taken things into her own hands and contacted her friend, Howard, a senior partner with the law firm Black, Walsh & Co. He was with her now, reading through the files on the disk.

Telling her there had been another murder, but not the details,

Sandra made Fiona promise to be careful then asked about the girls.

"They're upstairs, can't you hear the music?"

"No, but I can imagine!" Two opposing styles: Rave intermingling with Country. They were like chalk and cheese. Sandra had wanted to chat about the girls, but Fiona had too much on her mind.

"There's a letter here for you Sandra; American postmark?"

Sandra closed her eyes tightly and sighed. "It's okay; I know about that. It's something that will have to wait until I get back."

"Okay; you sound very down, are you okay?"

"Just tired; tired of the whole lot of it. There are things I need to talk to you about, but can it wait until tomorrow?"

Sheila McBride's eyes opened to darkness. Her head throbbed, her mouth was dry. She was sitting on the floor, her arms tied up together stretched above her head. Pain streaked from her wrists down to her shoulders. Rope bound her feet; at least she thought it was rope. Her ankles ached. Drowsy, her head heavy; she found she could not move. She faded again to a darker place.

42

Westport: Friday, 2nd November

"Three hundred and sixty five of them there are or so they say; one island for each day of the year; the saying goes." Michael stood beside her as they waited for Keith Jones to pack.

Sandra smiled. "You're lucky to be blessed with such a view." She scanned the bay below them. The water had taken on a deep green hue in the morning light. Hundreds of islets dotted the water, some edged with sand. It was breathtaking, unspoilt. To her left was Croagh Patrick, its peak hidden in low cloud. "It's like a pathway to heaven," she laughed, slightly embarrassed. She need not have been. Michael understood.

"I've climbed it on her birthday every year since I lost her. For now it's the closest I can get to her. Jones explained about your husband, Sandra, why didn't you tell me last night?"

"Trust Jones!" Sandra turned to look briefly at Michael before turning back to the water below them. She shrugged, "I didn't want to impose on your loss. There is no comparison: Gerry and I were estranged and I guess I didn't want your sympathy – it is not the same for me as it is for you."

He placed a hand on her shoulder. "I'll not tell you it gets easier; I haven't reached that place yet; if it exists. But bearable; yes, it becomes bearable over time."

She forced a smile aware that he didn't believe her. Feeling undeserving, she quickly changed the subject. "I was looking at the images again last night, Mike. I can't help feeling that we should be looking for more than one killer. Even though the murders are so similar, there are differences that just don't tie up."

"The sexual thing?"

"Yes, principally."

"Mm, perhaps you are right."

After stopping off at the cottage where Gracie had died they went on to the parochial house. Father Tom Devine, who welcomed them in, was clearly still shaken by Gracie's murder. Showing them to Sheila's room, he explained briefly that he had not seen her since before her heart attack. It had been quite sudden; touch and go for a time. She had spent some weeks in hospital in Galway. Then she had called him to say she was going to England for a brief holiday to convalesce before coming back to work. As they knew, Gracie had been covering for her.

Keith Jones took a few notes, but there was nothing new. Michael had already told them this. He had told them also about the property Sheila had inherited, which brought her quite a sizeable income and explained how she had managed to make such generous donations to the Priory. Sandra sat in the room for a time, but she could get nothing from it, there was nothing to give her an image of the woman who lived here. Nor was there any indication of where in England she might have gone. As far as the investigation was concerned, this had been a wasted trip. From a personal point of view though, it had been good to make contact with Michael again. When they parted company at the airport, she promised to keep in touch – and meant it.

The flight home was on time. By late morning, Sandra had dropped Jones at his flat and was parking in front of her house. She noted two uniforms in evidence, as well as a squad car across the road. It made her feel slightly reassured.

Two hours later, having greeted the girls as cheerfully as she could, she had sat down with Fiona, listened to everything she had to say and looked at the copies she had made of the disk. What she saw worried her greatly. She wondered briefly why Noble had not seized Fiona when he had the opportunity, but perhaps at the time obtaining the files to locate his mother had been more important to him. Or was it that he had somehow known Fiona was his sister and hoped she would lead him to Sheila? He would have known from his lover that Fiona was looking for her. She shuddered. Was that why he had killed Simon Alexander; had he been getting too close?

It was becoming increasingly apparent that there had been a miscarriage of justice in the Katie Smyth case. There was not enough evidence to clear Mark Jakes without further investigation, but enough questions had been raised to justify reopening the case. Fiona had already persuaded Howard Black to take her up to Broadmoor to see Mark. He arrived to pick her up just as Sandra had psyched herself up to tell Fiona about Sheila.

In a way, it was a blessed relief that Fiona was so preoccupied. She was so wound up with the thought of seeing Mark and at last being able to justify her insistence that he was innocent, that the momentous news about the identity of her birth parents and how it had been uncovered, seemed hardly to impinge on her consciousness. She sat for a time as it sunk in, calculating events in her head.

"At least now I can give her a name – and him too. I hadn't expected that. It feels kind of weird. How strange that it should be someone you know. Mum and Dad must have known him too; perhaps that's why they adopted me... but no, they couldn't have known it was him because they didn't know..." her voice faltered.

"What, Fiona?"

Fiona looked down at the floor, shrugged, "I already knew I was swapped for another baby. I read about it in Gerry's journal," she flushed, looked up, meeting Sandra's eyes defiantly. "When we were kids, Gerry always used to say that being chosen made us both special. He lied, they didn't choose me, Sandra, but they *did* make me feel special. I always felt loved and secure." She was silent for a moment, looking inward; a slight smile curving her mouth. "I have been wondering why my birth mother did that. Swap me, I mean."

Not wanting to muddy the waters just yet, Sandra had told Fiona nothing of the circumstances surrounding her conception and birth; only that her father had, until recently, believed she was dead. How on *earth* had Gerry known about the swap and why had he never said anything? What else had Fiona read in those journals? She wondered how she should disclose what she had learned from Jeff about Sheila's past, but it was delicate. Before she could choose the words, Fiona spoke again.

"I guess I am glad my father is looking out for me now he knows about me," she smiled a little shakily. "I must say I had begun to feel a bit paranoid about the policemen crawling all over the garden! I've told the girls it's nothing important, just something to do with the case you're on; didn't want to scare them." She looked up at

Sandra and grimaced. "It's funny, though, how it has consumed me all this time: the need to know who I really am. I thought it meant everything, but now, hearing their names I just feel flat; deflated, you know? Maybe we can talk some more later, when I've had a chance to think about it. Perhaps you can tell me more about her then? It's all too much to take in just now. I must go, Howard's waiting." Her eyes sparked with tears and she grasped Sandra's hands. "This might be Mark's only chance. I have to see to this first; I owe him this much. I loved him, Sandra; I think I still do."

Let off the hook for now, Sandra breathed a sigh of relief. Fiona left soon afterwards, leaving her alone with the girls. She picked up the letter waiting for her on the hall table. At the foot of the stairs she took a few deep breaths trying to lift her spirits so her voice gave nothing away. Keeping Suzi's advice in mind, she went slowly up to their rooms. It was time they had a talk.

Jeff was at that time standing on the beach beneath the cottage in Dover watching the dog handlers. The evening before, they had at last located the lodgings where Sheila McBride had been staying for the past few weeks; it had been a lucky break – they were overdue for one – a member of the Dover team going off duty had called in at the Fiddler's Rest on his way home; heard gossip about a woman with a horrifically scarred face. He'd called Jeff; she wasn't there now, but she hadn't checked out yet and was expected back. She'd gone for a walk on the beach, so the landlady said, grumbling that if Ms McBride came back now she was too late for supper, they'd stopped serving food! Jeff had asked him to wait and to call him immediately Sheila McBride turned up.

No call came. First thing this morning, Jeff had gone over there, relieved the bleary-eyed constable, and asked to be shown to Sheila's room. With alarm bells ringing in his gut, he had inspected it: of average size for a pub and dated, the curtains and bedding floral-patterned; the paintwork a sickly salmon pink, discoloured with time. The small suitcase yielded nothing of use; two changes of clothes, some underwear and toiletries. A plain, brushed cotton nightgown was folded neatly on top of the pillow. Pulling on a pair of gloves, Jeff lifted it and bundled it into an evidence bag before returning to White Cliffs. It was by no means certain that Sheila had gone to the cottage; she may well be lying dead somewhere by now, her guts cut open. How the hell did this bastard Noble manage always to be one jump ahead?

The coastguard had been alerted, but had reported nothing back as yet. Teams of officers were combing the beach beneath the cottage and a special dog unit had been called out. Handing over the nightgown, Jeff watched as the handlers held it over the dogs' noses. With the scent of Sheila McBride in their nostrils, they roamed the beach aimlessly for a time, dragging their handlers along behind them. Jeff paired up with DC James Creighton and his partner, a German Shepherd named Sonny.

"The tide coming in last night will have washed away any trace of her down here," Creighton said. "We'll try further up the beach. There's a pathway through the rocks over there."

In moments Sonny, nose to the ground, tail waving, was moving eagerly up the cliff path. Struggling to keep up, Jeff followed them into the field beside the cottage. Apparently, Sheila had indeed been close to the scene yesterday. Had she witnessed the murder? But no, Sonny did not make for the cottage, instead he ran along the edge of the cliff. There was no mistaking the dog's eagerness. Again it was off, nosing the ground, running along close to the hedge. Suddenly Sonny stopped, craned his neck into the hedge and jumped up barking. Creighton pulled him back and scouted all around the area. The dog followed the trail to a tree, excitedly nosing the ground around the exposed roots; then he ran back to the same point of the hedge. From there, the trail seemed to lead nowhere.

They headed back down the path to the beach. Officer Creighton's radio crackled. He called to Jeff who had sat down on a large, flat topped rock at the foot of the steep climb.

"One of the dogs has picked the scent up about a mile further down. Leads up to the road there then stops."

Jeff looked up towards the cottage then turned to view the long stretch of beach. Robert Canning had estimated that Anita Hunt had been dead only a short time before they had discovered her the evening before. It would have taken some time to move from the field all the way down the cliff path and across the beach to the road. The check points would have been set up by then. How had they missed her; besides that, she had no vehicle at her disposal? He thought of Sonny straining to find the scent in the bushes. Sheila had been carried, that much was obvious. Alive or dead?

Some twenty minutes later, Jeff left with Stevens to drive to London. Stevens had called King's College yesterday for information about a past student: David Shaw. The college had said the records would be made available to them today. They should ask for Molly Knight, the Students' Mentor. They parked up and were directed to her office by a student who happened to be hurrying out of the main entrance.

Jeff lost no time in explaining what they wanted: "We understand that David Shaw excelled at his studies, completed his degree and signed up for his Masters, but then he dropped out of sight. Why did nobody think to report him missing?"

"There was no reason to suppose he was 'missing'," Molly Knight said, her face blank. "Happens every year; we get more dropouts at undergraduate level, but even the post-grads change their minds sometimes. The cost involved in long-term study means making sacrifices; some of them decide to take up paid employment instead." She looked down at the records on her desk, "We had a letter stating he was not intending to complete his degree, it was not regarded as anything unusual. Has something happened to him?"

"We don't know. Do you still have the letter?"

"No, once it had been noted on file, it would have been destroyed. We try to keep the amount of paper down, Inspector. His name is on this list of undergrads for that year, if that is of interest."

Jeff studied the list she handed to him. One name stood out from all the rest: Jason McMasters. Jeff's eyes narrowed; "Tell me about this fellow here," he pointed.

Glancing at it, Molly looked up at Jeff and grimaced. "We get hundreds of students through these doors, Inspector; rarely does one stand out in my memory, but this happens to be one of them. I remember him alright. He was strange that one."

Jeff looked at Stevens then back to Molly. "Strange in what way?"

"To sum it up in one word: creepy. Funny you should ask about him though, he was close to David. It's coming back to me now: there were rumours at the time that they were a couple; nothing overt, but they were a lot in each other's company; shared digs. Maybe that was what started the rumours. Anyway, they were like chalk and cheese. David, as I remember, was a lively fellow; bright too. His tutor was convinced that Jason's marked assignments were actually David's work, but nothing came of it; Jason was too clever for that," she shuddered.

"You said he was creepy; in what way do you mean?"

Molly frowned slightly, looking at the desk as if trying to recall something. "Best way I can describe it is to tell you what I was told by his tutor, Professor Hutton – he's principally a behaviourist, but he took first year students for Anatomy. He was concerned about Jason, wanted my advice about counselling. It was about his behaviour when they were using the cadavers. There is a viewing platform above the theatre we use. Hutton was sitting there reading through some notes before class one day. The table was all set up ready with the cadaver: a woman it was, but the theatre was empty. Jason came in, looked about but didn't see the Professor. He went right up to the body, pulled back the cover and stared at the dead woman, then started stroking her face. Then, would you believe, he knelt up on the table beside her, ranting something. Hutton said he couldn't make out what he was saying, but Jason moved himself until he was on all fours over the corpse, rocking from side to side."

"Why ever didn't Hutton intervene?"

Molly made eye contact with Jeff. "Before anything else, the Professor was an academic, if you know what I mean. He confessed that he was completely fascinated by Jason's behaviour, wanted to see where it was going. There are many first year students who react peculiarly when they see their first cadaver being opened up, you know, pass out, vomit, and so forth, but Hutton hadn't seen anything like this before, so he stayed watching."

"What did Jason do next?"

"Well that's the creepiest part. He got off the table, lifted a dissecting knife from the tray and started slashing the woman's face. That was when Hutton reacted."

Molly straightened herself in her seat. "But it was the weirdest thing. By the time he got down to the theatre, Jason was on the ground rolled up in a ball, weeping like a child. The Professor picked him up, but by then the other students had started to arrive, so he asked David to take him back to his digs. Told the others it was some kind of reaction to seeing a dead body for the first time. It was reported to me, of course, and we discussed it, but decided to let it pass. Least said soonest mended, you know, and Jason seemed perfectly normal the following day as if he had forgotten all about it. However; a few weeks later, Hutton told me he wasn't entirely convinced; said there was something strange about the way Jason acted whenever he was in the dissecting suite."

"What action was taken?" Stevens asked, looking at Jeff, his expression one of stunned disbelief.

"It was hard to pin down anything in particular, so nothing. I confess that I shied away from tackling Jason about it. But there were no other incidents and he graduated successfully, though as I said, it was suspected that he'd cheated. Mind you, he had a career already cut out for him with his uncle's company, McMasters Pharmaceuticals, you know of it?"

Jeff nodded and exchanged glances with Stevens. Within minutes they had thanked Molly Knight for her help and left.

McMasters Pharmaceuticals was situated north of Maidstone. Comprising of four large factory-like buildings, the head office was located in the oldest of the buildings. Built of brick and somewhat Dickensian, it was most probably the original, Victorian factory.

Henry McMasters wore a white chemist's coat over a brown checked shirt and green tie. Nearing seventy, he was tall and wafer thin with straggly wisps of hair shooting out from his scalp. He wore dark-framed glasses with lenses that doubled the size of his eyes as he peered out studying each of them in turn. "Good afternoon, gentlemen. Please take a seat. How can I help you?"

"Actually, it is your nephew, Jason, with whom we wish to speak," Jeff said, noting out of the corner of his eye that Stevens, pen in hand, had his notebook at the ready.

Henry's gaze dropped to his hands, which were folded on top of an open log on his desk; his fingers had a slight tremor.

"I can't help you there I'm afraid; haven't seen him in at least a dozen years; not that that concerns me."

"Why would that be; weren't you his guardian?" Noting the change in Henry's demeanour, Jeff watched as the chemist walked to the window; turned to face them resting on the window ledge.

"We didn't get on," he explained. "Suppose it was no fault of the child's; though it's hard to imagine that's what he once was. A child, I mean! My brother, as I'm sure you know, was a nasty piece of work. A vicious, cruel bastard if I say so myself. Not that anyone outside the family realised it at the time, of course, him being a respected MP and what have you. But he led that boy a dog's life – and his mother too."

Stevens moved to the edge of his seat, about to interrupt. Jeff glared at him and gave a small shake of his head. Stevens subsided and with a shrug looked back at his notebook.

McMasters blinked, fished a tissue out of his pocket to clean his glasses then rubbed his nose with it before returning it to his pocket. "He married a lovely slip of a girl: Elizabeth Reid; most beautiful creature I ever laid eyes on..." Lost in memory, a smile came to his face; he held it for a moment before darkness crept over his features.

"Go on," Jeff prompted.

"Treated her badly; Kenneth was incapable of loving anyone; anything; except money; money and power. Well, she managed to get permission to help in the office here. No point now in hiding the truth I suppose, not now they're all dead and gone. But, well, not to put too fine a point on it," he cleared his throat, "we became close, if you know what I mean."

"You had an affair with your brother's wife," Jeff stated baldly.

"That's right, Inspector. When she fell pregnant, she told me the child was mine; I don't know why she tried to deceive me. I realised later that he wasn't, but at first, even though there was nothing of a likeness, I still felt him to be mine. She would get the nanny to bring him over so as I could see him, but then my brother found out and put a stop to it. I never saw the boy again until after the accident. But he wasn't mine; I knew it then. Evil; pure evil he was, just like his father. Kenneth had found out about our affair when she was about three months gone. He brought her here one day; pulled her by the hair into one of the labs. I was too weak to do anything. I could never stand up to my brother. Not that Elizabeth's own brother did anything to help her either. He was with them you see; Frank and a couple of other men. They tied Frank to a bench, and then..." the chemist's voice shook, his specs misting. Once more he attempted to clean them off.

"What happened?" Jeff asked.

"Strapped her to the bench beside Frank; wild he was, Kenneth, mad with rage. Had her head strapped down too. I guess we thought he was going to kill her at first. I thought he'd kill me too. I never understood why he didn't. His men had guns trained on me and Frank. We couldn't have moved a muscle to help. We both would have died trying. I guess in the end we both realised we were no help to her dead. I think that's why Frank didn't try. I think if it wasn't for her, he'd have been glad if they'd killed him." Again he paused, lost in thought, his face screwed up as if he was about to burst into tears.

"Go on," Jeff said quietly.

"Poured acid over her eyes he did, laughing he was; laughing so loud we could hardly hear her screams. I hear them now though, night after night in my dreams. My brother was mad, Detective; completely insane."

"Why didn't you report any of this to the police, Mr McMasters?"

The chemist looked down at his hands, shrugged, said sadly, "Maybe I should have, but it was too late for Elizabeth, there was nothing I could have done for her by then and I had my own family to consider, Inspector. As I said, my brother was completely insane."

Jeff nodded. "What about the boy, Jason?"

"Kenneth made out it was his own son – and as I said, I am certain that was so. I never saw Elizabeth again. When the accident took her I think it was a welcome release. It was sad about the little girl, though. God help Elizabeth having to bear him another child after what he did to her."

"She didn't," Jeff intervened. "The girl, Jenny, was adopted."

McMasters sighed; walked back to his chair. "I wouldn't have known about that. I knew to keep my distance by then. I got a call from Elizabeth one time though. She was hooked on cocaine by then. My brother was evil; evil. He fed it to her; chained her to him with an addiction. She was completely blind and always in pain; were it not for the drug she would have run away. She had tried before, you know, but he beat her so savagely she never tried again. She was delirious by then; too far gone even to take her own life. She had called to tell me our son was dead. She rambled on about Kenneth replacing him with another boy and passing him off as their son, but she said she knew; even blind, she knew."

Jeff sat forward. "Can you remember when that was; roughly even?"

"Yes, as it happens; not that it matters. Like I said, she was ranting; doped out of her head. I contacted Frank Reid at the time; worried about her, told him what she'd said. He said she was mentally unstable, not to take heed of it and that the boy was fine. So I thought no more about it, but I remember it well because it was the last time Elizabeth and I ever spoke. It was 1971, the night after bonfire night."

Jeff stood, eager to get back to the station. "Do you have an address for Jason?"

"No, but I can give you a bank account number if it helps. Jason is still half-owner of this company; his dividend goes into an account set up in his name."

"He inherited his father's share of the business then?"

McMasters gave a wry, pained smile. "No; long before he died my father saw through my brother. He changed his will; set up a clause that Kenneth's share of the company would skip him and go straight to his son."

Some time later, Jeff lay back in his chair in his own office. The Hynds's story was piecing together. The body of the boy in the Thames was undoubtedly that of Elizabeth's son, Jason McMasters. Whatever had landed the child in the river, it was clear in Jeff's mind that McMasters, always suspected of firing the Hynds's houseboat, had needed the boy alive because of the inheritance. His own son by some mishap had been killed and the devious, twisted, evil bastard had simply found another: Andy Hynds. On his desk lay the photo of 'Jason', retrieved from files held at King's College. Beside it he placed the artist's sketch drawn from the description given by Alexander's housekeeper. Beside that the curled, coloured snap taken of Andy when he was a small child; all were one and the same person, he was sure of it: Andy Hynds a.k.a. Jason McMasters a.k.a. Richard Noble.

"Stevens; National Records Office; get onto them. Find out how and when Jason McMasters changed his name to Richard Noble. Also, see if there's any change of name record – a deed poll maybe – on the name of David Shaw."

Jeff checked his watch; he had a meeting with the Chief Super and the Commissioner later. It was going to be a long night.

43

Broadmoor: later that day

Howard Black shuffled his case notes, setting them down on the table. Beside him Fiona sat silent; her eyes fixed intently on Mark, who sat whimpering, head sunk listlessly to his chest, staring at the floor. Fiona, trembling with shock, engulfed by rage and fear in equal measure, struggled to remain outwardly calm.

"Mark," Howard looked up, "it appears we may have come across something that gives us grounds for an appeal."

Mark Jakes slowly lifted his head to look at Howard. He avoided looking at Fiona. His whole body was trembling. His hands held together by cuffs, he brought his elbows to the table using them to steady himself.

"Fiona has discovered a computer disk sent to her by Katie Smyth," Howard said gently. A mildly mannered man, his face was filled with compassion for the pathetic creature that had once been a man.

Suddenly, Mark's breathing changed; he began to hyperventilate, panicked, gasping for air as if he was drowning.

Fiona leaned forward, "Mark; it's alright. It's me, Fiona. It's alright," added in an aside to Howard, "It's her name; he's reacting to her name." Reaching across the table she took hold of Mark's hands, holding them tightly. "It's going to be okay, Mark."

Looking at her for the first time, Mark held his head on one side as if listening to her voice. Suddenly he released a heavy sigh and ceased trembling.

The white-coated orderly standing with his back to the door intervened, "He has waking nightmares; screams and cries in his sleep. He often calls out your name, Miss Reid. Cries out that you are an angel come to take him away from the beasts that are coming to get him; we have to keep him under sedation for most of the time or he would harm himself."

Horrified tears starting to her eyes, Fiona gasped, swung round to Howard, unable to speak.

Meeting her tortured gaze, Howard turned his attention back to Mark. "It's still not enough; not on its own but it certainly raises some questions. We are here to help you, Mark."

Mark remained silent, but a tremor ran through his hands.

Still holding onto them, Fiona caressed his fingers, said softly, "I need you to be strong Mark; we have to go through this again. Please let me help you this time."

For a moment Mark gazed into her eyes; tears welled, spilled over. He began to sob, dropping his wet face into her hands. Cupping his cheek, she stood, hunching over the table leaning her head against Mark's. Gently withdrawing her hand from his grasp, she ran her fingers through his greasy hair, soothing him, whispering; her lips touching his ear. "I've never doubted you all this time; I've never let go. I'm bringing you home Mark; soon. I'm bringing you home."

For over an hour they sifted through Mark's confession; showed him printouts of the disk. Neither Fiona nor Howard could be sure exactly how much of it he took in; but slowly he began to respond and in a halting voice he started to speak.

Later, driving her back to her hotel, Howard mused on what they had heard. "It's odd that he remembers Richard Noble bringing them coffee after lunch on that day, and then nothing more. And yet he can describe the murder scene so clearly. I suppose it was the shock; it seems to have destroyed all his other memories. I think you are right, though, Fin. There's something decidedly odd about this. Also, all that business about Katie Smyth's supposed pregnancy. You say the autopsy report found that she could not possibly have conceived a child. I need to look into that. I fail to understand why that was discounted, given her possible pregnancy was cited as a motive. Look, if you want me to take this on, I am sure I can build a strong appeal out of what we have. I will have to investigate further, of course, talk to the officers who were called to the scene and so forth. And I will have to square it with Mark's own solicitor, but we're old friends, so I don't think it would be a problem."

Gratefully accepting Howard's offer, Fiona said very little, still reeling from the shock of what had happened to Mark. She could not recognise in the quivering wreck he had become, the man she had once loved. It broke her heart.

Back in her room, she ordered a sandwich and a coffee from room service and sat down to wait for it to arrive. Howard had offered to drive her home, but for reasons that she could not have explained, she had declined. More than anything, right now she needed to be alone; needed time to think. The news about her birth parents had remained on the fringes of her mind, but it was now almost completely submerged. She could hear Mark's halting voice as he had once again grappled with the blanks in his memory; the horror stark as he described seeing Katie's body, the blood all over his hands, his clothes.

Once again, Fiona examined the contents of the disk and read Katie's letter. 'I think he's stalking both of you,' she had written. Katie had arranged to meet Mark at their flat. Why not just tell him and give him the disk at work? Surely she could have slipped it to him; there must have been plenty of opportunity. Why did she go to the flat in the first place? Fiona found it hard to believe that Katie had really meant to help him with the engagement party. And in any event, had she offered, he would have refused.

A tap on her door heralded the arrival of the sandwich. Fiona found that she had no appetite, but gratefully downed the coffee. She thought back to the trial. All of it was still clear in her mind, etched on her brain. Simon Alexander had given a sworn statement to the court. He'd set up the meeting between Mark and Katie. But he had stated that Katie had come to him needing to talk; she'd had a problem. Fiona glanced again at the photos taken of Mark and herself; flicking from one image to the next. Stopping suddenly, she raised her head. It was Simon who had said Katie was pregnant: rumours he'd said; rumours around the office. But apparently no one else knew of these rumours and in any event, as she had told Howard, it could not have been true. Why would he have lied about something like that?

Fiona leapt off her chair; of course! If Noble had told him; put the notion in his head; got Simon to arrange the meeting and made Katie think Mark had done it. They were lovers after all, he and Noble; maybe he had thought Noble was just being kind. Then there was the coffee: Noble had brought them all a coffee. Could it have been drugged? If so, it would take time for it to work. Enough time for Katie to get to the flat. Would it explain why Mark remembered nothing afterwards? Why had nobody thought of this before? With a surge of anger, suddenly she needed a drink.

With everything going round endlessly in her head, Fiona made her way down to the bar, ordered a large scotch; was conscious that she was surrounded by couples. In between the songs playing out in the background, she could hear snippets of conversation above the clinking of glasses, see hands reaching out to hold and caress. It brought to mind the romantic evenings she and Mark had spent together; so many. In her mind's eye she saw him as he used to look; it stung her heart. Unable to bear it, she ordered another scotch and took it up to her room.

Knowing that if she thought about Mark any more it would drive her crazy, she turned her mind to her mother. "Sheila," she whispered the name over and over. It was strange; she had never expected to find a father too. For the first time she had doubts. Was it possible that her mother had known all this time where she was? If so, why had she never contacted her; had the shame of having an illegitimate child been too great? Then there was the other thing: the secret Gerry had kept to himself all those years; she was sure neither of her adoptive parents had known about the swap – had they ever found out? She cast her mind back to Gerry's journal, couldn't quite remember. She would have to read it again.

Sandra had explained about her brother; supposed dead. She had often wondered if somewhere she had other siblings. Had even wondered if that was what Gerry had feared. For so long he'd had her to himself; had he been afraid of losing her undivided attention? She found she was still angry with him. She was no longer sure why; she had been angry since the day he had killed himself. She knew in her heart that was what made her angriest of all; that he had left her.

What she had now discovered was not what she had searched for. She remembered Gerry's warning: 'When you find it; it might not be what you want.' This brother Sandra spoke of was suspected of being this Richard Noble. Suddenly her eyes widened as she remembered something that had come into her head just yesterday. That first appointment with Simon Alexander: coming up the stairs to his office; the man blocking her path. She had looked into his face. He had glared straight into her eyes. Stood over her unmoving until eventually she had pushed past him, her skin recoiling from his touch. At the top she had stopped and turned, slowly sensing a sort of dread inside herself, not knowing why. He had been looking up at her and she had turned swiftly and hurried on. The memory made her shiver. She thought of the artist's impression Sandra had shown her. Not perfect she thought; except for the eyes; yes they'd certainly got the eyes right.

Then another thought crept into her mind, a childish little thought that hurt. Like probing an aching tooth with her tongue, she couldn't stop thinking it: why had her mother come looking for him – her brother – and not for her?

Fiona called reception to extend her reservation for a few days. Then she called Sandra to explain that Howard was going to deal with the appeal and she intended staying close by so she could visit Mark; she wanted to keep stirring his memory. Also, she wanted more time to think things out.

That done, she showered and went to bed: her last thought as she drifted into sleep was of her parents. What did she want from them? It was something she no longer understood.

44

Police Headquarters, Maidstone: Saturday 3rd November

"Thank you McAdams for coming in this early – and on a Saturday too," Commissioner Hunt poked his head around Jeff's office door. "I know you've not had much rest."

"Probably more than you have, Sir." It was barely 7.30am Jeff had gone home at 5am for a shave, a shower, and a change, but had been working all night.

The Commissioner's eyes were puffy and bloodshot, the grief and stress stamped across his face made him look ten years older. "I daresay you are surprised to see me still here," he said. "I need to be doing something, McAdams."

"Believe me, I quite understand. I promise you, Sir, we are doing everything possible to find the man who did this to your wife."

The Commissioner raised his hand in acknowledgement, walked into the office and shut the door, leaning against the wall. "I knew from the beginning that Anita had born a child before we met. 'No Secrets,' she said. If only she had divulged the rest I could have protected her. It didn't occur to me that she was at risk." He swallowed, cleared his throat. "I wasn't aware until Chief Superintendent Millar came to see me on Thursday morning that the McMasters case was connected to Anita's past."

"No, Sir. It must have been a shock. We've traced the emails on your wife's hard disk. They came up blank I'm afraid: public computer, a library in London, much as we thought. Nothing else that was helpful. One thing we did find, however, was that it was your wife who placed the various advertisements calling the meeting at the cottage."

"Yes, I knew that McAdams; she said it was her bit of fun – made her feel like Agatha Christie contacting her old friends in this way. She wanted to talk to them about her book." He paused, the shadow of a smile hovered, quickly vanished. "She wanted me to be there for the reunion dinner on Thursday. Unfortunately, I had to be in London to meet with the Chief Constable concerning some very delicate information given me by Leonard Millar about the McMasters case. I don't doubt he will bring you up to speed, if he has not already done so."

Jeff nodded, "Yes, Sir."

The Commissioner slowly turned back to the door, paused, said, "Do you know, it's the first time I had ever lied to Anita; didn't want to alarm her. Maybe if I'd been straight with her..." he left the sentence hanging.

Jeff came round the desk, awkward, not really knowing what to say. In the end he hedged, "Sir, forgive me, but it might be best if you avoid the incident room just now. It goes without saying that we will treat the whole matter concerning your wife with the utmost respect."

Although the room was full, the manpower having doubled since Friday night, there was little chat. Most people looked very subdued, not just from tiredness, but from the appalling images around the boards. Another one had been added: images of Anita Hunt, but on Jeff's orders, the lower portion of her corpse had been deliberately obscured.

He saw that Sandra was sitting on a desk gazing up at the boards, looking from one to the other, reflecting quietly on the images. He had already explained to her how the killer had arranged Anita's body.

"Still no contact from Sheila?" she asked, twirling a pen in her mouth.

"Nothing; we've got an eye witness come forward; a woman matching Sheila's description was seen on the beach below the cottage just after 3pm on Friday afternoon. We were already fairly certain from the dogs that she was at the scene, but that confirms it."

"Chances are he already has her."

"It begins to look like that I'm afraid."

"What about the road blocks?"

"Again, nothing; hardly any cars went through and nobody matching Noble's description. Any word from Fiona yet?"

"Yes. She went with Howard Black to see Mark yesterday."

"The solicitor? I know him. Nice chap."

"Yes, he's offered to handle the appeal. Fiona phoned last night from her hotel; she's staying up there for a while." Sandra chewed heavily on the pen. "She was adamant they will prove Mark is innocent; I'm not so sure. The disk she found in Gerry's drawer; the letter from Katie, I'm not sure they're permissible. Could easily have been faked; Katie may have had some reason of her own for getting at Fiona; jealousy for one."

"There are other things, though," Jeff said thoughtfully, "the condensation in the bathroom and now this business about the drugs. His confession aside, it seems to be pointing away from Mark the more you look at it."

"What do you mean -- what condensation?"

"Sorry, didn't I mention?" Jeff shrugged and proceeded to tell Sandra about Stevens's involvement with the case and what he had said.

Sandra released a heavy sigh. "Poor Mark; poor Fiona. We none of us took any notice of her misgivings. I'd be happier if she came home. I'm worried about her, Jeff."

"Maybe you're right to be in the circumstances. I don't know if Millar's still got a tail on her. Look, I'll send a car to fetch her; no arguments. I'll have her arrested if necessary!" Jeff grinned, stood, walked to the boards, paced along their length.

"I never knew Frank Reid owned a cottage in Dover."

"Me neither. I have since discovered that Gerry sold it last spring. He never mentioned it to me at all. I suppose the estrangement between him and his father was so painful he just put it out of his mind. He hardly ever spoke of him, you know; Frank had been dead some years before Gerry and I met. I wonder what made him decide to sell it this year – and to the Hunts of all people. You know, Jeff, I begin to think I was married to a man I didn't know at all. Do you think Gerry knew about his father's involvement with McMasters?"

"I very much doubt it. Don't see how he would have. It was all news to me and I was involved in the Hynds case latterly. Something Millar said still bothers me: Sheila wrote to him over the years, yet she never told him about his daughter. I wonder why."

"I think she must have found out about Frank Reid; maybe he

was in some way involved with that fire at the cottage. Was he the mole, do you think?"

"I'm not sure. Millar hasn't confirmed that, only that Frank was in with McMasters more heavily than they realised at the time. It is always a risk in undercover operations like that; especially with evil bastards like Kenneth McMasters. From what we learned from his brother yesterday, Frank Reid was in over his head. There's more to all of this than we know yet, Sandra. I am convinced that Lady Clara is still hiding something. Trying to investigate this case is like feeling our way through a fog. It's been like this from the beginning: no answers, just more questions."

"I feel that too," Sandra agreed. "Weird isn't it that Millar is Fiona's father. Remind me, when did he come back to Kent?"

"When he got promoted to Chief Super about eleven years or so ago — it was just before you and Gerry got married as I recall. Why?"

Sandra shrugged, "No reason; just curious. I don't think Gerry knew him. We never met him socially."

"No. He never did much socialising. I suspect he spends most of his spare time on his knees!"

"It's strange that Fiona's never mentioned wanting to find her father; it's always only been her mother. I wonder how she's taking that news. She didn't say much on the phone." Sandra slid off the desk and surveyed the room. "Where's Stevens he's usually here before now?"

"He's spending this morning with his mother. She's explaining her story apparently, then I've an appointment later so she can explain it to me! I doubt either of us will get the whole truth."

Sandra gave a low chuckle. "Rather you than me! I'm off to see Leslie; see if she can enlighten me on a few things I discussed with Michael before I left Westport. Oh, and I know it's not great timing, but can I knock off around lunch time? I've things to sort out with Elle and Sam about this America thing."

Jeff frowned, "Yes, of course. What America thing?"

On her way to the door, Sandra turned back. "They've heard from their mother. She wants them to move over there to live with her."

"Ah," he nodded slowly, keeping his expression blank. He watched as Sandra left the room. When she'd gone he walked to the window, gazed out at nothing in particular. Oh dear; poor Sandra, he thought. Leslie was not anywhere to be found at the morgue, her office locked up. Robert Canning was whistling along to the radio as Sandra knocked on the open door of his office.

She smiled, "I though Leslie was due back yesterday. Has she been called out somewhere?"

He turned down the radio. "Phoned in this morning; her mother was taken ill in the night; very low she said. Went downhill yesterday; there's a history of hypertension, apparently."

"Is she in hospital?"

"I'm not sure. I imagine so. Leslie said she could be contacted on her mobile if it was urgent."

"Oh, Lord; poor Leslie; no, I won't trouble her just now. It's not important. I just wanted to bounce a few ideas off her that's all."

Robert lowered his feet from his desk. "Terrible business this isn't it Sandra: the Commissioner's wife; who'd of thought it! We haven't had one as bad as this in a while. Poor chap too; I thought he was remarkably composed yesterday considering. I suppose he was spared the worst of it; Jeff took steps to ensure he didn't see her as she was found; covered her up first. Her sons took it badly, though. Jeff had his work cut out holding back the older boy, Justin; bit of a struggle; I thought he was going to bloody Jeff's nose for him!"

He passed over a sheet of notes, "Here, you might as well read through this now – I keyed it in late last night so excuse the typos!"

Perching on a chair to scan through the preliminary findings, Sandra looked up quickly. "You found needle marks in Anita Hunt's neck?"

Robert nodded. "She was allergic to needles: the red patching at the back of the neck highlighted the spot. Took a sample of urine from the bladder too; used a dipstick on it; showed positive for GHB – Gamma Hydroxybutryic Acid. You know it?"

"One of the date rape drugs?"

"That's right."

"Thanks, that explains a lot. I think Gracie and Peggy must have been drugged too; possibly Katie Smyth, also. I'm surprised it wasn't found in the autopsies."

Robert pursed his lips. "Mm, mind you, the bodies were very badly mutilated. Still, now you mention it, I'll re-check the bloods."

"Would you? Thanks Robert. Look, I think I'll give Leslie a buzz anyway; she was a great support to me when Gerry died. I should return the favour; see if she needs any errands running; perhaps she needs someone to talk to."

"She'd appreciate that, I'm sure," he smiled.

As she left he had turned up the radio and was cheerily whistling again.

Getting back to her car, she saw there was a missed call on her mobile from Michael. She tapped in the number; he answered almost straight away.

"Hi Sandra, thanks for getting back to me. I just had a few thoughts I wanted to share with you. You remember saying you thought there might be more than one killer?"

"Yes, but—"

"Well, I've been thinking. I remembered a similar case in Florida some years back: a series of murders, all of the women killed were prostitutes; the circumstances of their deaths were much the same, and yet there were differences we couldn't explain; like as if the signatures were different, you know? Anyway, we got him in the end – a sad case it was too: DID; a classic."

"Dissociative Identity Disorder?"

"Yes, sorry; what we used to call Multiple Personality Disorder."

"Yes, of course; please go on Mike."

"I just wondered if that's what you've got here. One killer who thinks he is at least two different people. You know how it is: different personalities routinely take over the individual's behaviour. Often crops up in adults who've been abused in childhood: there's frequently severe memory loss associated with it too."

Even as he spoke, Sandra felt a growing certainty that he was right. She should have thought of it herself. She was supposed to be a profiler, for God's sake! The trouble with this case, as Jeff had said, was that it was blurred around the edges; nothing clear cut. Aside from which, she knew she had too much on her mind; was not operating at full capacity.

Thanking Michael, she told him about Anita Hunt and what Robert Canning had discovered.

"We were right, then. GHB, eh? That makes sense. I'll get onto Brian Quinn, tell him to have another look at Gracie's blood tests.

Look, you take care, Sandra. And don't hesitate to call me – any time."

For a few moments after he'd gone, Sandra stared unseeing at her mobile. The more she thought about it, the more she knew DID fitted the profile absolutely, even to her suspicion that to have perpetrated such vicious cruelty, the killer had at some time been systematically abused. In a way she had been right in thinking there was more than one depraved mind at work. If Andy Hynds a.k.a. Richard Noble had this condition, he would have no concept of what he had done; no blame would attach to him, it would always lie with one or other of the personalities that controlled him at any one time. With a heavy sigh, she punched in Leslie's number.

"I'm sorry to disturb you, Leslie, but Robert told me about your mother, how are you holding up?"

"I'm afraid she's very weak; floating in and out of it mostly. I think it will be a long drawn-out process until the end. There's still so much that I wanted to say to her, but she's not very coherent. I just hope she's strong enough to understand."

Sandra could detect the strain in Leslie's voice. It was hard to think of what she could say that wouldn't sound like a platitude. "At least you are with her, that's what is important. What hospital are you in? Are you on your own? Would you like me to come over – can I help?"

"That's kind of you Sandra, but I'm waiting on my sister; she'll be here today I hope. That's what's keeping her here; my mother, I mean. My sister was always her favourite. I've told her she'll come. I think she is hanging on for her."

"I didn't know you had a sister, you've never mentioned her. I'm so glad. You need family round you at a time like this."

"Did I not? No; I don't suppose I did. We're not close; not close at all. Our lives took very different paths; though it now appears we will be forced to spend some time together; catch up on lost time. It should be fun for all of us, don't you think!"

Sandra was taken aback. But Leslie had always come across a touch sarcastic; obviously the stress was getting to her. And then again, Sandra reminded herself, she and Suzi had been estranged for years until their father's death brought them together. "Well, if you're sure I can't help. But let me know if you change your mind, okay?"

"Okay, thanks. How's the investigation coming on? I'm sorry I had to relegate the most recent victim to Robert."

"Nobody would expect otherwise in the circumstances, Leslie. Work should be the last thing on your mind right now. I don't think it will be long now before something breaks; they're working on several leads trying to hunt down the prime suspect; this Noble guy. We're running a couple of names through the system, so something should come out of it by the end of the day. Actually I'd hoped to run a few things past you about Peggy Lyons, but..."

"Okay, fire away."

"If you're sure you don't mind; the timing's not great, I feel terrible intruding on you."

"Go on, Sandra; ask the question."

"I just wondered if you'd tested Peggy Lyons blood for drugs? It's just that there was a murder in Ireland a few weeks back that has all the signatures of Peggy's death – and Anita Hunt's now as well. Robert had already got a positive for GHB on hers."

"Has he indeed? Well nothing showed up; I would have told you."

"Yes, of course you would, I'm sorry."

"It doesn't matter. Peggy died from massive shock. I already knew that from the nature of the wounds; the burn marks from the ligatures on the wrists and ankles were conclusive evidence that she was alive and struggling when she was cut. That kind of stress at her age would have stopped her heart."

"Right; I just wanted to check. Look, like I said, forgive me for bothering you. Phone me if you need me to do anything for you; anything at all."

"What about Fiona? Any news? Is she okay?"

"So far as it goes, yes; she's in Berkshire, staying at a hotel near Broadmoor. There've been some developments concerning the conviction of Mark Jakes. She has always insisted he's innocent and, well, you know Fiona! She's determined to stay up there for a few days to be close to him. I won't bother you with the ins and outs of it just now, but we think she might be a target. Jeff has sent a car to bring her home, whether she likes it or not. I'm expecting her back later today."

"That's good; don't want her to end up dead now do we!" Leslie chuckled.

Hearing it, Sandra grimaced. It was a brave attempt to lighten the tone, but it failed. "I don't intend for that to happen, Leslie."

"No, of course; look, Sandra, thanks for your concern, but I'd better go, she's calling for me again."

Almost overcome with sadness for her friend, Sandra put her phone into her jacket pocket. Leslie seemed to be married to her work; dedication to the job often hid emptiness in one's life. All those affairs she was always talking about, trying to hide the lack of a stable, loving relationship; nobody to go home to at the end of the day. Sandra's eyes filled with tears. She found herself hoping that something good would come out of all this for Leslie. Maybe like herself and Suzi, she would be able to resolve at least some of the issues that separated her from her sister. She found that she was weeping; deep sobs of self pity racking her chest: was her life any different to Leslie's? Gerry was gone and now even the girls were leaving her.

"Pull yourself together, Sandra," she said, turning the key in the ignition. Driving away, she became aware that Leslie had not said which hospital she was in. Not that it mattered; she had her mobile.

45

GERARD REID
DIED FRIDAY 10 AUGUST 2007
BELOVED HUSBAND,
FATHER AND BROTHER

Getting up off her knees, Sandra ran her hand along the words. It had been hard choosing them given the circumstances of his death. In the end they had elected for simplicity. This was the first time she had seen them; Fiona and the girls had visited often since the day he had been lowered into the ground. She had not been able to bring herself to come here until now. Even now, she wasn't sure what had prompted her to come today. She lifted the fading bunch of Michaelmas daisies and replaced it with a spray of Windflowers from the garden. He had always liked them. Numb she had felt then; still did now. "Who were you Gerry? Hell; who were *we*?"

At home she waited for the girls. Fiona had called to say only that she was on her way home. She had not mentioned her mother and father and Sandra thought it better not to pry. They would talk about it eventually, when Fiona was ready.

Mulling over her increasing belief that Noble had been involved in Katie's death, she retraced her reasons. Calling Stevens, she asked him to find out if Mark had been tested for drugs at the time of his arrest. Something struck her as odd about Stevens' voice over the line. He sounded different; usually so confident, he sounded almost defensive – and then she remembered he'd have had that talk with his mother. She had never liked him much, but at that moment she felt sorry for him.

Walking to the foot of the stairs she called the girls; it was time to talk about Rebecca; the conversations they'd had since yesterday had developed into heated arguments between them. She wanted this issue resolved.

Sam sat on the couch alongside her; Elle chose the opposite couch.

"I've often wondered about her; Daddy threw out all the pictures; wouldn't talk to us about her at all," Elle said, fiddling with her fingers, now and then chewing on a nail.

Sandra sighed; she'd often spoken to Gerry in the early days about keeping the girls in touch with Rebecca, but the very mention of her name only angered him and eventually she'd given up.

"Tch! Why do you want to go to her," Sam cried. "She never cared about us then – why now all of a sudden?"

Sandra brought an arm around Sam. "Look; sometimes things happen in life and people who are close become distanced."

"She ran away, abandoned us. All the way to America – how's that for distance! It isn't as if she's ever tried to get in touch with us before."

Sam was upset and Sandra felt unable to ease her pain; the pain of rejection that she had carried around on her young shoulders since Rebecca had upped and left when Sam was only five.

"I know it's hard to understand, Sam, but I think perhaps you should give it a try. Get to know her; listen to her side of things. Maybe she felt she was doing the right thing at the time; staying out of your father's way. Think how dreadful it would have been if you had been forced to choose between them. And anyway, nobody's perfect; just give her a chance." She looked across at Elle, noted the spark of hope in her dark eyes that quickly died as Sam made a face at her.

Sandra tried again. "Look, I don't want you feeling that you owe me anything. You don't have to stay here just because of me. I'm here for you and I always will be. You know that I love you, both of you; nothing you do will ever take away from that. Why not go and see her? You can always come home if it doesn't work out. Who knows, maybe in a few years' time you'll regard her as a good friend – maybe even be able to forgive her. She is your mother, give her a chance," Sandra repeated. It was full of maybes; but it was the best she could do.

Sam sat forward, her face flushed, angry tears spilling down her cheeks. "She isn't *my* mother. *You* will always be my mother." She shot off the couch and ran out of the room, her footsteps receding up the stairs.

Sandra's heart felt heavy with guilt. Hadn't she been about to abandon them too; had Gerry not taken his life that day she would not be here now. She would have walked out on them just like Rebecca had. How had she even contemplated it?

Elle slid off the couch and came to sit at her side, throwing her arms around her. Unlike Sam, she had always worn her feelings on her sleeve.

"Are you hurt at me wanting to go? I do love you, you know I do. It's just that…well, you know."

Sandra forced a smile. "No Elle, not hurt; I shall miss you, of course, but that's not the same thing. I want you to take it easy; don't expect everything to be all rosy. It may not turn out as you hope. What I really think is that it's a great chance for you both. Your mother may be able to open doors for you that I can't. You can come home for the holidays and we can talk on the phone – and like I say, I will always be here for you if you decide you want to come back. I just want what's best for you; that is really all that I want."

"Truly?"

"Truly. Well no, actually there's something else I want. I want you to make it up with Sam. Don't keep saying things that you know will upset her – you may not think it right now, but she is your closest friend as well as being your sister. Try to understand how she is feeling," Sandra smiled, added, "and if you don't understand, then use some of that great acting ability of yours and pretend that you do – is that too much to ask?"

"I will, I promise." With a grin, Elle kissed her and went after Sam.

Breathing a sigh of relief and thinking that when it came to acting, she deserved an Oscar herself, Sandra felt suddenly very alone. The girls were talking quietly upstairs; she could hear the low murmur of voices. At a loose end, she found herself drawn to Gerry's study.

Fiona had left several of his journals in a bundle on the desk. Lowering herself into his chair she lifted one, randomly selecting pages to read; it was an early one, written in a child's handwriting. It was not something that would ever have occurred to her to do before, to read his private journals. Even now it made her feel uncomfortable, as if somehow he was watching. Setting it down, she sat back in the chair, looked out of the window, her gaze moving around the room. She cried out as she had at the graveside, "Who were you Gerry?"

Restlessly, she leaned forward again, running her fingers over the spines, "Why do I feel as if I never really knew you?" the words escaped almost as a sigh. Choosing a journal from the bottom of the bundle, she drew it forward, opened it. The writing had advanced to an adult hand. By the date Gerry was eighteen. Feeling like an intruder, she began to read, her eye caught by the words heading the page: 'I hate him..."

***

September 1984

'I hate him and all that he stands for.' Gerry laid down his pen, got up from his desk and went to Fiona's bedroom door. Music; Duran Duran belted out; Fiona slightly out of tune singing along. Hesitating, he turned away, went back to his own room, closed the door behind him and flung himself onto his bed. For a time he lay staring at the ceiling, his arms folded behind his head, going over and over everything in his mind. Suddenly swinging off the bed, he went back to his journal and continued writing, his anger scoring heavily into the paper.

'Mum is so caring and loving to him; loyal without question and this is how he has repaid her.'

'I am the son of a slut. Some fancy piece of skirt that he got mixed up with. How can my mother still love him? I shall never understand.'

'All for the love of his sister; and what of us; where do we fit into this world of his? Him; this public figure that commands a force of goodness; hiding behind it his devilish wrongs; he has cheated us and them.'

'To think all this time I have grown in his shadow; worshipped the very ground that he walked on; stood proudly by his side. Now, today, he has destroyed my life; told me the truth of what he is and who I am.'

'I did not care to know yet he insisted; moved the burden of his sins onto my head. I have always known that Mum's love for me was tinged with a great sadness. Fiona always outshone me, but then she would with anyone such is the happiness, the vitality she breathes into our lives.'

'Watching him sit there, a grown man crying like a baby, made my skin crawl. This picture of her in the back row: her dark head of hair; her devious smile; my birth mother, his slut and a little away from her the one I thought of once as an angel. Another slut. What a fool I was.'

He heard a noise at the door, quickly closed his journal, seized a book and opened it pretending to read. It was his mother. Gerry looked up and forced a smile. She looked so worn, so tired. She didn't love him; he could tell. She came in, shut the door and perched on the edge of his bed.

"Please Gerard; don't dwell on his wrongdoings. It's easy to lay all the blame at his feet, but it wasn't entirely his fault. Try to understand."

"He cheated on you; with her. She was a slut. How can it not hurt you to be near me?"

Alice Reid sighed, placed her arm around him. "You are my son in every way that matters. What is past is past. Maybe we have protected you too much; made life too sweet."

Gerry felt the hand come to rest on his shoulder. A sad feeling engulfed his being; her touch felt different. She spoke softly with a tremor in her voice.

"He was a loving man your father; still is; a family man. He had a sister; Elizabeth."

"I know; he told me. Why has he never mentioned her before?"

"Because of her husband; he never wanted you ever to go anywhere near her husband. You see, she was a real beauty. Married above herself; a very wealthy man; a politician. Your father had worked his way up to inspector at the time. Soon after they were married, Elizabeth's husband started to abuse your father's trust; little things at first, but soon they got bigger; it got out of hand; he made threats. You see, the man Elizabeth had married was cruel; so very cruel. He treated her worse than an animal. I do not want to tell you what terrible things he did to her, it's not fitting for your ears to hear, but every time your father said no to turning a blind eye to the unlawful activities his brother-in-law engaged in, Elizabeth suffered terribly. In the end, your father got dragged in deeper and deeper. And then there was no going back. He became very troubled; he had to do terrible things and I suppose, because this young woman, your birth mother, understood this other world, your father became close to her."

"Did you meet her; when you adopted me did you meet her?"

Alice shook her head. "No; that would have been too much for me; to have actually seen her for myself."

Gerry could no longer hold back his tears. "You must hate her. How can you even bear to have me near you; I am the sin between them. I am dirty; dirty," he sobbed.

"No! Please Gerard!" his mother gasped. "Please don't speak of yourself in such a way. I was desperate for a child; you were born of my husband; I merely put her out of my mind. Yes, at times I was torn. This woman could give my husband a living baby where I had failed. If I hated her at all it was for that, not because of you."

Gerry felt her arms go round him; she held him like a child to her bosom. "You were beautiful. You were mine in a way you would never be hers. Your father loved you from the moment he saw you. Remember all your times together, Gerry, don't hold that one fault against him. He promised it would never happen again; he didn't love her – it was me he loved. I forgave him. I gave him a chance; I forgave him because; well like they say, every cloud has a silver lining; for me that was you."

Gerry said nothing further; his mother was dedicated to his father. He could not bring himself to tell her the promise had been broken; that his father had cheated on her again; craftily succeeded in having another of his offspring supplanted: Fiona. But he loved Fiona.

As they sat there in silence Gerry promised himself that there was no way his sister was ever going to feel like this.

Later, after she left him, he took out from under his mattress the photograph his father had given him and tucked it into his journal.

46

Police Headquarters, Maidstone: Sunday 4th November

Sunday morning brought the return of the rain. Searches through the National Records Office had yielded no new leads. The previous evening, the coastguard and various search teams had shut down their efforts to find a trace of Sheila Hynds, also known as McBride. Officers had carried out enquiries at all boarding houses and hotels in and around Dover taking in several of the surrounding towns and villages; nothing. All the signs pointed to the fact that Sheila had been encountered in the field beside the cottage and taken from there, possibly by force, probably by Mrs Hunt's killer, but as this was not substantiated, the effort had to be made.

The team had broken for lunch. Stevens, in a reflective mood all morning, entered Sandra's office with two mugs of coffee and a bag of sandwiches under his arm: a peace offering.

"Coronation chicken on brown; all they had left I'm afraid. It's never so good on a Sunday."

Sandra smiled her thanks; anything would do as long as it was food. She indicated for him to shut the door and sit down. Stevens appeared to be putting on a brave face considering the conversation that had taken place between him and his mother the day before. Relieved that at last they were on the same level, Sandra felt she could finally talk openly to him.

"I'll be frank; Jeff has told me what your mother divulged to you yesterday; I—"

Stevens put up his hand. "It's okay; really. I don't want any sympathy, thanks all the same."

Sandra felt a touch embarrassed; working alongside him all morning, she had managed to avoid eye contact, sensing his mood, surreptitiously studying his features when he was distracted by other members of the team.

She shrugged, "I don't mean to sound patronising, but we all have secrets – or at any rate, things in our past we prefer to forget; me included."

Stevens reached for his own packet of sandwiches. "Been a noisy weekend," he said, changing the subject. "I used to enjoy fireworks as a boy, but these days all I can think of is the fire hazard! Not to mention the number of children who will be hurt. They'll be busy in casualty tomorrow night I daresay."

Nodding her agreement, Sandra tucked into her sandwich. Creamy chicken spilled out dropping into the cellophane and she scooped it up with her fingers. Catching Stevens's amused glance, she grinned. "Waste not; want not! It was a favourite saying of my mother's."

He smiled distractedly, said suddenly, "I guess I've known for some time that it was all a bit of a fairy tale: the son of a bishop made cardinal!" He gave a hollow laugh, "She has a great imagination my mother; I'll give her that."

Sandra took a huge gulp of her coffee, burning her mouth in the process. She cleared her throat. "I suppose Lady Clara was over-compensating; trying to make you feel special in her own way. I know from Fiona how tough it is; this longing that becomes almost an obsession to know who you really are. It's easy for me to say, of course, since I was not adopted, but I have always thought who you really are is not so much about who gave birth to you as who raised you. You know; that old nature/nurture debate."

Stevens sighed, crumpling the sandwich wrapper into a ball. "I spent hours walking the streets last night thinking it all over." He looked up at Sandra, pulled his mouth down, his expression forlorn, his eyes sparking with anger. After a moment, he said in a halting voice, "He abused her you know, McMasters, from when she was just a child. I wasn't her firstborn; she had another when she was just fourteen years' old. She said she didn't know what happened to it. Not too sure I believe that. It will take time to sift through everything she spoke about: what to believe; what not to believe."

With a wave of sympathy, Sandra leaned forward, briefly touching her hand to his knee as she bent to retrieve her bag. She took out the old black and white photograph she'd found in Gerry's journal the evening before. Reaching for one of the snaps she'd taken from Peggy

Lyons's collection she handed both to Stevens. After a few moments he looked up at her, raising his eyebrow in an unspoken question.

"I came across it last night in one of my husband's journals. When I first found the group photo at the Higham crime scene, the image of your mother puzzled me. It's not a good focus so it wasn't clear. I couldn't place her then, but I had this feeling that I knew who she was. Last night the recognition was instant."

"She's this one in the back row," he pointed.

"Yes; from what I understand, she is or rather was my husband's mother too, or so he thought. You say she was fourteen when she had a baby; was it a boy?"

"Yes," he looked back at the photograph, "but she's a few years older here; I'd say nineteen maybe twenty."

"Do you believe she is telling the truth about McMasters; the abuse?"

Stevens looked up from the photo. "Oh; yes, no question I'm afraid. Why would anyone lie about that?" he grimaced. "She talked much of it; I think I'm the first she's unburdened it all to. It was all very disturbing. It appears that my natural father was a gangster: an insane, brutish, power-crazed, violent paedophile." As he spoke, Steven's face went stark white, his hands clenching and unclenching. "How will I ever come to terms with that?" He attempted a lop-sided smile: "A bishop was better!" added, "And my mother is surely an actress!"

Both appalled and touched by his attempt at humour, Sandra did not know quite what to say. She waited while he regained his composure, asked, "Are you sure? I mean, did she actually tell you that?"

"Not in so many words. She said she didn't know who had fathered me, that she couldn't be sure, but I think that's because she finds it too hard to admit to – or maybe she is still trying to protect me."

Sheila nodded, "That may well be so. According to what my husband wrote in his journal, he believed Clara was his mother, his birth the result of her liaison with Frank Reid. Apparently, Frank was under the thumb of McMasters. I wouldn't be surprised if he took on Clara's child himself to save it from—" Sandra broke off, choosing her words, feeling awkward: "well, he would have known what McMasters was capable of. If the pregnancy of a minor had been discovered it would certainly have ended the man's political career. I think he may have arranged for Frank to dispose of the child, but being the man he was, Frank smuggled the baby away; reared it as his own son. Perhaps, like your mother, Frank and Alice couldn't bring themselves to tell Gerry about his parentage. Put together a history for him that they hoped would make him feel he belonged; unfortunately for them it backfired when he discovered the truth."

Stevens nodded slowly, his expression wry. Again he smiled, but there was no humour in it. "I believe that makes me your brother-in-law, Sandra! There is a certain irony in that," he said, adding bitterly, "how do you feel about having a gangster's bastard as part of your family?"

Sandra shrugged. "I don't know about that. Like I said, it's not who you are, it's what you make of yourself that matters." She smiled, added, "And if I am honest, right now I could certainly do with some family. If you want my advice, just cherish the relationship you have with your mother as it stands now. What I have learned from reading through my husband's past is that his soul searching destroyed him. Take my advice, Gareth, and live for the present."

Not far away as the crow flies, Sheila McBride lay in a darkened room. She knew she was getting weaker. There was a dull pain in her chest. Her vision was blurred and she could no longer focus on the figure ranting before her. Were it not for the eyes, she would not have known him. She knew there was something she needed to say; she was gripped by the urgency of this need, but when she tried to speak no words came out. Hunger pains griped her stomach; her tongue was swollen, her throat parched; she ached for water. My son; my son... The ranting continued. Weird sounds and unrecognisable smells invaded her senses.

Then she was falling; falling into an abyss.

47

Police Headquarters, Maidenhead: later that morning

"What is paramount for now is that we trace this Richard Noble or Jason McMaster's or whatever alias he's using and fast." Jeff paced the floor of the incident room where the murder boards now took up two complete walls. All the senior detectives, not entirely happy about working on a Sunday, had gathered to report their morning's activities and were seated, staring up at them.

As Christine walked laboriously around the room handing out copies of an image, Jeff raised his voice above the buzz: "DC Blake has run the snapshot of Andy Hynds as a child through a morphing program; it has calculated the ageing process and given us this photo fit. I think you'll agree, it confirms what we already suspected."

Without a doubt they had a photo fit; a lifelike copy very close to the artists' sketches they had been working from. Jeff lifted another photo fit from the desk in front of him. "This one here was produced from a year-book image supplied by King's College. As you can see, Jason McMasters is a clone of Andy Hynds. They are the same person. Our joint efforts today will involve putting together everything about him that we can. Money is paid into an account for him by his uncle's company, and we have records of withdrawals – interestingly, all made here in Maidstone at various cash points. I want two men at each location."

"We've got hold of CCTV tapes from most of the locations he is known to have visited over the last few weeks; Jones will be sifting through them for the rest of the day. In the meantime, we need to find out whatever we can about him: check out what vehicles are registered in his name; what property he might own or rent. Where he gets his hair cut; where he buys his newspaper; anyone who knows him or knows of him. Anything at all that might give us a lead as to his whereabouts. You've got a mug-shot; use it."

There was a chorus of groans. Jeff waited until it had died down. "It's legwork and it's laborious, I know, but get on to it; time is of the essence. If as we suspect he has Sheila McBride, we may be too late; but there is always a chance she is still alive. Even a monster like this one may baulk when it comes to killing his own mother." He looked around the room. "Okay people; let's move on it."

"Not you Stevens," he called above the general hubbub as everyone got up to go. "I want you to keep searching for David Shaw. Sandra thinks the murders are indicative of DID. Alternatively, it is possible that Andy Hynds and David Shaw are working together. They were rumoured to be in a relationship at college and we know Simon Alexander was gay. His death may have been a straightforward case of jealousy. You had your doubts about the Katie Smyth case; perhaps they were not unfounded. Maybe Andy Hynds is bisexual and was screwing Katie Smyth or Mark Jakes, or both! Unlikely, but not impossible: I guess what I'm saying is, think outside the box; search a wider area and see what you come up with."

As Stevens headed back to his computer, Jeff beckoned Sandra into his office.

"He's very capable; isn't he," she said, closing the door behind her.

"Knew that as soon as I read his record; dedicated too. If David Shaw is still with us, Stevens will be the one to find him. It occurs to me that he seems to be taking everything he discovered yesterday a bit too well, if you know what I mean."

"Delayed reaction, probably; I'm sure it will hit on him eventually, but he seems to be coping for now. As for Sheila; you think she's already dead don't you.?"

Jeff sighed scratching the side of his jaw. "Don't you?"

"I wouldn't put any money on her still being alive; but then again, if he took her on Thursday evening, why haven't we found her? All the other bodies were posed for us to find; he takes great pride in displaying them. She would be his greatest triumph. I begin to think the only reason we have not yet found her is because he is waiting for something."

"Do I detect a puzzle here?" He smiled, "Is there something in that head of yours you're not telling me?"

Sandra glanced towards the window collecting her thoughts.

"I've been thinking. This is a mission for him. Every killing has a purpose; follows a pattern all leading to the ultimate prize. If we place everything in perspective – his that is – he is searching for justice."

Lifting the tear off calendar from Jeff's desk she turned up the days and placed it in front of him, the number '5' stood out in bold, red lettering. "*Remember Remember, the 5th of November...*" she quoted. "Yes, well I won't go on. Think, Jeff! Does that date hold any significance for you? Might it for him?"

Slapping his leg, Jeff let out a gasp of exasperation. His gaze moved from the date to Sandra's face. "Why didn't I think of it before? As far as he is concerned it's the date he was abandoned: Bonfire Night, 1971. We know his life was pretty bleak even before then, but at least he had his mother. We have pieced together that McMasters almost certainly discovered Jack Hynds was double-crossing him, working as a snout. That will be why he fired the houseboat, but he took Jack's boy to replace his own son, Jason – the one we pulled out of the Thames. God alone knows what happened to him! McMasters wouldn't have cared much; he knew by then that Jason might be his brother's son. Any boy would do so long as he could get his hands on the inheritance."

"Surely people must have noticed?" Sandra asked.

"If they had they'd have been too scared to mention it. Andy was just an infant then: five or six he would have been. By the time he was grown they'd have forgotten."

"But *he* wouldn't. He would always remember that his mother never came for him. At that age he couldn't possibly have understood why. In his eyes she left him to the mercy of McMasters; and we know what that must have meant. I spoke to Stevens yesterday, and I've read your notes on your meeting with Lady Clara: McMasters was undoubtedly a sadistic paedophile." Sandra paused, her brow creasing with concentration. "Andy was five or six, you say; I wonder if that's significant."

"In what way?"

"I was thinking of the lamps. Could that be why he surrounds his victims with five lamps? Maybe they symbolize the five years when he had his mother; five years when there was light for him, so to speak. From what I've learnt of Sheila McBride, whatever misfortune befell her she was a good person; was doubtless a caring mother. He would have fretted for her – at least in the beginning."

Sandra leafed though her summary of notes. "The McMasters adopted a baby girl in 1972; perhaps Kenneth was tiring of Clara; needed to groom a replacement," she shuddered. "Death in an RTA was way too good for him. I hope he suffered."

"Try to stay detached, Sandra. Difficult I know, but you need to distance yourself."

"Michael Delaney said something very similar," she smiled. "I'll try. I've been reading Gerry's journals. As I told Stevens, Gerry found out that he was Clara's son; the one she had when she was fourteen."

"Really? So you think Gerry and Stevens were actually half-brothers?"

"It rather looks that way. What's been niggling away at my head, though, is the bond that existed between Gerry and Fiona. They say blood is thicker than water. Those two were not related by blood, but I have met few siblings as close as they were. Even when they were constantly arguing the bond between them held true."

"What about it? It's not uncommon you know; they were raised together in the same loving environment. Kids don't know about genes; they were simply brother and sister."

"Yes, but what if such a bond existed between Andy Hynds and the little sister who came into his life when he arrived at the McMasters's house."

"You mean Jenny; the baby McMasters adopted thinking she was Sheila's child?"

Sandra nodded. "Have you never wondered why McMasters deliberately chose Sheila's baby?"

"Millar said it was because he enjoyed teasing his victims. Assumed it was McMasters's way of letting them know he was onto the Priory."

"That may be so, but think of how he operated. He coerced Frank Reid into following his orders by intimidating him with threats to his own sister's life. Suppose he intended to follow a similar practice with Andy. He needed Andy for the money from the old man's inheritance; needed a way of controlling him when he was older; something to use against him if he didn't comply. Suppose, thinking they were brother and sister, he deliberately encouraged the two children to forge a loving sibling relationship. Lord knows, they would most likely have clung together anyway given what must have gone on in that household – it doesn't bear thinking about."

Sandra fell silent; the awfulness of the picture she was painting made her want to weep.

"I'm still not sure what you are driving at. Surely that would have been the one good thing in Andy's life if what you say is true."

"Jeff, the car crash that killed McMasters; the notes on file suggest it was sabotage don't they?"

"Yes – you've lost me, Sandra. What are you saying? That Andy was unhinged by grief at Jenny's death?"

"Yes, in a way, but more than that: I'm thinking Andy might have tampered with the car."

Puzzled, Jeff thought it through; shrugged; "Well, it's a theory I suppose, but it doesn't tie in with what you've just been saying. If he had bonded with his little sister as you suggest, he would hardly have set out to kill her would he?"

"He might have, if McMasters was abusing her – to save her, maybe. She was only five years' old for God's sake."

"Even so, a bit drastic I would have thought. Why not just run away and take her with him?"

"Jeff!" Sandra jumped up from her chair. "Of course! That's it. That's exactly it." She shot out a hand and grasped his arm. "Don't you see? If Andy wasn't expecting her to go in the car and planned to run away with her, he might have set out to ensure McMasters couldn't follow them. Maybe he didn't mean to kill them, just incapacitate them. After all, he couldn't have predicted there would be another car involved. Just think about the effect that would have had on him. In a mind already so damaged, how would he cope with the knowledge that he had caused Jenny's death? She was the only person left that he loved and he killed her."

Jeff looked at her and slowly smiled, "Sandra, that's brilliant; you're wasted in this job! He'd have been about twelve or thirteen; hormones kicking in; part child, part man. Probably confronted regularly with devastating abuse – it would have driven him completely insane."

"Exactly so; it is precisely that kind of trauma that leads to DID; the only way in which an individual can cope with it is to disassociate from it. Now put together the events of the last year and the connections with the Search Agency. Here," she paused to rummage in her bag. "There's something I want to show you. Fiona has told me that she remembers meeting Richard Noble at the agency. It was just the once and with everything that happened, she had forgotten until yesterday. What she has now recalled is seeing his expression when he caught sight of her; she described it as venomous; as if he hated her – and yet he didn't know her. She couldn't understand why. Here it is," she pulled a photograph from her bag. "I found it in one of Gerry's journals; look."

Pointing to Sheila Hynds, she watched the recognition spread over his face. He looked up at her, eyes wide.

"Jesus Christ! How did I not see it before? I suppose the image I retained of Sheila was of a grief-stricken mother. I met her only briefly a few times after we found her son – well, what we thought was her son. She wore no makeup, she was bowed down with grief, weeping, hysterical – and even then her beauty shone through – but I never saw it until now. It's an amazing likeness; uncanny; a few tweaks here and there and it is Fiona!"

"Yes; Andy's half-sister." Sandra walked restlessly to the window, perched on the ledge. "Can you imagine how it must have been for him when he first caught sight of her? Think about it: here is a girl the spitting image of his mother; he must have seen it instantly. The way Sheila looked when he last saw her would have been frozen in time; stamped on his brain like a photograph. The effect must have been devastating. He stalked Fiona; made it his business to find out about her. And what does he find? A highly successful TV presenter who benefited from an idyllically happy childhood; who is about to be married and is enjoying a happy, normal love life. His own childhood by comparison was unequivocal hell. But more importantly, so was that of his sister: Jenny, the little girl he loved – and killed. Guilt, Jeff. It's all about guilt. After years of torturing himself, he had found in Fiona the embodiment of his mother; someone he could blame. He was able at last to shift his guilt, transfer it to her."

Sandra shook her head, her brow creased in a worried frown. "If Fiona had never gone to live and work in the States, this could all have started years ago. As soon as he first saw her, his rage was unleashed and it resulted in a string of murders. He is a man with a mission: revenge. Now he has Sheila and it's mission accomplished. Or is it? In his warped mind, both women have committed a crime:

his mother abandoned him and Fiona stole his little sister's life. What is sending shivers up my spine is where Fiona fits into his plans. How he must hate them. All the suffering he has endured he has laid at their door."

Jeff got to his feet. "Where is she now?"

"She was going into the studios; said she could get more done on a Sunday when it was quiet. She wants to finalise that series she's been doing; the one about searching for lost birth mothers." The irony struck Sandra as she said it. Helplessly she looked at Jeff.

"Give her a call; tell her to come home. Try not to alarm her any more than you have to, but we need to get her somewhere safe. To my way of thinking an animal as enraged as Andy Hynds is right now will be incapable of restraint. He'll not have been waiting for the date, Sandra. He wants his mother to see what she is responsible for. It'll be Fiona he's waiting on. He'll keep Sheila alive until he has Fiona, and then he will make her watch."

48

The Reid's house, Sunday evening

The answer phone was flashing as Sandra shut the front door. Throwing her bags to the ground she raced to pick it up thinking it might be from Fiona. It was from the estate agent, yesterday. He had called to confirm a completion date. Why hadn't she seen there was a message before now? Not that it mattered; she shrugged. Walking back to the front door she swung it shut and collapsed onto the bottom step of the stairs.

"Well; that's it then; goodbye house," she murmured, her heart sinking at the thought of everything that now needed to be done. Sitting there for a few minutes she started to panic: was leaving this house the right thing to do? The purpose had been to make a new start for them all, but what did that matter now? Her family was disintegrating around her: chances were the girls would be gone in a few weeks. Fiona being here had only ever been a temporary arrangement; who knew what plans she had for herself in the long term. Soon, Sandra thought disconsolately, I will be alone. Too late to worry about that now, she told herself. The deed is done.

Determinedly she pushed herself to her feet and went through to the kitchen to prepare some supper. The girls had both gone out to a party, but Fiona would be back about 7pm She had sounded surprisingly upbeat on the phone when Sandra had voiced her concern. Fiona had told her not to worry, that she had a couple of colleagues helping her and one of them would drive her home. Sandra had not, of course, told her everything. She chopped an assortment of vegetables to go with some pasta thinking that while they were cooking, she would read some more of Gerry's journals.

Selecting the one at the bottom of the pile, she went into the snug, settled on a couch and switched on the reading lamp. This was the last of his journals; only partially filled. She was tempted, as she had been since she had first started reading them, to flick forward to the last entry. She so badly wanted to know what his thoughts had been on that last day and in the run up to it. The suicide note had seemed so... what exactly? Sandra wasn't sure; maybe 'impersonal' was the right word. But then, what did one say when one was planning to kill oneself. She didn't know; knew only that she desperately wanted something to cling onto; anything that would take away from her guilt.

Refusing to succumb to the temptation, she turned resolutely to the first page. The entries here were much shorter than in previous journals. The tumour by then must have been making its present felt. With a pang of remorse, she wondered how much pain Gerry had succeeded in hiding from them all. Looking up at the gallery of photographs on the wall, she remembered back to earlier in the year. Gerry had often been irritable; tiring earlier than usual in the evenings; frequently re-scheduling consultations with his patients – something he had always avoided doing in the past. How blind she had been; blind and selfish; too wrapped up in her own troubles. The guilt washing over her was hard to bear as she commenced reading.

Reaching entries for the start of February, she glanced at the clock; 6.40pm Bringing Fiona's number up on the mobile, she waited until it rang through to the messaging service; must be on her way home. A few more entries and she would go and cook the pasta.

The diary entry for February 14th was much longer than the others, taking up the allocated space for the following two days as well as its own. What was so different about that day that he should have had so much to say? Staring at the date, Sandra thought back, gasped, suddenly aware that it was the date of Katie Smyth's murder.

***

14th February, 2007

Gerry Reid left the house, his energy drained. Fiona was not answering her mobile, but Sandra had made a few calls and discovered she was at the police station in Highgate making a statement. Relieved that she was safe, his fear had turned to anger. He was much too angry to deal with her just now. It was past 7pm and he was late; he hurried out to his car.

At Brampton Manor he parked near the entrance and headed straight to the steps. Through the clear glass panels of the door he watched as a figure dressed in a nun's habit made her way slowly to greet him.

"Sister Agatha? Dr Gerry Reid; I'm sorry I'm late. I was unavoidably detained."

"Dr Reid; no matter, please come in. I've brought the records you asked about to the library; we will not be disturbed there at this time of day." She smiled, "*EastEnders; Emmerdale* and *Coronation Street* are, I fear, a much bigger draw for girls these days than private study!"

She ushered him into a large room, its high ceiling decorated with square panels of coving. Three walls were taken up with oak bookcases packed floor to ceiling with books.

"Please make yourself comfortable." Sister Agatha indicated two winged chairs at one side of a marble fireplace where a fire burned fitfully in the grate. A bundle of folders; tattered and faded, rested on a small table between them.

"I'll arrange some tea," she smiled. "It won't take long."

As she glided away, Gerry sat, pulling the small table over in front of him, leafing through the folders. Midway down the pile, a name burned into his brain: 'Clara Stewart'. With shaking fingers he opened the folder, saw the words on the yellowed page: 'Admitted March, 16th. 1964: aged fourteen years'.

Sick to his stomach he released a sobbing gasp, gorge rising in his throat. Motionless, he stared at the age. For half a lifetime he had hated his father; he would not have believed it possible to hate him more profoundly – until now. Clara, the woman he knew to be his natural birth mother, had been a mere child.

Slowly he turned the page: clipped to the top of the next one, a childish face stared up at him. Stunned, tears starting to his eyes, he dashed a hand over his face.

The rustling behind him announced the return of Sister Agatha carrying a tea tray. She was at least seventy years old by his estimation, maybe older. Striving to compose himself, he stood to help her, pushing the bundle of folders out of her way.

Placing the tray on the table, she peered at the photograph and nodded. "I remember her quite well."

Gerry was surprised. "I hadn't realised the sisters were housed here back then."

Taking the chair beside him, she poured the tea, handed him a cup. Short and plump, she squashed herself into the back of the chair, rested her cup and saucer on her lap and regarded him with a slight smile.

"I'm sorry Dr. Reid; you don't understand – not that you would. When I first came here, it was not as a nun. One of those folders is mine. Just like Clara, I came to the Priory needing help. I had got myself into trouble, as they used to say – and still do I believe. I was not as young as Clara – few were – but my baby boy was stillborn."

Flabbergasted, Gerry stuttered, "I... I'm sorry... I didn't mean to pry."

Sister Agatha's eyes focussed inward, the hurt evident in her features. Steadying her cup on the saucer, she shook her head. "It was a long time ago, but I still grieve for him – and will until the day I die. After the birth, I stayed on to help Mrs Lyons; my family shunned me and I had nowhere else to go; she offered me a home. Then, when the sisters took over many years later, I took the veil."

"Do you remember anything about Clara's background; the circumstances surrounding my birth?"

Sister Agatha studied his face for a few moments then nodded. "So sad it is; what some children are made to suffer. She was brought here in the middle of the night. It was your father who carried her in; into this very room in fact. Terrible state she was in too. Were it not for him acting fast like he did, both she and you would have died."

Gerry tightened his fists at the mention of his father. He sat forward unable to hide his hatred. "Were it not for him, she would not have been in such a state in the first place," he spat. "How can you condone him; she was a mere child for God's sake." He seized the photograph, held it up to her nose. "Look at her! He was a beast; a pathetic child-molester, a cheat and a liar."

Sister Agatha; looked at him. She frowned, seemed puzzled. "Like I said; had he not brought her here she would have died. She was a frail slip of a thing; you were breech. Dr. Lyons got us to carry her back to his surgery. Operated on her minutes later; there was no time you see. The baby – you – were stuck. Clara had lost a great deal of blood." She sighed, her fingers going to the rosary at her belt. The Good Lord acts in mysterious ways, Dr Reid. You and Clara survived and Kenneth McMasters got his just desserts; he paid for his sins in the end."

Gerry's eyes narrowed. Was the old woman gaga? What did that corrupt villain have to do with anything? Before he could speak, Sister Agatha put a gentle hand on his knee.

"I can see from your expression that you are under a misapprehension, Dr Reid. It was Kenneth McMasters who abused your mother. It was he who was your natural father. Superintendent Reid came across Clara writhing in pain and bleeding. He brought her straight here to Dr Lyons."

Gerry closed his eyes; tried to comprehend the enormity of what she was saying. Numbly aware that she was still speaking, he grappled with his horror to make sense of her words.

"I gave birth to my own son just two days later. By that time Kenneth McMasters had discovered what had happened, though not where Clara was. Naturally, he wanted nothing of the child to be traced back to him. He was at the time a respected Member of Parliament. We were more than shocked when we learned what he really was."

"So he left my mother and me here; didn't take us back?"

"Not exactly: your father confessed that he feared for your safety at McMasters's hands. My son was to be buried that day; Superintendent Reid asked if he could take my baby's body to McMasters and tell him it was Clara's child."

Sister Agatha removed her hand from Gerry's knee, once again fingering her rosary. "You can imagine how hard that was for me, but your father had told me what evil that man was capable of, and after a lot of soul searching, I agreed. The subterfuge worked; McMasters never learned the truth. Clara went back to him still very weak; she had been sedated after the operation. Never knew anything about what had taken place; was never told that you were her son. Superintendent Reid insisted on it. Your father was afraid that if Clara knew you were alive, she would break down and tell McMasters – she was in thrall to him you see. So young, that poor, poor child," she paused, dabbed her veil to her cheek. "Not long afterwards, the Superintendent adopted you, but such was his fear for you, he didn't even tell his wife what had happened: let her think you were his own son. Only Peggy, Matt and I knew the truth. His sole concern was to protect you. He was a good man, your father, Dr Reid. I was sorry to hear that he had died before his time."

Driving home Gerry was numb. Instinctively he knew now that Frank Reid had never been unfaithful to his wife; that Fiona was no more his natural daughter than he himself was Frank's son. The bond with Fiona, his sister, was forged not on shared blood, but on the love lavished on them by their adoptive parents.

Flashing before him were images of his past: the bitter arguments with his father; the hatred that had seethed in him against a man who was then aged and ill. So ill that he had felt he must unburden himself to the son he loved.

Barely aware of the direction he was taking, Gerry made his way unerringly to the graveyard. Parking by the gate, he stumbled along the row of graves at the far side, stopped at one of them and fell to his knees. He tried to picture his father as he used to be: the fun times; football matches; fairgrounds; cricket on the heath. Dark memories laced with bitterness and hatred crowded in. He remembered all the little ways in which he had deliberately set out to hurt Frank Reid as he himself was hurt. The child within him had never forgiven his father; never given him the chance his mother had pleaded for; he had destroyed him and in so doing, he had destroyed himself.

Shuddering with sobs, his heart pounding in his chest, Gerry at last gave vent to his grief, his cries shattering the quiet darkness of the graveyard. Wrapping his arms around the cold, hard granite of the headstone, his mouth against the engraving of his father's name, he hugged it to him.

"I'm sorry, Dad; please listen to me. I didn't know... I'm sorry... so very sorry."

49

Sandra put down the journal, threw another scrunched up wet tissue onto the growing soggy pile beside her and drew a fresh one from the box. Gerry had been going through such awful torment and she had known nothing about it. What kind of a wife did that make her? What Sister Agatha had told him, coupled with the constant pain in his head, was enough to drive anyone over the edge. No wonder he had killed himself. Dear God, how could she not have noticed? Because he had held her at arm's length for all those months, she told herself. Or had he? Was it more that she had distanced herself? If she had not been planning to leave him, would she have seen the change in him? Torturing herself with questions for which there were no answers – nor would there ever be, not now – she reached for the journal; put it down again. Suddenly she couldn't bear to read any more.

Sobbing, she went through to the kitchen. She had long since left the supper keeping warm in the oven; it would be all dried up by now. Where the hell was Fiona? Stopped for a drink with whoever was driving her home, probably. Sandra put some pasta in a bowl, took a few mouthfuls; pushed it away.

Her mobile bleeped: Fiona?

It was Jeff: "How are you fixed? I know it's getting late, but could you come in? We've made a few discoveries."

Scrawling a note and leaving it on the table, she was soon in her car and heading for the police station. The sky was lit up with sparkling cascades of colour, the air thick with the smell of sulphur and wood smoke. Most of the official displays had taken place last night; now parents were doing their own thing. It was always awkward when Bonfire Night fell in the week; firework displays seemed to go on for days because of it.

By 7.45pm, she was pulling into the car park.

"Jason McMasters has a string of properties. Most of them are here in Maidstone," Jeff handed her a printout as she pulled up a chair. "We'll be checking this lot out tonight. Thought you'd want to be involved. So far nothing has come up with the cashpoint surveillance; we've turned up a vehicle registered in his name, though: a yellow Ferrari Spyder would you believe. Shouldn't be hard to spot! We've got a call out, but no luck so fa—"

"Got 'im!" Stevens's shout resounded exuberantly from the other end of the room. "Sir, come and have a look at this."

Those of the team who were still working in the incident room rushed over to gather round his computer, Jeff and Sandra in the lead.

"A pathologist in Glasgow," Stevens said, pointing to the screen. "Five years ago; name of David Shaw; forced to resign for removing organs without permission. Guess what the organs were?"

"Don't tell me!" Sandra murmured.

Jeff grimaced, "How did we not know about this?"

"We wouldn't necessarily have a record of it," Stevens said. "It wasn't reported as a crime. Shaw would most likely have been investigated internally through the hospital's medical board."

"Okay. See if we can get a photo of him will you?"

"I'm running a search for one now, Sir, but there seems to be no record of a David Shaw employed elsewhere in Scotland since then. I'm waiting on a call back from Edinburgh to see if they've got anything on his NI number."

"Keep up the good work, Stevens. Call me on the mobile if they come up with something. Okay people, back to work."

"Okay, Sandra?" Grabbing his coat from his office, Jeff led the way down to the car park. "Forgive me for saying so, but you look tired," he said, opening the car door for her.

"That's because I am; aren't we all? If you're going by the state my eyes, it's because I've been having a good cry. I've been reading more of Gerry's diary entries; it makes for sad reading. I almost wish I hadn't opened the damned things at all," she said, seating herself in the car.

Jeff settled in beside her, reached for the ignition. "What does Fiona say about it?"

"She's not back yet, but don't worry. She's being sensible; said a mate was giving her a lift home, and don't forget there are still two uniforms watching the back and front of the house. I've asked them to be extra vigilant and I've left a note asking Fiona to call me as soon as she gets in."

"Okay. Where's the first address?"

Sandra peered down at the printout. "It's a Victorian conversion job near the river."

Four properties later they had nothing. All the buildings were let through an agency. No one they interviewed knew who owned their homes. The name Jason McMasters meant nothing to any of them.

On their way to the next property, a block of modern lets near the hospital, they stopped at a vending machine to pick up a coffee. Between mouthfuls, Sandra filled Jeff in on Gerry's discovery about his mother's past.

"So in fact, Stevens and Gerry were *full* brothers. Hell, poor old chap; what a discovery to make. That bastard McMasters had a lot to answer for. It explains why Gerry was so distracted last spring. I'd put it down to his illness, but it must have really grieved him."

"Yes; apart from anything else, when he found out as a teenager about Clara, he thought his father had cheated on his mother. From what he writes, he loathed Frank for that and went out of his way to make sure he knew it."

"I saw a bit of that myself before Frank died. The atmosphere between them certainly wasn't great." Jeff squashed his cup and winding down the window took aim sending the cardboard into a waste bin beside their parked car. It was almost 10pm A crowd of youths went by, laughing and shouting, bangers going off and echoing resoundingly in the street.

"Silly young sods!" Jeff muttered. "I suppose I must have been that age once." With a heavy sigh he stretched his seatbelt around his stomach, "But I'm damned if I can remember it. Ah well, best get a move on; can't be knocking people up much later than this on a Sunday!"

Sandra looked down at the printout: "Wait a minute; I know this address. King's Place, that's where Leslie's flat is – surely you can't have forgotten?" she teased.

Jeff took hold of the printout, holding it up under the courtesy light. "Suppose I did a good job then; I've spent most of my time making myself forget I was ever there."

Sandra dug her elbow into his side. "Go on, you old fibber. Leslie would be a perfect companion for you. What the hell happened between you two anyway? I know you've been avoiding her since that night."

"Nothing happened, Sandra; absolutely nothing." Jeff turned the key in the ignition, waited for a gap in the traffic, added, "And nothing ever will. Despite what you say, she's not my type. To be perfectly frank, she's too... well, promiscuous for me."

"Don't tell me she jumped on you?" Sandra cracked out laughing.

"And anyway," Jeff ignored her, "I'd already met the love of my life; it doesn't happen twice in one lifetime, Sandra. All I'm really missing now is a friend; someone to share a little companionship if you like."

Sandra raised her eyebrows, but said nothing as Jeff slid the car out into the traffic.

King's Place was an up-market, new development near the hospital. It boasted an underground private car park with an automatic door. "You and me; we're in the wrong business, Sandra. What would the rent be on one of these each month?"

"I wouldn't dwell on it if I were you; probably both our pay cheques put together at a guess."

A uniformed concierge was seated behind a desk in the marble entrance hall. Flashing their ID cards they made their way to the lifts.

"I'll take the top floor," Jeff said, hitting the buttons on the pad.

Sandra screwed up her face. "That wouldn't have anything to do with the fact that Leslie's apartment's on the floor below, by chance?"

"Not at all; she's going through all that stuff with her mother; women are better in those situations than men; I'm just being diplomatic about it."

"Of course you are, Jeff," Sandra said, her face dead pan. But in truth, she wasn't too happy about pestering Leslie at a time like this. They parted company as the lift door opened into a hallway decorated much like the entrance below: all marble slabs and bronzes.

Leslie was in 4A at the bottom end of the hall. Sandra buzzed the bell and waited.

"Sandra! I wasn't expecting… I said there was no need…" Leslie appeared dishevelled; her face strained.

"I'm sorry Leslie; I shouldn't really be intruding, but this is official business. Please forgive me for disturbing you at a time like this, but it appears that your building is owned by a Jason McMasters and, well, we were curious to see if you had ever met him or maybe knew anything of him at all?"

Leslie stared at her blankly for a few moments as if trying to place the name. "She shook her head; sorry Sandra; I'm stressed out. Come in; you've only just caught me actually. I've just this minute come back to freshen up."

"How is your mother?" It seemed a silly question, but it was all Sandra could think to say.

"Not good, I'm afraid."

Sandra's mouth dropped open as she followed Leslie into the living room. She had never been inside the flat before: was taken aback not only by its neatness but by the statement it made; sheer class. Although they had been friends for some years and Leslie had been to her house on a number of occasions, when it was Leslie's turn they had always met at Gianni's. Leslie wasn't the kind who entertained as she did herself; not other women, anyway, Sandra thought, unable to quell a sudden shard of envy. Compared to this, hers and Gerry's home was shabby; way down the social scale. In some ways it reminded her of Michael's house: the same luxurious comfort and touch-button convenience.

Sandra's gaze was drawn to two large prints on either side of the fireplace set high in the wall, a false flame dancing seductively against its backdrop. She stepped towards it, her feet sinking into the thick pile carpet, looked up at the prints: Monet's depictions of the butterfly garden in Giverny were beautiful; as indeed was the garden itself, she thought. She and Gerry had gone to see it while on a trip to Paris some years ago. For a moment she was lost in the memory.

She was brought down to earth as Leslie repeated the name: "Jason McMasters you said? Please, Sandra, do sit down." She indicated a pair of enormous black leather Chesterfields positioned in front of a huge, wall-mounted bookcase opposite the fire, waited while Sandra perched on one. "Afraid the name means nothing to me. I only have dealings with the letting agency. Why the interest? Is this McMasters attached to the case?"

Somehow disappointed, Sandra drew a deep breath and gave Leslie a brief summary of how they had arrived at the line they were chasing. She went on to explain about David Shaw, and how in her view they were possibly dealing either with two killers working in tandem, or one with a multiple personality disorder.

From time to time, Leslie nodded in agreement. "It sounds as though you've got it all falling into place. I'm sorry I can't enlighten you concerning this McMasters character."

Getting to her feet, Sandra shrugged. "Look Leslie; like I said; we're closing in; something will break soon. I am truly sorry I had to bother you. Are you sure you're coping alright? I take it your sister arrived? Is she with your mother? Have you had a chance to talk with her yet?"

Leslie seemed distracted by the questions. Before she could reply, Sandra added, "Oh goodness, I'm sorry, you must think I'm being nosy. I don't mean to be, it's just that I've been where you are now—"

"Have you Sandra?" Leslie interrupted, looked her straight in the eye. "I really don't think so."

Sandra leaned towards Leslie, placed a sympathetic hand on her arm. "I mentioned to you before that I was distanced from my sister; we fell out big time when I was eighteen because I... well, I have never mentioned this to anyone before, but I had an abortion. My sister couldn't come to terms with it. So in a way, I underst—"

Leslie started; flinging Sandra's hand from her arm, she backed away. "You had an abortion?"

Sandra flushed, shame flooding through her as she caught Leslie's expression. "Yes; I was only very young; trying to escape from a life I didn't want. I've regretted it often since. I'm sorry if I've shocked you. I only wanted to say that my sister forgave me and that when my father died we became quite close. That's what life's all about I guess; learning to accept faults in people we love; making compromises."

Leslie was backing away towards the door. "Yes, I hear what you're saying, Sandra," she said dismissively, "but I really need to get back to them. Can we talk about this some other time maybe?"

Going down in the lift, Sandra decided to check out the underground car park. Might McMasters have left his car here? As expected, she was met with a dream collection of wheels. The nearest vehicle was a silver Jaguar and beside it, a red Lamborghini. What kind of lives did these people lead anyway, Sandra thought as she surveyed one car after the next. But there was no yellow Ferrari. She paused by Leslie's white MR2. How much did forensic pathologists earn these days anyway? Ten times her own salary, obviously, she thought, running her fingers along the smooth, cold metal of the bonnet.

Joining Jeff in his car, Sandra's mood was down beat. There were times when she cursed her intuitiveness. She had sensed the change in Leslie as soon as she had mentioned the abortion. Her friend had seemed suddenly so cold. But she had a lot on her mind, perhaps it was understandable.

"Find anything useful?" Jeff handed her the printout.

"Zippo."

"Me too," he turned the key in the ignition. "Seven apartments on the first floor; all the same; they deal only with the letting agency. You okay? You look a bit stressed."

"I had a bit of a run in with Leslie. I expect it's because of her mother – and also her sister's arrived. She's at the hospital."

"Her sister?"

"Yes, they don't get on. Leslie was decidedly cool towards me – there was something a bit odd about her. I don't know what, exactly, but it took me by surprise, that's all. I'm okay."

"So where are we headed next?"

"There's a row of town houses on the way back to the station. Jason McMasters seems to have inherited a great deal of property; must be an extremely wealthy man."

"Yeah – beyond Andy Hynds's wildest dreams I would imagine!"

"I suppose; though his mother also seems to have done quite well out of inheritance."

Sandra checked her mobile; nothing from Fiona. She bit her lip; it was getting on for 11pm Should she be worried? She was about to voice her concern when Jeff broke into her thoughts.

"You don't suppose..."

"What?"

Jeff shrugged, "Oh, nothing. Just thinking how strange it is that this McMasters, Hynds or whatever you want to call him, always seems to know what we are about to do before we know it ourselves. It's uncanny."

"You're not suggesting someone on the team—"

"Lord no! Course not. Oh, I dunno, it's getting to me this case, Sandra. Do you know what I did this morning? I put a teabag in my mug, forgot to switch on the kettle and poured cold water over it. Talk about early onset of Alzheimer's!"

"Well at least you remembered to put in the tea bag," Sandra forced a smile.

Twenty minutes later, they had knocked up two very unsociable solicitors and one rather the worse for wear – and scantily clad – young blonde, none of whom had heard of Jason McMasters.

"Time to go back to the station and see if Stevens has turned up anything more on David Shaw I think, don't you?" Jeff said as once more they got back into his car.

"I think, if it's okay with you, I'll just nip home. Fiona's mobile is still going straight to messages. She's probably tucked up in bed by now, but I'll feel better if I see her. I ought to check up on the girls anyway. They should be home from the party by now." She checked her watch. "Jeff; we're running out of time. In half an hour it'll be midnight. Maybe we were wrong about this. Maybe Sheila is safe somewhere."

"We can but hope so," Jeff said, subdued.

Fiona wasn't at home. Putting her head round the kitchen door, Sandra grimaced at the remains of the pasta on the kitchen table along with a pile of dirty crockery. She checked the answer phone in the hall. No messages. Where the hell was that sister-in-law of hers? Again she tried Fiona's mobile; same as before. Once again she repeated her previous message: "Call me, please."

Slipping upstairs she checked on the girls; both were asleep. As peaceful as they looked, it brought her no comfort; in a couple of weeks their beds might be empty. She would rather have the mess to clear up behind them than not have them here at all. Then she would be totally alone. That scared her.

Taking a quick shower, she picked out a pair of clean black jeans and a black turtle neck sweater. Fumbling through her dresser she found her clasp, ran her fingers through her curls and retied her hair in a twist. A glance in the mirror depressed her; she looked like shit. That wasn't all; she felt like shit too.

From the moment the word 'abortion' had fallen out of her mouth she had regretted it. She certainly hadn't expected Leslie's reaction: it had made her feel so ashamed. Had she imagined the disgust she thought she saw in Leslie's eyes? Was it in fact self-disgust that had made her feel as though her skin was crawling? It would be a shame if this were to upset their friendship. She would have to square it with Leslie when there was more time to discuss all the ins and outs of it. She was a woman of the world; would surely understand.

In the kitchen Sandra uncorked the bottle of wine she had put in the fridge for dinner and pouring a small glass, took it through to the snug. Again she hit the redial button trying Fiona's mobile, praying for the ring tone to be interrupted and Fiona to answer; no such luck. Sandra cursed; why hadn't she thought to ask the name of the friend from work who was supposed to be driving her home. Hell, Sandra thought, she didn't even know if it was a male or a female friend. Had Fiona hooked up with another man? Surely not! And what of the tail; hadn't Millar still got her under surveillance? What could possibly be wrong? And yet, somehow, Sandra knew something was wrong. She could sense it; feel it deep in her core. Sick with anxiety she tried the mobile again. It was pointless, but she had to do something. Would any of Fiona's colleagues know? Dared she start calling them at this hour? And what if she was wrong and Fiona was happily ensconced on somebody's sofa for the night having had a few too many; she would never forgive her.

And yet there was this feeling; this instinct that would not let her rest. Lifting the glass, she gulped down most of the wine, went to the hall table for the telephone directory, came back with it to the snug and sat with her hand on the mobile, undecided. Would the producer know? Maybe the cameraman, what was his name? Robert Watts; that was it. She turned to the Ws; the directory slipped out of her hand and fell to the floor. Maybe it was a sign she shouldn't phone. Almost she giggled; hysteria was setting in – or was it the wine? She sighed. Tonight would be a long one. She thought through the fruitless evening she had spent with Jeff. Evening? Hell, it was half the night! What would their next step be?

Swishing the last mouthful of wine round the glass, she sank into the sofa, lifted her head and drained the last drop, savouring the taste; staring into the ceiling, thinking. There was something edging into her mind; something perplexing, like a burr on her brain; something she couldn't quite pin down; a strand of memory too elusive to give form.

And then she had it! She jumped forward dropping the glass; it caught the coffee table and smashed. Sandra barely noticed. How had she not realised it while she was there?

Grabbing her keys, she ran into the hall, words chasing each other in her head; conversations; yesterday and this evening; no! It couldn't be and yet that gut feeling persisted – and she had rarely been wrong.

50

Fiona struggled to open her eyes, but her eyelids seemed to be weighted down. She felt nauseous and her head was pounding. Where the hell was she? What had happened to her? Had she passed out or something? She remembered Robert giving her tail the slip; it was easy on a motorbike. He'd thought it was great fun. She'd asked him to drop her off at the end of the street. Couldn't bear the endless speculation; so what if she had spent half the night with him; actually he was gay, but it was nobody's business. She had needed someone to talk to and he was a nice enough guy. Her stomach cramped; feeling she was going to be sick she tried to sit up, but found she couldn't move. What was wrong with her? Had she really been that drunk? She began to feel afraid.

She held her head up and again tried to force her eyes open. For a few brief seconds she saw only whiteness all around her. It was like a mist, only not, and where it touched her skin it felt clingy, like plastic. She became aware of movement; noises; strange flapping sounds as if a curtain was moving in the breeze. Except there wasn't a breeze: she felt warm; sticky and warm. Yes it was definitely a flapping sound. Why couldn't she see properly? Fear turned to panic. A sharp pain deep in her head forced her head back down. Releasing a faint cry, she caught her breath waiting for it to subside. It was brutal; a thousand times worse than a migraine. Tears of pain spilled out of her eyes. She swallowed, almost retched.

She heard footsteps. Was she floating? No; she was moving; gliding. Wetting her mouth she gulped. There was another sound; she tried to place what it was, a kind of snuffling and whimpering, like an animal in pain. It was close to her. The heaviness of her eyelids became too much, she succumbed. A buzzing echo filling her ears; the whiteness darkened to grey then to black as the drowsiness overcame her.

The coffee was way too strong, verging on rancid, but Jeff was glad of it, almost instantly feeling the kick as it reached his stomach. Picking up an anxious call from Millar, he ground his teeth, swore and rejoined the team in the incident room. All of them were groping about the office like a crowd of guys the morning after a stag do. The air was stale; most of them could have done with a shower. They had been working since the early hours of Sunday morning – some of them even longer than that. Most had now come back to the incident room with nothing to report. They all looked up as he stood in the doorway. The look on their faces said: 'demoralised'. He walked straight to the boards and turned to face his team.

"You don't need me to tell you how tired we all are. But this fellow here," he pointed to the photo-fit of Jason McMasters, "so far he's kept one step ahead of us. It's now the 5th of November, if only just. For him this is where it all ends; back on the same date where it all began. It's what he's been working towards all this time. I'm afraid that for us time is running out, so I have to ask for another all-night session. I'm sorry."

Nobody raised any objections; all of them were keen to get this bastard, Jeff thought. They may be demoralised, but the camaraderie in the team was great. "Okay then; everything points to the fact that he has Sheila McBride. We have to surmise that if she's already dead, by now we would have another crime scene on our hands. For whatever reason, it seems he is waiting. Either that or he has changed his mind."

"Or we've got it all wrong, Guv," Jones piped up. "It's not beyond the bounds of possibility that they are in it together."

There was a murmur of agreement.

Jeff waited. "From what I knew of Sheila Hynds a.k.a. McBride, I sincerely doubt that; but it's a fair point Jones. However, for the time being this David Shaw is perhaps our only lead. We need to find him. The clock is ticking."

He stared at each group of detectives before adding. "Sandra has tried all evening to reach her sister-in-law, Fiona Reid. I've a bad feeling our killer might see her as the icing on the cake and that it is she he has been waiting for. It might be his wait is over. You know she has been under surveillance for the last few days; well I've just now had a call to say the tail has lost her. She was seen going into

407

the home of a Robert Watts shortly after 8pm They left together on a motorbike just after 1am, last seen heading out of town on the A290. Jones; get onto it. See if they've been traced. Find out about this Watts guy. I think we have two women's lives at stake here. Take five everyone, you're doing great. Have some more coffee and then get to it. Let's give it all we've got, eh?"

Jeff went back to his office. Maybe he was just imagining it, but a clean breeze of fresh air seemed to waft past him bringing with it a new lease of life. Hell, he thought, I'm starting to get powers myself. Either that or I am having way too much practise at giving pep talks!

Sheila McBride stifled a sob; this time when she woke she found she had been moved from the floor and was now strapped to some kind of metal table set on a slope. Leather straps bound her wrists holding her weight. Across her chest too, something was tightly bound beneath her breasts.

From somewhere above her, two pulleys hung down. Straining her head she followed them, a scream rising in her throat as she saw that they were attached to her legs, which were strung up and angled outwards. She couldn't feel them; it was as if they were someone else's legs. After days without her special moisturisers to keep her scars supple, her mouth wouldn't open wide enough to scream; it came out as a gurgling gasp.

Tangled all around the room were green-leaved vines; the stems were clinging to vertical structures, snaking over surfaces. Huge, winged insects fluttered restlessly around them. Sheila felt one close to her head, the air moved her hair as one of the creatures spread its wings. Paralysed with fear, her heart pounding against her bonds, the sharp pain in her chest increased each time she took a breath.

"Glad to see you're awake. I have a visitor for you, Mother!"

He was back. Her body cringed. His voice was shrill, menacing. Slowly she turned her head. Beside him was some sort of trolley covered in plastic sheeting. She watched, apprehensive as he wheeled it into view positioning it directly opposite her. He bent and started to pump with his foot; the back half of the trolley rose. Suddenly he stopped; straightened and turned to face her. Smiling at her with that horrid, devious grin, his eyes glinting with delight, he waited like a conjurer about to take a rabbit out of the hat. In a swift motion, he tore the plastic sheeting from the trolley and Sheila's worst fears became reality.

Directly opposite her, unconscious, bound as she was herself, was the young woman from court house steps. The woman her son had stared at so viciously. There was no question of her identity: her flawless features, golden hair and unmarked face were like looking into a mirror that had turned back time. Sheila knew that she was looking at her daughter. She had known it then, too. Her heart lost its rhythm, beating sporadically as she convulsed against the straps that held her, her instinctive reaction to shield; to protect.

Loud ridiculing laughter shattered the silence; her struggles were futile. She gasped; sobbing, gasping breaths rent her throat as her tears flowed, blurring what she had seen. But beneath her grief and pain, like an uncapped gusher, there welled a surge of white hot anger. She sucked in a breath, licked her cracked lips.

"You make me sick to my stomach, Andy Hynds. You're just like your useless shit of a father! Spawn of the Devil the pair of you, God knows, I wish it had been you they pulled out the Thames."

Spurting out the words, careless of the consequences, Sheila knew that whatever hopes she had envisioned weeks ago of reaching him were fruitless. This thing before her was beyond help; his soul stained beyond redemption. He was devoid of compassion; not even a hint of humanity resided in this travesty of nature that was her son. The effort left her limp, her heart staggered, her breathing slowed. In her mind's eye, she saw him as he used to be: her little boy. "Oh, Andy," she breathed.

His face bleached white; he shot out a hand to strike her, pulled it back, smirking as she struggled. "Patience, Richard, patience," he murmured, his voice suddenly deeper. Straightening his dress, he swung round as a buzzer sounded, a startled expression crossing his face. "I'll leave you two to get reacquainted," he said, and was gone.

Sheila focused her gaze on her daughter. The face was peaceful, blissfully unaware of the hellish situation in which they were both trapped. She's like a sleeping angel, Sheila thought, hopelessly, her tears beginning to flow again.

There was nothing she could do except hang her head and weep and try not to hear the interminable fluttering of wings that shivered the air around her.

51

Sandra looked at her watch; it was almost 1.30am It's too late she thought; too late. She knew she should not be driving after all that wine, but right now it seemed the least of her worries. Punching the wheel she reversed up the street and headed for the station.

Turning into the car park she killed the engine and sat for a moment. Something else was bothering her. Something Jeff had said leaving King's Place. Sifting through the printouts, she pulled one out resting it on the steering wheel as she clicked on the courtesy light. There it was: the list of apartment numbers and owners; eight of them on the top floor. Jeff said he had seen only seven. Had he missed one or was it a slip of the tongue? Sandra shrugged, more important at the moment was the suspicion that her friend and colleague was covering something up.

Resting her head on the steering wheel, Sandra again asked herself: Why had Leslie lied to her? It was probably nothing; just that she was distracted about her mother. And yet she *had* lied. She heard Leslie's voice in her head: 'You've only *just* caught me.' She had been wearing her coat; had only just got back to the apartment. And yet, the bonnet of her car had been *cold*; stone cold.

Perhaps it was nothing; maybe she wasn't using her own car. Maybe her sister had dropped her off. But no; that couldn't be it either. The sister would have had to stay with the mother. And in the circumstances, Leslie would hardly have walked. What did it matter? Sandra asked herself in despair. Why was she letting her instinct drive her like this? What had made her drop everything and come rushing back to the station intent on checking out Leslie's background?

"Why am I doing this? She's my friend!" she said out loud. Lifting her head, she stared up at the night sky, but it was clouded over now. Resting her elbows on the steering wheel she knew she was desperate; desperate to catch this killer and worried; worried sick about Fiona.

So now she wasn't thinking straight. That had to be it.

Unable to stop a steady stream of tears washing down her face and dripping onto the printouts, Sandra had to admit to herself that she was hurting. Not so much about the lie – there was most likely a simple explanation for that – but about what had happened between her and Leslie tonight when she had told her about the abortion. For a few seconds it was as if Leslie had bared her soul. Her honest reaction to what Sandra had disclosed had been one of revulsion, utter abhorrence. So much so that Sandra had felt ashamed; almost dirty. But more than that; she had seen anger in Leslie's eyes; a flash of pure rage that was akin to hatred.

Could she have been mistaken? Surely it was a misunderstanding. How could Leslie of all people have this reaction? Never once in the last few years had she come across a person less concerned about morality! Surely Leslie could not be that much of a hypocrite? It made no sense to her the more she thought about it. But more than anything else, what was bothering Sandra as she sat motionless in the car park, trying to decide what to do about it, was that whenever she had these intuitive feelings she was almost always proved right.

With her hand on the car door handle, she looking up at the lights blazing out of the incident room high up in the building. She could not go to Jeff and Stevens with these strange, half-formed suspicions based on so small a lie. Maybe, despite her promiscuity, Leslie drew the line at abortion. Millions of people would share that view. She thought back over their friendship: Leslie had stood by her during her breakdown after the kidnapping. Had been there for her when she needed a shoulder to cry on; had even been there for Gerry when he lay dying. It was Leslie who had found him: by sheer chance she had called in to borrow a book; they had often exchanged books, she and Gerry. She it was who had called the ambulance. Afterwards, she had reassured Sandra that he had not suffered, that it had been very quick. She had kept in close touch throughout the inquest and had been with them at the funeral, openly sharing their grief. How *can* I believe anything ill of her, Sandra asked herself, when she has been so good to us?

Coming to a decision, Sandra reached for the ignition key, slotted it in and turned it. Something was happening with Leslie right now; something had made her angry. Surely it was more about her mother dying and her estrangement with her sister than about anything else. I am supposed to be her friend, Sandra thought. I am not going to let her cope alone.

She would go back to the flat, see if Leslie was still there; offer support and give her a chance to explain why she'd lied. And while I'm there, Sandra thought, I can double check the floor above. Turning her car she headed back to King's Place.

There were no lights on in Leslie's apartment. The block was as quiet as the grave; but then, it was now after 2am Sandra tried Fiona's number; it rang out; nothing. She locked the car and headed towards the building. She would check out the layout on the floor above to see which apartment Jeff had missed. The concierge was nodding off. He grinned at her sleepily, waved her through.

Exiting the lift she found the hallway replicated the one below, except that to her left, just where Leslie's door would have been on the floor below, there was nothing but a wall. Jeff had been right there were only seven apartments. It didn't mean anything; it must be that the printout was wrong.

As the lift door jolted open on her way back down, she realised she'd hit the button for the underground car park. Still sitting where she'd seen it before was Leslie's car.

She went back up to Leslie's floor, held her finger on the buzzer. No reply. She turned, leaned against the doorframe, once more bringing up Fiona's number; nothing.

Checking her watch she saw it was now 2.15. There was no good reason for Fiona to be out of touch for this length of time. It was wrong, all wrong. And where was Leslie?

All Sandra's instincts screamed at her that something was wrong there too.

She heard the lock click open behind her; it made her jump.

52

Jeff was holding for the switchboard to connect him to the morgue. There was as good a chance as any that Robert Canning would have some knowledge of the incident in Scotland concerning this Shaw fellow.

"Grizz, old boy; what can I do for you? I was just about to call your number. Is Sandra with you?"

"No, she's not come in yet." Jeff cut straight to the question, but all Canning was able to recall was a similar case involving the organs of children. He'd never heard of David Shaw.

"Thanks for hearing me out anyway, Bob. Do you want me to give Sandra a message – or you could try her home number."

"Done that mate, several times; both the house line and the mobile are ringing out until the messaging services pick up. It's just that—"

Jeff tensed; interrupting. "Are you sure? I can't think where else she'd be. The girls might not be up yet, but Sandra should still be there; probably having a kip."

"Sure I'm sure. I'll keep trying then. I want to talk to her about the Smyth girl. I gather there's a move afoot for the Jakes verdict to be declared unsafe? Anyway, on that, something's come up that is *most* interesting."

Jeff waved his arm high to get Stevens's attention and switched the phone to loudspeaker. "Don't keep it to yourself, Bob. I wouldn't mind hearing it too. It would seem that our case and the one you're talking about are connected in some way."

"I'm aware of that, Grizz, though I'm not sure this will help your present case any."

Jeff exchanged glances with Stevens, who had come over, his expression one of keen interest.

"Try me," Jeff said.

"Right well; what do you think about this? Last time I spoke with Sandra, she asked me to double-check the blood test results for Peggy Lyons – you know we found GHB in Mrs Hunt?"

"Yes. Go on, I'm listening."

"Well, Sandra said while I was at it, would I check out Katie Smyth's too. So I did. The thing is, Grizz, the lab must've mixed up the samples, I've checked and double-checked. The results we got back were the wrong blood group. I only know this because I got hold of Katie Smyth's medical record. I was curious about her reproductive organs. Women born without a uterus are quite rare: one in four thousand; most interesting. Did you know that in cases where the uterus is atrophied it is almost always the case that the vagina is also? It is likely that there will be found an unusually high level of testost—"

Jeff tapped his fingers, "Sorry to butt in, Bob, but never mind the lecture, what about the bloods?"

"Yes, sorry. Well, as I said, if I hadn't known what her blood group was, I would never have known. I double-checked, went back to her medical record, and sure enough, it was a mismatch. So then I got hold of Mark Jakes's medical records too and guess what: same thing. The point is, Grizz, the results we got back from the lab could not possibly have been for either Katie Smyth's or Mark Jakes's bloods."

"Now that *is* interesting. What about Peggy Lyons?"

"Haven't checked yet, but I will. Look, Grizz; in my line of work a mistake like this simply doesn't happen, not with the labelling and code system we have in place. I don't know about you, but I got to thinking and, well, not to put too fine a point on it, the phrase 'tampering with the evidence' comes to mind. I can't think how else it could have happened. Someone's buggering us about. I'm going to chase it down with the lab, but—"

"What lab, Bob: what company did the testing?"

"McMasters Pharmaceuticals, same as always."

"Okay, thanks mate. I'll tell Sandra as soon as she comes in." Jeff rang off as Stevens slammed his fists on the desk.

"I knew it! I just knew it."

Jeff, frowning, was already trying Sandra's number. There was no reply. He tried her mobile; same result. Concerned, he stabbed in the number of the Uniform on duty outside the Reid's house; spoke into the phone. Looking up he saw that Stevens had gone back to the image boards and was standing deep in thought in front of the images of Katie Smyth. Setting the phone back down, Jeff walked over and stood beside Stevens.

"What are you seeing? Enlighten me!"

Stevens released a sigh his eyes remaining focused on the board. "Well, Sir, only three groups of people – sorry, four if you split the attending officers from the SOCOs – had access to the scene or evidence from the scene. My colleagues from the station would have used their usual reference number. So we need to check our copies of the report, see if there's a mismatch. I mean, what Canning says isn't *always* true. He's covering his professional back; they do make mistakes sometimes, if only rarely. On the other hand," he paused, thinking.

"Go on, penny for 'em?"

"Well, Sir; if we're still working on the assumption that these cases are connected, and you factor in the apparent medical knowledge of the killer, it could point the finger at someone from the path lab. They would have coded the samples for Katie."

Stevens left Jeff's side and rummaged through the filing cabinet to retrieve the case notes from the Smyth murder.

Walking along beside the boards Jeff studied each of the harrowing images in turn, his thoughts coming at random. "A person who possesses or is trained to have knowledge of the human anatomy. A noted skill with a knife too; a pathologist would tick all the boxes – but who?"

"David Shaw, Sir."

"It would be tidy, I agree, but sadly it has to be someone who has access to the forensic labs here in Maidstone. It was the Coroner's office here that got the Katie Smyth case because at the time, if you remember, the whole of London was taking part in that Major Incident Exercise between the 14th and 15th of February. And nobody here has heard of a David Shaw."

"Could have changed his name; even his appearance."

"True. Who did the Smyth autopsy? It wasn't Canning; I distinctly remember that Leslie was away at the time."

"It'll be in the Coroner's report," Stevens made his way back across the room. "Hang on; I've got it here, Sir." He retrieved the report from the filing cabinet and scanned the pages. "It was a chap called – hey, that's a coincidence, I wonder if they're related."

"Who?"

"His name's Fenton; Max Fenton." Stevens carried the report back to Jeff, "Here's the signature, look, Sir, at the bottom of the autopsy findings."

Jeff looked where Stevens was pointing, read the name. Dropping the report on the nearest desk he took out his mobile and searched his directory for Robert Canning's home number.

"Bob, it's me again. The office that carried out the autopsy on Katie Smyth was ours her in Maidstone right?""

"Yes, why?"

"A Max Fenton signed off the autopsy; do you know of him or if he's related in some way to Leslie?"

"I don't think so, but it's not a 'he', Grizz. It's Maxine. I never got to know her very well, she wasn't here long. Trained at King's as I recall, but why do you ask?"

"Did she indeed. Can you describe her?"

"Well, like I said, I only met her the once, but by all accounts she seemed to know what she is doing. Let me see now; quite tall; slim build, wore heavy framed specs – you know, the kind women choose who want to look authoritative," Canning chuckled. "I tell you what though, she had amazing hair. It was red; the kind of red that doesn't look quite natural, didn't match her skin type, if you know what I mean. Anyway, what's the interest?"

"Wouldn't you have expected this Max to spot the difference in blood groups? She would surely have checked the medical records?"

"In theory, I suppose, but in practice not necessarily. We don't always have time, Jeff."

"Okay, Bob. Thanks. Get back to me when you've spoken to the lab, will you?"

He shoved the phone into his jacket pocket; stood with his back to the room gazing out of the window, hands behind his back, rocking on his heels. Something Canning had said had struck a chord. What was it?

Suddenly he swung round to Stevens.

"What is it, Sir?"

Jeff was shaking his head. "How the hell did we miss it before, Stevens. All this time. I always said there was something odd about the woman; never really liked her."

"What is it Sir?" Stevens repeated, frowning.

"It's the red hair, Stevens." He strode to the door. "Come with me. We need to find Sandra. She left the house just after 1.10am and Uniform haven't seen her since." He was punching in the number of her mobile as he spoke, this time with even more urgency than before.

Mystified, Stevens shrugged on his jacket and followed.

53

Fiona came to drowsily. Her head was hanging down, her chin resting heavily on her collar bone. Feeling disoriented, she fought off the throbbing that was drilling deeper and deeper behind her eyes. Aware of the bindings she struggled, panicking, squinting to protect herself from the brightness of the room. Where was she? What was this place? Why couldn't she remember how she got here?

"You're not alone. I'm here."

The voice sounded frail. Fiona lifted her head, searched it out. It seemed to come from directly opposite her. Her vision was blurred, the shape vague. She closed her eyes tight, opened them again. Saw a woman; a woman with only half a face. She was lying on some sort of table; her legs seemed to be sticking up in the air.

Fiona gasped. She strained against the ties that pinned her to whatever it was she was lying on. Her throat ached, her mouth was parched.

"Who are you? Where am I? Who is doing this?" Fiona's voice died in her throat. This wasn't real; it was a nightmare. Her mind was playing tricks. She squirmed against the bindings that trapped her. All she had to do was to wake up.

"It's some sort of tropical garden room, but where I don't know." The woman's reply was no more than a whisper.

I might as well go along with this, Fiona thought. I will wake up in a minute. "Who are you?" she asked.

"My name is Sheila McBride. I'm... I'm your mother."

So that was it. She'd finally flipped; the stress, it must be the stress. Finding out her mother's name and seeing Mark like that, no wonder. Wake up, Fiona; for God's sake, wake up. More than anything, she wished this migraine would go away. It was making her feel sick.

"I'm sorry," the woman whispered, "so very sorry. I saw you on the TV and I saw him watching you. You were outside the court house. I hoped to find him before he got to you, but I failed. I'm so sorry," she said again.

Fiona went rigid, her whole body numb as the horrifying possibility that this wasn't a nightmare impinged on her consciousness. "My mother?" she gasped.

"Yes. You are my daughter; mine and Leonard Millar's." In a voice quavering with despair, she added, "I should have told him; he would have protected you."

Fiona did not know how to react. All the feelings she'd dreamed of: the excitement and the longing; the certainty that they would somehow know each other; have instant rapport, did not belong here. Not in this sick nightmare. Whatever image she'd had in her head of this first meeting, she could never have imagined anything like this. Slowly gazing around the room, Gerry's warning began echoing in her head. But even he, surely, could not have meant this.

The weird, yeast-like odour that filled the air was sickening; sweet, like stale beer. A paralysing sense of dread took hold of her. The migraine was getting worse, affecting her vision. Lowering her head she closed her eyes. With all her being, still clinging to the hope that this was some kind of dream, she wished herself away, anywhere but here.

"Fiona? Are you still with me?"

How did this woman know her name? Raising her head to see, Fiona found her vision had deteriorated even further: brownish, vein-like streaks criss-crossed her eyes. Anguished, she tried to scream; it came out as a sob.

"My eyes! I can't see; what's wrong with my eyes? They're bleeding."

"Oh my poor love; no! No, they're not. I expect it is the vines you can see. Don't be afraid. You will see the insects too, but they won't harm you. Don't be afraid," Sheila repeated.

Even as she spoke, Fiona sensed rapid movement close to her hair; a flapping sound like a bird trapped in a cage.

"Don't panic, Fiona. I know they're huge, but they're only butterflies; just butterflies. Harmless. Noise – any kind of movement – startles them."

Fiona froze again. Vines; yes, she could see them now; leaves hanging down, tendrils clinging to the ceiling – and huge insects with brilliant colours gleaming on their wings. Almost afraid to breathe, she whispered, "How do you know my name?"

"I have always known it. I named you; the little boy, your brother, was so taken with you. I knew he would insist that it would remain yours." Sheila paused, licked her lips. Her voice sank almost to a thread. Fiona strained to hear.

"I named you after my great-grandmother; your great-great-grandmother. She was born during the famine in Ireland, but by some miracle survived. She lived through many a hard time after that too. She was over a hundred years' old when she died. They said she was one hundred and eleven and that she was the oldest person ever to have lived in Ireland, but I don't know if that's true. I can remember her well. I suppose I hoped you would inherit something of her toughness with her name – and although I knew you would probably never know of it, I was trying to keep part of your past alive in you." Shelia's head lolled back, her eyes closed, her breathing coming in spasmodic, ragged gasps as though the effort of speaking had taken all her strength.

Suddenly afraid for her, Fiona was silent. Nothing the woman had said had any meaning for her. It should matter, but it didn't. She felt her lids growing heavy again; a sinking sensation pulling her down.

Suddenly, several loud bangs shattered the silence and footsteps sounded, coming closer and closer. A mocking voice chanted something. It was an inhuman, echoing sound.

As if in harmonious accompaniment, agitated butterflies flapped and fluttered all around them.

Fear gripped Fiona's stomach; she tried to block out the sound.

"Remember, remember the fifth of November! Mother! Dear Mother!" the voice wheedled.

"Fiona," the woman's voice brushed across Fiona's senses like a caress. "Whatever happens I have always loved you; walked every day alongside you. I gave you up to protect you. It is the hardest thing I have ever done. I am so very sorry. Please forgive me."

Fiona could only look at her blankly; the plea from this disfigured woman – a stranger claiming to be her mother – was incomprehensible. They shared just one thing: fear; they were both utterly terrified. That at least she could recognise.

"Be strong child; be strong—"

The warning was cut off as the door flung open. Her heart thudding, Fiona turned her head to look at the figure in the doorway.

54

"Where are we going, Sir?"

"Leslie Fenton's apartment in King's Place," Jeff drummed his fingers on the steering wheel as a car cut in front of him.

"Do you mind telling me why?"

"Sorry. It's just a theory, but one or two things are beginning to sound alarm bells for me. As daft as it sounds, I think Leslie may be involved with Richard Noble."

"What? No disrespect, but that's preposterous, Sir."

"Is it? Why?"

"Well... aside from anything else, for starters she's Sandra's friend—"

"That, Stevens, is precisely what I am worrying about." He handed over his mobile. "Here, try her number again, will you."

"Gone through to messaging, Sir," Stevens said after a moment handing back the phone. "What makes you think Leslie might be in cahoots with Noble anyway?"

"I think she and this Maxine Fenton are one and the same person."

"I can't see it myself, Sir, but just supposing for the sake of argument they were; wouldn't someone have noticed? Leslie's quite well known after all."

Jeff cleared his throat, "Yes, well... the thing is, Stevens, I went back to her place one night after we'd been out and, well, something stands out about the occasion in my memory." Jeff coughed. Obviously he sounded as embarrassed as he felt because Steven cracked out laughing.

"Well I imagine so, Sir; she's one sassy lady!"

"No, that's not what I meant. Her dressing table looked like a make-up artist's."

"That's women for you," Stevens chuckled.

Jeff ignored him. "Along with all the makeup, she had an assortment of wigs. I thought little of it at the time—"

"Had other things on your mind I expect, Sir?" Stevens smirked.

"Okay, Stevens, that's enough: joke over! Women like to change their appearance from time to time – even I know that, but it was more than that. Something Bob said reminded me: one of them stood out particularly."

"A red one by chance?"

"Exactly so."

"Well, again meaning no disrespect, but aren't you overreacting a bit, Sir? It's a bit flimsy."

"On its own, maybe, but there's more; she's a pathologist for one thing, and she tells lies for another. She has told Sandra that she has a sister, but she categorically told me she was an only child. Why would she do that? And another thing: think about the Peggy Lyons autopsy. Don't you think it rather odd that Leslie filled out the cause of death as heart failure even before the results of the blood tests were known?"

"I'd call that over-confident and somewhat negligent rather than odd, Sir. But it would certainly explain how Noble is always one step ahead of us."

"Exactly! If I'm right then Sandra's theory that there are two profiles – two different killers – is spot on."

"I still can't picture Leslie Fenton in that mode, Sir. If she's involved at all, isn't it more likely that she's being used without even realising it?"

"Maybe, but let's keep an open mind, Stevens, eh? Here, try Sandra again will you? And if there's no joy, radio in for backup – preferably armed; I've got a nasty feeling about this."

Jeff parked alongside Sandra's car. He rested his hand on the bonnet. It was stone cold. He checked his watch; it was just after 9.30am "She's been here a while," he remarked to Stevens. "Must've come straight here last night." Again, he tried her mobile. Nothing. "She's switched it off," he muttered.

As he spoke, two patrol cars rounded the corner; not the back-up he'd hoped for. The two armed support units had been called out and were unavailable.

Not knowing exactly what they were facing, he detailed four uniformed officers to the rear of the building, sending two more to the car park beneath.

"What the hell's that?" Stevens looked up at the apartment block.

"Lord knows!" Jeff could hear it too: loud music, the din travelling down to street level. Bit early for a party, he reflected; and on a Monday too. Maybe it was someone elderly and deaf – except that it wasn't that sort of place; all the tenants were yuppies. As they ran towards the entrance, Jeff thought about Sandra. Why had she come back here? Had she worked something out about Leslie; she'd said last night there was something odd about the pathologist's behaviour and Sandra was nothing if not intuitive. Even without news of the mixed up blood tests, she might have put two and two together. He tried to convince himself that he would find her safe inside; that his fears were unfounded. Like Stevens had said: it was flimsy. At the same time he was angry; increasingly angry. What the hell was Sandra thinking of coming back here on her own? If she'd reached the same conclusions he had, why hadn't she contacted him?

Jeff flashed his card at the concierge; a different one from last night: a pimply youth not long out of school by the look of him. "Any disturbances?"

"No; dunno; I've only just come on."

"Well don't move; I'll get a statement from you later," Jeff said over his shoulder as they rushed to the lift.

The youth sat back in his chair, his mouth dropped open.

They found Leslie's apartment door open. On the ground near to the wall and broken into several pieces lay a mobile phone: Sandra's; Jeff recognised the distinctive case. Whatever hopes he'd had that she was safe were now shattered. Inside the apartment there were few signs of a struggle. They circled, scanning the room; saw a smudged smear of blood just around head height on the door; it was still slightly tacky.

"Noble must have been here," Stevens said. "He must have been here when Sandra arrived. Do you suppose Leslie called to ask her over?"

"Almost certainly; probably fed her the line about her sick mother," Jeff agreed bitterly.

Jones and two more uniformed officers arrived in the doorway.

The vibrations of the music boomed somewhere above their heads. "Jones; for pity's sake, find out who's responsible for that and get it stopped!"

Dispatching the two officers to watch the front of the building, Jeff stood with his back to the door as Stevens searched every room in the apartment.

"Nobody here, Sir; it's empty. I can't see any more blood; nothing to indicate a struggle anywhere else."

Jeff walked over to the window and stared out. It wasn't a good sign. Living people kept on bleeding; in dead people it stopped. He felt the tension twisting his guts, butterflies fluttered in his stomach as the seconds ticked by. He swung round, remained where he stood, studying the room. Think man, think!

"Sandra must have determined that Leslie was involved in this somehow," Stevens offered as Jeff growled once more about the din.

"Damn that noise! Who the hell would want that ringing in their ears?"

"It's opera, Sir. Puccini's *Madame Butterfly* unless I'm mistaken; actually, I quite like it."

"What did you say?"

Stevens was taken aback, "That I quite like it?"

"No, you idiot! What did you say it was called?" Jeff shouted above the noise that was now swelling to a thunderous volume.

"*Madame Butterfly.* What's that smell, Sir?" Stevens, distracted, walked across the room sniffing the air like a dog: "It seems strongest just here, behind you; coming from the fireplace. I'd say it was ether; no – more like formaldehyde."

Eyes narrowing, Jeff walked over to the fireplace, for the first time noticing the prints: Monet, butterflies. Everything seemed to be about bloody butterflies. He sniffed; smelt the chemical; could see nothing to explain it. The fireplace was made of marble; there was an ornamental Buddha standing in the hearth.

"It probably means nothing. She works with the damned stuff – they use it in the morgue. It probably clings to her clothes."

As Stevens tampered with the fireplace, Jeff paced the room, his thoughts coming thick and fast, He spoke them, shouting above the sound of the music.

"Let's think about the sequence of events: Katie Smyth murdered or rather mutilated. You were first to arrive straight after, Stevens. You sensed something was amiss. The culprit was there drenched in her blood and yet you found condensation in the bathroom; heat from the steam created by the shower still present. Now we have mixed up blood vials. Three women murdered; carefully sliced open, this time in a more ordered fashion. Incisions not haphazard cuts like Katie's; their wombs cut out and taken. This building here: it's owned by Jason McMasters. He has access to the labs. Sandra's car sits abandoned outside. This is Leslie's apartment. Door left open; blood smeared; Sandra gone. Where would they go? Where is it leading us, Stevens?"

Back to where it started, he thought to himself, frustration hammering at his head. A sudden holler from Stevens behind him tightened the screw in his nerves.

"Sir! I think you'd better look at this!" Stevens was wrestling with a piece of plasterboard set into the hearth that moments ago had formed the backdrop. Finally freeing it, he threw it out of his way; inside the hole a glow of light was emanating from a battery lamp.

Dropping to his knees beside Stevens, Jeff reached in to lift out what he'd found: a worn rag doll and several dog-eared children's fairytale books. They looked at each other baffled; scrawled on the inside of each hard cover in faded pencil was the name 'Jenny McMasters'.

"Guv!" Jones called from the door. "That music; it seems to be coming from the flat above here; but it's not and I don't understand how it's not because it's as if it's directly over our heads. But there is no entrance to a room above here on the next floor."

Mystified, Jeff and Stevens turned to see a puzzled Jones staring at the ceiling. "Somebody seems to have made a few adaptations to this building. At least that's what we think. There has to be a second level to this flat but there's definitely no way of getting in from the floor above. We've just looked outside to see if there are windows, but the only ones in about the right place belong to the next flat. The tenant was in the hallway complaining about the noise, he let us look around inside. He's only just got back from the Himalayas early this morning, Guv. The music is deafening – I don't wonder he's complaining. The thing is, from inside his place it sounds like it's next door – except there is no next door. Is there any sign of a staircase in here or some kind of access to a room above?"

As Jeff was trying to make sense of this garbled account, Stevens answered for him, "No. I've checked every room. What does the concierge say?"

"He doesn't know anything; it's his first day in the job," Jones grinned as Jeff rolled his eyes in exasperation. "He's trying to get hold of the boss, but he's not answering; still on his way home the lad said."

"Okay," Jeff nodded, "let's have a look at it from the outside." Following Jones back down to the street, they scanned the outside of the building. "Look," Jones pointed. "See what I mean Guv? Those three windows up there and the French doors with the balcony belong to the bloke we met in the hallway. But if you look inside his flat, it isn't as big as you'd expect for the external wall space. The only thing that makes any sense is that there's a penthouse to Leslie Fenton's flat! And look, see there," he pointed to the roof, "skylights – there has to be some kind of access."

Racing back inside, they began to search for a hidden entrance to the floor above.

55

Fiona's eyes flicked from one figure to the next not knowing which one scared her the most.

Their captor entered the room dragging Sandra along behind her, raising her up with such force that Fiona heard the seams of Sandra's shirt rip apart. Horrified, she watched as Sandra was flung towards the wall. Limp and bloodied, bleeding from a wound visible on the back of her head, her body hit the wall and slumped to the floor. Her face was pale, almost grey.

Fiona screamed. 'Please God!' she prayed. 'Please let her still be alive.' She tensed as the terrifying woman came towards her, bent over her; she saw the eyes were crazed with hatred, a hatred she'd witnessed only once before. The eyes! She knew those eyes. But he had been a man; this was a woman. Or was it?

From across the room, Sheila's voice was a cry of fear: "Leave her alone! I beg you! You have me please; please leave her alone! Do what you like to me, but not her. She's your sister! For God's sake, Andy! Fiona is your *sister*."

Andy? Not Richard? Sister? How could she possibly be this animal's sister? Rigid with terror, Fiona felt as if she were a fly caught in a spider's web; she couldn't move. As she watched, hypnotised by those eyes, she saw the pupils grow larger, blacker. Suddenly he straightened, throwing himself in the direction of Sheila's voice he lashed out smashing his fist down on her face.

The sound of bone cracking forced another scream from Fiona. As Sheila's head lolled to the side, he stood over her; slowly he put up his hand, pulled off the blonde wig and flung it to the floor. His shaven head glistened with sweat.

Fiona couldn't breath; each gasp was a cry. Oh yes. She knew him. She watched him return to her; could see a vein pulsing in his forehead as he bent over her. His face was flushed, he was breathing deeply, almost growling. The growling deepened; it was as though he was changing in front of her eyes, becoming wolf-like, his mouth started foaming, drooling as he exerted pressure on her chest. Fiona's lungs collapsed; deprived of oxygen, she started to hyperventilate.

"My sister?" he snarled. Without warning he released the pressure and spat in Fiona's face. She writhed, sucked in air, her body cringing in disgust as his spittle landed on her cheek. She could do nothing but shudder, retching as it slid down to her jaw.

In his right hand he held out a crumpled photograph. He smoothed it with his fingers, crooning he stroked it, turned it towards Fiona and shoved it up against her face. Grabbing her by the hair, he forced her head up against the image.

"This is my sister!" His voice was no longer shrilly feminine, but deeply masculine. Suddenly he jumped backwards and in a quick swipe grabbed hold of Sheila's head, shaking it violently.

"Jenny! Jenny is my sister! Do you hear me! My Jenny! You killed her; both of you. You killed my Jenny." He began to sob, great racking sobs. Mascara mingling with his tears incongruously streaked his cheeks. He wiped them with the back of his hand, smudging the slash of red lipstick on his mouth.

Fiona winced; helpless; unable to look away, unable to block out the faint cries of pain from her mother whose shattered jaw streamed blood where her face had caved in.

Gerry's warning sounded again in Fiona's ear and listening to it she began to shiver; suddenly she felt as though she were drowning in guilt. 'This is your fault,' his voice said in her head. 'I told you not to seek out your mother. You are to blame for this. It is you who have unleashed this evil. I warned you. Why wouldn't you listen to me?' Closing her eyes, Fiona clung to the imagined sound of Gerry's voice; at the moment, the only thing that seemed real to her.

Her eyes flicked open as Andy screamed. "You will pay! I promised Jenny I'd make you pay; both of you!" He backed away from Sheila, looked across at Sandra. Moving towards the door, he lifted his foot and drove it into Sandra's lifeless body. "And you're no better than the rest of them," he shrieked. "You didn't give yours away; you killed it," he kicked her again and walked out of the room.

The man was completely, utterly, inhumanly, insane. Fiona focused on Sandra for some sort of movement, a sign that she was still breathing, but there was none that she could see. Turning her gaze apprehensively towards her mother, she saw that Sheila's head drooped down over the bloodied neckline of her blouse; she too appeared lifeless.

Feeling terribly alone, Fiona released deep sobs, her tears flowing freely, running into her brother's spittle, washing it from her face.

The butterflies rose frantically from the vines as music filled the air. Beautiful, soaring music: a soprano and a tenor combining in a heart-rending duet of love and abandonment. The volume was almost unbearable. Fiona jerked against her restraints, turned her head to watch the door, whimpering as she waited for him to return.

After several journeys in and out of the room, he came to stand over her again. He had cleaned his face and was dressed in a green suit like surgeons wore. He had wheeled in a metal trolley, it rattled as he pushed it towards her. From the corner of her eye she could see a set of surgical instruments and a row of glass jars: six of them. Four contained a flesh like substance; two were empty. Fiona's fear was now so great that she lost control of her body; her bladder voided its contents onto the floor.

He was pushing, pumping something beneath her; the apparatus to which she was secured began to sink. Helplessly, instinctively, she sought her mother, but lying flat now, Sheila was gone from her view. Suddenly she was blinded by lights and he was reaching towards her.

"Fiona!" Sheila's voice came to her across the void. "Listen to me my darling; I am here, I am with you. We will be together soon. It will be over soon. I love you. Pray with me. Our Father that—"

Without warning, Andy lurched across the room screaming, his voice shrill again, horrifying; triumphant.

"You dare to use those words!" He brought his fist down into Sheila's stomach; she cried out and was silent.

With a shout of laughter, Andy came back to Fiona. Again the arm was raised; the steel blade caught the light and glimmered. Her most dreaded fear realised, Fiona drew her eyelids down to shut out the sight in front of her and saw that in his other hand he held an empty jar.

56

Sandra's eyes opened wide. Immediately she tensed; a clawing, rending pain in her gut. Her head was hurting, her vision blurred. She was on the floor. In front of her she could make out the wheels of a trolley and one pair of legs encased in white boots; wellingtons; green plastic trousers.

One by one her senses gathered momentum: the sweet smell of rotting fruit and the hint of ammonia; the sound of voices, contorted, moving about, the pitch changing seeming near then moving away – as if she were under water – and music; loud; singing. Lights; bright, bright lights; everything seemed white. And a sense of danger; fear so tangible, she could almost smell it.

Instinctively stifling a scream of pain, she raised herself onto one elbow, felt the quickening throbs of a migraine attacking the back of her head. The hallway outside Leslie's apartment flashed into her mind and was gone. A fuzzy feeling enveloped her; a wooziness. Twisting upwards, she clutched her stomach; a ball of fire seemed to rage inside her crippling her every move. It came to her then that of course, she was in hospital; in an operating theatre. She relaxed her back against the wall. Why had they left her here on the floor? And what was the pain? She couldn't remember. She had been outside Leslie's door; had she had some kind of stroke? Leslie must have brought her here. Thank God! But why was no one helping? Couldn't they see her?

Above her someone screamed: a shrill cry of despair. A man's voice shouted in response; a deep, angry roar. This couldn't be right. Where was this place? Another tirade ensued; another woman's voice; a woman sobbing.

Gripped by a sudden rush of sensation, Sandra came at last to her senses and recognised whose voice it was.

Slowly, slowly; wishing herself invisible, she edged to the left of the trolley. She could hear steel clashing; light objects not heavy.

What was happening? From here she couldn't see. Sheltering behind the trolley, she looked around her, her gaze settling on a mirror propped against the wall to her left. By dragging her legs to the side she was within reach of it. She tried to ignore the pain; it was almost unbearable as if her ribs were broken, but she was near enough now to lean forward. The tilt of the mirror afforded her a view of the room and what she saw horrified her to her core.

Jesus! Almost she cried it out loud. Sheer will power kept her silent; she knew that silence was imperative. On the trolley above her, she could see a woman thrusting her head from side to side. She was restrained by leather straps and horribly injured, her garments smeared with blood. It was she who had screamed. Her screams had subsided to whimpers.

Nearby, strapped to an adjacent trolley was Fiona. A bald-headed man was leaning over her wielding a knife, the blade poised as though he were about to operate.

Sandra gasped.

He frowned, paused, turned.

She closed her eyes, let her body go limp, held her breath. But it was the injured woman lying above her he was addressing.

"No Mother! As the sins of the father are visited on the son, so the sins of the mother are visited on her daughter. Your sins have become hers. Here it will end. You left me that night Mother. Why did you lie to me? 'Soon; soon!' that was what you said. 'When you are scared close your eyes,' you told me. 'Picture my face and it will all go away.' And I did. I did. But it didn't go away. I waited and I waited. But you never came back."

Sandra stuffed her hand into her mouth to stop herself from gasping again. Between sentences his voice was changing from adult to child and back again. There was something familiar about him. She couldn't place it.

"I found a sister; someone to share the loneliness; someone to love me. Do you know what our father did to us? Can you imagine it? But we held on. We loved each other me and my Jenny. And because of you she was taken. I have waited so long to fulfil my promise to her. Answer my questions Mother! Can you tell me why? Why did you make sure this child of yours had a good life and not me? Why didn't you care about *me*, Mother? Why *her*?" He looked down at the operating table, "This is the one who stole my Jenny's life from her. She lived and Jenny died. Why Mother? Why?"

Sandra's eyes darted back to the woman he was addressing; saw beneath the dreadful injuries that she was horribly scarred. Realised this must be Sheila. The man could only be Andy Hynds, and on the trolley beneath him, Fiona was in mortal danger. Gripped by stark terror, Sandra knew she had to do something. Slowly she started to move.

"Your daughter, Mother, has nothing left. I've already seen to that. I've taken everything she loved, one by one: the man she was to marry, the brother she adored, his wife, this pathetic creature who presumed to be my friend—" his voice stopped abruptly as he saw that she was no longer there.

Recoiling in horror from his words, Sandra had slid along the floor to the end of the trolley. She knew she had a split second to act. Gritting her teeth and screaming with pain, she sprang to her feet, flinging herself at his back.

It was a futile attempt. He turned before she reached him.

As he crushed her chest with one swoop of his elbow and she heard her ribs crack, she saw again the livid hatred that had dwelled earlier in the eyes of Leslie Fenton. And then she understood.

57

"This is just wasting time; time we don't have!"

Jeff vented his anger, pounding his fist along a wall in the bedroom. Behind him, covering the scalps of featureless porcelain heads on the dressing table, were several wigs: the blonde swirls of Leslie Fenton's hair in a variety of styles; the red one that she had used as 'Maxine', and another, black. He stared at them in dismay. Two years ago, one quick glance had led him to assume they were to satisfy some lewd night-time activity; the fantasies of a promiscuous, forty-something woman. But no; they were for the day-time masquerade of a depraved killer. That much was apparent to him now: two signatures; two profiles; two killers – and she is one of them, he thought. What had she planned for him that night, he wondered. If he had gone along with it, would he be standing here now? He shuddered. Who was she really, and what tied her to Jason McMasters? Presumably sex; he couldn't imagine love came into it.

He looked up at the ceiling, reached a decision. "Right; there's only one other way. Jones and the rest of you keep on looking. Stevens, you come with me. We've some climbing to do. Thank God it's stopped raining!"

"Shouldn't we call out the fire service," Stevens looked doubtful.

"No time," Jeff snapped.

Minutes later they were standing on the balcony of the upstairs apartment staring up at the roof; there were two skylights a few feet apart; the furthest one was slightly open, the sound of *Madam Butterfly* pulsating through it. The tenant, who had earlier complained about the fracas, had listened to Jeff's hurried explanation and gladly given them access. He said his name was Jeffries; Dr Lance Jeffries. As Jeff and Stevens were examining the roof, he burst through the French doors carrying a bundle of ropes and two climbing harnesses.

"These should help; they're part of my kit," he said, laughing at Jeff's bemused expression.

"Sorry, didn't I say? I'm a geologist, not a medical doctor. I've been working with a team in Tibet monitoring climate change at high altitudes." As he spoke, he was pulling on a harness.

"Hey! Hold up a minute. What do you think you're doing?" Jeff shouted, putting out a hand to stay him.

Jeffries looked pointedly down over the balcony railings, "I'm trained for this, Superintendent. Let me help you; you'll need me if you slip."

One look over the railings and Jeff, his head swimming, agreed.

Jeffries grinned, "Good job it's a tiled roof; not as slippery as wet slates. I'll go ahead and guide you up. I'll take him up with me," he pointed to Stevens, adding, "no offence, but he's smaller and fitter. Once he's got up to the skylight, I can lower his harness down for you."

"None taken – and thank you. Lord! I hope we're insured for this!"

Stevens was already locking on his harness. Jeff tried not to look down. He'd never been one for heights, but somewhere under this roof were two missing women and an injured officer – he prayed it was nothing worse than an injury – and one thing was for sure; he wasn't going to let Sandra down again. Not this time.

He watched as the pair hauled themselves up onto the lower part of the roof. Within moments Jeffries was up on the roof ridge and Stevens was crawling towards the first skylight. Reaching it, his face pressed close to the glass, he suddenly ducked sideways, lay back flat against the roof. He gesticulated sideways to Jeff; put his fingers to his lips and rolling onto his stomach, started moving towards the other, open skylight.

Jeff wondered what he had seen. At least the volume of music would cover any noise they were making. As he watched, Stevens reached the skylight. Sitting upright he discarded the harness and signalled to Jeffries to pull it away. Raising the skylight window, he knelt and looked inside, straightened and manoeuvred his legs into the opening. Then he turned and stuck his thumb up to Jeffries, who began lowering the harness to Jeff.

As it dropped down over the edge of the roof and he reached up to grab it, Jeff saw that Stevens had disappeared from view. He struggled into the harness and clipped all the safety catches into place. Giving each one a few tugs to make sure he'd done it right, he stood and judged the distance between the edge of the roof and the balcony. Only too aware of his own mass, he shook his head despairingly. Above him, the scientist waved, smiled encouragingly and gave a tug on the rope. Thank God for Jeffries; his being on the scene was an unbelievable stroke of luck. Someone up there must be looking out for them!

Hauling himself up onto the metal railing, Jeff steadied himself against the wall behind him. In an instant everything around him seemed to be swaying. The movement of air, no more than a breeze, seemed suddenly to have assumed hurricane proportions. A car turned the corner into the road below him; hoping it was the armed response unit, Jeff, without thinking, looked down. Wobbling, he grabbed onto the rope. Way beneath him, the car slowed passing the patrol cars and then picked up speed again disappearing up the road.

Disappointed, taking several deep breaths to quell the surge of nausea, Jeff turned to face the wall, sliding his hand along it to feel for the edge of a coin stone. Avoiding the guttering, he raised his elbow onto the edge of the roof at the same time bracing his foot against the wall. He grappled in desperation several times before he was able hoist his whole body up onto the edge of the roof. Without Jeffries' continued pressure on the rope, it would have been impossible. He tried not to look down, but way below him out of the corner of his eye he could see a small crowd of people had gathered and were staring upwards. Police officers were endeavouring to move them on. Two more squad cars had arrived; Jones must have called them. Getting his breath back, Jeff proceeded to climb; a roof tile dislodged beneath his foot and was sent spinning over the edge. He paused and waited for the crash, but the noise of the opera vibrating underneath him blocked out all other sounds.

Slowly, moving one limb at a time, he made his way over to the first skylight. The glass was clouded with condensation. He put his face against it. What he saw made him jerk upwards. He lost his hold, slipped backwards on the tiles.

Astride the ridge, manfully hauling on the rope, Jeffries mouthed, 'You Okay?'

Jeff nodded, adjusted his hold and edging back towards the skylight peered through. In a gap between the dense foliage of what looked like vine leaves, he had seen Sandra writhing on the floor beneath him. He picked her out again, saw that her hair was stuck bloodily to a wound at the back of her head. Jeff's surge of rage at the sight of it made his eyes water. Blinking the tears away, he made out the shape of a body strapped to some sort of apparatus and across from it there was another similar. A shape was leaning over it; a man; dressed in plastics. Jeff couldn't see what he was doing; he could only guess. The gorge rose in his throat and he retched.

His eyes focused on Sandra again; she was moving on all fours, trying to raise herself up off the floor. Jeff saw the man straighten, wave his arms. He didn't wait to see any more. Without a thought for where he was, careless of his own safety, Jeff clambered towards the skylight through which Stevens had disappeared.

Huffing with the effort, he squeezed through it and dropped with a grunt to the floor. The rope joining him to Jeffries like an umbilical cord broke his fall. Jeffries – bless him – had moved down from the roof ridge and was looking through the skylight. Jeff motioned up to him to stay where he was.

Springing open the catches of the harness, Jeff climbed out of it and looked about him. He was in a brightly lit bathroom.

The door was ajar; Stevens hunched beside it. Finger to his lips, he nodded at Jeff, put out his hand and flicked off the light switch, plunging them into darkness.

58

"It's him; Jason McMasters!" Stevens urged in a strained whisper. "He has them in the room at the far end of the hall. We'll have to get up to the door without alerting him; it's open but he's facing away from it."

Jeff, his eyes getting used to the dimness relieved only by the light filtering through from the skylight, moved up beside Stevens as he slowly pushed open the bathroom door. Some ten feet away, they could see McMasters had his back to them. Halfway along the hallway there was a break in the wall.

"I think that's an alcove," Stevens whispered. "It'll give us some cover."

Silently they slid along the wall. It wasn't an alcove, but a stairwell. Steps spiralled downwards.

"Take a look and see if it leads to a door into the flat below. We must have missed it somehow," Jeff breathed in Stevens's ear, for once entirely glad of the music that beat ceaselessly in his ears. They could be talking normally for all anyone could hear them. The opera was playing continuously, round and round. Jeff was beginning to recognise the melody. It was enough to put him off opera for life he reflected.

Stevens was quickly back, speaking breathlessly into his mobile in a stage whisper, a finger stuck in his other ear. "It has to be in the living room, Keith. There's a huge bookcase in about the right position opposite the fireplace; it must form a concealed door. Break it down if you have to!" He listened to something Jones said, added, "Well bloody well find one. There must be an axe somewhere in the building!" He shut off his mobile and shoved it in his pocket.

"Might be an idea to shut yours off, Sir?"

"Good thinking. Not that anyone could hear it above this racket,"

Jeff reached for his mobile and held the off switch until the light died.

Together, backs to the wall, they edged their way towards the open door at the other end of the hallway. McMasters had disappeared from view, but they could hear his voice fragmented between the haunting wailings of a soprano. Slowly, slowly, Jeff leaned around the door frame. The apparatus he had seen was a kind of stretcher trolley; strapped to it was Sheila. Her nose was smashed, her mouth a mess of blood, but he could see that she was breathing; still alive. He caught a movement beneath the trolley; it was Sandra. Her face deathly pale, she was on her knees frantically struggling to unbolt the straps that held Fiona's mother.

He turned back to Stevens. "We can't hold off any longer. We'll have to jump him."

Stevens nodded, turning to lean against the wall so that he was facing the open door. Suddenly they heard a sound from behind them. Jeff swung round. Lance Jeffries had followed them through the skylight, stumbled against something in the bathroom and sent it crashing against the tiled floor. He stood in the doorway, a mortified expression on his face, mouthed, 'Whoops! Sorry!'

Still focused on the room ahead, Stevens made eye contact with Sandra. She had heard the noise. Before she could react, Stevens raised his finger to his lips. McMasters, it appeared, was too hysterical to notice. They could hear him shouting now; his voice rising and falling, alternating between a childish whine and a deep bellow. The man was raving; stark staring raving mad.

"He's a bloody lunatic!" Stevens whispered. "You ready?"

"No, hang on a minute." Jeff went back to Jeffries, reached out and hauled him angrily into the stairwell. "God damn it man! There are lives at stake here; yours too if you're not careful. For all we know he is armed. Stay here! Don't move!"

As a shaken Jeffries nodded, Jeff crept up beside Stevens. Sandra had seen him. He sent her an encouraging smile, indicated that they were about to move. She gave an imperceptible nod. "Okay Stevens; ready when you are," Jeff said, feeling for the cuffs in his pocket.

Stevens bursting through the doorway was the first to see McMasters. He was kneeling on top of the other trolley, his arms raised, a wicked looking, thin-bladed knife glinting in his hand.

For an instant, following close behind, Jeff saw the killer's expression change to fear as Stevens lunged at him, then he was through the doorway himself, racing forward, grabbing the arm that held the knife.

All of them fell grunting to the floor.

McMasters was the first to extricate himself, brushing Jeff aside as though he was swatting a fly. Jeff's head crashed against the wheel of the trolley. Momentarily stunned he watched helplessly as Stevens scrambled to his feet, held his arms above his head to fend off the knife that was slicing through his clothes into his flesh. He ducked, attempted to rugby tackle McMasters to the floor.

Howling like a rabid dog, McMasters grabbed hold of Stevens's shoulders and smashed him against the wall. Stevens's eyes disappeared into his head and he slid slowly down the wall coming to rest in a crumpled heap on the floor, blood pouring from his scalp.

"Fuck you, McMasters!" Struggling to his knees, his anger giving him the strength he needed, Jeff threw himself at the killer and brought him down. Bringing up his knee, he pinned McMasters's leg to the floor, tried and failed to reach the cuffs. The man's strength was superhuman. Clasped together like lovers, they rolled around in a tangle of limbs, grunting and cursing. Screaming with rage, McMasters threw punch after relentless punch at Jeff's head. Jeff fought to move out of the way of McMasters's fists without letting go of his grip on his leg, but on top of the blow to the head he had already received, it was a losing battle. Where the hell was the back-up when you needed them!

Crying out in agony with every move, Sandra crawled slowly out from under Sheila's trolley and hauled herself upright. Since the last series of kicks she had received after her futile attempt to pull the killer away from Fiona, she had found it difficult to breath. She knew from the excruciating pain that she was bleeding internally. There was a red mist in front of her eyes and it came to her in a detached kind of way that she might be dying. It was probably no more than she deserved. At her side Jeff was losing his battle. Both men were covered in blood – whose? She searched their entangled forms for the knife but was unable to see it. What could she use as a weapon? Reaching blindly to the metal trolley, her hand came up against a glass jar.

Suddenly, in a shocking cessation of sound, the music was cut. The room seemed eerily silent, but for the rushing of frantic insects and the grunting, gasping men. There was a sound at the doorway. Sandra turned, saw a man running into the room; wide eyed he focused on Jeff and McMasters struggling on the floor. In one rapid movement he stepped over to the table and lifted the jar from Sandra's hand. She screamed out Jeff's name in fear, but avoiding Jeff, he brought the jar smashing down on his opponent's bald head.

In the mess of splintered glass beside the unconscious McMasters, a dying butterfly, its body crushed, spun in helpless circles and was still.

Jeff lay on his back gasping; his shirt covered in blood. "Glad you're not the sort who does as he's told," he grinned weakly.

Jeffries dropped to his knees took hold of Jeff's shirt ripping it open; searching for a wound unable to find one. "I think you're stabbed but I can't see where!"

Jeff pushed him back, "I'm okay, quit poking me there's a good chap. You'll find a pair of cuffs in my pocket. Get them on him for God's sake, before he comes round. The man's got the strength of an ape."

While Jeffries did as he was bid, Jeff struggled to his feet, stood there swaying. A quick glance showed him that Sandra was alive. He couldn't tell if Sheila was still breathing. Stevens was up on all fours, attempting to get to his feet.

"Jeff, help me." It was Sandra. Stumbling over to her, he helped her to her feet. Holding her against him he could feel her shuddering, could see from the grey, waxy texture of her skin that she was in agony. "We must get you to a hospital," he murmured into her hair, reaching for his mobile.

"Fiona! Jeff, please tell me the truth; how is Fiona?"

He turned to the trolley where McMasters had been poised with the knife. Fiona lay silent, there was no blood on her body, but her eyes were glazed staring at the ceiling and she was shivering violently.

"She's alive, not cut, but in severe shock." Still supporting Sandra with one arm, he handed his mobile to Jeffries. "Could you phone for an ambulance; tell them there are six of us, some in need of urgent

441

medical attention. And thank you, again Dr Jeffries. As it turns out, slipping off the roof was the least of our problems! Thank God you were here to help us."

"The name's Lance and I am glad to have been of service. I've never seen anything quite like this before," he said, taking the mobile and looking up at the vines and the insects hovering in the foliage. Tearing his gaze away, he looked back at Jeff, "I think you and the young lady had best sit down before you fall down."

As Jeffries took the mobile out into the hallway, Jeff leaned Sandra against Fiona's trolley and leaving her there, walked over to look down at McMasters. There was a trail of blood where Jeffries had pulled him face down to cuff him to the base of Sheila's trolley. Blood was creeping out beneath the green plastic suit, pooling on the floor.

Above him, Sheila was moaning, trying to sit up. "Let me see him, I want to see him," she breathed, her voice barely audible.

"Stevens, are you okay? Could you give me hand?" Jeff called.

Between them, they lifted Sheila from the trolley, but she was unable to stand unaided. Stevens held her up, half leaning against the trolley so that she could look down on her son.

Jeff left her side and knelt down beside McMasters, turning him over and feeling for a pulse. The knife was embedded deep in his chest.

"He's alive; but barely. I'm sorry Sheila; it must have happened when I brought him down," Jeff said, unlocking the cuffs. He was amazed that McMasters had managed to fight as ferociously as he had with this wound. He had been powered by hatred; that was for sure. It was only then that Jeff, getting a clear, uninterrupted view of the killer's face, placed his features. It was like looking at pictures he'd seen of a young Jack Hynds. No; it was like looking at Leslie Fenton's twin brother. Confused, he dashed a hand over his eyes, shook his head.

Without warning McMasters's eyes blinked open; his body tensed and he spoke. His words were slow and barely strung into sentences. "Mummy… Mummy… I'm scared Mummy…. It's dark!"

Shocked beyond belief, everyone in the room started down at him and then looked up at each other, stunned.

The voice issuing from the killer's mouth was clearly that of a child: a little boy.

"Andy!" Slipping out of Stevens' grasp Sheila crumpled to the floor.

"Mummy! Help me Mummy. I can't see your face."

With a faint cry, Sheila crawled to her son. Reaching for his hand, she lifted it and held it to her breast. "I'm here Andy," she spoke shakily in a soft whisper, her fingers gently stroking his hand. "I didn't leave you. I thought you had died with your father. I never knew, I promise, I never knew."

Unbearably moved, Jeff stuck out his arm to hold Stevens back. He could see that Sandra's face was streaming with tears.

Jeffries had come to the doorway, "Emergency services on their way. There's a lot of banging going on at the bottom of the stairs; I think your men are breaking through."

Jeff nodded, held his fingers to his lips. Jeffries faltered, stayed where he was.

"Mummy, where are you? I'm scared. I can't see you."

"Here Andy," Sheila sobbed, raising his hand to her shattered face. "Here I am; look at my face, look into my eyes. Hush, my darling; it's all better now."

McMasters's face was ashen, all vestiges of blood drained out of him. He looked up at his mother, the little boy's voice sinking to a thread: "Night, night Mummy; I love you." With a sharp intake of breath his head dropped, his eyes stared, glazed over.

Along with the sound of feet pounding up the stairwell, ambulance sirens could be heard nearing the building. Jeff prised Sheila's fingers away from those of her dead son and with Stevens's help, lifted her back onto the trolley. She was no longer conscious.

Suddenly the room was full of people. "Ah: the cavalry!" Jeff said in aside to Stevens, who smiled wryly.

"About bloody time!"

59

Maidstone Hospital: later that day

Oh God! No! Please! Don't touch me! Sandra pleaded under her breath. She would have shouted it out loud if she could bring herself to face the agony of drawing breath to speak. Her chest was swathed in heavy bandaging, as was her head. The pain pulsating through both was worse than anything she could have imagined. It had taken her several long minutes since groggily coming to, to sit up and get her legs over the side of the bed.

Reaching towards her to lift them back and manoeuvre her against the pillows, the nurse was all businesslike and cheerful. "Where do you think you're off to?" she said, pulling down the uncomfortable hospital gown that was bunched up, pulled tight round Sandra's middle. "You'll not be going anywhere soon my dear. Take these," she held out two fat, white capsules and a plastic cup of water. "They'll help the pain."

Obediently, Sandra did as she was told.

"Now lie back and get some sleep, there's a good girl." The nurse smiled, tucking her under the covers.

Sandra groaned. Unwelcome images kept flashing through her mind. The last thing she could recall with any clarity was when the paramedics had helped her into the ambulance. She was, she supposed, lucky to be here at all. She closed her eyes and began to die all over again.

The next time she woke, her bed was in deep shadow; the door was ajar, a dim glow of light filtered through from the corridor. Silhouetted against it was a black, burly shape.

She caught her breath, whispered, "Is that you Jeff?"

From the chair beside her bed there came a gentle snore.

"Jeff!" she strained in a theatrical whisper, not wanting another unwelcome intrusion from the nurse.

He stirred, whispered, "Yes, it's me. How do you feel?"

"Like shit! How's Fiona?"

"She's fine; she's fine. So is Stevens, damned lucky though, all of you. That fellow Jeffries deserves a medal." He stretched over and flicked on the shaded bedside light.

"God! You look awful!"

"Thanks!" Sandra made a face at him. "I feel as though I've been in a fight with a bull and I don't think I'll ever be able to move again, but aside from that I'm fine. What about you?"

His face was dreadfully bruised; a cut on his head had been taped up. He was still wearing his reefer jacket; she saw that it was torn at the shoulder and spotted with dried bloodstains. Lowering her eyes she turned her head away.

"A few nicks here and there but nothing to write home about. What a day, eh!"

Jeff sighed, relaxing back in the chair. "Right in front of us all the time and we never saw it. One hell of a psychopath; and that voice at the end; weirdest thing I've ever heard. But anyway; case closed thank God!"

"How did I not see it?" Weakly Sandra fought back the tears as it all came flooding back. It was she who had unwittingly given so many opportunities to someone she thought she could trust. She who had invited into her home her husband's killer.

Jeff reached forward and awkwardly patted her arm. "There'll be none of that blaming yourself. He was clever, Sandra, and cunning. None of us could see what he was."

"But I should have done," she protested. "How did we not see through it? I mean, the very way he walked, talked? I know the make-up was always heavy, but mature women often try to camouflage signs of ageing. There was nothing to suggest that Leslie..." she faltered, drew in a painful breath as she spoke the name. Leslie had been her friend; she had *trusted* her, been close to her: but it had all been a ruse to gain a window into Fiona's world. How could she *not* have seen it?

"He will have been popping hormones for years; must have got access to medication through his uncle's company. That would account for the womanly curves, the husky, female voice; the lack of facial hair. As I said, he was clever. He used overt sexuality, adopted a predatory style of catwalk walking. And his features were very fine; much like his father, handsome in an effeminate kind of way." Jeff stretched and settled himself more comfortable. "As I said, you mustn't blame yourself."

"He killed Gerry," Sandra said, her voice breaking. "He systematically killed everything Fiona ever loved. Had I seen through the disguise, my husband would still be alive."

"Would he? Are you sure about that?"

Sandra gazed at him for a moment then looked away. "I don't know," she acknowledged in a small voice.

"If you want to blame someone, why not blame me? I saw all the wigs, the make-up and what have you in the apartment that night. Hell, I wouldn't have gone back there had I not been tempted to sample the sex that was so blatantly on offer! The mind boggles. I have been wondering what would have happened if I hadn't cut and run," he grinned, embarrassed. "It was the nun's habit that really got to me! Seriously, though, we often don't see what is right in front of our noses; our perceptions of people are based on what we believe about them. There was no reason to suspect that Leslie Fenton was Andy Hynds. In our eyes he was a woman; that's how he presented himself and that's how we saw him. As I said, you must not blame yourself."

They looked at each other. Sandra nodded slowly, not entirely convinced. "What do you mean the nun's habit?"

"Well actually, it wasn't a nun's habit, but that's what I thought at the time. It was hanging up in the closet; a black robe, white collar and what have you. I assumed it was all part of the..." he coughed, "well, you know; kinky stuff. Anyway, I spoke to Henry McMasters earlier; had to tell him his nephew was dead." Jeff shifted in the chair, bent his arms up, linking his fingers behind his head.

"He always suspected Jason might be his son, you know. Henry had an affair with Elizabeth Reid; well, she was McMasters then – his sister-in-law. He couldn't have known the boy was really Andy Hynds. Kenneth McMasters passed him off as Elizabeth's son – Jason was the one we pulled out of the Thames – for the inheritance. Did I mention it before?"

"Not that I remember, go on."

"It was perhaps why Henry McMasters took such an interest in

Jason and was so cut up about him turning out bad. When he took over the guardianship, he arranged for the boy to attend a boarding school in Surrey run by a retired missionary. Apparently Jason – or Andy as we know him – settled in well and formed a close bond with the priest. Unfortunately he died."

Sandra shot Jeff a look.

"Of old age!" he said.

"Oh."

"Andy must have kept his robes to remember him by. Henry confessed he had never understood what the priest saw that was good in him, but he had a calming influence on the boy."

Trying to move up in the bed, Sandra caught her breath, bit her lip. "Nobody is born evil, Jeff," she gasped, "maybe if Andy hadn't been so damaged the priest might have been able to help him. As it was, the only bit of religion and kindness he encountered in his miserable existence got distorted; twisted. His souls were too stained by then to save."

"Souls?"

"No, you're right: just one soul. Several identities though: a small boy's desperate coping mechanism that went horribly wrong."

"It's a sad fact of life that children get abused, Sandra; they don't generally end up as depraved killers!"

"God, Jeff. I'm not excusing it. I am only making the point that even in a depraved animal like Andy Hynds there was some good. Look at how much he loved his sister, for example. For whatever reason, the child within him never grew up; his development was arrested, if you like. It isn't that he was *pretending* to be other people, Jeff; he actually *became* them. They took him over. That is why the signatures of the murders were not the same; it would depend upon whichever identity he was at the time he killed." She gave an involuntary shudder and cried out in pain.

Jeff frowned, leaned forward, "What's wrong? Are you okay? Shall I call for someone?"

"No; sorry, just a twinge," she lied. "The hurt child wanted revenge for what he had suffered. Women who had in his view so carelessly given birth and then abandoned their babies" – or aborted them, she thought, but did not say – "deserved to be wiped out. Their wombs were trophies. He didn't just kill women, of course, but hatred of women is what drove him." She thought for a moment, asked, "Did Stevens ever find David Shaw by the way?"

"No, not yet, but I think it is fairly obvious that Andy killed him and took on his identity before he went to Scotland. When we all get back to work, I'll have Blake go through the database for unidentified remains. But we may never find him. I suppose I will have to break the news to his Dad, poor old sod." Jeff sighed. "I don't look forward to that, I have to say. That'll be something else he'll lay at Sheila's door."

"How is Sheila? You didn't say."

"Not so good I'm afraid. Her heart stopped; the medics managed to resuscitate her, but she's very low. Last I checked she still hadn't come round, but Fiona's sitting with her." He stretched again, pushing himself to his feet. "I ought to go and you ought to rest. I'll get one of the nurses to bring you some tea or something shall I?"

"That'd be good, thanks Jeff."

As he turned to go, the room was lit up suddenly by a scintillating flash shooting into the night sky; a fountain of lights fell to earth, sparking and glistening like coloured rain.

They both stared up at the window. "It's still bonfire night," Sandra said disbelievingly.

"So it is," Jeff answered with a smile, leaning across to close the curtains. "Do as you are told: get some rest!"

Reaching the private ward in the intensive care unit he paused at the window catching a glimpse of the back of Fiona's head. She was sitting at one side of Sheila's bed. On the other side was Leonard Millar, his chair pulled up close. Between them Sheila was strung up with tubes. A drip trailed up to a bag of fluids above the bed, a row of monitors beeped and flashed behind her. She was motionless, her eyes closed.

Millar was leaning forward, both of Sheila's hands clasped in his own. Jeff had never imagined he would ever look upon this man with pity; but for the second time in a week he did. For the three people in the room this case was far from closed. Jeff backed away, walked down the corridor and headed for the exit. There would be the press conference to attend to in the morning. He needed to get home, have a shave, tidy himself up. His whole body ached as if he had been run over by a bus; but a soak in a hot tub would help. Of them all, he was the least injured – except for Fiona, and her injuries were not physical.

Leonard Millar looked down at the hands he was holding and back up at Sheila's poor face. They had patched it up as best they could, but had decided against operating. It would be too much for her heart, they had said. In the last few hours, her condition had deteriorated. Now, looking at her swollen, broken features, Leonard saw for himself the enormity of her suffering: the dreadful scars left by the fire years ago, her skin shrivelled and red beneath the fresh wounds inflicted by her son. In his mind's eye he saw her as she once was; the delicate beauty that had captured his heart so long ago.

Fresh bruising had spread along her arm, radiating out from beneath the tape covering the drip needle. He gently ran his thumb alongside it, wanting only to soothe her into her final sleep. So long, it had been so long that he had carried this love in his heart: the longing to hold her once again, the yearning to be with her. Now all he could do was keep her company as she began the journey she must take alone. Struggling to find comfort in his faith, he prayed for her. He tried also to pray for her son; the child she would find again as she drifted from this life into the next. To pray for both their souls was as much as he could do for her. For himself he doubted he would ever come to terms with the evil unleashed so many years ago that had led them to this moment.

On the other side of the bed, Fiona's chair was placed a respectable distance away. She perched awkwardly on the edge of it, a spasmodic tremor shaking her drooping shoulders as she gazed at her mother's face. He found it hard to look at her; her face transported him to another place in another time; the resemblance to her mother was as cruel as a mirage. Had their paths ever crossed before, he would have known her as Sheila's daughter. The need to break the silence between them was overwhelming but the words just seemed to slip away from him as he tried to speak. What should he say? How would he start? He wondered what thoughts would be running through her mind. Again he bowed his head to avoid eye contact as she looked up at him.

"I think I need some air. I won't stray too far. Please call me if…"

"Yes, of course..."

She got up from the chair, studied the monitors for a moment, walked to the door; leaving him alone with her mother. She did not look back.

A muffled whisper brought his focus to Sheila. Her eyes were open a little, the lids puffed and purple with bruising. She was attempting to speak. Her lips were dry, cracked and swollen. He reached for the small, wet sponge and gently moistened them.

"It's alright Sheila, you're safe now," he said softly.

"Leonard?"

"Yes, it's me." He lifted her hand and caressed each of her fingertips with his lips.

"Leonard," she breathed, tears trickling from the corners of her eyes to puddle beneath them.

"F... Fiona..."

"She's here. She's safe."

Helplessly he watched as drawing her hand away, Sheila reached out blindly, splaying her fingers as though she thought Fiona was there to grasp them.

Then the arm dropped.

Her breath rattled in her throat and the monitor began to bleep.

60

Driving home from the hospital, Jeff wished Angie was there waiting for him; he could do to talk to someone who had nothing whatever to do with police work! During the afternoon, he and Stevens had talked at length, pooling what they knew, drawing together all the ins and outs of this convoluted case. He now knew why Lady Clara Smith-Stevens had fast-tracked the Jakes case. It appeared that when her son had started to search for his father and had mentioned Katie Smyth's suspicions concerning misuse of information at the Search Agency, Lady Clara had panicked. Afraid that too much delving into adoption records would reveal her past identity, she had taken steps to ensure Jakes was tried and convicted as quickly as possible. From what she had confessed to her son, she had used Jack Hynds as a tout in a blackmailing scam. That would explain why she had seemed so discomfited when Millar had bared his soul the other night at White Cliffs. Did Millar know? Had he known that Hynds was also working for Frank Reid? He'd lay strong odds that Clara knew. Hynds had been playing a dangerous game, but so had Reid with a foot in both camps. Millar had never confirmed the identity of the mole in the undercover operation to collar Kenneth McMasters, but it seemed highly likely it was Frank Reid. Maybe he had tried to make some redemption: he had adopted Gerry, and someone had got Sheila out of the fire at the cottage that night: Frank? Was it a mistake; in all the confusion, had he thought it was Gerry's mother he was rescuing? If Sheila recovered, maybe she would be able to tell them. But really, did it matter? It was all a long time ago – and it was over now.

Stevens had said that his mother had promised to resign her position as Parliamentary Under-Secretary and take early retirement. That whole business about Cardinal Carlosanta had been a cock and bull story: a way of giving her son some kind of a history that he could be proud of and also an attempt to keep the investigating team from the truth. She would have known he would follow the link to her former husband, Peter Smith, add two and two and come up with five. He should have known better. And as for Opus Dei! Jeff almost chuckled; the woman had a rare imagination, he had to hand it to her! Millar should have objected, but he had fudged the truth every bit as much as she had. Gone along with it because he'd known Fiona was in danger and it had given him a reason to place her under surveillance, for which read protection. Neither he nor Clara had wanted the investigation to uncover the past. Nor, come to that, had the Commissioner. Well not about Frank Reid's involvement, at least. The hushed-up corruption of a Chief Superintendent! The damage to the Force if that got into the newspapers would be incalculable, particularly now at a time when funding was such an issue.

Mind you, Jeff reflected thinking about the Commissioner's wife; it had been her imagination, not Clara's. According to Stevens, Anita Hunt, a.k.a. Claire Hamilton, had sent the draft of her latest book to Clara. The thriller, which would never now be published, was about a Vatican plot to kill off the mistress and child of the new Pope! Jeff snorted: gripping stuff he was sure, but sometimes the truth was even stranger than fiction. The plot had included the whole story of the five women who had born their children at the Priory, even to the fire and escape down the cliff.

Clara had much to answer for: she had known all along about Anita's writing retreat in Dover. Was it possible she had actually *hoped* the killer would find Anita, kill her off as he had done Peggy Lyons? Kill off all the people who could identify her as McMasters's former mistress? Surely not! What was he to do about Lady Clara Smith-Stevens? It was a problem. Strictly speaking he could have her for perverting the course of justice, not to mention wasting police time. But Gareth Stevens was too good a fellow to destroy in the process. Maybe her resignation and retirement were enough. Maybe it was up to Millar to sort it out and not his problem to worry about at all. What would Angie have said?

Jeff pulled into his driveway, killed the engine, cut the lights and pulled on the handbrake. He switched on the courtesy light, leaned over to the glove compartment and retrieved the tattered folder that had been sitting there all week. It could be filed away now. Laying it on the passenger seat, he flipped open the cover, stared down at the snap of the little boy with wide, round eyes: Andy Hynds.

"No," he murmured, "you weren't born evil were you – you were made that way." If anyone was destined to be born evil it should be Gareth Stevens. He was Kenneth McMasters's' son, and yet look how he'd turned out: a regular guy and an excellent copper. Andy's childhood had been wretched beyond imagination; Gareth's had been nurturing, surrounded with love. Something DC Blake had said came into Jeff's mind: the 'Law of the Free Womb'. Was there such a thing at all, he wondered. What say had any child on leaving the womb, no matter which one it came from?

Epilogue

20th December 2007

Leaving the house in the late afternoon, Sandra took a walk. It was warm for December and although the light was fading and it would mean walking home in the dark, she needed to do this. Tomorrow she was flying out to join Fiona in Ireland. Two weeks after Sheila's death, Fiona had taken her mother's remains home to Westport for burial. She had decided to stay on; with the money and property she had inherited, she could afford to take a long break from her career. She still had to come to terms with what had happened to Mark, who was now a patient in a private hospital. It would take years of therapy before he was able to live a normal life. On the laptop computer taken from the King's Place apartment, Keith Jones had found digital images of each murder, filmed in painstaking detail by Andy Hynds. It was no wonder that Mark, drugged and forced to watch Katie's horrific death, was still living the nightmare. Quelling a surge of nausea, Sandra wondered if any of those involved in this case would ever be able to forget what they had seen.

She turned to look back at the house that had been her home for the past twelve years. Tomorrow was completion day and all her furniture was going into store. She still did not know where she was going to live; what she was going to do. Her life seemed empty of purpose since the girls had gone to live in the States. Maybe a trip to Westport would help – and it would be nice to see Michael again. It had obviously done Fiona good to get away; she had sounded quite upbeat on the phone last night. Sandra had gladly accepted her invitation to join her there for Christmas. For now, it was enough to think only that far ahead.

For both of them it had been a great comfort to learn that Gerry had not intended to take his own life. It was clear, now they knew the truth, that he had not written the suicide note. Either he had overdosed on the opiates by mistake, or his killer had forced them down his throat before tipping him off the steps. Either way, he had not committed suicide.

She stopped to buy a bunch of roses: white ones. His favourite; they would wilt by morning, but never mind. From the garden she had gathered some holly to put with them; the berries were good this year.

The graveyard was quiet as she walked the narrow paths. It was such a lonely place. How easily the dead are forgotten, she thought, staring at all the headstones, the faded inscriptions, the tufts of overgrown grass and wilted posies.

She stood for a time at the foot of his grave not thinking anything in particular, just staring at his name inscribed on the headstone. Reaching down she placed the roses in the centre and straightened again. Life could be so unfair. One day, God willing, all she would remember would be the happy times and the love they had shared.

Turning, she walked back to the gates and made her way home.

The End

FORTHCOMING FROM FERRAN O'NEILL

SOUL CLEANSING